Praise for *What We Devour*

"Wickedly clever, bloody in the best way, and with a cast of characters who are all delights however dubious it might be to root for them. *What We Devour* is a book after my own heart and an instant favorite."
—Emily A. Duncan, *New York Times* bestselling author of *Wicked Saints*

"A triumphant dark fantasy, *What We Devour* serves up an incredibly smart magic system with a side of eat-the-rich energy. Perfect for fans of *Wicked Saints* and anyone who likes their romances equal parts swoony and stabby. This is my favorite Linsey Miller book."
—Rosiee Thor, author of *Tarnished Are the Stars*

"*What We Devour* has my new favorite magic system. Miller pulls no punches in a stark examination of class structures and the consequences of conflating worth and wealth set against the backdrop of a postapocalyptic fantasy world. With a cunning main character and visceral prose that will leave you haunted, this book is a dark delight."
—Kalyn Josephson, author of the Storm Crow duology

"*What We Devour* is a brilliant and bloodthirsty read that pulls no punches, makes us question all of our actions, and begs us to find a way to change the world."
—Laura Pohl, author of the Last 8 duology

"Dark, mesmerizing, and wildly original, *What We Devour* is a captivating fantasy you won't be able to put down."
—Andrew Shvarts, author of the Royal Bastards trilogy

"*What We Devour* is a twisting, complex puzzle box, effortlessly weaving sinister bargains, deadly magic, and the ethics of power and sacrifice. With an unforgettable cast and themes achingly relevant to today's readers, this book is not to be missed."
—Margaret Owen, author of the Merciful Crow duology

ALSO BY LINSEY MILLER

Belle Révolte

MASK OF SHADOWS DUOLOGY

Mask of Shadows
Ruin of Stars

WHAT WE
DEVOUR

LINSEY MILLER

sourcebooks
fire

Published by Sourcebooks Fire, an imprint of Sourcebooks
P.O. Box 4410, Naperville, Illinois 60567-4410
(630) 961-3900
sourcebooks.com

Library of Congress Cataloging-in-Publication data is on file with the publisher.

Printed and bound in the United States of America.
VP 10 9 8 7 6 5 4 3 2 1

Brent,
none of this would have been possible without you.
Here's to another fifteen years.

Alistair's Laboratory

ANDERS

THE NEST

ANGDEN

SUNDER

Noshwright

THE WHEELS

GYLDEN

AVINITY

The Tongue

ARWEL

THE WORKS

The-Vile-Wallow-in-the-Waters
The-North's-Welcome
Prosperity-Rolls-Off-the-Tongue
The-South's-Rest
Forget-Them-Not
Death's-Last-Chance-to-Lay-Claim
Good-Fortune-Favors-the-Faithful
Order-and-Chaos-Work-Side-by-Side
A-Good-Night's-Rest
Wheels-Carry-Us-to-Riches
A-Warm-Welcome
A-Noble-Order
Study-Under-Watchful-Eyes
Gold-Yields-for-Everyone
A-Vile-Necessity
A-Noble-Garden

part one

MOUTH LIKE NIGHT

*If you can't tame your demons,
set them free.*

one

I T WAS AN HONOR TO WORK WITH THE DEAD, BUT Rylan Hunt—*four stone, fifty-two inches, eviscerated*, my notes read—had died two days before his thirteenth birthday, and no funeral rites would fix that. I uncurled his clenched fists, the tense muscles creaking like tinder, and peeled off his sodden gloves. His mother had made them last autumn, and they'd been blue yesterday. Now the whole of him was red and brown and purple, the stains of death settling beneath his skin. I turned and tossed his gloves into the compost pile that would become his funeral plot. The collecting pool sloshed about my knees.

Every part of him loved and every part of him returned to the earth except for the parts that seeped into me. I was a graveyard so no one else needed to be.

Felhollow's only undertaker: it wasn't a title I wanted, but there had been nothing else left to do in this town when I arrived seven years ago.

"And it means I'm here for you," I said, one shaking hand on his arm.

Rylan's skin was in tatters, ribs splayed open like a hurricane lily. I collected what blood I could, but there was barely enough for funeral rites. There was hardly anything left of him.

The person who'd done it had been captured, but breathing still tasted bitter. What good was vengeance? Rylan was dead.

We feared the old tales of our long-gone demigod overlords,

the Noble and the Vile, but we mortals were far worse. They might have ruled over us, warred with us, and dined on us, but the haughty court of peers with its money and soldiers was far more vicious than any old gossip's tale.

I covered Rylan's torso with a sheet of canvas. My needle slipped through his skin easily, stitching the canvas to him to hide the wound. The stitching was an old comfort, the steady movement the same sway as the river waves I'd been born on. Death was as common there as it was here. Only the wealthy—or more often, the peerage who had long ago been gifted titles and holdings by the Crown and ruled over Cynlira—could avoid it.

"You look older." I brushed his hair from his face. "I know you liked that."

Most twelve-year-olds did.

"I've never understood how you can stomach standing in that mess," a familiar voice said behind me. "It makes my skin crawl."

I sighed and leaned my head back, letting the midday sun soak into me. The open-air pool where I performed funeral rites was a shout away from the church doors. Rylan rested on a stone slab in the center of the pool, and if needed, I could sprint to the church and heal anyone who took a turn. The bandits who'd tried to raid us this morning were all dead save for one—the vilewrought.

"Don't be rude, Jules," I said without looking.

"Am I ever?" He huffed and dropped something with a sickening crack. "Lore?"

I turned. Julian stood over the crumpled vilewrought bandit and held out his bruised hand to me. He was Felhollow to the bone—pine green eyes, lean muscles from years felling trees, and a deep distrust of anyone not from Felhollow.

I held up my hand. "Almost done."

I laid two square halfans atop Rylan's eyes to hold them shut. Everything had a cost, including death. Most Felfolk could barely afford it these days. Well, except for Julian.

"You don't have to follow the old traditions, you know," he said. "You're not from here. No one would blame you."

"His mother asked for them," I said and stepped out of the pool, pale pink water muddying the dirt. "How am I supposed to convince Felhollow I'm good enough to marry you without your traditions?"

He shrugged. Julian didn't follow them. I was as good as adopted by his family, but I'd be an outsider till we married, probably a little while after too.

"You up to healing this trash?" asked Julian, nudging the vilewrought with his boot. "Fix her enough to talk. We need to know if we got all them bandits."

The vilewrought at his feet flinched. Magic rolled off her in waves, raising the hair on my bare arms. I knelt down before her and touched her bloody hand. Her shoulders shook.

"Sure," I said. "Go look after the others and make sure none of my healing comes undone while I'm working."

Julian did what I asked without so much as blinking, and the dying girl's laughter rattled out of her with a cough. I pulled my knife from its sheath.

"You're vilewrought," I said. "That's rare."

She lifted her head, blue eyes set in bruised white skin, and nodded to Rylan's body. "He the only dead?"

"He is." I touched the dried blood coating her arms. The only wound I could see was a ragged one gouged across her chest. "Any of this yours?"

"Probably," she said. Her hands twisted in the tightly knotted ropes. I'd told Julian a dozen times vilewrought could still work even with bound hands. "What good's a healer all the way out here?"

"Lately, barely any." I pressed the knife to my arm. My noblewright, a force of magic I could feel but never see, unfurled from me like smoke from fire. "Hold still."

She groaned. "No use healing me. There's nothing to tell."

"I don't care," I said. "You're hurt, so you're getting healed."

Take it as sacrifice, I prayed and cut a strip of flesh from my arm, *and heal her wound.*

A shiver like a cat's tongue ran down my arm, and the blood and skin vanished. Noblewrights, like the Noble they came from, could only create, and they always needed a self-sacrifice to create from. I dropped the knife, hands shaking. She hissed.

New flesh wove its way across her wound and settled as a shiny pink scar.

"Noblewrought." The girl stared at the scar. "You're noblewrought."

Before the gods abandoned us and when the Noble and the Vile still walked this world, mortals hadn't been able to use magic. They fought back against the Noble and Vile to no avail, and then, they were left with only one option. There was only one way to escape the terrifying grip of their immortal tyrants— they devoured the Noble and Vile and took their magic.

We noblewrought and vilewrought were the legacy of those who had feasted.

"You're good." She prodded the new skin and stared up at me. Even her shiner was gone. "Real good."

My noblewright was like having a god in my veins, answering my prayers when I made the right sacrifice.

"Thank you." I sat back and studied her. "Who did you sacrifice to kill Rylan?"

"Right," she said with a sneer. "Vile me, always sacrificing others. Maybe I'm tired of killing."

"Did you kill him?" I asked and pointed to Rylan.

"The blond one did." She scratched at her chest and winced. "I didn't bother learning names."

There had been two blond bandits, and Julian's father had ordered both killed this morning after questioning them.

My noblewright shivered. A thrum, bees in a hive, started in my chest and spread through my hands.

"You're hurt elsewhere," I said. My noblewright could only heal so much. I twisted my trembling hands together. "Tell me why you picked Felhollow, and I'll fix it."

"I know what's wrong with me, and you can't fix it. Bleeding out. Or in, I guess." She chuckled, and blood bubbled in the corner of her mouth. Her bound hands tugged at her shirt. "We didn't pick Felhollow. He did."

Her vilewright, invisible and nearly intangible, hung between us like roiling storm air. She narrowed her eyes at me.

"They bound me with Chaos's sigil when I was seven and made me a soldier, and I can feel their terrible commands even now. I can feel what I'm supposed to do gnawing at me," she said and yanked her shirt open.

Beneath the new scar, a jagged sigil like a closed, bleeding eye had been carved into her chest and filled with red ink. All wrought, even the dualwrought Crown of Cynlira and her vilewrought son, were bound to serve and obey the court and common council. It kept their magic limited and tightly controlled, each sigil denoting what magic their wright could perform. The magic in hers ate away at her bleeding skin.

"This will kill me if I don't do what I'm supposed to, and I'm going to let it. The only self-sacrifice my vilewright would ever accept," said the girl with a laugh. "It'll be enough to destroy our tracks and erase everything that might lead him here."

"Who?" I asked. Mother had always told me to never let them bind me no matter what, so I'd run to Felhollow. What was this girl running from?

I reached for my knife, and she kicked it away.

"That man deserves what's coming for him, but you don't," she said. "That vile boy's going to love you, and I'm so sorry."

I shook my head and pulled her hands from her chest. "Who? Tell me, and I can fix this."

"This is my choice." She smeared her hand through the blood on her chest and drew her fingers down her face. I knew the moves. All wrought did. Five lines over a half-moon, like a hand grasping from an open grave. Death's sigil marked our final sacrifice, one last contract with our wrights. "My first real choice. Don't worry. My vilewright will make it quick."

"You don't have to do this," I said and leaned over her, the prickling of her vilewright's presence an itch I couldn't scratch.

"Tell that man I'm no assassin. Not for him." She drew a line of red across her mouth. "And run. If he's already here, run, because he will never let you go. You can't fight him."

But I could. An uneasy ache, a need to destroy, rose up within me, and she reared back.

"Oh, my noble sister," she whispered. "That noblewright the only monster in you?"

I didn't answer, and she didn't speak again.

The only redemption for vilewrought was death.

two

I STUMBLED TO MY FEET. JULIAN APPEARED IN THE doorway of the church, a broad shadow cut in two by the rifle on his back. I was sitting on the edge of the pool by the time he got to me, my head in my hands, and he crouched down before me. His calloused fingers pried my face free, and the warmth of his hands was uncomfortably sticky in the late summer sun. He glanced at the vilewrought girl, fingers flinching toward his knife. I shook my head.

"She said someone was coming." I sniffed, drowning in death, and gestured to her. "She destroyed their tracks leading here—"

"So she told you," said Julian with a scowl.

"—and told me to run if 'he' found me."

"She's got a piece of Vile soul attached to her. Who knows if she was truthful?" he said and grabbed a rag. "Chin up. If anyone was chasing her, we can take them."

Felhollow could handle most bandits, and Julian's father, Will, was in the good graces of enough peers to keep them from doing anything untoward. He was the richest person in town and kept it flush with munitions. Not that anyone ever came to Felhollow.

"I should know what she meant." I rubbed my face. "It's on the tip of my tongue."

"You've been awake since yesterday morning." Julian kissed

my cheek, knelt before me, and gently cleaned the blood from my hands and legs. "Go rest. I'll handle this. I can sleep through the funeral tonight, but you can't."

"You should be there. Rylan looked up to you," I said. I'd never be able to rest after what that vilewrought said.

Julian tossed the rag into the compost pile and wiped his hands clean. "I wish you hadn't sent me away. She could've hurt you."

"My noblewright could have handled her if she tried. Or my knife." I cracked my neck. "You sure no one needs me?"

"I need you to pretend you've got reasons for keeping me around," he muttered and helped me stand. "Or are you just with me for my money?"

Standing, we were eye to eye, and his smile was tight.

"You got any other good qualities I don't know about?" I asked and took his hand. Seven years I'd known him, and it still wasn't enough. We'd been best friends long before we started stepping out. He was kind and comfortable, the first spring rain after a dreary winter. "Stay with me. Ivy and the others can handle the rest."

Julian stripped off his coat and draped it over me. "Deal. Let's—"

The sharp cry of Felhollow's warning whistle cut him off. Julian spun, hand going to his rifle. I grabbed one of my bone saws and took off running for the center of town. He sprinted after me. My noblewright hummed in anticipation. I shivered. Magic was never sated.

We ducked between the houses to the center square. A crowd was gathered around the water pump, forming one solid block of shoulders that barred the way for a group of soldiers. Old Ivy, the head of the guards and town council, stood before the five soldiers with her arms crossed. Her wife was behind her, an ax in her hands. The soldiers each held a rifle and carried a sword on their belt. None, so far as I could tell, were wrought.

Behind them, a carriage black as pitch blocked the road leading out of town.

"—killed a twelve-year-old this morning," Ivy was saying with her mortar-on-pestle voice. "We want nothing to do with you."

Julian and I nudged our way to the middle of the crowd. Will hooked one arm through Julian's, forcing him to sling his rifle back on his shoulder. They were two of a kind, same corn silk hair and green eyes, and they scowled as the soldier sneered at Old Ivy.

"Thought you ordered all the bandits executed?" Julian asked.

Will nodded and whispered, "They're here for someone else. Do not antagonize them."

"Bandits don't concern us," said a soldier with a gold collar on his long red coat. I'd not seen a warrant officer since leaving the capital. Almost all of them were the second and third children of peers who hadn't inherited the title. "We have a warrant for Willoughby Chase, and we won't be leaving without him. If you do not present him, we are allowed to acquire him by any means necessary."

Julian stiffened next to me. Will didn't so much as flinch.

"Which peer did you piss off?" I whispered.

"Suppose we're about to find out," he whispered back, hand slipping around Julian to squeeze my arm. "Don't worry."

How often had he said the same for me? Will had treated me like kin since I got here, keeping me fed and sheltered till I earned enough healing and undertaking. Twelve years ago, he'd finally done what most of Felhollow dreamt of and cut a deal with several peers for lumber, and now he had a seat on the common council. He was Felhollow's point of contact with the rest of the world and rich enough to get out of jail time, surely. He'd breathed life into Felhollow and me. I grabbed his hand.

"Here is the warrant," said the officer, pulling a thick letter from the inside of his coat. "Read it for yourself if you doubt me."

He tossed it to the ground before Old Ivy, and she passed it back to Will.

Will picked it up with trembling fingers. The smooth paper was bleached to pale ivory and stippled with gold flakes. Blue ink so dark and thick my skin grew cold just looking at it lined the front, and the colors of the wax seal bled into the envelope. I'd never seen the seal of the Sundered Crown of Cynlira in person—red and blue phoenixes twisted together in a writhing circle and eating each other's tails. Inside the ring was Will's name. No one in Felhollow had ever received a royal summons. There was only one reason anyone would.

"A sacrificial summons," I whispered.

Will ran his thumb across his name, and the ink smeared. I reached out and touched the wax. Still warm.

"From the desk of Her Most Serene Excellency Hyacinth of the House Wyrslaine, the Crown of Cynlira and What Else Remains," Will read aloud, a flush speckling his face like watered-down blood on fresh snow. "Information has been laid before the Peers' Court that Willoughby Chase of Felhollow in the South of Cynlira has engaged in fraud, larceny, and treason against the Crown and her great nation. He is summoned to Mouth-of-the-River-of-Gods to be held until he appears in court to answer for this information. Should his answers prove unsatisfactory, he shall be sacrificed for the good of this great nation."

Beneath it was the signature of the Heir, Alistair Wyrslaine, in swirling blue ink and the date Will was set to be sacrificed—ten weeks from now.

"Treason?" Julian's voice cracked.

Will shushed him, folded the letter shut, and cleared his throat. "This summons was obviously just written. What evidence is there of these charges?"

"Evidence is for the trial," said the officer. "Chase is to be remanded in custody until then."

"Willoughby Chase is a productive and beloved citizen of Cynlira backed by the court of peers and common council," I said loudly. "Even if this hadn't been written when you got to town, he could be trusted to appear for court. There's no need for this threat of sacrifice."

"We are not judges. We have orders, and we will follow them." The captain glanced back at the soldiers under his command, and they squared their shoulders. "We have work to do, and you are wasting our time."

"Hand him over to be killed for our Crown's fun?" asked Old Ivy. "I don't think so."

Will slipped his hand from mine. Sweat gathered in the wrinkles of my palm, the terror of losing the only family I had settling over me. The sacrificial trials were a sham. Outlandish rumors about them haunted Cynlira, and the official statement from the court didn't quell them. They started decades ago and occurred every few years and then once a year. Now once a month, the Crown sacrificed the guilty "in order to keep the Vile from returning."

Even peers and councilors got sacrificed when they moved against the Crown.

"Orders are orders," said the captain. "Any issues you have may be taken up in Mori."

"Well, that's horseshit," shouted someone, and I peeked around Julian to see who. Kara, strong arms bare and bandaged from the fight this morning, leveled a carrot at the captain. "We're supposed to let you take him with no evidence of wrongdoing and expect you to give him back when he's proven innocent? When I can see the ink's still wet from over here?"

"Yes," said the captain. "You will, or we will take him by force."

"Will you now?" asked Kara, snapping the carrot in half with her teeth.

One of the soldiers raised their rifle toward Kara. Next to me, Kara's partner, Ines, stepped forward. I tugged them back.

"Our benefactor is eager to continue his journey," said the captain, "so please know that we have no qualms about how we acquire Chase, so long as it is quickly."

"Julian," I whispered, "we can't win this fight. Trust me?"

"Course." He squeezed my hand, gaze fixed on his father. "Is there anything you can do? Anything at all?"

I swallowed and nodded. My noblewright flattened against my back, uncomfortable and out of the way. It wasn't the only god in my veins.

Take Julian's memory of his eleventh birthday, I prayed, tightening my grip on his arm so my vilewright would know what to do, *and destroy these officers' memories of coming here for Will Chase.*

My vilewright tore away from me like a scab, and I gasped. A shudder racked Julian's body. I looped one arm through his to hold him upright. A soldier turned to us.

Take my memory of Mother's laugh that night before she died, and create a new memory in the minds of the officers. They came here to arrest the bandits, not Will.

My noblewright drifted to the officers. A glaze passed over their eyes, each of them blinking.

Dualwrought, my mother had called me with a stifled sob, like Her Excellency the Sundered Crown. I'd a noblewright who could create, a vilewright who could destroy, and so few memories of my mother. But Will was worth it. He would be family. He was as good as family.

The officer took a deep, steadying breath. "If only we had gotten here in time, those bandits wouldn't have been a problem. We will keep our ears to the ground for word of any more bandits in the area."

Every single face in Felhollow turned to me except for Will's.

"We understand," he said, hands clenching and unclenching at his side. "Your work is much appreciated." And he bowed his head slightly to the man who'd been threatening to drag him to his death not five seconds ago.

Ines looked at me, their eyes wide at my untouched flesh. People were so unimaginative. They always expected sacrifices to be physical.

"Memories," I whispered to them, "work just as well."

I'd told no one I was vilewrought, not even Julian. The only other dualwrought alive was the Crown, and I knew what folks thought of her. I'd no desire to be her competition or her plaything, and I knew well what Julian thought of people with a vilewright. I wanted a home. They didn't need to know.

Old Ivy whispered something to the folks next to her, and they whispered to the ones near them. The knowledge of what had happened—or at least what Old Ivy thought had happened—spread. They would think I had used my noblewright in some curious way, and Julian would only notice his missing memory if he thought on that day too hard. I didn't worry. He wasn't one for reminiscing.

My wrights returned, their presence little more than a breath against my skin. They always preferred to huddle at the back of my neck, but now they lingered over each shoulder like an invisible, intangible mantle. My vilewright let out an appreciative hum.

"Now," said a new voice, "which one of you did that?"

A knife of a man stepped from the carriage. He wore a sharply pleated shirt of pure white silk with a red waistcoat and cravat beneath a black greatcoat, and a single red thread ran down his coat seams like a vicious drizzle. His black hair hung in a fishtail braid over one shoulder, feathery pieces framing his pale white face. The weight of his vilewright knocked the breath from my lungs.

Everyone but me sunk to their knees and pressed their foreheads to the dirt.

"Fascinating," said the Heir to the Crown of Cynlira, the red-eyed vilewrought more feared than any army, Alistair Wyrslaine. He adjusted his scarlet glasses and pinned me with his bloody gaze. "You're not the vilewrought girl I was looking for, but you'll do."

three

I WAS SEVEN THE FIRST TIME I SAW THE HEIR. MY mother was dead, and I was living on my own in the Wallows, trying to hide my wrights and survive. Processions weren't uncommon, but the Heir hadn't been seen since his vilewright had been discovered and he'd been bound to serve his father. His mother had paraded him through the city, the white and red greatcoat that marked him as a vilewrought in the service of the Crown swallowing him whole. He was nine and barely bigger than me.

He'd returned a month later with the two thousand or so rebels of Hila—peer and common alike—trailing behind him like dogs, their free will destroyed by his vilewright. His father had gifted him part of his army to assist him in proving his worth by crushing the rebellion, and instead he had used them as sacrifices. Children thought in terms of equivalent exchange, so he had done just that—sacrificed the free will of his father's soldiers to destroy the free will of the rebels. His vilewright, of course, had demanded a larger sacrifice than two thousand, so all four thousand soldiers had lost their will. His father had been horrified. His mother had thrown him another parade.

"What use are soldiers who question orders?" she had asked, so the rumors said.

The binding on Alistair Wyrslaine's chest may have stopped him from killing with his vilewright, but his wright wasn't what made him monstrous. He'd shed no blood in Hila, but that didn't mean he hadn't killed them.

They had all killed themselves without question the day after returning.

"You're mistaken," I said, trying to reckon this looming sliver of a man with the small boy barely able to ride a horse from my memories. "I'm not anything to you, and I never will be."

"I don't make mistakes." He smiled and laid one hand atop the officer's head. "She destroyed your memories of the true warrant. Be on guard."

The soldiers all rose, but now their hands trembled as they tried to hold their rifles steady. Another soldier, this one in the black uniform of the Wyrslaine army, slunk from the carriage and followed in the Heir's footsteps. Her uniform was thin silk and peppered with tears. Scabs lined her knuckles.

A sacrificial guard—the Crown and Heir had a whole group of soldiers employed solely to serve as sacrifices to their vilewrights.

The Heir approached. His gaze swept across the Felfolk prostrate around him, and he looked at them the way a hawk might glance at ants. He was hungry, but they would never be enough. I stared up at him, my noblewright pressed flat against me. He stopped only a step away.

I'd a whole wright he didn't know about. I could get out of this.

"Is there another vilewrought here?" the Heir asked. He didn't even lower his chin to look me over, his expression hidden behind large, round glasses. The Vile could look like anything and anyone, but their eyes—the same sanguine color as the god of Chaos—had always given them away. The Heir wasn't one of the Vile, but he had fashioned himself to look like one with those red glasses. No one had ever seen his eyes. "Who trained you? What was that contract?"

Contracts: I'd always called them *prayers*, but this was what proper wrought called them. They wrote contracts, specifying *exactly* what to sacrifice and *exactly* what they wanted to be created or destroyed, and then hoped they were specific enough. If they weren't, their wrights took liberties—frequently, dangerous liberties.

The Heir had been trained in writing contracts. His vilewright required them, even if he could speak them in a pinch. Mine didn't.

"That vilewright's dead," I said and lifted my chin.

He chuckled. "Fortuitous for me, then, that the universe loves balance so much that it put you in my path after removing the other vilewright from it. We are very rare, you know."

No mention of me refusing him.

"Ah, Your Excellency," said Julian, trembling hand closing around my ankle. "She's not vilewrought."

"'Your Majesty,' actually." The Heir tucked the toes of his boot beneath Julian's wrist and lifted his hand away from me. "We always know one another. It's not your fault that you are unobservant, but try to keep up." The Heir raised one hand to my face, not touching but intending to, and let it fall to my shoulder. "May I?"

No wasn't a real word when speaking to royalty.

I inclined my head. More delicately than I would have thought possible for the red-eyed vilewrought, the Heir pulled back the collar of my shirt and revealed the bare flesh over my heart. A thrum, his vilewright drawing nearer, shuddered from him to me. He let go and stepped back. His fingers never brushed my skin.

"You're not bound. You're self-taught." His voice was the low, breathy rasp of sleepless nights. "You're perfect."

"I'm not anything," I said. "I'm not—"

The Heir smiled, clapped his hands together once, and spun to the officer. "We must finish our business here. Willoughby Chase—acquire him."

"Who?" the officer asked and swallowed.

The Heir's sacrificial guard pried the summons from Will's hands. "The traitor you were supposed to be taking into custody."

"He's not here," I lied. "So you can't take him."

"By law, we must take him. Rules are meant to be followed. Contracts are meant to be obeyed." The Heir took in the crowd and beckoned his sacrificial guard and the soldiers near. "The vilewrought girl will ride with me. Acquire Willoughby Chase however necessary."

Fear roiled my stomach. I could bear the aftertaste of Rylan's death and maybe even the rotten winds of Mori as the Heir's plaything, but I could not let Will be taken by the Crown. He had given me a family and a home. I couldn't let him die for some trumped-up scam.

But they knew now. He knew.

I was vilewrought, and the folks paying attention would have realized I was dualwrought like the Crown. They would hate me for lying or fear me in that quiet way small towns feared newcomers. If I let them take Will, they'd never forgive me.

I grabbed the Heir's hand. He spun, arm tearing from my grasp. A needle as long as my forearm appeared between his fingers, and he held it over his sacrificial guard's hand. Blood welled near its point. I held up my hands in surrender.

"I will go with you, willingly, no fight," I said, "but only if Will Chase stays free until his trial and you don't bind me."

"No!" Julian lurched to his feet.

Our friend Mack caught Julian around the knees and yanked him back. One of the officers aimed her crossbow at them. Mack locked his arms around Julian's chest and whispered in his ear. Julian stilled. Across the crowd, behind the Heir's back, Kara and Old Ivy lifted their heads. Kara slipped the whittling knife from Ivy's boot. The Heir's head tilted slightly toward them.

I'd a bargaining chip, and at least this way, Will had a chance.

"That's my deal. Do you want it or not?" I asked.

"Why do you think you can bargain with me?" He smiled and turned his back on me.

"Because I bring something to our fight you can't." I caught my cheek in my teeth and bit down hard. "So start haggling."

Create a flat tip like a nail's head on each end of his needle. Make it useless, I prayed to my noblewright. *Take my blood and pain as payment.*

This was the boy who'd downed a peer's whole rebellion, ripped the will from people's minds without a thought, and collected his fellow wrought for his research, using them until they died. His mother sacrificed her enemies to the long banished Vile, and he didn't so much as blink.

Now, he shuddered.

"You're dualwrought," he said, breathless and flushed. His hand fluttered toward me before he pulled it back.

Good. He wanted me.

I nodded. "You really want to see what I can do with both of them?"

"You've been in hiding," he said and crossed his arms. One thumb ran across his bottom lip. "You aren't trained."

"No," I said, "but how do you think I've managed to stay hidden?"

A wild dog was as dangerous as a trained one.

"You'll cooperate?" he asked. "You'll work with me?"

With. Not for. Curious.

"Yes."

He smiled. "It's illegal, you know, for a working wrought to not be bound."

For the nation's protection, the court and council said, so we couldn't kill everyone and take over.

"You're the Heir to the Crown of Cynlira," I said. "Nothing is illegal for you."

"Still, there is an order to things." He stepped closer to me. "You will work with me, and you will do what I say."

"I will work with you," I said. "I will not only do what you say."

"I think we will work together quite well," he said slowly. "We will draw up the contract on the way to Mouth-of-the-River-of-Gods, but for now, we have a deal."

A contract. He said it as if simple words on paper could hold someone so rich, titled, and powerful to their word.

"Your Majesty," his sacrificial guard whispered, head bowed, "Her Excellency will not be pleased. Will Chase is still wanted."

"My mother won't know anything about this," he said. He eyed me, head tilted to the side, and ran his thumb across his bottom lip again. "You said there were bandits. That's the memory you gave them. Where are they?"

"Dead," shouted Ivy, voice muffled by the ground. The coils of her white-streaked black hair shook as she spoke, and her fingers dug into the earth. "We executed six after they killed one of our kids."

"My condolences," he said without any change in expression at all. "Willoughby Chase must appear in court on his appointed day, or you will die, my new dualwrought. He must answer for his charges. Where is he?"

Beside me, Julian sucked in a sharp breath. Will glanced up at me.

"Traveling," I said. "He's a busy man."

The Heir beckoned me close, his red gaze never leaving me.

"He will appear for his trial, and you will work for me. If he is found guilty, he will be sacrificed," he said and held out his hand. "Do we have a deal?"

"If he is not found guilty, he lives and goes free."

I took his hand. A shiver ran through him to me, and he only touched me for as long as was polite. Such a considerate monster.

"Deal," he said. "Come with me."

He took off for the carriage without looking back.

"Lorena." Julian crawled to his feet and grabbed my arm. "You don't have to do this."

"Find me," I said, prying him from me. "Please. Find me in Mori, and we will fix this."

I looked to Will. His eyes were hard and his mouth set, the tremor in his hands gone. Julian nodded, and I squeezed his hands once, twice, before pulling away. The Heir waited at the steps of the carriage, holding out his hand to me, and helped me inside. He followed me in, and his sacrificial guard shut the door behind him. I tucked myself into the corner farthest from the door. The Heir sat across from me.

"We," he said with a shuddering breath, "are going to create such wonderful things."

four

THE CARRIAGE WAS THE NICEST THING I HAD EVER sat in. Dark-blue velvet coated the benches, soft and warm beneath my hands. The window let in enough light to see but not so much that it was unbearably hot. A stack of books, bound in leather and gilded down their spines, teetered at the Heir's feet, and he handed me one as if it didn't cost more money than I could even conceive of. The carriage kept a steady pace, and the Heir let me stew in silence. I dragged one finger down the gold edges of the book.

"I have been looking for another vilewrought for a very, very long time," he said, and his glasses cast twin blood moons across my lap. "Surely, you have been curious about vilewrights. I can tell you anything you want to know."

He was fishing, offering me a worm, but I knew what happened to fish.

"You said we would draw up a contract." I dredged up all the confidence I could muster and smiled. City people adored rural girls who smiled at them. They called us quaint. Let him think me untrained and naive. "Please don't take this the wrong way, Your Majesty, but you are exactly that—the Heir. Laws and contracts do not bind you as they do me."

I had heard of his deals, of course. Gossipmongers said it was like making a deal with one of the Vile. Word it right or write your will.

"True. I have power many don't." He settled into his seat and crossed his spindly legs ankle over knee. "If you do not contract your vilewright in just the right way, it will take liberties. Imagine I am your vilewright. Think over exactly what you want from me, and we shall draw it up once we are in Mouth-of-the-River-of-Gods."

"But you will keep me safe until we draw it up?" I asked.

"You're too valuable to waste." He popped the joints of his hand finger by finger, never once breaking eye contact with me. "My mother has a bad record with prior vilewrought, however, so we must make sure your introduction to her is as innocuous as possible."

I'd never heard of any other vilewrought, which meant she had probably killed them.

"What if I don't want to meet her?" I asked.

"Then, like everyone else she has ever met, you are cursed to be disappointed." He pressed his palms together and rested his fingertips against his chin. "You possess both a noblewright and a vilewright?"

I nodded.

"When did you know? My mother recognized my vilewright when I was six but didn't let them bind me until after Hila. Which wright made itself known first? Did you feel it move about you? Did you feel its hunger?" He leaned forward, elbows on his knees. "My mother thinks it is absurd to ascribe movement or wants like that to them, but they have imperatives like anything else. Vilewrights yearn. I have always wondered if it's actual hunger or me projecting after the contract saps my strength, but I have never had anyone to ask before. It's odd, but..."

He spoke for hours, referencing a dozen ideas I didn't know but grasped from context. I had grown with these wrights, and they had grown with me. I didn't need the words of his academic texts to know what was mine and what was theirs.

"You're describing them like a soldier talks about their sword," I said as the carriage rolled to a stop in a dark, quiet town. "They're not tools."

He licked his dry lips and nodded. "Of course not. They are alive in a way, but they cannot exist without us. You should read this tonight. We can discuss it tomorrow."

"My schedule is rather full right now," I said, "with nightmares."

He snorted. "Read it."

We slept at an empty inn. I stayed in a room with his sacrificial guard, Hana Worth. He slept alone. She loaned me a small bag with a change of clothes, tooth cleaner, and other small necessities, and I slept swaddled in Julian's old, brown coat, my nose tucked into the collar. By dawn, we were awake, and I tossed the book he had given me onto his bench. It was gilded and lovely but utterly unreadable. The Heir didn't so much as glance at me when he entered the carriage. He only had eyes for the book.

"Did you read it?" he asked.

He still hadn't asked for my name.

"No," I said. "It's in Old Liran."

"All wrought can read Old Liran, Madshavi, and Krate." His dark brows drew together. "Surely, you were taught?"

"You accepted our deal because I'm self-taught," I said. "Remember?"

"Of course I remember." His top lip arched into a half sneer. He took a breath and slowly let it out. "It describes vilewrights as parasites."

Both of my wrights bristled at that, the feeling like a metal knife scraping against my teeth.

"But you understood me last night?" His hand drifted to his chest. I couldn't see the sigil the court and council had placed on his chest but knew it would be as red as the heart it had been carved over. How could he stand being bound to serve and only using his vilewright in ways they approved? "You must understand me."

He said it the same way my mother, feverish and dying in the days after the factory fire, had asked for water.

"That our vilewrights are hungry?" I asked. "That noble-wrought can't understand the way a vilewright will thrum in your chest until you sacrifice something, anything, to it?"

Sometimes, in the dead hour before dawn when Felhollow was quiet and all I could hear was the nothing in my life, I was so hungry for something more—more than hiding, more than settling down, more than the monotony of everyday life—that my bones ached. I wanted something. I wanted everything.

My vilewright loved those hours.

"Our vilewrights are not parasites. They hunger," I said. "I understand perfectly."

He sighed, the tension in his shoulders slumping, and leaned back.

"Most of us have the same teachers. Each peer has two or three that they loan out for a price to others, partly to spy and partly to make sure none of us learn to do anything dangerous," the Heir said, glancing at the blushing dawn outside the carriage window. "They taught me to make my contracts longer and more precise. They feared my vilewright would take liberties. What are your contracts like?"

I shifted. We were to be stuck in this carriage for days, and already I was tired of it.

"I don't write long, exacting contracts like you do, and I have never written one down," I said slowly. "My wrights were all I had as a child."

He looked up, mouth hard.

I shook my head. "However lonely you think you were, you at least had somewhere and someone that was yours. I didn't. I only had my wrights. I ask and offer a sacrifice, and if they're pleased, they do what I ask. If they're not, I get sick, and they sulk and take the sacrifice but don't do anything. Keeping me alive keeps them alive. Our relationship is—"

"Curious." He smiled so widely it upset his glasses. "A monster in our veins. We feed the monster, and it does something akin to what we asked."

A god in my veins who answers my prayers in exchange for a sacrifice.

"I need another vilewrought so that I can conduct my research without anyone being aware of it." He flicked his hand out, and a long needle appeared between his fingers. He spun it across the backs of his knuckles. "I am limited by my binding. You are not."

"No one knows what you do with the wrought in your collection," I said. "It's unsettling, not knowing."

"It certainly is." He glanced up at me, the light flickering in his glasses. "Would knowing make you feel better?"

"I would feel better if you put that away." I nodded at the needle. "And yes. I want to know why you want me."

"Ah. A nervous habit." He smiled crookedly and tucked the needle into a pocket in his sleeve. "Before we speak of particulars, let us speak of what you do and do not know about wrights."

He did not answer my question that day or the next.

He was good at speaking around true answers. He had to be, growing up around his mother and the peers. They collected all the wrought they could find, bound them to their service, and trained them to write out contracts so long and convoluted that the wrights could only ever do precisely what was asked of them. Most noblewrought couldn't function without contracts either.

Any rebellion would be stalled by the time it took to draft and enact a contract.

The Heir didn't mention that, but it was obvious why the court and council insisted on them.

I contented myself with questions I figured he would like and kept my more pressing ones closer to my chest.

Would Julian and Will come to Mori? Would Felhollow disavow me? Was anyone angry about me lying? What had Will done, and what was he doing? The warrant had been written right before the soldiers confronted us, but he'd been so calm that it was like he knew it was coming. Even if he had broken some law, it surely wasn't anything worth killing him over.

"You must have more interesting questions?" the Heir asked. "Contracts are so dry, and you will see plenty once we begin work."

I shrugged. "How can wrights hunger and consume sacrifices when they have no physical forms?"

"A curious conundrum," he muttered and slid to the window, pushing open the little pane of glass. From its other side, he peeled a dirt-sodden spiderweb, and it clung to his hand like a second skin. "This web is real even though the spider is gone, but at certain angles, we cannot see it. In certain lights, we can almost see our wrights even though the Noble and Vile are gone."

"We're not at the right angle, you mean, to see wrights," I said.

The Heir turned his hand over, and the threads of the web vanished. The spider, not gone after all, scurried across his palm. He moved as if to kill it, and I grabbed his wrist. He raised one brow.

"Perhaps the Vile will return one day," I said, coaxing the spider to me and cupping it in my hands. "They're scary, but they're not bad. They eat pests, you know."

He didn't speak to me again until the fifth day. We were traveling next to the Tongue, the river that ran through Mori and into the south of Cynlira. A musky sulfuric sting rose from it that left each breath tasting of sun-dried fish and thick, clinging mud, and it dredged up all my old, worst memories. I read one of his books, my hands shaking. The Heir handed me a flask of cold water.

"You're nervous." He closed the journal he had been writing in. "Why?"

"I grew up in Mori," I said. "Didn't want to come back."

"Really?" asked the Heir. "How did I not notice you?"

The catch in his voice made my chest ache. "I grew up on the north end of the first wall behind Formet district."

The church district Formet had been mostly abandoned, and the water of the Wallows was seeping into its long-unused churches. The gods had possessed names once, but after they abandoned us, we stopped using them. Now they were just concepts—Order, Chaos, Life, Death, and Time—and their churches were rotting. Last I'd been there, most of the buildings were caved in or housing folks with nowhere else to go. The guards had gone through every few weeks to clear them out.

"The Forget-Me-Not district?" His head tilted slightly. "You grew up in The-Vile-Wallow-in-the-Waters?"

No one used the old names anymore, but of course he did.

"You didn't visit the Wallows." I shrugged. "And I've lived in Felhollow for years."

He stared at me for a long moment, his mouth slightly open. "What is your family name?"

Lirans always took the name of the parent who brought the most to the partnership, but it wasn't like he'd recognize her name as if I were some peer's forgotten kid. She'd simply had two copper halfans more than my father.

"Adler," I said. "Do most people answer that with their full name and forget you never asked them all together?"

"Forgive me." He adjusted his glasses and leaned back. "What is your name?"

"Lorena Adler," I said. "You're forgiven if you tell me exactly what it is you want from me."

"I want you, Lorena," said the Heir, long fingers tapping against the side of his face. "What do you want? Other than aiding Willoughby Chase, you have made no mention of what you want."

Another distraction. I said nothing.

The Heir sighed. He slid from his seat to mine, his thigh knocking against my knee. One finger hooked around the wire connecting the lenses of his glasses, pulling them down and off, and he unknotted his cravat. He cleaned his glasses with it.

"When I was a child, I wanted a dog," he said, "but it wasn't a dog I truly wanted."

He set his glasses on my nose. With one finger beneath my chin, he turned me to face him. Lurking in the space above his shoulders as if it were a person leaning to whisper in his ear, a faint smear of dark red hung. I reached out, fingers gliding through the shape. I felt nothing at all.

"That's your wright," I whispered. "You can see wrights."

He laughed, head thrown back and neck bare. A faint scar ran from his left ear to the hollow of his throat.

"They only show vilewrights." He nodded to the space behind me. "Yours hides when I look at you."

I would've hidden too.

"Did you make these?" I asked, leaning around him to study his wright, but it vanished beneath his coat. This boy was as clever as he was monstrous.

"My mother said I could have a dog if I did something with my vilewright that she had never seen before," he said, "and I very much wanted a dog, though the contract nearly killed me."

"You didn't want a dog." The glasses slipped down my nose until his mouth was halved by a thick red line. "You wanted someone who didn't mind you were vilewrought."

He had wanted someone who loved him and wasn't scared of him. An equal—something impossible so long as the peerage existed and he was the Heir to the Crown.

"And now I have you." He took the glasses from my face and pushed them to his forehead, black hair and red lenses a crooked crown. His eyes were a soft, ashy gray. "What do you know of the Door?"

"Just rumors." I shook my head. "When the gods banished the surviving Noble and the Vile who escaped mortal appetites, the Vile cheated. They didn't leave our world completely, and they made sure there was a way for them to return. Deep beneath the heart of Mori is a Door. It demands blood sacrifices to stay shut."

They ate us. We ate them. The survivors hid behind a Door that ate us. The cycle continued eternal.

It was what they wanted to sacrifice Will to.

"It's very real, and it requires more and more souls to sate its appetite and stay shut. One day soon, we will not be able to feed it enough. It will open. The Vile will return. Many will die, and the survivors will live under Vile rule again." He tilted his head to the side and let his glasses slip into place, adjusting them with one unsteady hand. "I want you to help me shut the Door—no more sacrifices and no more death—for good."

five

MORI WAS BUILT IN THE CROOK OF THE CRESCENT Mountains. The royal grounds resided at the top of the cliffs, looking down upon the rest of us. The river split the city in two, winding its way from the palace, and mortal-made creeks carried water to every district and tinged them sulfuric yellow-brown. Boats and barges crept through the wide gates between districts like words through crooked teeth.

If the gate leading out of Mori was a mouth, the Wallows was a constipated gut full of crumbling buildings, half-sunk houseboats, and stagnant water with nowhere to go. Without it, Mori would cease to function; Wallowers did all the work no one else wanted to do. It was more profitable that way, ignoring the Wallowers who lost a hand in the mines or finger in the factories, and it wasn't like anyone would do anything about it if they could. The common council—a few dozen seats set up by the court to check the power of the court—was stocked with folks who wouldn't make a fuss or had too much to lose if things changed. Of course, if they ever tried to really change anything, the court needed only to outvote them to overrule it. There were over two hundred families in the peerage, and each one had a representative who sat on the court. Those courtiers determined everything that happened in Cynlira.

The whole setup was a joke.

My mother had been burned so badly I hadn't even recognized

her, and the peer who owned the factory had sent her home to die. Some newcomer had taken her place on the line the next day. A new death every few weeks, and it was still open. The peer who owned it still profited.

"Welcome home, Lorena Adler, to the longest-standing city in what's left of the world, the Crown of the Shattered Continent, our capital of Cynlira, Mouth-of-the-River-of-Gods." The Heir opened the curtains and stretched out, still sitting next to me. "Did you miss it?"

"Can't say I did," I muttered.

The Heir laughed, one gloved hand closing around mine, and nodded toward the tallest tower at the top of the palace.

"Deep beneath that tower, behind locked doors and down stairs older than this city, in a cavern with no other exit, is the Door my mother sacrifices mortals to," he said. "The Vile are gone, but anyone who sees that Door is infected with their odd chaos. Noblewrought can barely stand to be near it, and I only know one who can look at it without flinching—my mother. It tempts us into opening it. It wants to be opened."

"What happens if you don't feed it?" I whispered.

"It opens a little bit more each time it is denied a sacrifice, but it demands more and more. It is very real, it is very danger-ous, and it is the only thing keeping the Vile from this world." He dropped my hand. "I want to destroy it. I want to create a stronger Door that doesn't require sacrifices to stay shut. I want you to help me build that new Door and save the world."

I pulled away from him.

This was the Heir to the Crown, the boy so dangerous his first instinct as a child had been to destroy people's free will in Hila. There was no world where I believed he would undertake something so kind.

"It's such a fascinating puzzle to unravel," he said, already turning back to one of his books.

So that was his motivation—curiosity.

"Well," I said, "at least you finally hinted at what I would be doing here."

He chuckled. "I'm sure my collection of wrought will be more than happy to explain our work."

It took us an hour to reach the royal grounds. I'd never crossed all of Mori so quickly. Outside, tall trees shaded the clearing we were in, and the sounds of a stable came from over a wall of holly bushes. The Heir nodded to me.

"We are in my private residence," he said, glasses shielding his eyes yet again. "You will have to bow to me in public, you realize?"

"Of course, Your Majesty." I didn't bow.

He didn't say anything and swept out of the carriage.

"Come." Hana stuck her head in. "You will have a room with the rest of His Majesty's researchers."

These grounds were too opulent for me to comprehend. The gardens were so neatly ordered I could tell the time by where the shadows fell against the garlic stalks, and tulip blooms in every color lined the paths as markers. One building had a small greenhouse full of ripe fruits all to itself, and another had a shooting range of pockmarked targets and marked trees denoting the start of hunting grounds. Servants in plain clothes and soldiers in colors for families I didn't recognize darted down the paths. Hana led me to the last door in a distant hall. The name plate had recently been pried off.

"This building belongs to His Majesty and houses those within his employ," she said, holding out a key to me. "It only locks from the inside. Lock it at night. Vilewrought are particularly susceptible to the Door."

"There are only two other vilewrought," I said. "How do you know all vilewrought are susceptible and not just them?"

"They sleepwalk to it." She crossed her arms over her broad chest. The silver bell necklace at her throat jingled. "They're as deadly asleep as they are awake, by the way. Don't get any ideas."

I'd sleepwalked as a child, too, but it had stopped when I left the Wallows. I fiddled with the handle. My neighbor—Carlow by their nameplate—had left their door cracked. A meticulously kept room covered in a thick coat of dust lay beyond.

"Good luck with her," Hana said. "Please don't try anything. I'd hate to kill you."

She said it so lightly I almost missed it.

"He's killed thousands," I said. "Does he really hold to his contracts?"

"As strictly as a wright," said Hana with a laugh. "He's got his own logic, so make sure you word your contract right."

She pushed open the door to my room. The room was sparse, only a raised bed and writing desk. Hana lingered in the door.

"No one is to know you are dualwrought except for the others within the lab," she said. "However, you will need a reason to be here."

I ran my hand across the plain brown clothes—one dress, one linen shirt, one waistcoat, and one pair of trousers—laid out on the bed. So plain yet smoother than the homespun clothes I'd worn in Felhollow.

"I'm an undertaker," I said. "Surely, he needs one of those."

Maybe he wasn't lying and the Door really did require sacrifices, or maybe his mother and he just liked killing. Either way, they left plenty of corpses behind.

"Of course you are," muttered Hana. "The ones in Mori wear gray greatcoats."

Bones and ashes: everyone's final sacrifice to Death.

Undertakers in the Wallows had never bothered with the coat. We all knew them by name, since death came so often.

"Don't bother with a real one," I said. No one suspected some Wallows-born girl from the root end of nowhere of anything. It would be to my advantage. "If you have to, get me an old one."

Within an hour, the Heir stood at the threshold of the room and carried a frayed gray coat. He had changed out of his black coat into the white one of wrought, the red sigil on the back identical to the one carved into his chest. The sigils were a holdover from before the gods left and denoted what kinds of magic a wrought could do. The bindings prevented any other.

The Crown had been bound to Life and Death and forced to serve her nation as a healer and undertaker. My similarity to her was already too great for me to stomach.

"May I enter?" the Heir asked.

"Am I allowed to refuse?" I pulled out the chair at the desk. "Your Majesty."

"It is important for powerful people to establish clear boundaries. My father never did." He stepped into the room and laid the coat on my bed. No sigil decorated its back. From the bag over his shoulder, he pulled a thick stack of papers. "This is the structure I use for all my contracts."

The closer he came, the angrier my noblewright grew. It was a fuzzy stuffiness in my ears, like staying underwater too long.

"Did your father teach you these rules?" I asked, trying to shake my noblewright's fury away.

"In a way." The Heir straightened his glasses. "Did your life in the Wallows teach you how to use your wrights without such contracts?"

"Do you treat your vilewright like you treat conversations? An equal exchange of information, like our wrights?" I asked.

"There is no such thing as an equal exchange, especially between wrought and their wrights." He snorted. "They're not sentient. They don't infer or know. They obey."

Wrights didn't demand a sacrifice equal to their action. They always demanded more. To destroy a life, a vilewright couldn't simply sacrifice one life, and it was trite to say wrights obeyed when they were the ones setting the sacrifices.

"I wasn't speaking literally." I sighed. "My wrights know I trust them. They can infer what I need them to do. Perhaps yours can't and require long contracts because they know you don't trust them. My wrights and I understand each other."

If I died, they died.

"Surely, they don't always do what you want," said the Heir.

"What we want and what we need aren't always the same." I kept the chair between us, but he still didn't sit. "We survive."

It was why I could do so much so quickly. The Heir couldn't do something like he'd done at Hila unless given permission by the court and council.

"Are you telling me that you leave the destruction up to your vilewright?" he asked, voice soft and controlled. "We spend years studying contract language, and wrought still die every month because their noblewright takes liberty with the wording. Do you know how many people I have—" He let out a shuddering breath and shook his head. "Wrights are not people. They are, at best, feral dogs with some hope of training."

A tingling weight settled over my shoulders. His gaze flicked up, the corners of his eyes crinkling.

"I think," I said slowly, "you offended my vilewright."

"It's not a person." He held out the papers to me, but his gaze remained glued on the space above me. "It can't get offended."

I sat and read over the contract in silence. He pulled a book from his bag and made notations in the margins. I looked through the contract three times, picking through the wording, and made sure to mark anything that could be interpreted in multiple ways. If he knew how to be specific for his vilewright, he knew how to be vague to his advantage.

"What does this mean?" I asked, having already worked it out but wanting to know if he would lie. I pointed to one section of the contract. "'Except for the rights granted in section twelve of this contract, the former party shall retain rights to knowledge developed during employment and will not be held accountable for damages in perpetuity.'"

"Anything you develop during the course of working for me shall be my property," he said and adjusted his glasses with two delicate fingers. "It is simply protecting my research."

What a poor liar he was. I drew a line through the sentence, and he winced.

"I will have to rewrite the whole thing now," he said.

He didn't have to do that, but he was so peculiar about this. "You and I both know that line means you own everything I create and it's not your fault if I'm injured forever. At the very least, you're paying if I get hurt."

Still, he hadn't explained what his research with the Door involved.

"I don't suppose you'll tell me exactly what I'll be doing and if it's dangerous?" I asked. "How long will I do it? I'm not signing this, you know, with that line about length of employment to be determined by former party. What if I can't help you with your work? Is our agreement null?"

"You are far too useful to be put in harm's way." He never approached the desk and never sat.

I nearly snapped the quill. As if my worth were tied to my usefulness.

"I have some questions that must be answered before I agree to anything," I said, "and I want your answers in writing."

He pulled out a fresh sheet of paper, the ghostly watermark of Felhollow shadowing the center, and handed it to me.

"You know, Will Chase is the reason you have nice paper like this," I said.

The Heir hummed. "So long as I have paper, its acquisition isn't pertinent."

"Of course it isn't." I wrote out the majority of my wants— Will and any of his companions would have safe passage to Mori, Will would stay in his lodgings in Mori until the trial, we would be granted access to the evidence against him, and if he was innocent, he and the Felfolk would face no retribution. We simply had to prove his innocence to the court and council. "What if you break the contract?"

The floorboards creaked, and I turned. He loomed over me.

"I never break my contracts," he said, hands clenched around the back of my chair.

I leaned away from him. "You're the Heir. You can do whatever you want."

"If either of us break this contract, my vilewright will extract a price," he said.

This was what made the Heir so dangerous. There were so few vilewrought, and he was the only one who could instill pieces of his wright into materials. He could have contracts extract a price or explode incendiaries long after the contract was written. His designs left no survivors.

Once the contract was written and we signed, we would be bound to obey it. We would be bound to follow the contract through.

He ground his teeth together. "I would be more worried about Chase if I were you. What if he runs?"

"He won't," I said. He loved me. "What if I can't help you?"

Even through his glasses, I could see the eye roll.

"What if he's guilty?" he asked.

"He's not," I said and stood. "Here. Write your new contract then."

He took a seat at the desk and opened up a fresh pot of sky-blue ink. He wrote out the contract in painfully precise penmanship, quietly asking me questions as he went before adding an addition or changing the original wording of his contract. I stood behind him, leaning against the desk, and told him everything exactly as I wanted it worded. On the third page, he thinned out his ink with water.

"Did your mother sacrifice your ink supplier too?" I asked.

His shoulders tensed and his fingers tightened. "You could say that."

"That's everything for me," I said. Julian, Will, and the rest of Felhollow would be safe unless they broke any existing—the Heir had balked when I added that specification—laws, and if Will was guilty, he would be sacrificed. He wasn't guilty.

Will had always been as cleanly cut as they came, and he had Julian to think of. He would never have put Julian in danger. He wouldn't do that to us.

I'd also slipped in a line making sure no more sacrifices came from Felhollow. We were so few and too far out of the way to make that worth it. The Heir agreed.

"Then we have a deal," he said. "A copy will be delivered to you tomorrow morning. For now, I simply need biographical information and a piece of you to make sure the signatures are appropriately binding."

"That's a lot of pages to say you're using me," I said, pulling out a few strands of my hair.

The Heir peeled back his glove and nicked the back of his hand with the nib. "You are capable of using your wrights without restriction, and you are using me as much as I am using you. Unless I have misunderstood?"

"No," I said, "you're just being very upfront about it when that contract was anything but."

"Good," he said, dipping his quill in his ink once more. From this angle, I barely caught his smile. "You currently reside in Felled-Noble-in-the-Hollow, yes?"

"We just call it Felhollow these days."

He jotted down the full name and said, "Your birth date?"

"I'm a seventeen-year-old child of winter. Not very specific after that." I shrugged at his sigh. "It was probably the first day of Byrdaffin, and that's what I always say, but might've been the second to last day of the year. You've got five days to pick from."

He looked up, quill dripping ink on the page. "My mother kept extensive records for my siblings and me."

"My mother worked sixteen hours a day in the Northcott munitions factory, and paper was expensive."

It hurt that I could remember such a simple fact but not her face or voice. I'd sacrificed them all to keep Felfolk alive over the years. I'd kept my memories of the peer she'd worked for. Sixteen hours per day for ten years she'd worked for Lankin Northcott, and all she'd gotten for her troubles was killed in a perfectly avoidable accident. Northcott hadn't wanted to pay for upkeep, so my mother and a dozen others had paid with their lives.

One day, I'd pay Northcott back.

"A Wallower with connections to Felhollow and a dual-wrought daughter?" he asked. "Someone with no cunning would assume you used your wrights to get where you are."

And I prayed, *Take the stain from the paper and the ink from the quill if needed. It's his favorite. Destroy his memory of what I said about my mother.*

Surely, that would be enough for only sixteen words. My mother was mine and mine alone. I had few memories of her. The Heir could keep thoughts of her out of his head, or I would make him.

My vilewright lunged, the Heir flinched, and then he dipped his now-empty quill into the bottle and let the ink refill it. "We'll say the first day of the year, then."

I smiled.

This was why the concept of nonphysical sacrifices was such a revolution and never taught to anyone. It was why they'd bound the Heir as soon as he returned from Hila. No one knew when a wrought was using them, and they didn't require the wrought to act. Blood left a stain. Sacrificing a feeling didn't reveal anything.

No one had known what Alistair was doing in Hila until it was already too late.

With no binding and using nonphysical sacrifices, I could use my wrights without anyone the wiser.

To use the Heir's blood as a sacrifice, I'd have to stab him. To use his memory, I only needed to be near him.

The Heir signed his name in the blood from the back of his hand, offered me a fresh quill with a sharp nib, and had me sign in my own blood as well.

"I will need your assistance with the sacrifice," he said once I was done.

I glanced at him from the corner of my eyes. "What did you have in mind?"

"I need either quite a bit of blood," said the Heir, "or a very treasured memory. Perhaps something to rival whatever memory of mine you destroyed earlier? I'm assuming it was about your mother."

I stiffened. He smiled.

"My first taste of honeysuckle." I held out my hand to him. "It was summer, I was ten, and it was my first time out of Mori."

"That will do." He took my hand, bare fingers cool and dry against mine, and chuckled. "You're wasted on Felhollow."

I knew that, but obscurity there had been better than danger here. Though now I could help do something.

"Is Willoughby Chase really worth dying for?" the Heir asked, rising from the chair, my hand still clasped firmly in his. A crack in his lips bled when he grinned. "Destroy a memory of mine again and you'll forget you even have a wright." He dropped my hand and turned away. "Lock your door behind me. There are worse things in this palace than me."

I slept hard, waking only when Hana rapped at my door and rattled the lock. Blood speckled my bed and clotted my nose. The ink I had sacrificed had not been enough. My vile-wright sat heavy on my chest.

Nothing was ever enough.

six

I COULDN'T STOMACH THE THOUGHT OF SEEING
Julian yet. Julian and Will had not recoiled when they
learned I was dualwrought, but it had been an emergency.

Would he only stay friendly with me out of duty now that
I'd handed myself over in exchange for his father? Would Will
feel beholden to me? I'd found them and made them family, but
this could ruin it.

I peeled Julian's coat off and laid it across my bed, smoothing
it out. It barely smelled of him now. The plain clothes and gray
coat fit fine but felt heavier. A stifling sweat crept over me.

The door rattled.

"Adler!" called Hana. "His Majesty prefers early starts."

I opened the door. She was leaning against the wall, a dozen
new cuts on her hands and a moon pendant spinning between
her fingers. Her gaze raked me over.

"Let's go," she said and walked away.

The red Wyrslaine sigil spanned the back of her black uniform. The shoulders of her sleeveless coat pulled taut across her
broad shoulders, and the only delicate part of her was the way
she tucked her necklace beneath her shirt. White scars marred
her pale skin, crisscrossing her arms. Even her boots bore the
Wyrslaine sigil.

My mother had spent the last six years of her life trying to keep
me from this. If she saw me now, she'd have died all over again.

Hana led me to a small building nestled in a clearing of fruit trees. The names Baines, Carlow, and Creek were burned into the wood of the door, and bursts of swallowwort grew from the wood around Creek's name. Carlow seemed to have ripped away the purple hyacinth growing from hers. Another name beneath Creek's had been scratched from the wood entirely.

"This is the only day I'll show you where to go," said Hana. "I'm His Majesty's guard, not a nanny."

I was desperate to ask her how she could stand to be his sacrificial guard, serving as the sacrifice that allowed his wright to work, but the tilt of her thin lips and bulge of her biceps wouldn't let me.

"Consider me sufficiently nannied." I touched the door—no handle—and knocked. "Only one question: did you choose to be his guard?"

She flinched. "Like most of the people in his employ, he offered me a deal. I took it."

She looked me over once more and left.

No one answered the door. I knocked again, and a muffled "open it" slipped through. I pushed. Something blocked the door.

"Open the door."

I sighed and shoved. "I'm trying."

The door groaned open. It clunked against a foot, and I stuck my head through the gap. A noblewrought with Life's green sigil stretched across the back of their pale coat was curled up on their side. They didn't budge when I knocked the door against their foot, and I had to force the door open with my shoulder, pushing them away. They'd a lithe body, pink skin tanned from days outside, and their brown hair was blond in sun-bleached streaks. Their lips were a pale gray-blue.

I rested my fingers against their neck and cursed.

"Hello?" I asked.

The room was long and lined with desks and shelves. Every

surface was covered in books, bowls full of metal and bone, and glass apparatuses I didn't recognize. There was room for five people to work comfortably, but only four of the desks were in use.

The one near the door was neatly ordered and pristine, only a stack of too many books marring its surface. I could feel the Heir's need for rules rolling off it. Next to it was a table littered with dirt and rot, the wood blossoming with oleander and pansies, and worms churned in the old papers and earth. On the other side of the room near the door was a desk drowning in hand-drawn maps and diagrams, and a crossbow half taken apart sat in the corner. Solid bone bolts were lodged into the ceiling above the desk.

And at the far end of the room, at a table overflowing with crumpled pages and old quills, sat a noblewrought with their back to me. The blue sigil of Order—they specialized in technology, then—was stitched into the back of their greatcoat.

I cleared my throat. "There's a corpse blocking the door."

"Good for him." The noblewrought grunted, narrow shoulders hunched up to their ears, and ripped a page from a book. "Kick him aside and come in."

It must've been Creek then. He was the only man in the Heir's employ according to Hana.

"Are you Carlow or Baines?" I shimmied the rest of the way into the room and stepped over Creek's corpse.

"Rule one," they said, fiddling with whatever was on their table. "Do not interrupt my work."

"Rot will set in soon, and he needs—"

"He'll be fine. He always is." They shook out their knotted mantle of black hair and stretched. "Baines will be here shortly. They were supposed to deal with you."

So this was Carlow, the girl I lived next to.

"No sigil," said Carlow, sliding from her stool. Her brows furrowed above a pair of thick, dark goggles. She was slight and barely put together, as if she'd last changed her clothes and braided her hair a month ago. Freckles dotted her nose. "You're not bound at all."

"I'm an undertaker," I said. "Least I was until I used my wright at the wrong time."

Carlow's coat hung from her shoulders. The sigil carved into the flesh over her heart oozed blood and blue ink. She must have disobeyed it constantly.

"He finally found a live vilewrought," she muttered, scratching at the raw skin of her binding. "You may call me Carlow if you must speak with me at all."

She would've been scary if she weren't so short.

"Don't be dramatic." Carlow kicked Creek's leg and stomped back to her desk. "You don't get to die until I do."

I was wrong; she was terrifying.

I leaned down to check Creek again, and he jerked up, drawing in a deep, rattling breath.

"How long?" Creek asked and coughed. The color returned to his face. "How long was I dead?"

"Five minutes," said Carlow. "The formation collapsed a minute after death. I told you—our deaths aren't accepted as sacrifice. We're not enough."

"Ah, the dulcet tones of an 'I told you so' upon revival do soothe my soul." Creek shook his head, straggly hair sticking to his gaunt face, and stumbled to the messy desk. Standing, he looked more like a costume stretched over a wobbly frame than a person. He raked his fingers through a pile of tinder-dry twigs. "Damn. I thought we were onto something."

"The new vilewrought is here." Carlow went back to her table. "Deal with her."

"You die often?" I asked, my noblewright shivering against the back of my neck.

Creek let out a bark of a laugh and turned to me. I stepped back. His eyes, pupils and whites and all, were a bright blue. It was the chosen color for the god Order, and the Noble created by Order had marked every mortal they cursed with those blue eyes.

"I am Delmond Creek, gardener and noblewrought, but you may call me Creek," he said and held out his hand as if nothing were wrong at all. "You have already had the displeasure of meeting Carlow. Ignore her. Her bite is as bad as her bark, and I've run out of muzzles."

"He's a poisoner," said Carlow. "Don't touch him."

I took another step back. The Noble and Vile had been banished centuries ago. To have been cursed by them, he must have been ancient.

"I had been wondering when you should show up, Lorena Adler," he said, tucking his hands into his pockets. Grass stains colored the pale knees of his breeches. "Ignore her. Dear little Franziska Carlow is an ornery thorn in my side. I derive new medicinals from natural substances."

"Poisons spelled with more letters," said Carlow.

I meant to ask how he knew my name, but what came out was, "You're cursed."

The Noble were creatures of order and rationale, easily angered when mortals interrupted their work of balancing the world, but I'd never heard of any living Noble-cursed.

"How old are you?" I asked. "Did you know the Noble and Vile? Does the curse affect your noblewright? Did you get it for eating one of the—"

"My tastes are much more refined than that." Creek sliced one finger open, took a moment—contracting his noblewright probably—and created an iris from the wound. He tucked the blue flower behind my ear. "While curiosity is certainly better than screaming, it's still rude. Even if we are accustomed to rude here."

Carlow snorted.

"Play nicely," he said, but I couldn't tell if his gaze shifted to Carlow. His eyes were hungry slivers of sky and impossible to follow.

"He's sixty-nine," said Carlow, turning to stare at me. "His curse is generational. Mine is infectious."

She pushed her goggles to the top of her head. Her eyes, too, bore the mark of a curse, but they were so red and deep and dark I feared the color would spill down her cheeks and drown us all.

The Vile, creations of Chaos, had always favored red.

"Don't worry. It only passes to people I love, and I hate everyone. You're safe." She jerked her head, goggles falling back over her eyes, and turned away. "Mostly."

"Ignore her. I'm only twenty-five." Creek cracked the joints of his neck with a sound like branches under foot. "Carlow and I are not truly immortal. No need for such a scowl, Lorena. We can only die of old age or if we fulfill the covenants of our curses, though I doubt I will ever grow a perfectly blue rose, so that's no threat to me, and Carlow's not going to love anyone ever again, so she's safe."

He led me around the room. At the very back, there was a small door that led to a washroom with a full copper tub with a web of pipes that rained water from the ceiling. Creek warned that it was for decontamination and placed me at the table next to Carlow, closest to the washroom "just in case." He dragged over one of the two spare stools, declaring it the one least likely to be missed.

"The other's too squeaky," Carlow muttered.

"We haven't had to use the washroom since Baines arrived. They're quite militant about safety," he said and patted me on the head. "We'll keep you safe. You're our secret weapon after all. Her Excellency and the court have been rejecting our recent contract proposals. Since you're not bound to anyone, you should be able to continue our research without them knowing. You being dualwrought is—"

Carlow swept her arm across her table, knocking a whole slew of wood shavings, dowels, and dovetail puzzle pieces to the floor. "You're what?"

"See what you miss by being ornery?" Creek asked. "You didn't listen to His Majesty at all this morning, did you, darling? In order to remake the Door into one that doesn't demand payment, we must remove it without letting loose its charges. Only a vilewrought can destroy the Door, the first step, and the Heir cannot disobey his mother. The court and councils consider this too risky. If we attempt to experiment with such a task, the employer we're bound to will know immediately. They won't know anything about you though." He stepped back and studied me for a moment, one hand coming up to my shoulder. "Have you heard it yet?"

"No," I said. "I barely thought it real until recently."

"It's very real and very alluring." He leaned in close and whispered, "Open the Door."

I jerked away, and he laughed.

"You had better get used to that," said Creek.

"Her Excellency has no inclination to stop the sacrifices," Carlow said quickly, scurrying to me and shoving Creek out of the way. "Her court of peers agree, and even the council is lenient when it's not them being sacrificed. They think it keeps people in line."

"Doesn't it though?" Creek glared at me from over Carlow and set his chin against her head. "She doesn't look very impressive. Dualwrought should be impressive. They're chosen by the souls of the devoured Noble *and* Vile. Why this mortal?"

Carlow elbowed him. "Being wrought is essentially glorified possession, and when the immortals were still around, it was impossible to determine why and how they possessed certain mortals."

"Mostly wore whoever fit, I imagine," muttered Creek.

"The Heir is really trying to shut the Door?" I asked and

pointed to her goggles. If they were always like this, we'd get nothing done. "Do those show you noblewrights? The Door?"

"No." She pulled her googles down over her eyes, slipped out from under Creek, and returned to her desk. "They keep me from having to look at all of you."

"Access to the Door is limited," Creek said. "It is weak from hunger, and the Vile Crowns, the strongest of the Vile, are capable of infiltrating this world through it. 'Open the Door, Lorena Adler,' they'll say, and eventually, you will."

The door to the laboratory flew open. I startled, tearing my gaze from Creek's cursed blue eyes. A noblewrought—short, chubby, and grinning from ear to ear—gasped when they saw me and shooed Creek away. He slunk aside.

"I'm Basil Baines," they said, taking my hands in theirs and looking me over so quickly their brown curls bounced. "You're Lorena, yes? The dualwrought? May I call you Lore? Call me Basil."

I laughed. "Yes and yes and if you insist."

"Smashing!" They tugged me away from the others. "Ignore them. They're always weird and terrible. How do you use both wrights? Did you learn? I heard you weren't bound. You have to teach me how you use your noblewright."

"I'm not," I said slowly, "but I don't know as much as you lot."

"Don't worry. No one knows as much as Carlow," they said and plopped down onto the stool at my table. "She doesn't pay enough attention to be patronizing about it usually, right, Carlow?"

She grunted and turned a page in her book.

"She's trying to figure out the pattern behind the number of sacrifices the Door requires," said Basil. "It's very dry."

"That's beyond me." I hopped up onto the table. "All right. I'll answer your questions if you answer mine."

"You're supposed to be reading," muttered Creek, but he shrugged and went to bother Carlow.

"Deal." Basil nodded, tongue pinched between their teeth. "How did you learn to use your wrights, and how are you not bound?"

"My mother told me to keep it a secret, so I did," I said. "I never learned to use them really. I ask, and sometimes they answer."

Basil leaned across the tables and grabbed a notebook, their freckled nose almost to the pages. "Only sometimes?"

"Sometimes," I said, "they think I have bad ideas."

seven

THE HEIR DIDN'T APPEAR THE NEXT DAY EITHER. Three days I'd been stuck in this city, and already I itched to leave. I hadn't heard from Julian or anyone else in Felhollow, and the lack of news or even attempts to contact me ached. I had gotten used to loneliness in the Wallows as a kid; for all of the Felfolk's jokes about my home, Felhollow *had* become my true home. I'd have sacrificed anything for Julian's familiar presence or Mack's soft laugh. I missed them.

Carlow set a covered bowl on my desk, and Basil peeked over my shoulder.

"Maybe," they said and nudged my side, "Carlow will be bowled over by your work."

I laughed into my hand, and Basil shook beside me. Carlow pulled out a knife.

Basil—even Carlow and Creek on good days—made this new loneliness bearable.

"Leave that covered for now," said Carlow, handing me the knife. "Creek, you fail first."

We had been trying to replicate the Door, but so far, nothing had resisted my vilewright's destructive abilities.

"Your lack of faith withers my heart." Creek cracked the knuckles of one hand against his chest. "Life is a doorway to Death after all, so what better to make the Door out of?"

The man was inscrutably philosophical. He worked primarily

with organic material and let Carlow handle the inorganic. The Door was Vile-made and unnatural, and Creek insisted on using the plants his noblewright made to try and shut the Door. He said their opposition would cancel each other out.

He placed a small replica of the Door wrapped in a lattice of vines on my desk. "I am sure this isn't enough, but I am eager to see you open the Door, Lorena Adler."

My vilewright destroyed his vines with only a memory from Carlow as sacrifice; they would never keep the Door shut or be strong enough to replace it.

"The Vile are incompatible with mortal life." Creek shrugged. "Perhaps a lattice of wrights and wrought would be more apt."

"Thank you for volunteering to be the first to test that out." Carlow sharpened her quill. "Now, the real test please, Adler."

Creek mumbled under his breath, and a bloody lattice of plants, red blooms and bone-white thorns, grew across his arm. They moved as if woven by unseen hands, and my noblewright grumbled against me. I tucked my hands into the pockets of my trousers to hide their shaking. By the time Creek was done, even my teeth hurt. Carlow prodded the odd plant life with her quill.

"Why is it always vines?" she asked.

"I prefer their companionship over yours," said Creek. He caught me wincing at the way some still moved beneath his skin and winked. "They are still drawing blood from my veins, and they are connected to my noblewright, so they are not strictly mortal. There is magic in them not in my other works. Her Excellency forbade His Majesty from destroying works still connected to their noblewrought, so we haven't been able to test creations like these. She said it was too akin to attempting to kill a wright."

Of course she'd put a pin in anything that could result in her losing power.

"What if I do destroy your noblewright?" I asked. He was

as old and as sharp as the shears in his pocket, and they had already tried so much. Creek and Carlow had been working on this for years. If they thought this was the direction to go in, it probably was.

"Don't worry, Adler," said Carlow, her quill scratching through a series of calculations. "If we get lucky, you'll destroy Creek entirely."

"A pity we're stuck together forever," Creek said and blew her a kiss.

"Hush, you two." Basil yanked a vine from Creek's elbow, and it crumbled between their fingers. "We have to get them to stay alive once plucked from you."

The spare stool in the corner squeaked, and Creek said, "It appreciates me."

"Please shackle him to the Door," murmured Carlow, setting her journal aside and tugging Creek to her eye level by his collar. She examined the slivers of skin where flowers and vines crawled out of Creek. He rested his chin atop her head. She licked her finger.

"Did you use bone for these?" she asked and touched the stem of a bright red poppy. It stuck to her damp skin.

"I did, and my arm will be rather useless the rest of the day," he said.

"Like the rest of you, I suppose." Carlow plucked the poppy free, and it collapsed in a splash of blood. "Perhaps a new Door made from us would work since we're immortal."

She pulled away, and he stumbled into the space left behind. I shuddered. They had tried everything to permanently shut the Door, it seemed, but none of it had worked. Everything made by noblewrought broke down within a few days when exposed to the Door. Carlow had managed to extend that to a fortnight by adjusting the wording of some of the contracts and using herself as sacrifice. Her Excellency had forbidden Carlow and Creek from using their lives as sacrifice after that.

They couldn't die, but they had too many other uses to risk it all on theories.

"I'll put in another request to Her Excellency so I can get started on murdering you for a sacrifice," said Carlow, sharpening her quill. "Given your inability to keep your mouth shut, you're the closest of any of us to being a door."

He tugged her close, one arm around her waist, and tapped his fingers along the arches of her ribs. "All mortals are doors if you pry hard enough. Do you think I would find a heart in there or only a withered poppy?"

Basil sucked in a deep breath and turned away.

"You're slipping, Creek." Carlow dug her penknife into his upper thigh and ripped open the artery. "You know there's nothing in me. We've both ripped me open enough to know that."

Creek was dead before he hit the ground.

"Baines, give me my notes back," said Carlow, holding out her hand. "I have work to do."

Creek came back to life laughing, peeling aside his torn trousers to examine the scar-less stretch of skin. "And back to work."

"Ignore them," Basil muttered to me. "They do this all the time. It's easier to be dead than deal with life, I think, and things haven't been the same since... Well, they were never good friends, but it's gotten worse lately."

I nodded. Being alive was already like standing before a cliff. Each trouble was another hand on our back pushing us toward the edge, and being wrought was a whole other set of hands on our shoulders. We were useful, but only if we hurt ourselves. We were worthwhile, but only if we hurt ourselves. We were in control, but only if we hurt ourselves.

"If none of your noblewright creations work," I asked slowly, loud enough for the others to hear, "why not have the Heir use his vilewright?"

"What will we do when his vilewright destroys the Door? Kindly ask the Vile to not eat us?" Carlow asked, turning to me with one black brow arched over her goggles. "We must be careful. Her Excellency is aware of all His Majesty's contracts, and anything that could be viewed as treason will get us all killed. He might be her heir, but she has no intention of letting him rule until she's ready to step aside. She doesn't want us stumbling upon how to kill wrought—or their wrights—in our research."

Right, those bindings.

"That is why you're here though." Creek narrowed his eyes at me and tapped his vine-covered skin. "Try to destroy these. Don't be afraid. You're not good enough to destroy my noblewright."

I nodded. It wasn't an insult, only a fact, but my vilewright still grumbled.

Creek held out his arm, and a white rose twined about a vivid blue pansy grew from his open skin. My vilewright slipped down my arm, shivering the whole way. I braced myself against his desk.

"Memories work best as sacrifices from Carlow and me. Our curses make bodily sacrifices insufficient since we cannot perish, so physical sacrifices are either useless or leave us dead for days at a time." He picked up an unlabeled vial from his desk and held it out to me. "It took me nearly one hundred deaths to create this, but there's only enough to kill ten people."

"Only ten people?" I asked.

Carlow snorted, and Creek crossed his arms.

"I'm rather fond of my first memory of Carlow dying," he said. "Use it as sacrifice and destroy the plants only."

Destroy these flowers, I prayed to my vilewright, *and take Creek's first memory of Carlow as sacrifice.*

My vilewright whined, and pain like an ice pick stabbed at the back of my eyes. It wasn't enough.

Destroy what you can of the flowers. The mortal parts.

I squeezed my eyes shut. A warmth like spring sunlight streaming through leaves and the damp scent of turned earth settled over me, and my vilewright swept over Creek. Creek gasped. There was a clatter, glass against wood, and a drawer shutting. I opened my eyes, and my vilewright trilled as if it had been waiting for me. The flowers rippled, and their petals fell away. I stumbled. Creek picked me up and sat me on his stool.

"Now that is curious," he said.

All that was left of the flowers were veins, red and thin, standing upright in the shape of the plant they had once laced.

Basil came to my side. "Is it still attached to your veins?"

"Truly," said Creek, "what is the difference between the veins of a leaf and the veins beneath my skin?"

"So many things." Carlow leaned over the odd leftovers of my magic and touched the veins. "It feels as if the petals are still there even though I can't see them. What was your contract?"

"I had it destroy the mortal parts," I said. "Those must be the immortal parts. The sacrifice wasn't enough to destroy them."

"That's it?" she asked. I nodded, and she sighed. "I knew Creek and I weren't completely mortal, but if a vilewright can't destroy creations using our bodies, perhaps the Door can't either."

"I'd need a bigger sacrifice from one of you all though," I said. "I've never destroyed anything immortal."

Carlow gestured to her knife in my hands. "Kill me. I'll revive eventually, and it should be worth more than Creek's memories."

He frowned. "You cannot predict how long it will take you to revive from that."

"I need a break from you lot anyway," she said.

"No." I dropped her knife. "I've never killed anyone, and what if it takes ages for you to revive?"

"Then I'll revive more well rested than I've ever been," said Carlow. "Will your vilewright obey if you specify how much to destroy to ensure I am only dead for a few days at most?"

It purred, the answer rumbling out of me with a stutter. "Yes."

"Half of one petal should allow her to revive tomorrow," Creek said and handed me the knife. "It's not murder. It's a sacrifice."

"Those aren't exclusive," I said.

My stomach rolled. Even if Carlow and Creek could revive, this line of research ended at only one point—to destroy the Door, many wrought would have to die.

"They are today." Carlow let Creek pick her up and sit her on the desk before me. She opened her coat. The binding on her chest was a brilliant, weeping blue. "Do you know what your contract will be?"

"Accept Franziska Carlow's life as sacrifice," I said, "and destroy half of a rose petal."

Basil held up their hand.

"That's a very simple contract," they said, nose wrinkling. "It might not work."

"It'll know what I mean." My grip on the knife grew slick with sweat. "I had to learn to work with them quick. Didn't even know most words when I started. It'll know."

My vilewright, always a sharp pain or low growl, let out a soft hum.

"It doesn't matter." Carlow prodded a spot directly over her heart and felt for the gap between her ribs. "So long as we can find a way to destroy something immortal-made, we have a chance at destroying and replacing the Door. Pretend that petal's the Door. Stop worrying about killing me. All that matters is finding new, better ways to affect the Door. Destroy it. Lock it. Anything."

"Most people dream of doing it," said Creek, "so enjoy it."

Take Carlow's life as sacrifice, I prayed to my vilewright, *and destroy half of that petal, immortal parts included.*

I jammed the knife between Carlow's ribs, and she died in minutes, slumped across the desk. Creek held up his arm. Basil tested the petal.

"Destroyed completely," they said, fingers moving through the space where it should have been. "It's not growing back either."

Creek closed Carlow's eyes. "Promising."

eight

I VOMITED IN THE WASHROOM. BASIL HELD BACK MY hair, washing Carlow's blood from my hand with a damp cloth. Because of the bindings, none of them had ever been able to create ways to trap immortal things or destroy them, since that was too similar to trapping and destroying wrights. The Crown would never have allowed such experimentations, but I wasn't bound and could undertake whatever contracts I wanted. We repeated similar contracts for the rest of the day, learning that physical sacrifices worked best for destroying immortal objects.

It made sense. The Door required physical sacrifices to stay shut. Why wouldn't creations made by the only other immortal things left, wrights, require the same to be destroyed?

"However we deal with the Door, it will require blood," said Basil, glancing from Carlow's corpse to the watered-down wine sky outside. "Why is it always blood?"

"It won't be if you open it," Creek said. His body was pocked with holes left by my vilewright's destructions. "Carlow had to die for you to manage even this little bit. Imagine what destroying the Door would require?"

"Imagine what remaking a version that didn't demand sacrifices would require?" countered Basil.

"Let me think on it tomorrow," I said. Carlow's body, still and silent, made me shudder each time I saw it in the corner of my sight. My wrights were overworked and lethargic. My head ached from all the contracts. "I doubt anything will ever be enough."

"Not from us alone." Basil shooed me out the door. "Go rest. We'll resume tomorrow."

By the time I got to my room, I was too tired to sleep. Restless energy raced over my arms and legs.

I never heard Carlow return. That was another way Cynlira scarred us; it was how Cynlira had scarred my mother and all the folks in the Wallows. It pushed us to work and work and work until our bodies broke down and we couldn't remember the last time we slept. It told us that if we worked hard enough, we could be rich.

We couldn't be.

The peerage would work us until we died, bolster their bank vaults with our work, and then leave all the money we'd earned them to their heirs. It was what it had done to my mother. It was what the Heir was doing to Carlow. It was what the Crown was doing to all of us. Overwork, be it from too many sacrifices or too tiring jobs, kept folks too exhausted to resist the way things were.

Someone knocked three times on my door, and I hesitated. The Door would try to lure me to open it.

"Lorena?" came the voice of the Heir.

He would be a terrible lure.

I opened the door. "Your Majesty?"

"I fear I have neglected you, but my mother required my presence for these last few days," he said and swept into the room. "Next time, make sure it's me at the door before you open it. Ask me only something I can know."

"Excessive, but if you insist."

"I do." He set a small glass bowl of red dirt on my desk, leaned against the wall, and clasped his arms behind himself. It was the same bowl Carlow had presented me with but never deemed me ready to work with after all our tests. "Basil told me of your experiments today, and if you are up to it, I have another for you. Can you destroy this?"

The dirt was impossibly smooth, each granule the same minuscule shape and color. I tipped the bowl, and the dirt spilled out. It pooled like water.

"What is it?" I asked, and an oily, bitter taste coated my tongue. I had not been up to it, but now I wanted to know. "It's not dirt."

"Do you know why blood is red?" asked the Heir.

"Iron." In order to create or destroy blood with my wrights, I had to know what everything was made of. My work as an undertaker had given me excellent knowledge of how the mortal body worked. "Iron doesn't make dirt perfectly ordered like this."

"No, but this isn't really dirt so far as I can tell," he said. "It's part of the Door, or at least a physical manifestation of the Door. It took us two years to figure out how to separate it from the Door's cavern."

"What?" I yanked my hand away from it. "What do you mean by physical manifestation? A door is a door."

"Not always." He raised one shoulder and lowered it slowly. "We know this isn't truly dirt, but what it is eludes us, just as the Door's true form eludes us. Can you destroy it?"

He eyed me over his glasses. I followed his line of sight to a little spot above my shoulder. He nodded to the empty space.

"Your vilewright is..." He waved his hand back and forth. "Listing?"

"Tired," I said.

"If you insist. Can you do it?"

This was a challenge then. Could the dualwrought girl who'd threatened him in Felhollow back up her confidence?

"Of course I can attempt it, but I have questions. Can I touch it?" I asked. When he nodded, I swept the dirt back into the bowl. The grains made a sound like shattering glass, and a few clung to my skin, their touch oily and damp. I scraped them into the bowl and sniffed my hand. It smelled of nothing. "Have you tasted this?"

"It tastes of nothing as well," he said. "Several people and wrought have tasted it, myself included. Touch appears to be the only sense through which we can accurately perceive it."

I rubbed my fingers on my shirtsleeve. It was like I had dunked my fingers in lard.

"How many people did you feed it to before trying it yourself?" I asked.

"I am the Heir to the Crown of Cynlira. I am too valuable to be tested so freely, but I did test it myself last year." He bowed his head, hair covering his face, but he couldn't hide his smile. "You understand that, don't you?"

Because all lives could be reduced to value. The peerage never saw the nuance in such a statement.

My teeth clenched together, and he glanced up at me.

He inhaled, exhaled, removed his glasses, and cleaned them against his shirt. "You are upset by this?"

"Yes," I said.

The disappointment of his sigh was palpable, and I remembered clearly how he had once said, "You must understand me."

If I was to be here, help Will, and stop the sacrifices, this boy was my best chance.

"I understand why you did." I touched his arm. I did not let my thumb slide a hairbreadth to the left and beneath his sleeve. I did not curl my fingers around his wrist. He stilled. "That doesn't mean I agree with it."

He was as twitchy about touch as me. He wore his clothes like armor, the sleeves always buttoned tight against his wrists and his cravat knotted about his neck. I loved touch, to be touched and to touch, but so often, others expected more afterward and didn't know how to stop when I drew back. I used undertaking as a shield: no one wanted to touch the girl who touched death. It saved me from expectations. The Heir used fear and finely tailored suits.

The Heir's jaw tightened. I withdrew my hand.

"What would you have done?" he asked.

Not approached those certain to say yes if you offered them enough money. That was too easy and led down too many dangerous paths.

But I lied and shrugged. "I don't know."

"I hate not knowing," he muttered. He unbuttoned his greatcoat and sat at my desk. "I have not yet explained to my mother that you are here. I do not know how she will react to our deal involving Willoughby Chase. You realize that not sacrificing him will require another sacrifice? Can your conscience bear to send another in his place?"

Will had helped me when no one else would, and now I could finally help him.

"My conscience can't bear letting an innocent man die," I said and leaned against the desk. "Does she select the sacrifices?"

He nodded. "Now that it's one sacrifice every month, she discusses it with the court, and in the event the court betrays her, she alone will decide. She hardly needs them to do what she wants, but it is easier for all when she agrees with the court. They could kill her, but she would kill them. Everyone would die. She could kill them, but they would kill her. Everyone would die. For now, it is a precarious peace."

For them. From the peerage warring over lands to the daily dangers of work, most of Cynlira had never known peace.

"If she goes ahead with the sacrifice, she'll be breaking my contract with you," I said. "How does she feel about killing her only surviving child?"

"Far less conflicted about it than you're imagining." He glanced up at me, gray eyes pale against the dark shadows beneath his eyes, and settled his glasses on his face. "How did your father die?"

"Mining accident." His hands had been ripped off, and the mine hadn't kept a noblewrought healer on-site like they were supposed to. "Let's get this done. I need a sacrifice."

The Heir laughed softly. He held out his arm to me and rolled back his sleeve until the tendons of his forearm were tense beneath my fingers. I tapped the nook of his elbow, holding his arm until a vein rolled beneath my fingers, and pricked it with the long needle he offered up to me. He didn't even wince.

Take his blood, not enough to kill him, I prayed to my vilewright, *and pain as sacrifice, and destroy this part of the door.*

If I knew something, my wrights knew it. They were like some distant part of me I could only access when I paid the price. I had never put boundaries on my wrights—I rarely used them in a way that could get someone killed—but if this was part of the Door, it was Vile. There was no telling how much blood was necessary to destroy it.

The blood dripping from the Heir's arm vanished in a stuttering motion as if some small tongue lapped it from his skin. Black smoke drifted from the bowl, and the scent of charred hair burned in my nose. The Heir and I leaned over the bowl.

Three little granules crumbled and drifted away in the smoke. The Heir made a small noise in the back of his throat. My vilewright trilled.

It wasn't a sound exactly but a feeling that rang in my head, like those whistles only dogs could hear. I knew the sound was happening even though I couldn't quite hear it.

"Wait," I said. "It's not right."

Three other grains twisted, the red rippling and *something* writhing beneath their surface, and each buckled about their middle. The grains split, and the three new ones wobbled atop the pile in the bowl.

The Heir hummed. "Only three. Curious."

"Baiting me won't work." I ground my teeth together

and took a breath. It did work, but I was too tired to rise to it tonight. "Same thing happened to you?"

"Every time," he said. "The Door is not a door, but it looks like one. This is the dirt that surrounds it. It is not dirt. The area around the Door is part of the Door as well, but we're not certain where that boundary ends. Carlow and I believe it's expanding."

"Who disagrees with you?" I asked.

"My mother." He swallowed. "The growth, when compared to the almost exponential increase in sacrifices necessary, is negligible."

"If we knew the mechanism it uses to replicate, we might be able to destroy that and then destroy the Door," I said. "Tried it?"

"Of course," said the Heir. "We even attempted to re-create it to gain some insight."

"You can't create, so who attempted it?"

"I am well aware of my ability to only ever destroy," he said, words clipped and teeth bared. They weren't as sharp as the rumors said. "Carlow. She was dead for a month after."

My day had been filled with Carlow moving—tapping her fingers against her desk, throwing her notes at Creek's head, and tugging at her tangled hair as she read—and then the sudden unsettling stillness of death at my hands.

"My mother discovered what we had done and alerted the court and council. We were forbidden from attempting it again. The court of peers and common council are often at odds, but they concur on this: we can do nothing with the Door that might open or destroy it." He chuckled, and my noblewright shuddered. "Keep the dirt. Do nothing that could harm you, but see what you can make of it."

I nodded. "So this is what my work will be—dirt."

"Dirt," he said and rose from my chair. He stopped in the doorway. "I have heard that Willoughby Chase will arrive tomorrow to begin mounting his defense and begin his house arrest. You are welcome to visit him. You will be followed. Feel free to inform him that we will be watching him as well. Do not think you can escape my guards or our contract."

"I would never," I said. "Are you going to tell me why I should make sure whoever knocks at my door is who I think they are?"

He shook his head. "No. You're a smart girl. You'll figure it out."

So he wanted to watch me figure it out. What a peer he was, playing with me.

I slid the lock into place. His footsteps faded down the hall, and I crawled into bed. The door rattled once. I didn't answer.

"Smart girl," I thought I heard, but by the time I opened the door, I was alone.

nine

I LEFT THE ROYAL GROUNDS AT DAWN. THE GUARDS were already up and about, winding through the gardens and buildings. From the doorway of a building I hadn't been to, Hana Worth watched me leave with her bandaged arms crossed over her chest as she scratched at old scabs. A hand gloved in healer's green tugged her back into the room.

It was so utterly normal, too normal for a place like this, to see the Heir's guard blushing and vanishing into the healer's room, as if this place were as much a part of the real world as Felhollow.

I flipped up the collar of Julian's coat, half hiding my face. Noshwright, in the Wheels-Carry-Us-to-Riches district where the newly rich rubbed elbows with the hoping-to-be-rich, was a sprawling inn that I had never entered. Will Chase owned quarters on one of the upper floors, and he always stayed there when in Mori. The Wheels was the fanciest of the merchant districts, full of people from all walks of life hoping they looked powerful enough to get what they wanted. None glanced at me twice.

Unassuming. Uninteresting. Unseen.

As a child, I would never have been able to walk the Wheels without getting accosted. There were too many city guards, their eyes sliding over everyone and people moving around them like they were scenery. One hustled a few Wallowers down an alley and to somewhere they wouldn't ruin the view of the rich merchants in from out of town or get in the way of any peers running about. No one paid the actions any mind.

City guards were soldiers from the army of the house running the city. In Mori, it was black-coated Wyrslaine soldiers with red stitching. Felhollow had been too small and unimportant to warrant any actual guards, even with all the recent bandit raids. It was impossible to see the dangers of politics while every law and rule, written and unwritten, benefited you. Unless the guards started rounding up councilors and peers, their rough handling of people didn't matter. But their shiny new rifles made my skin crawl. Nearly every soldier carried one.

It took me two hours to reach Noshwright, but I lingered in the street. Before the large front doors, a carriage came to a stop, and a man stepped out. He paused on the carriage steps, helping two toddlers down, and the family moved unhesitatingly to the doors of Noshwright. Two servants swept open the doors from the inside.

You could take the measure of a person by their shoes in Mori, and even the kids wore shoes worth more than my mother had made in her entire life. It was unfair of me to feel angry at this family, who looked perfectly nice. It was unfair how money opened doors most of Cynlira couldn't even approach.

Will was as rich as this man, maybe richer, and still wore his old boots. He'd not scoffed at Julian's relationship with me. He spent more money on Felhollow than the peer who ran the holding had in decades.

I couldn't let fate rip away the family I'd spent so long finding.

I shook my head, took a breath, and moved toward Noshwright. The doors didn't open for me, and I pulled one open a crack, slipping inside. A hand grabbed my wrist.

"Lore?" a familiar voice whispered.

I spun around. Julian stood at the edge of the street, staring into the alley I'd taken refuge in, and prodded my shoulder. I smiled.

"You're all right," he said and wrapped his arms around me. My nose squashed against his cheek, and he tucked his face into my neck. "I am so angry at you."

"What?" I asked and tried to pull away, but he tightened his arms and dragged me to a lift guarded by two Wyrslaine guards.

"I understand why you didn't say anything and all," he muttered into my scalp, "but you making that deal and taking off. That wasn't what I meant when I asked you to help, and you know it."

"I didn't have much time to think it over!" I swallowed my uncertainty and pushed his hair back from his face. Anger I could work with. "Are folks upset?"

"A few, and most of us told them they were welcome to find a new town." Julian wouldn't let me go, and we stumbled into the Chase quarters. "Mack, she found us!"

Mack Sarclaw skidded into the entryway. Stout and steady, as serious as Julian was confident, he took one look at me and smiled so widely I nearly cried. He gathered me up from Julian's arms and kissed my cheeks. We collapsed onto an upholstered bench, untangling ourselves enough to sit. They settled on either side of me.

The room was small but nicer than my little room back in Felhollow.

"It's just us. My father's talking to some friends but will return soon. He doesn't know how he can repay you," said Julian. "What were you thinking?"

"The Heir was taking me no matter what." I shrugged. "Might as well have gotten us something out of it, and if I'd tried to fight him instead, Felhollow was likely to be destroyed."

"Certainly got an earful out of it," muttered Mack. "Ivy threw a fit."

I winced.

Mack squeezed my hand. "Not at you," he said quickly. "She was furious at Will. Apparently a bunch of councilmembers have been getting investigated lately, but he was in the clear."

I relaxed against him. "Thank you."

"We've lived next to each other for nearly a decade." Mack sighed. His locs shifted over his shoulder with the soft clink of glass beads and gold cuffs, and I smiled at the sound. He'd worn his black curls in locs for as long as I'd known him. "So you're dualwrought?"

"It's why I left Mori," I said. "Lying to y'all was the bane of my existence."

"It's seeds already sown." Julian turned and draped his legs across Mack and me, raising one blond brow when I huffed. "How else am I supposed to make sure you don't run off again?"

He said it lightly, but his fingers laced through mine and held his hand against his chest.

"Anyway," continued Julian, "Mack's not angry at you, but I am. Dualwrought, Lore? I always knew you were keeping secrets, but dualwrought? I can't believe you didn't trust us."

"Better caught keeping secrets than dead," I muttered.

"You're too honest to get away with pithy statements," said Julian. He sniffed. "Maybe not, I guess."

"Hush," Mack said. "You were right to lie to us. Felhollow would've eaten you alive."

We were the only Felfolk in our generation left. I had been nine and new, but Julian had accepted me with no questions, and Mack had been thrilled at the prospect of a new friend. He'd smiled more then and been more talkative, but time wasn't kind. Loss was a fog that Felfolk couldn't shake, people always dying by bandits, disease, or nature, and we'd all been to far more funerals than weddings. I was unbound and dualwrought, and maybe I could've saved more.

"Will it not eat me alive now?" I asked.

"We're a bit put out you never helped more now that we know you're dualwrought," said Julian, "but you're family."

I winced. "I helped as much as I could with both wrights. I just kept it secret."

"We know," Mack said and shot Julian a look. "Are you safe?"

"As can be," I said. "The Heir and I have arranged a contract, which is working, since Will's under watch here rather than jail. Where is he? We need to know why he's being targeted."

"He's meeting with some council friends about the warrant. Since it was clearly slapdash, he's thinking they were after someone else and settled for him." Mack tapped his fingers along Julian's calf. "Tell her what Will told you."

"My father got a seat on the council a few months back," said Julian. "He was keeping the news to himself until the next session though. He and the rest of the folks on the common council think the Heir's up to something, and apparently my father had concerns about him traveling through Felhollow and those towns. Something to do with the sacrifices and the Crown," Julian said. "He and most of the council tried to force the Heir to show them his work, and he refused. So now a bunch of the council members are getting sent warrants for minor offenses—safety regulations in factories and towns, bribery, and other things they've never bothered with before."

"Minor," I repeated. Will wouldn't let his business break safety rules. He knew my mother died from that.

"They're angry he bought a munitions factory, too, and now Felhollow has guns." Mack snorted. "The peerage is all for arms until the wrong sort start arming themselves."

"Will and his friends are discussing what the Heir was even doing near Felhollow and why he'd chase one vilewrought," said Julian, sitting up and taking my hands in his. "I know what I asked you to do in Felhollow and what you've already done. I don't want you in danger. However, this is my father. He's all I've got left."

The truth stole my breath.

"You want me to spy on the Heir," I said. "But you already know what I know. The rumors are true—he's researching the Door his mother sacrifices people to. He says it's to stop the sacrifices and lock the Door for good."

"That seems likely," mumbled Julian. His hands slipped from mine and curled around my wrists. "You believe him?"

I shrugged. "That's what I'm working on with him, so if he's got ulterior motives, I can't see them yet."

"I want you to help me build that new Door and save the world," the Heir had said, but saving the world could mean anything for a boy so versed in pedantry.

"It's less spying and more you telling us what you're doing," said Julian. "You really signed a contract with that vile boy?"

"He was willing to deal, and I got him to agree to keep Will here," I said. "So long as we can prove Will is innocent, it will be fine. Don't leave Mori. Don't threaten the court or Heir. Let's work on figuring out what their evidence is, if he's done anything that warrants sacrifice, and get him safe. Once he's proven innocent, he's free to go and can't be sacrificed. Even the Heir, for all his power, has to obey that contract. If his mother tries to sacrifice Will anyway, the Heir will die."

Julian's grip on me tightened. "So he's safe for now."

"If we can prove he's innocent," said Mack.

"Yeah," I said, "but Will would do all that."

Julian inhaled, nostrils flaring, and his fingers slid up my arms to my shoulders, pressing into my flesh like sigils. I dropped my forehead to his shoulder.

"Thank you," he whispered, one hand drifting to my head and stroking my hair. "You sure you're safe up there? You have to stay in the palace?"

"He will look into Will's arrest and trial so long as I help him with his research," I said. "You've heard the rumors; he always keeps his deals. I made it as foolproof as I could. He can't kill us or hurt us, physically or emotionally, on purpose, and even if we die, he's bound by the power in the contract to prevent Will's death if he knows your father is innocent."

Mack cleared his throat. "Your wright bind you to the contract or his?"

"Wrights," Julian corrected.

Mack shot him a look, and Julian flinched.

"His, but the contract cuts both ways. If he breaks it, his vilewright will turn on him." I inhaled the scent of the road still clinging to Julian and the woody musk of him I would be able to identify till I died. The tension eased out of me. I pulled away slightly and touched the collar of his coat I was wearing. "Do you want this back?"

"Keep it," said Julian. "Think of me."

"Like she's going to forget you." Mack squeezed my arm. "Are you free to move about? Is talking to us safe?"

"There are always going to be guards watching me, but I'm allowed to go wherever." I leaned back, morning light washing over me from one of the windows. "I should get back though. I'm working with three noblewrought—Basil Baines, Delmond Creek, and Franziska Carlow—and I think there used to be another one. Find out exactly what Will is being charged with and why they think he's guilty. We can work backward to prove he's not. Once that's done, I might be able to work out another contract with the Heir to get away from here."

Maybe. Probably. It all depended on how desperately he wanted my help with his research.

"Well, that's a plan," Mack said. "Keep our dualwrought undertaker alive and save Will."

"Don't joke about it, please." Julian wrapped his arms around my waist, hands slipping beneath my coat. "Do what you have to, Lore, and if anything happens, we'll go back to Felhollow. He can't touch you there."

Distance would not deter a vilewright. The contract would kill me if I went back on it.

"Sure," I lied to keep him from worrying. "Just find out more about the charges."

He could never tell when I was lying.

ten

THE NEXT MORNING, I ARRIVED AT THE LABORA-
tory right after the Heir. The sun had barely crept over the
mountains, red light seeping across the sky and tinting everything pale pink. His flaxen greatcoat hung on a hook near his
desk, the sigil of Chaos nearly black in the dim light, and his
shirtsleeves were rolled up to his elbows. Steam rose from a cup
of tea on the desk, and he gestured to the stool next to him. I
perched on it, setting my bag beside me. No one else had arrived.

"I have looked over the warrant for Willoughby Chase and
can deliver several documents to you," he said without looking
up. "I admit, however, to not having committed much thought
to the case overall yet."

Of course he hadn't.

"The contract only said you would allow me to look over
everything, not that you would," I said. "Julian, as a family
member, is allowed access as well. I'll get him to copy them and
show me."

"That won't be necessary," he said, straightening his
already straight glasses. "Court documents may not be copied.
Any information you need will have to be gleaned from them
directly."

"Well played." I leaned back and crossed my arms. "I suppose
this is what I get for assuming access to information included
the ability to copy said information to facilitate better access."

I had glossed over that aspect of the contract, and now I was paying for it.

"In that case, I will have to memorize what I read, and I won't have time to work much tomorrow I'm afraid," I said. "Until then, you can explain why you wrote the sacrificial summons for Will while sitting in that carriage."

The Heir sighed. "I assumed you knew."

"As well as I know Old Liran." I rolled my eyes while he wasn't looking. "I still want to know about that summons. The ink and wax were still wet."

"They were." He took a sip of tea and turned to me, glasses foggy. A coiled lemon peel dangled from the cup. "There was a warrant out for his arrest for lesser crimes, and I signed the sacrificial summons because he was the only councilor living in Felhollow. Once I realized that Felhollow was where the vilewrought ran to, I knew it was Willoughby Chase I was after."

"What lesser charges?" I asked. "Why did it matter he was the only councilor from Felhollow?"

If it had been a day ago, I would have found the idea of Will committing any crime without good reason laughable, but Julian had spilled Will's secrets. Will had funded a new factory in the Wallows a few years back with a few other councilors. Will wasn't paying for healers and was instead letting workers go when they got injured. It wasn't illegal, but it was infuriating. It was exactly what Northcott had done.

"I can't tell you that," said the Heir.

I exhaled loudly. "We had a deal."

"I wanted the vilewrought," said the Heir, which sounded true enough. "Chase stole her. That is crime enough. Worse, he deprived me of another vilewrought. Is that not enough to justify my actions?"

He adjusted his glasses.

"No, you're not that petty." I let him have this lie. He wasn't telling me what Will had really done anytime soon, and I'd have to wait or find out on my own. "You love contracts, and you like rules. You'd not break the rules so flagrantly by arresting him on false charges simply because he annoyed you. You'd find a rule that would let you arrest him."

Treason, the warrant had said, but what treason could Will of all folks get up to? It was the only crime on the warrant that made him a potential sacrifice. The Heir wouldn't have tacked it on without being able to prove it.

"Perhaps." The Heir inclined his head to me, fingers falling to his throat. He unknotted his red cravat twist by twist. "You should stay with me after his trial. If you don't, my mother will almost certainly pursue and bind you."

I watched his fingers rub at the pale skin of his collarbone and narrowed my eyes. "And you won't?"

"We should consider the terms of our next contract sooner rather than later," he said. "Tea?"

"Yes, please," I said and twisted fully to him, crossing my legs at the knees. "What if I wish to return to Felhollow?"

"I would try to dissuade you, but you are your own person." The Heir stood and stretched. "It is my mother you must watch out for then."

He drew a book from his desk, licked the tip of his finger, and parted the pages with a slow press along the edges. The book fell open, splayed before him. His fingers curled around it.

"I would like your opinion on several things," he said, voice low and deep in the back of his throat. He glanced at me over the rim of his glasses as if he were waiting for the answer to a question he hadn't asked.

He hadn't, had he?

"Is it about our contract?" I leaned forward and tried to see what book he was reading.

"It is a bedfellow of our contract, I would say." His tongue wet his lips, and he gently laid the book before me. He dragged his finger down the inside of the spine till his nail covered the first letter of a line. "What do you make of this?"

"Wrought," I read aloud, "are almost certainly the result of the union between the mortal and immortal souls, and their wrights are the remnants of the immortal souls left behind by the consumed Noble and Vile. These remnants, these wrights, attach to mortal souls at random, for this is the only way they may interact with our world. Through the union, both mortal and immortal are given new life."

I raised my gaze to his, and one of his brows rose.

"Dualwrought are the rarest of all wrought because the likelihood of two souls attaching to one person is astronomically low," he said, studying me as if waiting for me to react. "You are a singular creature."

"Like your mother," I muttered. "Tea?"

"Of course." Instead of moving around me, he stood right next to me and reached one arm across the table. His thighs pressed against my knees. "You are nothing like my mother save for being dualwrought."

"Don't we have the same hair?" I asked absently, skimming through the book.

He snorted. "No. Physically, you are nothing alike. Mentally, you share nothing except cleverness. Emotionally, I doubt she could even comprehend you."

"Lovely. I hate being comprehended." I looked from his hands—pouring a perfect cup of tea far more slowly than necessary with his fingers tracing the curves of the pot—to his face. His cheeks were flushed.

He laid his hand on my arm. "Honey?"

"Yes, please." I narrowed my eyes. "Why did you want me to read this?"

"I thought you might enjoy it. I did." He did not remove his hand from me. "During our travels, we touched on the nature of wrights."

Oh.

He set the cup before me, and I picked it up. He pulled away.

"Is it to your liking?" he asked, clearing his throat softly.

He was flirting with me. That could be useful.

"I did not mean to deceive you," he muttered after I didn't answer for a while, and he reached into his coat. A small brown paper envelope crinkled in his fingers. "I know how difficult it can be to live with gaps in your memories. A sacrificed memory cannot be reclaimed, but new memories can be made."

I took the envelope and flipped open the flap. A sweet scent I didn't recognize overpowered me. I tipped the five small flowers into my hand, their pale yellow petals like velvet against my skin, and frowned. Old memories—Julian barely twelve and laughing in a field of clover, my hands tangled in green vines at the edge of Felhollow, Mack kneading damp earth and tucking a seed beneath it—rose up in me, but none featured honeysuckle. My noblewright whined against me, its shivers oozing across me. The Heir took the empty envelope back.

"I can bring you Willoughby Chase's ledgers and some of the evidence gathered against him in the morning," he said, "but it cannot be removed from my sight."

"Thank you." I pinched the bottom of the honeysuckle with two nails and tugged, pulling out the thread of the flower with a bead of nectar. I touched it to the tip of my tongue.

The Heir glanced away, ears red.

Very useful.

"This," I said and held up the flowers, "is far more to my liking. This is kind."

Sex was all well and good, but there were so many other things to be done. Jules was a creature of habit, and I withered with boredom. I always preferred quiet evenings pressed to his side, discussing Felhollow or our friends or nothing at all, and liked to listen to the thump of his heart and huff of sleepy breaths. Intimacy, to me, was the way he curled his fingers around my wrist whenever we were near and how he knew what I was thinking with only a look. It was knowing that when I turned around, he would be there. But that wasn't intimacy to Julian Chase. It was just...snacks. Small bites before the main meal.

He always used food and hunger to describe sex—he was a wolf, so hungry sometimes he was howling, he said—but no one died from lack of it, and I'd no desire to be devoured. The metaphor left much to be desired in terms of *after*.

Hunger could be sated, and I didn't think my desire to be with him ever could. The Heir I had thought more like me based on the way he spoke of understanding, but perhaps I had been wrong.

"Your Majesty?" I asked softly.

He looked up.

"Can I say no to you without retribution?"

"Yes," said the Heir. "Of course."

"Of course." I couldn't keep all the scorn from my voice. "What am I to do if you accuse me of theft and get me arrested because I refuse you? If you make it hard for me to find a job? If no one of import deigns to hire the person the Heir is snubbing? Do you really think normal people can say no to the Heir? To any peer?"

He laughed, expression empty. "Would you like a lawyer to draw up a contract then? My last partner did."

"For a relationship?" I raised one brow and smiled at the flush tinting the Heir's cheeks. That was one way to put a partner at ease. "If you hurt your last partner, do you die?"

"Yes," he said quickly. "If I hurt him, I die. I am not completely oblivious. I am aware of power and its many obstacles. He is a peer, but I am the Heir. We were not on equal footing, so I equalized it."

"Everyone has to have one good quality, I suppose."

"Please," he said, but he was smiling. "I am powerful, rich, and not unattractive."

I shrugged and said, "I shall add 'humble' to your list of qualities."

"Humility is worthless. I know what I am." He reached back, the long scar bisecting his throat white in the dim light, and tossed me a thin notebook. "Be sure to keep the list up-to-date."

He knew what he was, not who he was? I opened the blank book and wrote a single word he would never agree with—*insecure*. He tried to peek.

"This is for me, not you." I snapped the book shut and set it aside. "We work together. We have a contract detailing that work. You're threatening to sacrifice my partner's father. Let us not distract from what we need to do."

He swallowed, disappointment darkening his eyes, and nodded. "Of course. You're right."

"I don't want to muddy what we have right now," I said.

At my last word, his eyes widened. He smirked ever so slightly.

"And I do have something I need from you," I said and swiped a finger across the rim of my cup, gathering a drop of honey that had escaped on my skin. I pressed my finger to my lips and met his eyes. I could play his game. "Teach me how you write your contracts. I want to understand you and your vilewright."

"Yes," he gasped and swallowed. He held out a thick, worn book to me. "Here. These are some of my old contracts. They should help."

"I'm sure they will."

eleven

B Y THAT EVENING, I HAD READ THROUGH THE FIRST
five contracts in his book. They all involved the odd red
dirt from the Door, testing different ways to destroy it or parts
of it. He hadn't succeeded, the dirt reforming itself no matter
what he sacrificed, and I traced the slightly frantic words of the
latest contract. Carlow and Creek argued the whole time, their
grumblings a reliable backdrop to my reading. Basil seemed to
be the only person who remembered I was there.

"None of us really formed a bond with our noblewrights
like you have with yours," they said. They'd been asking me
questions every few minutes and taking note of my answers in
the margins of an old tome on wrights and wrought, going so
far as to define what I meant by *prayer*. "It's why unbound and
untrained wrought are interesting. You work differently. Your
wrights work differently. It's fascinating."

I didn't feel fascinating; I felt picked apart.

"How do you know it's not your bindings that require
such specific contracts?" I asked. "To let your employer know
exactly what you want?"

"We don't," said Carlow darkly. "Which is why I find myself
dead so often. I don't like being told what I can and can't do."

She could create the most wonderful things, from bridges that
folded up on themselves to let boats pass beneath to hinges that
allowed prosthetic hands to work more nimbly than ever before.

She couldn't heal so much as a paper cut, though, and she pushed the boundaries of what she was allowed to do until her binding bled and oozed. She couldn't alter oxygen—it was too dangerous to allow the noblewrought to mess with something so important— and even iron was hard for her to work with. Changing the composition of metals to better suit her needs left her exhausted and sobbing. Ink and blood almost always stained her clothes.

"If not for your curse, you'd be dead five hundred times over," said Creek. "Your utter disregard for yourself is a thorn in my side."

"Why?" she asked. "Because I'm not dying fast enough? Perhaps putting up with you is the sacrifice I make."

"And what a good lesson that is—just because you cannot see the sacrifice or price doesn't mean it's not there," Creek said, coaxing an avens flower the same blue as his eyes from the dirt on his desk. It grew so quickly, dirt scattered across the floor. "You must always consider how your wrights interact with our world and how others perceive them. Seeing something doesn't mean it's here. Seeing nothing doesn't mean nothing is here."

He gestured to the stool in the corner, grinning when it squeaked and spun as if someone were sitting in it.

"If only Delmond Creek were neither visible nor here." Carlow sighed, stretched, and stood. "Or dead for good."

"I don't think this lab could take any more deaths," Creek muttered and turned a page.

Carlow inhaled.

No one spoke of the last wrought who had worked here, but it was clear they were dead and that Carlow and Creek had not forgiven each other for whatever had happened.

Basil cleared their throat. "We're supposed to be teaching Lorena. That's what His Majesty asked us to do today."

"I don't have any questions as of yet, so it's fine," I said, and Basil shot me a look. "I mean, will he be here today?"

"Most likely," said Carlow, creating a metal wire thinner

than a strand of hair and studying it through her goggles. The right lens, I'd learned, was a monocular. "His mother makes him attend court and council meetings, but he's probably bored of them by now. He'll go back to being here every day soon."

I shook my head. It was unthinkable, being so powerful and calling that power "boring."

"Do you think when he's the Crown, we can call him the Vile Crown?" Carlow asked. "Like the old ones?"

The most powerful of the Noble and Vile had been called Crowns and ruled over their weaker fellows, and we had borrowed their terms after they were banished.

"How infuriating do you think it is for them to know we use the term Crown?" She whined and rubbed her eyes. "I hope it's very. I hope they seethe every day thinking about us weak little mortals calling our leader the Crown."

"I'm sure they do," said Creek, rolling his eyes to the ceiling.

"You know, the rumors say some of the Vile Crowns weren't evil, just unpredictable and powerful," said Basil. "The Crowns could even possess dead mortals and take control of their corpses."

Carlow scoffed. Basil, bless them, had a penchant for taking things apart, history, and telling the same story over and over. Their eyes lit up when they did, though, so it was hard for even her to be mad. She must've heard this history many times from them.

Creek chuckled. "Powerful? Vilewrights are fragments of Vile souls and grant unimaginable abilities when used properly. Imagine what a proper Vile Crown could do and you're still thinking too small."

"Powerful enough that I'm still cursed even after they've been gone for centuries," muttered Carlow.

"Yes." Creek, smile falling, tucked a pale-blue bud behind Carlow's ear. "Perhaps they were so powerful they forgot what eternity and death meant to mortals."

She shook her head. The bud tumbled to the floor, rolling away under her desk.

"Rumors say the Noble weren't nice either." Basil tugged Creek away, pointing to his stool, and said, "Sit down and shut up, or I'll attach you to it."

Creek sat.

"They cursed folks too," I said, hiding my laughter with my hand. "Felhollow's named after one, you know. It was killed there after killing a bunch of townsfolk after they made a deal with the Vile to save themselves from the plague. The Noble didn't care about mortals. They only cared about keeping the balance between life and death."

"Death is the only discerning god, the stories tell," said Basil, "and will take everyone no matter who."

I let out a bark of a laugh, and Basil startled.

"Take it from an undertaker," I said. "Death's only as discerning as we are."

Sure, it took rich folk in due time, but it wasn't peers dying every day from exhaustion, disease, and accidents. They could pay noblewrought to heal them. My mother hadn't even been able to pay for her funeral plot, much less healing.

Basil shrugged. "I like the stories. They tell us we can be more. If they overthrew the Noble and Vile, we can do this."

They gestured to my desk and the bowl of odd red dirt from the Door.

"Stories say a lot of things and rumors even more." Carlow groaned and shut her book, pressing her palms hard into her eyes. "Rumors say moss only grows on the north sides of trees, but I'm not stranding you in the forest to check."

"And I thank you very much for that," Basil said.

"It doesn't matter what the Noble and Vile were," said Carlow. "We must be whatever tools this world needs."

"Who the world needs," whispered Creek. "You are a 'who,' Franziska, not a contrivance."

She stilled and nodded. "We should get back to work."

"Sure," I said slowly. "Basil, could I see one of your contracts? I want to compare it to the Heir's."

"Oh, of course." They shuffled through a stack of papers on their desk. "Anything specific?"

"You could say that." I grabbed the Heir's book of contracts and flipped to one of the attempts he'd made at destroying the dirt-like pieces of the Door. "How specific are your contracts?"

"Fairly specific," they said. "If what I'm creating is complicated, I have to state the makeup of what I want."

They showed me a page that included a steel beam for a bridge, and I frowned.

"You can just specify steel?" I asked. "You don't have to provide the percentage of iron and carbon?"

"No, not so long as I have it in mind. Why?"

"The Heir's contracts are far more detailed." I flipped through the book. Every single contract listed components and directions to an exactness that made my teeth ache. "I don't even do what you do, but should I be doing this?"

Basil sucked on their teeth and tapped their fingers against their desk. "Maybe. I'm not sure. I think you probably know what's best for your vilewright, but you should talk to His Majesty about it."

The door opened, and the Heir stepped through, a book under one arm and a knife in the other.

"Speak of the Vile," said Creek.

I froze, but the Heir only smiled.

"Ah," he said, "talking about me?"

"It was either that or work." Carlow jerked her head in the direction of his desk. "Lorena has been going over contracts and has some questions."

"Then I shall answer them," said the Heir.

I let him settle before approaching. He kept his coat on, buttoned from hip to throat. He adjusted his glasses, pinching the bridge of his nose, and the shadows beneath his eyes were as black as his hair. I leaned against his desk so the others couldn't see either of us and rested my hand on his arm. His muscles clenched beneath my fingers.

"You care about them," I whispered. It was hard to imagine this boy caring about anything with a heartbeat.

"They are my wrought," he said. "I have little choice."

He did, but I didn't say anything.

"All your contracts can't be this convoluted." I flipped to a random page from his book. The contract was three full pages, specifying the amount of red dirt to destroy down to the weight and exactly where it was in the palace. He had even written out what similar things his vilewright shouldn't destroy. There were caveats in case his vilewright needed more of a sacrifice to accomplish it: take the first layer of flesh or one pint of blood. The precision felt unnecessary.

"I have certain contracts that can be executed with only a word and a sacrifice," he said. "Destroying bullets fired at me is doable because my vilewright is familiar with the wording of the contract. I need only know I have been shot at. Of course, my vilewright is only one wright. It can only destroy three to five. Anything more and I'm a mess for the healers to deal with. Bolts and other projectiles require a different contract and sacrifice. Sacrifices work best when the wrought enacts them, of course, but on those occasions, my vilewright will take the sacrifice without my having to lift a finger. I have it well trained."

Magic was always more powerful when the wrought did the sacrificing, cutting an arm or offering up a memory. It was why he had Hana—stabbing her was more powerful than his vilewright simply claiming the blood from her without the Heir's intervention.

My wrights weren't as finicky as this though. A projectile was a projectile, and my vilewright would've known what to do with either a bullet or a bolt.

"That's all well and good, but what about this? The red dirt-like substance in the oak bowl in the center of the room in the east wing of my quarters," I said and held up the journal. "What's your vilewright going to do? Destroy the other wooden bowl full of dirt?"

"It's done similar things in the past," he said. "It's not me. It knows a bowl holds things, but bodies hold blood, do they not?"

I shuddered. "Why do you care if it hurts someone?"

He had killed so many. Did one more death matter to him, or did he simply not want to deal with the political consequences?

"I'm not a monster," he said slowly, as if the words were too heavy for his tongue. "I admit to having leveraged my past and the rumors about me to my advantage, but I take no joy in killing. Some deaths are simply necessary sacrifices. Why waste a life if I can avoid it?"

"What about Hila?" I asked.

"Hila was a tragedy of my own making, but I was told at the time it was a necessary one. I know what it's like to fear your own home," he whispered, shoulders stiff. "The peers fear me now, but that is a needed fear. They are the ones who can do damage, and through their fear of me, I get them to obey without question. Perhaps I am a monster, but what good are dreams if you've never known a nightmare?"

I did not need to have been stabbed to know that I preferred not being stabbed.

"You didn't want a dog," I whispered.

A pale pink rose in his cheeks. "There are a few who, like you, do not fear me—Carlow, Baines, Worth—and I have no desire to harm them. They are as important to me as my vilewright. Sometimes it is nice to be accepted, not feared."

And yet everyone in this lab used his title and not his name.

twelve

THREE DAYS LATER, THE HEIR PROVED CARLOW correct. He was in the laboratory every morning with me. The two of us read through his past experiments with his vilewright over tea in the lab, our quiet meetings lasting anywhere from an hour to three. The others rarely showed up until well after, and Carlow, the only one I thought might interrupt us, preferred to work late and sleep later. She had set a series of experiments for me, and the Heir observed my contracts as I attempted to fulfill her tasks. He hummed as I failed again, tapping the feathery tip of his quill against his chin. I groaned.

"I have to be able to see what I'm destroying," I said. "This won't work."

I was trying to destroy only the mechanism of a mechanical horse. The little horse had working legs that moved after a knob was wound, and Carlow had made it, working and painted, in little more than an hour. It was made out of the same type of wood throughout.

"It's a toy horse, not a torso." The Heir handed me a cloth from his pockets and made another notation. "How did you destroy those memories in Felhollow, or do you have a better knowledge of the mortal brain than I give you credit for?"

"I don't," I said and wiped my bleeding nose. There was not enough in me to sacrifice when I didn't know what I wanted.

My noblewright fluttered about me, all nerves. "That was different. We perform better under pressure."

"That's unfortunate," he said and closed his journal. "Rest. We'll try again in a moment."

He slipped out the door to the laboratory. I slumped against the table, a dull ache forming behind my eyes. I wasn't any good if I couldn't figure out how to perform all the time and not just when in danger, but my wrights understood danger. They knew that if I died, they died. They didn't understand pressure. They didn't understand ambition.

The door opened, slamming against the wall, and heavy footfalls rumbled toward me. I rose, and Carlow shoved me back onto my stool. The mottled red light of dawn seeped into her inscrutable eyes.

"The Crown knows His Majesty has an unbound dual-wright," she said quietly, her tangle of hair a curtain between us and the rest of the room. "The Heir is arguing with her outside."

Gooseflesh rose on my arms, and the tea in my stomach rolled. "Is she angry?"

The Sundered Crown Hyacinth Wyrslaine had only ruled for six years. She had been another nameless noble girl married off, a choice candidate given her wrights, and bound to the court so that she could only use her wrights for what they approved of. Then, she bribed enough of them to let her overthrow her husband and his supporters.

She killed his personal guards first. There had been a standoff between her and them, leaving all of them dead and her victorious. The old Crown had barricaded himself in the courtroom with their children, and Hyacinth had confronted him there. In the chaos, their two daughters died, and Hyacinth was caught off guard by her husband's most loyal guard. Knight Beatrice had struck out in that terrible moment, her sword sinking through Hyacinth's scalp, cheek, and shoulder before lodging in her chest. Some said a Vile soul where Hyacinth Wyrslaine's heart should have been stopped the blade.

I figured it was her clavicle and a well-placed prayer to her wrights. Hyacinth Wyrslaine was one of the best healers in the world after all. That was all the court had allowed her to study.

"She is never angry," said Carlow. "She is at her deadliest when she is calm. Don't underestimate her."

My wrights growled so low and so deep that my teeth shook. The door creaked open.

"Franziska," drawled a gentle voice, "you're ruining the surprise."

Carlow dropped to her knees, coat splayed out behind her like bluebird wings, and pressed her forehead to the floor. I copied her and waited. My wrights covered the back of my bare neck.

In the Wallows, royalty had felt like a distant dream. We all lived and died the same no matter who the Crown was because we had no way of changing the court. The peerage was unreachable. The Sundered Crown of Cynlira doubly so.

"Franziska, darling, we will have words about this, but I understand your hesitance." The Sundered Crown's voice bounced slightly with amusement. "You may leave."

Carlow rose. There was a shuffling of steps, the click of the door, and silence. I held my position, legs all pins and needles. Silk rustled over the ground. The Crown sat atop the Heir's stool.

"So," she said, "you have both a noblewright and a vilewright?"

"I do, Your Excellency."

"Come here, Lorena Adler." She patted the stool I had been sitting on earlier. "I have wanted another dualwrought my entire life, and now here you are. We must talk."

There were surely rules about looking at the Crown, but the moment I lifted my head, our eyes met. I froze.

She was plain—a small nose, a thin mouth lined fuller with coral pigment, and brown hair streaked with white at her temples—and even though her cosmetics were more expensive than my whole life, I might've overlooked her in a crowded room. I would have.

"Let us be honest with each other." The Crown took my chin between her fingers and turned my face from side to side. I would've been as plain as her if not for my red hair. "Your mother was the one who told you to hide, yes? The one from the Wallows? Do you take after her?"

"No, Your Excellency," I said. My mother had always said I looked like my father, but I'd no memories of him. Angular jaw, downturned hazel eyes, and thin lips gave me a perpetually peevish look. "I don't believe you would've ever seen her or my father though."

"No, I suppose I would not have." She smiled, letting me go.

I looked away. The two servants behind her kept their gazes down, but the guard kept their eyes on my hands.

"Did you think I would be scarred beyond recognition?" the Crown asked with a lilting laugh. A servant added honey to her tea and stirred it for her. "Or perhaps that I would be beautiful beyond reason, reworked and remade perfect by my wrights?"

There was a scar, a scar like any other, running from the center of her forehead, through her left brow and eye, down her cheek, and ending in her chest opposite the binding of green and white ink that the court and council used to keep her in check. Her dress was cut to show off both.

"Peers always make their enemies ugly or beautiful, never the between, and always whatever their narrow views of appalling and appealing are. Such unimaginative gossips." She laid her hands on the table and tapped the long, armored ring adorning her first finger against the top. The nail tips were sharpened for sacrifices. "But you, Lorena Adler, are neither beautiful nor unpleasing. You simply are. Like me. Overlooked. Underestimated. A simple girl amongst hungry wolves."

She said it so surely that I shuddered. She had healed a killing blow, which meant she was powerful enough to have healed the wound without it scarring. My skin was freckled with scars.

"I thought you'd be prettier," I said. "Rich people always looked prettier when they drove past the Wallows."

The Crown sat up straighter. "It's the money. Money does wonderful things for confidence."

And clothes. And health. And everything else.

"Now," she said, peering into the cup that had been her son's and holding it out. "What does my son have you working on?"

One servant refilled the cup while the other dropped two spoons full of honey into it, never hitting the rim. This woman had never been overlooked or underestimated. She, like her son, was unlike anyone else in Cynlira.

"He's mostly testing the limits of my contracts and sacrifices now," I said. There was no clause in my contract barring me from telling his mother what he wanted to do with the Door, but it was clear from our conversations that she didn't agree with his intentions. It was better to lie, and doing so was second nature now. If she thought me untrained entirely, she'd underestimate me. "I wasn't taught to contract my wrights, so my ways of working are quite different. It's not even working today. I'm nothing like you."

"Indeed," she said. "And what did my son promise you in exchange for this knowledge?"

"Information and protection," I said. "No more sacrifices coming from Felhollow. There aren't enough of us to last a year, and we're too far away to do much."

I needed to know more about her sacrifices and why she did them as she did if I was going to help Will.

"You're too far away to protest as well then," said the Crown. She sipped her tea, and her servants retreated. "How did you escape notice while living here? I employed a number of noble-wrought solely for the purpose of finding wrought children."

I swallowed. A sickly sweet bile rose up in the back of my throat. "I'm from the Wallows. I stayed out of the way and rarely used my wrights."

"Yes, Alistair said he was surprised by the speed with which you destroyed and created new memories for my warrant officers," she said with a smile. "He does love a good puzzle."

I clasped my hands in my lap, nails digging into my skin. My noblewright whined. My skin felt too tight for all the fear rising in me.

"How did you do it?" she asked.

I swallowed. "I've always been better with bodies and memories. I'm an undertaker. I know the mortal form very well."

"Please, how does someone who has never been trained know how to so quickly and cleanly alter memories like that? You can't see thoughts while preparing a body for funeral rites. You can't see feelings when observing mortal nerves. Those are all intangible things. Altering them requires practice." She leaned in close until I could taste the honey on her words. "You have practiced, though, haven't you? If you couldn't perform the most basic creations and destructions, you wouldn't be useful."

"No." I shook my head. "I told you. I haven't been very useful today."

"I'm aware," she said, gazing at me from over her cup, "just as I am aware that you are more dangerous that you have led everyone to believe."

She pulled a small pistol from the folds of her dress and pressed the muzzle into my gut.

"I'm going to count down from three," she said, "and you're either going to figure out how to destroy the mechanism of this gun without being able to see it, or you will get shot. I can repair such a wound of course, but an untrained dualwrought is hardly of use to anyone."

Use—there it was again.

"Three."

Destroy the bullet and gunpowder, I prayed. My vilewright tore from me and swept over her before I had even promised it a sacrifice. Could I even sacrifice anything? Would she fire if I stabbed her hand?

"Two."

Take her nails and the blood that comes from losing them. Take her bangles.

"One."

I flinched. She pulled the trigger, hammer striking with a sharp clank. Nothing happened, and she set the gun aside. The bracelets and rings that had decorated her hand were gone. She studied her bloody fingers.

"Well," she said and wiped her hands on the skirts of her dress. "You do work better under pressure."

"He told you to do this, didn't he?" I asked through clenched teeth. "That was not fair."

"His little tests are much better than mine." She bowed her head slightly, but I didn't believe her bashful blush for a moment. "The world is not fair. It is best you learn that now. I survived and became Crown because I am strong, not because the world is easy. I earned this, and I enjoy helping others with promise earn worthy lives as well."

Except she had been born a different sort of strong than us—noble and rich, noblewrought and vilewrought. If this world were a war, she had been born in armor with a sword in her hands, and we had been born with nothing but our teeth and nails and grit. She couldn't see our truth for the visor she had been born in.

"Do you really think that's why you survived? That's why you're the Crown?" I asked before I could stop. "Because you're stronger than all the people who work for Cynlira?"

The question struck her. She reared back and laughed, a

chiming sound. The Crown rose from her chair, white dress brushing along the floor like a low, shushing voice, and I stood. She was a full head shorter than me, but when she walked, all the presence I had thought she didn't have took my breath away. She moved as if the world was the one moving and it only moved for her.

"Lorena." Her hands closed around my shoulders, fingers curled over them as a mother might hold her child still before a mirror. Her blood dripped down my chest. "You may, of course, continue to aid my son, but the Door and who I sacrifice are none of your concern. The Door cannot be destroyed. Your deal with Alistair may stand since the contract is signed, but I would suggest being more honest with my son and steering his research toward something more useful."

I nodded.

"If you lie to me again, the name Felhollow will only be uttered in dark corners of this world as a word of warning—*we don't want to end up like Felhollow*. Do you understand?" she asked. "Do not lie to me again."

I bowed my head.

"No, no," she said and clucked her tongue. "I want to hear it this time, darling. You lied so well. Let's see how much feeling you can put into three words. Do you understand me?"

Three. Not one.

"Yes," I said. "Your Excellency."

"Oh, Lorena Adler, do be more careful." She squeezed my shoulders and let go, and one of her hands drifted to the top of my head. She tucked a few strands of hair behind my ear. "I hope you're useful for a while. I would hate to find you dead without me having a hand in it."

thirteen

W ELL, I'M ALIVE," I SAID AS THE HEIR ENTERED the laboratory. "Does that satisfy your curiosity about my abilities to work under pressure?"

He didn't even have the decency to blush. "To an extent. She was going to speak with you regardless. Now she knows you're capable at least."

"I hardly think that's in my favor," I muttered and dumped the tea she had been drinking over one of Creek's potted ferns.

"It is," said the Heir. "She, and I by extension, have no need for anyone less than capable."

So she would've let me bleed out on the floor if I hadn't destroyed the bullet because I wasn't good enough.

"She might have killed me!"

"But she didn't." He picked up the pistol. "Concise way to solve the problem. What was the contract?"

I'd no idea if this was better or worse than the forced flirting.

"Destroy the bullet and powder, and take her nails, blood, and jewelry as sacrifice." I winced. "She didn't even mention the sacrifices."

"She's sacrificed worse," he said and wrote everything down. "The two of you were alone. She knew who you would have to sacrifice."

I collapsed onto the stool near my desk, far from him, and

pulled the mechanical horse to myself. The Heir glanced up once and straightened his glasses. I shrugged.

"You wouldn't have died. You're too good for that," he mumbled. "Your contract is hardly precise though."

"She was going to shoot me," I said, drawing out each word. "I've had bandits give me more of a chance."

He bristled and shook his head. "You could have healed yourself."

"But you and she didn't know that."

"We inferred it." He finally looked up at me, glasses hiding his gaze, and gestured to the stool next to him. "Please. We need to discuss your contracts."

I relented. His desk was better for work anyway, the neat precision of his contracts reflected in the perfectly labeled shelves and boxes. Clean penknives and scalpels were aligned in neat rows at the back of the table, and on a shelf above them was a small box of quill nibs. The shelf above him was bending beneath the weight of all his journals and books. I picked up one.

The hand-painted illustrations on the first few pages of a Vile with strangling vines for a tongue retreating unhappily into a cave and a Noble with eyes like the sea locking itself away behind the moon were enough to tell me what it was about.

"You're very careful. Exacting," I said. "The Vile were creatures of pure chaos made to unbalance the world so that the Noble had something to balance. You're overcompensating."

The Heir's handwriting, each letter as if made by a press, was as ordered as his desk.

"Chaos is vile," he said. "I find there is beauty in the rational."

I set down the book on the edge of the table. His fingers tightened around his quill, leaving splotches on his paper. I looked away, and when I looked back, he had returned the book to its rightful place.

"Who didn't like that you were vilewrought?" I asked.

"It's nothing like that," he said quickly. "My father loathed mess, and I've never broken the habit. He feared chaos would lead me to Chaos, especially after Hila, but I am not some errant vilewrought. I will be better than he thought I was."

I knew so many rumors about him and his mother, but there were so few about the previous Crown. The Heir's grand-father was the one who had started the sacrifices. The Heir's father had carried it on "with great trepidation for the future of his country." The Heir's mother had no such hesitancy.

It didn't matter if I saved Will. It didn't matter if I made sure no more sacrifices would be taken from Felhollow. Cynlira was a mine threatening to collapse, and the Sundered Crown was taking a pickax to it still. She would destroy this nation.

"If I had used the contract you did with my vilewright, it would have destroyed one bullet." He picked up the pistol and opened the chamber, letting five more tumble to the tabletop. "There would be no guarantee it would be the one necessary to save me, and it might have taken the powder from another casing. This shouldn't have worked."

"It inferred what I needed," I said, and he scowled. "My vilewright's known me long enough to know what I mean, and it definitely knows that if I die, it gets no more sacrifices from me."

"But is it really aware of that?" He dropped his quill and leaned back.

"I don't know, and I don't know how to test that," I said. "How binding are your contracts? Could she break it for you if she wanted to sacrifice Will even if he were innocent?"

"She wouldn't."

"But what if she does?" I asked.

"Then I would most likely die, and she would have no Heir. She is fond of me, despite popular belief." He glanced at me over the rim of his glasses. "My mother, the court, and the council believe that replacing the Door will cause it to open permanently. My mother is many things, but she does not want all Cynlira to die."

I snorted.

"The dead can't bow, Lorena."

"How am I supposed to work then? I'm not you. You could say one word, and my whole town would be wiped from the map. Explain to me how I am supposed to trust you when I am a chick among foxes?" I asked. Kara, Ines, Old Ivy, Mack's family, everyone I had ever known—the Crown knew Felhollow mattered to me, and I couldn't save the whole town from her. "We're taught the only resource we have in excess is obedience, and you might pluck one of us up for sacrifice at any time. I trust our contract. I trust your mother's words far less."

I took his hand in mine, and he stared at our interlaced fingers.

"I understand," he said. "That is fair."

Sexual attraction and I might have been strangers, but I knew how it worked and that half of the Heir's attraction to me was our shared knowledge. He had nearly died when I told him I understood him that first time in the carriage. There was a yearning in his gaze that I could barely meet. He wanted closeness in body and mind. He wanted consumption. Coalescence.

"I understand your hesitancy," I said, squeezing his hand, "but I cannot live with it."

We had met, and now we couldn't resist the pull. Miscible, he would've called us.

"I will ensure that she understands that Felhollow is off-limits." He swallowed, throat bobbing, and did not pull away. "She would not anger you so though. She let you use her as sacrifice and left smiling. She is not happy about our contract, but she has not attempted to change it. That alone means she has accepted it. Please try not to worry."

"I will try," I said and slipped my hand from his. "I've

skimmed the documents from Will's original warrant. Why would she care about him acquiring old factories?"

He pushed his glasses higher up his nose and tugged the tie from his long hair, letting it fall before his face. "I'm sure I wouldn't know."

He was lying.

"I'll have to keep reading then, and I might not have time to do more tests. Julian can't accept that Will might not be perfect." I sighed. "I had forgotten how hard it is to get over."

The Heir stiffened.

"My father's parents are still alive, probably, but they never approved of my mother and definitely not of me. I went to them once after my mother died, and they turned me away. I always thought family had to love you," I said.

The Heir leaned toward me.

"It's enough to make you hate yourself even though you really hate them." He reached out, fingers shaking, and let his hand hang above mine. "It is difficult for some to see depravity where they naturally assume devotion."

"I look like my father, and I hate it." I closed the distance. "You look like your father, don't you?"

He nodded and pulled off his glasses. Curling strands of inky hair hid his eyes, rustling with his breaths, and I ran my thumb across the back of his hand. I did not look at his eyes.

"You don't hide yourself because of that, do you?" I whispered.

He laughed. "I would hardly call any part of my life hiding."

The door creaked. He tore his hand from mine, turning back to his books. I held back my laugh and slipped from the stool. Carlow hesitated in the doorway to the room, her goggles hanging about her neck, and she glanced up once. I had never thought of her as small, but she was. Even short and stout Basil seemed looming compared to her.

"Is she gone for today?" asked Carlow, clutching a notebook to her chest.

"So far as I know," the Heir said, voice rough. "You have my permission to leave for the day though."

Carlow darted back out the door.

"She's really scared of her," I said, and it was the most I had ever understood Carlow.

The Heir nodded. "I am, as always, the lesser of two evils."

"She's dualwrought, not immortal," I muttered. "Right?"

"She is very mortal. Using her wrights tires her out, just like us," said the Heir. "Mortals gained magic through a contract. Any mortal could do magic so long as they consumed a Noble or Vile. Through the conjunction of mortal and immortal came a contract, so pieces of immortal souls—wrights—attached to mortal souls—wrought—and did the bidding of those who had devoured them."

"You're making it toothsome. We mortals grew tired of our demigod rulers, so we ate them, body and soul, to obtain their powers. This new warfare so horrified the gods that they banished what was left of the Noble and Vile from this world." I twirled one of the knives from his collection between my fingers. "Good story. The powerful eat us slowly, so we have to eat them bite by bite to get back the power they stole from us."

He frowned. "For all our faults, my mother and I have never cannibalized anyone."

"It's a metaphor using very real history," I said, "and if I hadn't been able to stop that shot, if I hadn't been of use, she would've let me die."

"I know what a metaphor is," he said and frowned. "Soon after, as the original noblewrought and vilewrought began to die, their power cropped up in new children. Pieces of those Noble and Vile souls attached to new mortals at birth. Do you ever wonder—"

"Which Noble and Vile were devoured to create my wrights?" I took his hand in mine and pushed back his sleeve. "We understand each other too well for you not to know the answer to that."

The Heir grinned and offered me his arm. "You work better under pressure, don't you?"

I narrowed my eyes and cut into his arm and let his blood drip onto Carlow's mechanized horse.

Destroy the inner workings of this, and have Alistair Wyrslaine's sense of pain and blood.

My vilewright lapped up the blood that spilled from the Heir, hummed, and took a whole minute to sink into the horse and figure out which parts were the mechanisms. They vanished as if they had never been there at all. The Heir made a notation in his ledger.

"I will make sure you have time to research and tests." He stared at my fingers curled around his wrist. "It took longer than with the gun."

My wright rumbled against me.

I set the knife aside and let go. A headache pounded behind my eyes. "I took away your sense of pain. You should note how long that lasts."

"A better sacrifice, and yet it still took longer."

"Perhaps it's full," I said softly. "What was the first time you sacrificed something other than someone else's blood to your vilewright?"

He stilled. Licked his lips. Set the knife aside. "I sacrificed my sisters' fear."

A more merciful act than I'd have guessed.

"My father thought me unlucky. He wasn't pleased I was the oldest," he said, voice low and hoarse. "My sisters were far better than me in every way. They always felt terrible he preferred them to me. They shouldn't have."

"What happened to them?"

"Our mother." The Heir adjusted his glasses. "My father threatened to kill me. I was always her favorite. She threatened to kill them. He didn't believe her."

She had to be stopped. Even if Will survived, we'd all still be doomed if the Crown took a liking to me. She could kill them at any time. The Door didn't matter. The Sundered Crown had to be stopped.

And I would need the Heir to stop her.

"Let me call the healer," he said quickly. "You should rest, and she can heal my arm."

"We should keep testing." I pulled the Heir's hand back into my lap, my fingers loose around his wrist. "We're working together quite a lot. May I call you Alistair?"

fourteen

THE NEXT DAY, I WROTE A NOTE FOR THE HEIR that I would be visiting Julian to go over the case against Will Chase. I meant to leave it in the laboratory, but the way was blocked. A member of the court had Carlow cornered against the door.

"Do not interrupt my work for such a banal request again, Franziska. Such desultory behavior is unacceptable. His Majesty may indulge your appetite for disobedience, but do not forget that you and every other wrought are at the mercy of the court and council. You do as we instruct," the courtier was saying. "You don't know how to obey." She ripped open Carlow's coat and grimaced at the ooze of ink and blood covering her binding. "It's unbecoming."

"My dear Carra Shearwill," said Carlow with a grin, "I have not even begun to unbecome."

The courtier stalked away, and Carlow punched a tree.

"Enjoy the show?" she asked.

I shook my head. "She one of the twenty-five?"

Twelve councilors and thirteen courtiers, with the input of the rest of the council and court, controlled what the wrought could do with their wrights. Even the Sundered Crown was bound to prevent her from doing anything untoward. She'd only survived killing her husband and taking over because she had the twenty-five on her side. The split was to keep it fair and make sure the peers *and* common folk had a say in what work wrought did. "The Crown does some of our bindings now, you know. She decides what new wrought can study. Even before she was the Crown, she was one of the wrought in charge of binding new." Carlow brought a hand to her chest and closed her eyes. "I wanted to be a healer, but Cynlira needed more noblewrought good at building and supporting industry."

"I'm sorry," I said, knowing nothing would ease her pains. She'd no choice in any of it.

"I didn't want to be a healer and undertaker. I went through it and came out fine. It builds character," mumbled Carlow in a terrible, nasally impression of the Crown. She took a deep breath, drew herself up, and ripped open the door to the laboratory. "Come on. We have work to do."

Death or destruction was the only thing that could break the bonds.

"Not today," I said but followed her in anyway. "I'm going into the city to deal with some things."

"May I come with you?" Basil, standing at their desk, dropped their quill. "I need to requisition some things, and the walk to the Wheels is so much nicer with a friend."

"Sure." I smiled.

They beamed and led the way. By the time we reached Noshwright, Basil was in the middle of a delightful story about their parents, who ran a bar out west. I stopped at the doors to the large inn.

"...my parents are lovely, but I'm thrilled to be away from my more traditional neighbors," they said softly. "We've been cut off from the rest of the world for decades, but people can still be so isolationist."

Basil's family had come to Cynlira over a century ago from Krait in the far, far north and been stuck here once the gods left, cutting off Cynlira from the rest of the world with a deep chasm. The court hadn't made it easy for folks to settle after. Lots of Wallowers still grumbled over it.

"It's not the same, but Felhollow thinks it's them versus the big cities," I said. It wasn't something I could understand. "If you ever want to talk about it, that is."

We paused in the lobby of Noshwright. Basil stepped aside, pointedly looking away from me. Julian was too focused on his father to be good company, and Mack was friendly but slow to warm to new folks. The pair were across the lobby, and Julian spotted me first. He darted through the crowd and hoisted me up into a hug. His lips brushed my cheek. I leaned back but didn't pull completely away. We didn't have time for this.

"Who's that?" Julian asked, peering over me at Basil, who was giving me time to say hello by studying old cookbooks on display.

"Basil Baines," I said and gestured them forward. "This is Julian Chase and Mack Sarclaw, my dearest friends. Basil is noblewrought and as smart as they are nice."

I tried to infuse the words with the feeling that if either of them said a mean thing, I'd kick them.

"Nice to meet you, Basil," Julian said and nodded. "Thanks for watching out for our Lore."

"I think she could watch out for all of us and herself just fine." Basil laughed softly. "So you're from—did you make that?"

They pointed at the crossbow hanging from Mack's belt.

"Yes." He touched it. The bolts were gone—no loaded weapons in the inn—but I'd never seen Mack without the bow. "Why?"

"That's a modified wheel lock from an old pistol," Basil said, and I braced for the rambling. "But you can't have a spark on a wooden crossbow?"

"Oh no, it's repeating. I repurposed it. Holds three bolts now and spins." Mack trailed off, tongue-tied, and rubbed the back of his neck. "My other one's better."

Julian tugged me toward the lift. "If that Basil likes muck-ing about with metal as much as Mack, they'll be ages. Come up to my rooms. We need to talk."

His rooms—Julian only inherited them if Will died free.

Until Will was convicted and executed, his properties still belonged to him. After that, they went to the Crown.

"Your father here?" I asked.

Julian nodded, waiting for the clicking of the lift's counter-weights to stop. "Don't punch him."

"Why? What's he done?"

"At least one illegal thing," Julian said softly outside the door to the rooms. "But on the bright side, he put the old church he bought in my name as a gift, so if everything goes to shit, we can live there."

"Yes, consecrated ruins are exactly what I want out of a home." I wrapped my arms around myself, trying to ignore his easy acceptance of Will's crimes. "How illegal? My contract hinges on his innocence."

I had found nothing that made him guilty of treason; I had found plenty of things that made me feel guilty about helping him. There was a healer in Ipswit he'd fired for asking about injured factory workers being let go, the hours in a munitions factory at the edge of the Wallows had been lengthened, and the noblewrought in charge of the powder had been reduced from three to one. It was a recipe for disaster.

It was unconscionable. It was not illegal.

"Not terribly," said Julian. "Only some tax evasion. Not enough to warrant sacrificing him, certainly."

"Well," I said, "if it's only tax evasion."

Julian shook his head and nudged me through the door. "It's not, and you're not going to like it. I went through my father's ledgers."

"Which ones?" I asked. The Heir hadn't let me copy the evi-dence against Will, but he had been forthcoming. "I have copies of the relevant ones, and while tax evasion seems likely given the numbers, you're right—it's not enough."

"Trust me," he said, "you haven't read these."

The quarters had been transformed. Papers, ledgers, and pistols littered every surface, tepid cups of water teetering atop the listing stacks. The dining table had been covered in a map of Cynlira, pins marking a handful of spots, and Will Chase leaned against it. Nineteen years older than us, Will had always seemed jovial and untouchable, the sort of happy only a sudden windfall could produce, but he had aged these last two weeks. His blond hair was hoary, and the wrinkles above his brow were crevices. He smiled though.

"Lorena!" His arms opened wide and, enfolded in them, a part of me I thought I had snuffed out longed for the embrace to last. "My savior. I can never thank you enough, my dear girl. You didn't have to do that."

"You helped me when I moved to Felhollow," I mumbled into his shirt. "It was the least I could do."

I'd thought of him as family, and he'd been breaking the law the whole damned time, putting us all in danger.

"And you did a great deal." He patted my arm and sat me down in one of the clean chairs. "Now, I hear that you have been contracted to His Majesty?"

I nodded. "He's attempting to replace the Door with something that doesn't require sacrifices."

Julian sat behind me, and Will before me. He laced his fingers together, chin balanced on top.

"The council had gotten wind of such research, and it is troubling," said Will. "We had hoped he wouldn't do anything so dangerous."

That hardly seemed right.

"My contract with him concerns your trial." I glanced at the papers near me—they were business records dealing with wages and expenses. "Did you not pay your taxes?"

He had the decency to flush. "I made a mistake after purchasing a new plot of land on the border between two holdings, and unfortunately, the peer has been unforgiving."

Of course they were.

"It's not like he couldn't or wouldn't pay," said Julian. "He doesn't have access to his assets since he's set to stand trial, so he can't."

"That can't be it." I gestured to the map of Cynlira. "I've read through the documents they're considering evidence. It's like slogging through mud, but there are things that would worry the court. You bought a munitions factory and bought up a bunch of land. It's like you're making a move to buy into the peerage or establish your own holding."

It wasn't unheard of, but it was expensive. The court loathed that it was even an option. The last holding to be established was Hila, and then its leaders had fought for independence from Cynlira.

"Even if I were, it's not illegal." Will smacked the table. "Only treason, mass murder, and rape are punishable by sacrifice, and I've done none of that. The court's just threatened by council members broadening our horizons."

"Since when does the Sundered Crown need a reason?" muttered Julian.

I glanced back at him. "I've met her, and judging by what I saw, she doesn't. She prefers having one so no one can challenge her. As far gone as Cynlira is, if she broke the rules so blatantly, they'd stop her because it would mean she could the same to them."

Following the rules most of the time kept people on their toes.

Will paled, and Julian sucked in a breath.

"You met her?" he whispered.

"Can you think of nothing she would consider treasonous?" I asked them both, desperate to forget the way I could still feel the threat of her gun against my ribs. "You've increased rifle production, but that's hardly news. The current model breaks often enough, and bandits are getting worse in Felhollow. That we can justify."

"If it's not illegal, it's not too unscrupulous," said Julian. "He's playing by the rules. The court can't blame him for that. No justice to be had trying him for things that are legal."

I gripped my hands together, nails digging into my palm. Laws were not justice.

"I don't care what unscrupulous things you've done, but you have to get it all together and make sure it's legal," I said. I did care, and I hoped Julian hadn't already forgiven the legal but immoral things.

"Good lie. You've the mettle of Mori and the sense to deal with folks even when you hate them," Will said so quietly I was sure Julian didn't hear. "Dualwrought and clever. Dangerous combination."

I shuddered. The door to the rooms opened. Mack stood on the threshold, a tray of small lemon cakes in his hands and his bow gone. His locs were bundled up atop his head like he always did when working.

"Mack!" Will leapt to his feet. "Good. We were finishing up, but you can help me finish listing all the raids in Felhollow from this last year. We need to justify why Felhollow needed guns."

Will was hiding something, and I had to find out what before he got us all killed.

I rose. "I should go. I still need to get some work done today. How'd Basil treat you?"

"I don't know what happened," Mack said. "They asked to see the crossbow and we dismantled it, you know, to see the wheel lock, and then there was tea in front of me and I'd already told them my favorite kind. Then there was cake and they remembered they had to hit the market, so I said I'd take it up here."

"Basil's like that." I grabbed one of the little cakes. "They're the sort of chatty that makes other folks chatty. Even Carlow likes them."

She didn't mock them at least, which she did to everyone not royalty.

Julian grabbed my hand and held me back. "Lore, I want you out of here as soon as you can be."

"I can't break the contract," I said.

"We'll find a way," said Julian. "We'll find a noblewrought who can do it. This is too dangerous for you."

I shook my head. Julian would never understand the part of me that wanted to stay and learn what I had denied myself. Mother had always said I was better off alone, but Basil, Creek, and Carlow were like me. They understood how it felt to break yourself down for people who would never do the same for you. Even the Heir, for all his posturing, understood the dark part of me that wanted more.

It was why he hadn't included my future in the contract. I would never be able to leave now that I knew what living and working with other wrought was like.

"I cannot leave," I said slowly, "but I will be safe."

Mack swallowed and kissed my forehead. "Willoughby seems to think the Heir wants to free the Vile. Be careful. That boy's dangerous."

Everyone in this damned city was.

"Don't worry," I said and dragged my hands over my face. Mori would be the death of me. "I have a plan."

fifteen

THAT EVENING, I PROGRESSED FROM SIMPLY destroying the mechanisms in Carlow's little wooden horses to recreating them in perfect working order despite not knowing how they worked. Basil worked on their own research, something to do with the melting points of different metals compared to the red dirt. They had dragged their stool to my desk so they could work next to me. Creek and Carlow watched us, their heads bowed over a notebook. Only Carlow wrote in it.

"Carlow, Creek," the Heir said as he walked the horse to them. "What do you think?"

Carlow and Creek, Creek and Carlow. Their names were always together and awkward when they weren't.

"What's the point of evaluation until she actually does what she's supposed to?" Carlow asked.

Basil leaned in close to me and whispered, "It's her, not you, I promise. She's still sad."

"Why?" I asked.

"Before you, we had another noblewrought. Poppy was twelve and adored Carlow, like a sister would," said Basil quickly and as quietly as possible. "She died in her sleep two years ago. I think Carlow died a little too. Carlow loved her."

I swallowed, remembering the bleak months after my mother had died.

"Even Creek's been nicer since," Basil said. "He's like a different person."

"How could he have been worse?"

The Heir placed the bowl of red dirt on the table before me, and Basil leaned away.

"Try to destroy this for good," he said. "Even just a granule will do."

"It won't," said Carlow loudly, "but I suppose it's something."

"It's more than you can do," I muttered.

Imagine the Door is about to eat me and you have to destroy it. It's like the gun and horse but Vile. What sacrifice would be enough?

A hunger, deep and dark, opened within me. I gagged, heart in my throat, and lurched forward. My nails dug into the table, and the Heir pulled my hands away before I could split my nails. He placed a knife in my hands.

Only a granule. Only a granule. Not the whole Door.

Something cinched within me, and my vilewright growled. I focused on the minute ways mortal bodies re-created themselves. We were nothing but little pieces always working. My noblewright, after months of study, had created the knowledge in my mind. So many corpses, so much knowledge. I imagined the granules doubling and their centers, near bursting, pinching apart. I imagined their spindly insides dragging half of their vile bits into the new granule. I imagined reaching inside and plucking their insides away.

Take blood and a good memory of his mother from the Heir, and destroy what makes them repair themselves, I prayed. *And if that isn't enough, take blood. Not enough to kill him. If you need more, take it from the others. Don't kill anyone.*

I grabbed the Heir's arm and nicked a vein. The dirt rippled, grains rolling down the little mound and pooling around the rim, and one single granule crumbled. Black smoke spiraled above the bowl.

No new grains appeared.

"Well done," said the Heir.

His eyes fluttered shut, and he crumpled to the floor. Creek lunged, catching his head. I grabbed his coat and lowered him down. Basil ran out to call for a healer.

"No, don't. I'm fine." The Heir blinked, face suddenly pale and pinched, and glanced at me. "Did you specify that it shouldn't take enough blood to kill me?"

I nodded.

"Maybe make sure it leaves me awake next time," he said and groaned. "I should have given you Hana for this."

"I'm so sorry, Alistair." I helped him sit up, and he didn't let go of my wrist. "I should have thought that through more."

He stared at me, eyes wide behind his crooked glasses, and licked his lips. "It's all right, Lorena. If you help me stand up, I'll forgive you."

Carlow cleared her throat. We all froze and looked at her.

"Stay sitting. I have bad news," said Carlow, lips so worried her teeth were red. "I ran my calculations five times to be sure, and I can find no flaws. The Door will either open in five months when we fail to sacrifice enough mortals, or we will be forced to sacrifice a tenth of the Liran population to it within a single month."

I dropped the Heir. "What?"

He groaned. "At least it's only a tenth."

"That's six hundred thousand people. That's nearly all of Mori," I said. "We can't sacrifice over half a million people to buy us time to fix the problem."

"It wouldn't buy us much time. Twelve years ago, the number of sacrifices began growing exponentially. After five months, the growth is unpredictable save for the fact that it will be growth," said Carlow, pushing her goggles to the top of her head. Scratches marred the pale skin around where they'd rested. "I ran it five times and got the same answer each time. I haven't told Her Excellency yet."

"If the growth is exponential and increasing as Carlow says, one month is a blessing." The Heir adjusted his glasses with steady hands. "Don't tell my mother yet. This is good. This is leverage we can use to justify our research."

This was a tragedy. One tenth of Cynlira wouldn't touch the peers or even the councilors' families. Cynlira had been walking toward a cliff edge for so long, and now we were sprinting toward it without a care, the peerage and councilors at our backs. They'd herd us all off, sacrifice hundreds of thousands to the Door, to buy themselves time. Far-reaching solutions had been unnecessary fearmongering, but now we were too late. They'd take the easy path that would keep them in power the longest.

And if they could choose which six hundred thousand to sacrifice, they'd allow it in the blink of an eye.

A starving silence, desperate for words to soothe us, fell over the room. I touched Basil's shoulder, and they flinched. Creek sniffed.

"If we cannot save all Cynlira, then we will save what we can," said the Heir. "We will find a way to shut or remake the Door."

The peerage and council could've done it years ago, before it came to this.

"Maybe we should try eating it like we did the Vile," I said.

Creek turned so fast his neck snapped. "That's the only good idea any of you all have ever had."

"Please try it." Carlow tossed her journal aside. "Just wait until it's about to open so that the end of the world is an inevitability and not our fault."

"There is no time to waste then." The Heir struggled to his feet and clutched his desk for support. He waved me off. "Lorena, come with me."

He nodded to the door, and I followed. Carlow leaned forward against Creek's back, her arms dangling between them. Basil sat heavily on the Heir's abandoned stool.

"Where are they?" said Carlow. "The sky is infinite, but

the earth is not. There's no room for all the Vile the Door holds back. Space cannot be created or destroyed, so where are they?"

"If you had all the time in the world and all the books ever written, no knowledge would be safe from you," muttered Creek. "You've done well."

I followed the Heir outside before I could hear any more. I tried to ask him where we were going, and he held up one hand. His steps were still unsteady and his path winding. He led me deeper into the royal grounds, to a building I had never even seen, and the imposing stone carved straight from the side of the mountain gave way to marble floors and tapestry-covered walls. He tripped once, and I looped one of my arms through his. He leaned heavily against my side.

The Sundered Crown could not reign much longer, but to ensure that, I had to make the Heir trust me.

When we reached a stairwell at the center of the palace, the Heir spent a half hour contracting his vilewright to open a set of five doors. There were real locks and a key as well. Behind them all was a single staircase down into the depths of the mountain. We spiraled down it and deep into the earth, water oozing from the stone walls. Far-off screeches echoed down the halls.

"The sacrifices," the Heir said. "Try to ignore them."

This was where Will would've been.

We came to a stop an hour after leaving the lab. The near rush of water rumbled up my feet, a heavy damp hanging in the air. Salt and sulfur tinged the space, and a bone-white dust stuck to the wet walls dripped around us. The path dropped off, and the Heir offered me a hand as we descended into a cave system lit by the pale-green light of luminescent spiderwebs. My wrights writhed within me. Moss the color of old teeth lined our path.

And at the end, beyond dragging footprints and sacrificial stains, in the middle of a small sandbar encircled by salt-encrusted runoffs of river water, looming over me as it had that day more than ten years ago, was the door to my mother's sickroom. She'd only survived three days, but I'd still know it anywhere.

"What is this?" I whispered.

"The Door," he said. "It's different for everyone."

It was a crooked door set in a listing jamb. The wood was old and wet-warped, bug holes freckling the lower half, and the uneven slats left a gash of space in the middle. A brilliant white light spilled out through the cracks. No light so bright had ever existed in the Wallows.

This wasn't some specter created by a noblewright; I would've noticed. This was the memory that marked the loss of my mother in my mind.

I was not afraid, and in that clarity came fury.

"Get out of my head," I said, stalking to the Door. "That home's not real anymore, and I never wanted to open that door."

The Door grew, shrank.

A breath.

I leaned in close, unafraid, and whispered, "I burned that house. Did you miss that part of the memory, or are you grasping?"

And through the crack in the door came a soft, shivering laugh. I stumbled back.

I wanted to open the Door. Something in me whispered that my mother would be on the other side, her flesh healed. Her arms would fold around me, and she'd smell of soap and sawdust instead of seared skin and hair. She would laugh instead of scream.

I had never wanted anything so deeply. It was in my bones, my blood, every pounding thought in my head urging me to rip the door open.

"Messing with this will end the world," I whispered. There were dark things beyond that Door begging to be let back in. They were begging me to let them in. "What if we can't fix it?"

"There is no such thing as 'can't,'" he said. "There is only what we do not understand yet. This Door would not exist if it were impossible."

I turned him to the Door and held his face so that he had to look at it. "Only someone who's been handed the world would say that. It's not the rich who will die. It's not the peerage. You'll all be safe behind your soldiers, stone walls, and wrought. It's the rest of us who will die. You'll destroy us."

"No!" He yanked himself from my grasp and spun, red glasses cracking against the ground. "No, I can and I will. I was made to destroy. I have always destroyed lives, but for once, I can destroy this and create something better! I made myself a monster when it was expected of me, but I will not be that monster now!"

I knelt and picked up the glasses, far too aware of the Door at my back.

"I can," the Heir whispered, eyes wet, breaths stuttering. "I can. I can. I promise. I can create something better. I just need more time. I need to understand it. To know."

He sunk to his knees, gaze stuck on the door, and shuddered.

"I can create things. Good things." He looked to me. "Please, Lorena, you understand, don't you? My mother has never cared, but I do."

Alistair Wyrslaine, the poor boy desperate to understand everything because no one understood him.

"Alistair," I said, setting the broken glasses on his nose. For all the good I had ever done, I'd done it to survive. Not out of goodness but survival. We were not the same, but we were plucked from the same plot. "Of course I understand, but you have to be careful. Your mother has been down here an endless number of times. What do you think it's done to her? Those sacrifices? Alistair, they have to stop. Even without them, she's killed so many people. She doesn't want you to succeed. Why do you think that is?"

"They're guilty. Those are the rules," he said, his gaze stuck on whatever Door he saw beyond my back. "I tried—I didn't like..." He squeezed his eyes shut. "Willoughby Chase is an exception, not a standard. Most buy their way out of the sacrifice if they can. Perhaps you're right. He's innocent. If he weren't, he could've paid."

Oh.

Society was built on the corpses of those the court cast aside—those who couldn't pay a fine, those who stole to survive, those who couldn't afford an education and didn't know all the rules—and why should this be any different? Of course the wealthy only cared about the validity of the sacrifices when it happened to one of their own. Did Julian know?

"But then he did the one thing my mother cannot forgive," said Alistair.

I couldn't imagine the Crown forgiving anything and could not think of what Will must have done. It had to be insulting. It had to be demeaning. But Will didn't have enough power or money to degrade the Crown.

"Lorena?"

"I know what we have to do," I said, "but I'm afraid you won't understand me."

"Of course I will." He rose up on his knees, the unnatural light of the Door reflecting red in his eyes, and grasped my coat. "I do not want to be remembered as the red-eyed vilewrought monster of Hila. I can't be, and you understand that. I promise I will understand you."

Maybe I didn't deserve the people I was trying to save.

"We have to be very, very careful." I stroked his cheek, suddenly seeing the boy Julian and the others were so afraid of. "We must deal with your mother. The Door will open within five months. We cannot let her stop your research. We cannot let her continue killing. She must be stopped."

I had to convince him to kill the Sundered Crown.

sixteen

I T KNOWS YOU NOW," HE SAID WHEN ESCORTING ME back to my room. "It will try to make you open it. Don't."

It was the Door in the depths of the palace in a world where the Vile were banished. It had no power here.

"I understand why you think this about my mother." He adjusted his glasses—he was lying about something then—and moved as if to touch me but didn't. "But I need time. We'll talk tomorrow."

Long after he'd left, hours into the dark night, footsteps echoed up and down the hall, and someone who sounded like the Heir rapped twice at my door. I jerked up and was halfway to the door before stopping. The Heir always knocked thrice. I crawled back into bed. They knocked for an hour.

Perhaps the Heir was right: I had seen the Door, and it had opened another in me, letting the vileness in me free.

Dawn was bleeding through my window when I woke. A fat waxing moon still hung in the sky. Footsteps shuffled outside, and hushed voices echoed in the hall. Carlow's door creaked.

"I'm annoyed," said Carlow, her voice gritty from sleep.

"And I'm serious." Creek sighed. "Stay in bed today."

"I'd mock you for playing my father, but we both know what befalls people unlucky enough to be my family," Carlow said, her voice pitching. She laughed. "You never cared before."

"You were never so reckless before."

Before Poppy's death, he must've meant.

"Why are you doing this?" Carlow whispered. "I can't. You know what happens to the people I love."

"The heart is a garden, and a gardener does not always control what takes root and grows," said Creek, his voice steadier than I'd ever heard it. "Your curse should never have been inheritable."

"Well," she said, "when we ruin everything and accidentally destroy the Door, you can tell that to the Vile who placed it before I kill them."

"He deserves it, but that isn't how you break a curse, Franziska Carlow," he said, her name the pause between his quickened breaths. "I would know."

"Because you failed to break yours two years ago?" She let out a bark of a laugh. "We're going to be stuck together for eternity."

"Franziska, I'm not—"

A door slammed down the hall, and one of them stumbled. Carlow's door shut. A dozen people at least thundered down the hallway. I threw my blanket off and dragged a dress over my head. I pulled the greatcoat on just as the door rattled.

"The gall of him, installing locks," came the gentle voice of the Sundered Crown. "Lorena, I have come to speak with you."

"One moment, Your Excellency." I stomped toward the door so that she would be sure to hear that I wasn't avoiding her and shoved the ledgers and notes on Will's case onto my bed and under the blanket. "I'm sorry. It has been a slow morning."

When I opened the door, she was staring down her nose at me despite me being taller.

"Yes," she said, gaze rolling to take in the full room behind me. "My Door has that effect on people."

Behind her stood a host of guards and the Heir. His red glasses were pushed close to his eyes, and his black hair was twisted up in a smooth bun. The collar of his shirt could have cut his chin. Even his mouth was a sharp, little line.

"Would you like to come in, or shall we go somewhere else?" I asked, head bowed.

"I would like for you to bow properly." She inclined her head—not a bow but an instruction. "You're far too uncouth to be the only other dualwrought. We will remedy that."

I sunk to my knees and pressed my head to the floor. After a breath, she tapped her toes against the ground. I rose, head bowed.

"Good." She smiled, close-mouthed, and patted my hand. "Fetch another chair."

My mother's voice rose up in my head. "Beware of creatures hiding their teeth."

One of the guards darted away. I tried not to glance at the Heir. His mother glided past me and sat at my desk, the wide cut of her white trousers spilling across the floor like snow. Another guard set a covered tray before her, and yet another sat a new chair beside me. I sat, clutching my greatcoat at my stomach. Julian's coat was thrown across the end of my bed.

"We're going to discuss what you do know," she said, dismissing everyone with a wave, "and then I am going to teach you what you do not."

I glanced at the Heir. He stood, unmoving, at the wall behind his mother.

"Now." The Crown gestured to the tray on my desk and drew a cup of milk tea toward herself. "You know how to heal yourself, yes?"

I nodded.

"Good," she said. "Eat."

Slow-baked black bread slices lined the outside of the tray. Boiled eggs, seared tomatoes, and hard yellow cheese covered the rest of it. Poached eggs jiggled in the valley of a saucer, their orange yolks speckled with thick flakes of salt, and slivers of toasted white bread were stacked next to them. There were even three small cakes stuffed with candied peel.

"I am glad," muttered the Crown, frighteningly dreamily, "we got tea before we were cut off from the rest of the world."

There were no plates, only two knives and two spoons, and the Crown made no move for either.

"Yes, Your Excellency," I said and ate a tomato. "What is it you would like me to learn?"

"I am curious." She picked up the knife and twirled it exactly like the Heir always did. "All wrought have a preference— tangible or intangible?"

"Intangible," I said, and the Heir's jaw clenched.

"That won't do for most injuries." The Crown took a sip of her tea, licked her lips, and impaled her hand with the knife. "If I use a relatively simple contract to sacrifice a feeling and destroy this..."

The Heir's breath caught in his throat. I froze, one hand gripping my spoon. The Crown didn't even glance at him, her gaze focused solely on me, and the knife in her hand began to degrade. Her vilewright enacted the contract slowly, leaving a ragged and bleeding hole behind. The Heir pressed the back of his head against the wall.

"No weapon," she said, "but hardly enough to fully heal the wound. The invasive aspects that cause infection are still present, and the jagged pieces of bone are still where they shouldn't be. A feeling is not an equal sacrifice."

"I see." I sipped from a cup of water, tongue curling at the sweet hint of orange and almond syrup, and swallowed my first thought. She would never believe me unskilled enough for that. "How long did it take you to learn all this?"

"Years."

I cocked my head to study the wound. The knife wasn't completely gone, and rust floated in the blood.

"When did you destroy your ability to feel pain?" I asked.

"The day I was betrothed," she said with a smile. "Good. You're thinking how you should be."

I was thinking how she did, she meant.

She glanced at the Heir, and he rapped once at the wall. A guard in the same sleeveless uniform as Hana Worth entered. He kept his eyes down and held out his hand, fingers shaking. The Crown cut the tip from his littlest finger. It vanished. Her hand healed.

The long, detailed contracts were designed so that wrought knew exactly what to tell their wrights to enact the outcome they wanted, and she had been doing this for so long that she must have had dozens of contracts memorized. She could probably think specific contracts like I could, but it still took her longer than I would've thought. How had she not died instantly when Beatrice rent her in two? Was there always such a long moment between the wounding, the wright understanding the contract the Crown asked it to undertake, and the healing? Was there always a moment of weakness?

I gripped the desk edge to keep from flinching.

"Alistair," said the Crown, "ensure he does not collapse before reaching the healer."

The Heir followed the guard out of the room, and I picked up my knife, spearing a boiled egg. I held on to the blade even once I was done eating.

"It's good that you have a strong stomach." The Crown's hands curled around her cup. Not even a scar remained. "I could teach you how to do that, but your work with Alistair would have to end. The Door is a waste of time anyway. I require a certain dedication from my students. Could you do that?"

So Carlow and the Heir hadn't shared her calculations.

"Why don't you want him studying the Door?" I asked.

"It is useful for me," she said, "and it is better, in the long run, if we are not the cause of it opening, even by accident, but the peers who helped our people survive its opening."

"But what happens when it does open?" I asked.

"I'm sure that would be unfortunate for some," she said, "but my son and I are quite adept, and my peers have the resources to survive. A little chaos, like a wildfire, is sometimes necessary to keep the world in order. If the Door does open one day, then those who survive are certainly the ones worthy of rebuilding the mortal world."

No, they were the ones rich enough to survive. It was easier to survive the end of the world when you were healthy at the start of it and coddled by your safety net of resources. Those without would die first. Maybe a few would survive. Many wouldn't.

"You survived so long with so little." She reached across the desk and patted my hand. "After all, cream always rises to the top."

"Oh." I ducked my head, offering her a small half smile, and lied. "I see what you mean, but I signed a contract with him. I can't not help."

"You are a resourceful girl. I'm certain you'll think of something." She leaned back in her chair, poured what was left of her tea into my empty cup, and offered me the little tray with sugar and cream.

"No, thank you," I said. "It's still a bit too rich for me."

"Of course. It's a pity you're from the Wallows." She sniffed, nostrils flaring. "What is the worst wound you have healed for yourself?"

"Nothing like what you've done," I said. "Crossbow through the calf, probably? No one knew I was vilewrought, though, so I had to do most of it alone."

I'd sacrificed a whole hutch of chickens to keep from bleeding out, and still my vilewright had wanted more.

The Crown hummed and tilted her head. "Passable. You can do better."

"May I ask you something?" I forced myself to stumble over the words. "Please. I never had anyone else to ask."

The Crown grinned. "Of course, Lorena."

"Is it easier on your own body?" I asked and held out my arms. I had scars aplenty from my sacrifices and surviving, but the Crown only had one. "It was always easier to destroy or create something in me than someone else. I used to heal folks when I could, but some died. Was that me, or was that—"

"The curse of being vilewrought?" The Crown laughed gently and took my hand in hers. "Yes, it takes longer for our vilewrights to work than our noblewrights, especially when working outside our bodies. We are familiar; others are not. The vilewright must acclimate itself with the new body."

I ducked my head and let out a sigh. "So it's not just me."

"It will never be just you ever again." She untangled her hand from mine. "You're with people who understand now."

I understood perfectly—like me, if she used her wrights on herself, they worked faster. If she was to die, it would have to be quick.

seventeen

THE SUNDERED CROWN WAS RIGHT. I COULD DO better, and I did. She spent two hours going over the inner workings of my arm with me, pointing out the tendons, bones, and muscles that were the easiest to re-create if I needed to sacrifice them. She flayed herself open for me and asked for nothing—yet—in return. She let me use her for the sacrifices so long as I wrote beforehand what I was asking my vilewright to do. By the end of our meeting, I had repaired the shattered bones of my off hand's little finger.

The Crown, of course, had done the shattering. She said that I, like all wrought, would get used to the pain.

She said, for now, the pain was useful, but later I would need it as sacrifice.

The Heir's familiar three knocks rattled my door. I let him in, hands still shaking from the easy way the Crown had severed that guard's finger. He didn't linger in the doorway, this time slipping inside and shutting the door, and he sat gingerly on the edge of my bed. I sat next to him and wrapped myself in Julian's coat. He took a deep breath.

"You could have warned me," I whispered without meaning to.

"It's how I learned," said the Heir. "It's how many noble-wrought have learned how to heal. Warning you of something so natural did not even occur to me until I saw your face."

"That explains so much." I shifted, the papers under the blanket crinkling.

The Heir reached under it and pulled out my notes on Will's case. "You didn't have to do that. She knows about our agreement."

He rose and helped me organize them. We stacked them on the floor near the desk, each tower a different section. Business expenses, tax information, and citations from the court and council: I had read them all and learned little. There was nothing treasonous in the documents.

"It doesn't make any sense," I said. "He hasn't committed treason unless your mother suddenly cares about wage violations."

"She doesn't." He folded himself onto the edge of my bed and picked at the blanket. "You asked her some interesting questions."

"Alistair, it took everything in me to not just scream the whole time she was talking." I collapsed next to him. "Which question?"

His mouth quirked up. "Lorena, you asked her if her wrights were always so slow."

Had I made it too obvious what I was truly asking about?

"Like anyone else could have done anything faster or survived Beatrice," said the Heir. "I remember that day. I was there. The blow didn't sunder her face. It only tore it open. It was her chest that was sundered. I saw her heart, Lorena. We all thought she was dead. It took her hours to heal those wounds. I don't know how she did it. I don't know if she does."

So her healing wasn't fast. Mine wasn't either, but it didn't take hours. I'd never had my chest cracked open though. She would've had to slow her heart without killing her brain. To kill her, her heart had to go.

"I didn't mean it like that," I lied. "Do you think she's upset?"

"No. If she were, she would have said so." He straightened his glasses—it was such an easy tell—and froze with his fingers on the arms. "Her moods are hard to predict, but no, she is no more upset with you than she would be anyway. Even if she is, she's too thrilled by the concept of a dualwrought daughter to care."

I shuddered. "I don't want to be her daughter."

"Yes," he said with a laugh. "That would be awkward."

"Take them off." I tapped one finger against the back of his gloved hand. "It's me, Alistair. I know exactly who you are."

He pulled the red glasses from his face. The shadows beneath his eyes were puffy and tinged with red. "Who knows you best, Lorena Adler?"

"My wrights." They trilled, the sound inaudible but shaking within me. "They know me as well as I know them."

They were as harsh as the world, giving nothing without taking something.

"Not your mother?" he asked.

"I was so young when she died. She never really knew me," I whispered. "I never asked her anything important. I know her favorite color and joke, but I don't know what she wanted from the world beyond surviving. I don't know what she would've done if she left the Wallows. I never asked her what flowers she wanted for her funeral plot."

Maybe I was destined to be an undertaker the moment I heard her last breath.

"No one knows me now. My mother does but she doesn't," he said.

I nodded. "I know what my mother's heart looked like. We shouldn't have to know that."

The Heir's hand twitched. He laid it on my shoulder, fingers slightly curled. The warmth of his body seared. My mother and so many I had grown up with were dead and cold, and the memory of her death still haunted me, and the Heir seemed to know. He yanked his hand away and sighed. Laughter bubbled out of my chest as a sob. I pressed my palms into my eyes.

"I know what my sisters' blood tasted like," he whispered. "I know how blood arches from a slit throat. I know how knowledge of death makes nightmares of grief. I'm sorry."

"It's not fair."

"The world isn't fair," he said. "It demands we harm ourselves and others to manifest power. Without coldness, we would suffer. I used to care so much that it hurt and I thought I would drown in it. To care in a world so soaked in cruelty is to suffer. We can't afford to care."

"Is that what you tell yourself?" I lifted my face to him. "Everyone except you and the peerage has to harm themselves to survive. That back-breaking, finger-flaying work of factories and mines or the endless hours at any other job in Cynlira. My mother worked in a munitions factory. She was never not bleeding and tired. She had to be to keep us housed and fed, and that is not a fact of the world but a fact of Cynlira. She's dead because Lankin Northcott didn't care if his factory went up in flames so long as he got enough money out of it first. She wasn't even the worst off. You've always been powerful, even if bad things have happened to you, so of course the first time you noticed that power had a cost was with your vilewright. The rest of us didn't need wrights to notice.

"I am scarred not because I am noblewrought," I said and held out my arms, "but because I scrubbed floors till my fingers bled to pay for my mother's cremation. The world doesn't demand we break ourselves to survive; the people refusing to help us do."

He blinked at me and reached into his coat, pulling out a tall, thin flask. He held it to my head. The cold metal burned and eased the ache.

"Once the threat of the Door is dealt with," he said, "we may begin dealing with the other threats to Cynlira."

"You know I mean the peerage, right?" I took the flask from him and held it to my cheek. "You didn't tell her about Carlow's prediction."

He smoothed tendrils of my hair from my forehead, tucking them behind my ears. "No. I know what she will say—we will survive, and the strong will survive with us. Telling her now isn't beneficial."

"Does she always use you for sacrifices like that?" I asked, turning to face him. My cheek bumped his hand, and his fingers fell to my shoulder. "What did her vilewright take?"

"I have extensive journals, so I'll figure out which memory it was later." He held his breath for a moment and then let it out. "She makes sure I always fill in the blanks."

"Alistair," I said slowly, "how do you know she's telling you the truth after she sacrifices a memory?"

"She loves me. She is a monster, but she loves me." He pulled his hand away from me, gray eyes wide, and stood, looking nothing like the red-eyed vilewrought Heir his actions had made him. "How do you know Julian is not simply using you to save his father?"

Because he loved me, and I knew him better than he knew himself. He couldn't lie worth a damn.

"He's my best friend," I said. "He wants to marry me. I doubt he'd propose such a binding contract if he wanted to be rid of me."

The Heir's brows shot up. "Such a vivacious boy for a girl who survived by staying hidden."

"It's easy to hide in his shadow." I had made myself unassuming and standoffish to stay safe, but Julian was too cheerful to be scared off by sarcasm and jerked-away hands. Being an undertaker had kept nearly everyone at bay. "Are you jealous that I have friends and not contractually obligated business partners?"

He flushed.

"Don't worry. I understand. My wrights were my only friends for years until I moved to Felhollow."

He rose, cheeks still an unsettling shade of pink. "I'll have someone bring you lunch. I'm sure breakfast was unappetizing. Thankfully, I'm fairly certain my mother will leave you be now."

"Small mercies," I said. Five months—what a horrifying number. That was hardly any time, and it wasn't enough to get the Crown out of the way. Will would be safe by then if he was innocent, but how many would we be sacrificing every week by then? It wasn't enough to keep Will safe. Eventually, all of us would be sacrificed to the Door. Cynlira couldn't survive like this. "Have you eaten? I want to tell you about my time in the Wallows. I want to tell you what Mori is like for the rest of us."

eighteen

IT WAS ALMOST NICE, TALKING TO ALISTAIR Wyrslaine, during the moments when I forgot he was the Heir. He was intense but no more so than Mack when he got talking. He didn't try flirting with me again, and I was thankful for that. We couldn't both be playing each other.

It was harder to think of him as the Heir now that I was committed to using his name with him. He was barely older than me but so much bloodier.

The next morning, there was a flask of tart lemonade—barely any sugar and no poison—outside my door. I drank it sparingly as I left for the laboratory. Carlow's door was shut tight, voices whispering behind it, and a sound that might have been sobbing broke through. I stopped and touched the door. I'd never thought of Carlow as a crier.

I withdrew my hand and kept walking.

I didn't know her well enough. She would hate being caught crying by me. I decided to send Creek after her, but by the time I got to the laboratory, she was already there. There must have been a less winding path between our quarters and here.

"Within three months, the sacrifices necessary to keep it shut will equal the population of Port Altiver," she said, nose so close to her journal there was ink smeared across it.

"Well," drawled Creek, peering over her shoulder, "at least that's not a very large town."

I'd passed through it with the Heir on our way to Mori. Port Salt-Swallowing-the-River was as old as Felhollow and as deserving as any other town, no matter how many lived in it.

"We're going to have to decide how many people we're willing to let die before we try to replace the Door," I said. "We're at three a month now. Is five too many?"

"Not if they're rapists and murderers," Basil muttered.

"But what about when we run out of those?" I pulled the bowl of red dirt toward myself, hand shaking. "What about when we no longer have time to judge folks with wrights and must guess if they're guilty or not?"

"The more pressing question you're avoiding," said Carlow, "is how many innocent people are we willing to sacrifice to the Door so that we can buy ourselves enough time to replace it and save the rest of Cynlira, and how do we choose them?"

"Risk everyone now or sacrifice some to lessen the risk?" Basil groaned and closed the book they had been reading. "We can't decide that."

If we didn't, who would? The Heir? The Crown?

"I do not like either of those choices," said Creek. "Let's just not make a choice."

I laughed a bit too loudly and sent my quill nibs rolling across the floor. I stumbled from my stool, shooing the others away from my mess. Carlow snorted as I crawled under her desk. I swept all the odds and ends beneath it into my pockets.

"What is our number?" I said, kneeling. "What number of survivors makes the number of dead worth it?"

The door swung open. Hana entered first, followed by the Heir. He was dressed as he had been yesterday, as if he had an identical outfit for each day of the week, but his glasses hung around his neck from a thin gold chain. Basil dropped their inkpot, and Carlow screwed up her face. Even Creek stared at the Heir as if they had never met.

Then the Crown entered, and we all dropped to the floor.

"Since you seemed more accustomed to intangible sacrifices, I grew curious." The Crown wore white again, a tightly fitted bodice that showed off the carved binding on her chest. A few stray beads of blood welled across the tangling lines of Life's and Death's sigils. "I would also like to go over your numbers, Franziska, but first Lorena."

So the Heir had told her. She led me into the washroom and then behind a curtained door I hadn't noticed before. The little nook was hardly big enough for the desk shoved into it and seemed to be nothing more than a closet. I sat on the stool nearest the door. She laughed.

"Relax," she said. "I have two simple tests for you, hardly anything at all, and then you may return to fulfilling my Alistair's curiosity. He is only researching this because it is a great puzzle and he has no self-control when it comes to things that intrigue him."

I crinkled my brow and feigned confusion. "But what if Carlow is right? What will we do then?"

"We continue on as we have been, albeit slightly less populated." She pulled an old set of scales from the shelf beside us and walked her fingers along the top. "There are always people not valuable enough to keep around."

A chill crept down my spine.

"Of course," I said, afraid I'd pushed her too far already. "What were the tests, Your Excellency?"

"Ah," the Crown said with a sigh. "When I was your age, people always asked me why I did things, and they hated that my answer was 'because I wanted to.' Nothing I wanted was ever right, and then I realized that all I had to do was take what I wanted. I owed no one answers. I have read your contract with my son. You gain nothing from it."

How unsurprising that caring about someone else was such a strange concept to her.

"Intangible sacrifices were never really accepted or

considered until recently. When I was learning, memories were untouchable. Only tangible sacrifices were known, taught, and allowed." She took my hands in hers and ran her thumbs across the backs of my knuckles. It would've been loving if I didn't hate her. "I was tempted the moment I realized destroying memories and creating new ones was possible. Alistair opened my eyes with Hila. There was so much more possible than I had previously thought. I considered letting Beatrice live. She was the best fighter in Cynlira, and I could have destroyed her loyalty to my husband and created a whole new life for her where she was loyal to me."

My vilewright growled. For all the terrible things I had heard about the Crown, I had never heard of her destroying memories and creating new ones like that. When the Heir had destroyed the free will of the people in Hila, that had been the first time such a blatant intangible sacrifice had been made publicly.

"Did you ever alter someone's memories and free will?" she asked. "Did you ever want something enough to try?"

I knew want better than anything. I had grown up hungry, and food had never filled that need. My wrights were ever-growling with longing for something, anything, more than this, and my parents, too, had wanted. My mother had wanted to live. I had wanted to live.

I so rarely indulged, but I had. Altering a healer's memories so they wouldn't remember me stealing supplies to save my mother or a guard's so they wouldn't know which kid had robbed them. Memories made a person. What was the difference between altering them and changing someone's will?

"No," I lied, "but I thought about it quite a lot. I didn't think I would be able to pull it off. Those soldiers were my first. I panicked."

"Disappointing." She pulled away. "What do you want, Lorena Adler?"

"I want Will Chase alive," I said. "I want Felhollow to be left alone."

"I don't believe you." She took a breath, and the scales crumbled. A minute later, a knife appeared in her open hand. "What do you want?"

I forced myself to flinch, but this was good. Her contracts with her noblewright, just like those with her vilewright, took longer than mine to enact.

"I want to go home. I want to forget all about you and your son and your rotting city, and I want to live a life that never crosses yours again."

She pressed the blade into the back of my hand.

I hissed. "I want to tear this entire fucking city from its mountain. I want all your court to drown in the waters I was born in. I want to break you down like you lot break us till not even the historians remember your name, because I know what it means to survive, and for all your talk, you wouldn't last a week in your own city."

"Finally," said the Crown, grinning. "Honesty. You lie so often I was afraid I would never get the truth."

"You're not as terrifying as you think," I said, eyes on my blood welling around the blade.

"Have you been able to destroy any part of the Door?" she asked.

I jumped at the change of questions, and the blade sunk deeper.

"No," I lied.

She jammed the knife through my hand.

Pain.

My vilewright took my ability to feel pain, and I sighed.

Knife.

The blade in the Crown's hand slowly degraded till there was nothing there at all but a wound beneath her fisted hand. She reared back.

We sat in silence for a long while, our wrights working between us, and none of my blood spilled from the wound. Her vilewright was a whisper against my sore skin.

"That's better," she said, face pale. "I have destroyed your ability to lie. It seems that was all you ever did. I may not hold my son's interest for intangible sacrifices and destructions, but I am not inept. If you attempt to destroy the Door and create a new one, I will kill you. I will kill Willoughby Chase. I will kill Julian Chase. I will kill Mack Sarclaw. Felhollow will cease to exist. Do you understand?"

My tongue stuck to my teeth. Everything hurt. I nodded.

"Good." She rose and dragged me to my feet. "Alistair's contract with you will be difficult to destroy but not impossible. I like you, and Cynlira needs another dualwrought. Your less useful inclinations we will work on."

The rest of the laboratory was pretending to work, Creek going over Carlow's calculations and Basil reading a text upside down. They all looked up when we entered. The Heir stood.

"Now," said the Crown, letting go of my arm. "I must take my leave and deal with those calculations of yours."

"Perhaps I would be of help with them," said Creek, sliding his gangly body between Carlow and the Crown. "You know how she is sometimes."

"Unnecessary—the talking and the offer," the Crown said, crossing her arms. "Come, Franziska. Let us see about your guess of five months."

"Estimation," said Carlow, one hand clutching the back of Creek's coat. "My calculations are always correct. You know this."

"One day, your need to be right will get you killed." The Crown crooked one finger at Carlow. "Come."

I held back a shudder. At least Carlow couldn't die.

If only the rest of us were lucky enough to be cursed.

nineteen

I FLED THE LABORATORY AS SOON AS I KNEW I wouldn't cross the Crown and Carlow's path. The Heir chased after me, his voice wavering and unclear. He didn't reach out to stop me, and he didn't speak after I raised my hand for silence. By the time we reached my room, the unease rolling over me was worsening. He left the door to my room open, lingering near my desk. Basil's and Creek's footsteps echoed behind him.

"Shut it," I said. "Please."

He did and came to me. "What did she do?"

"Stabbed me," I said, and he nodded as if that were the most natural thing in the world. I tried to lie and tell him that was all, that she had done nothing else, but I couldn't. The words stuck in my throat. "She took away my ability to lie."

The Heir's head jerked up to stare at me, and he opened his mouth. I could see the "no" forming on his tongue.

"Alistair." I took his face in my hands, fingers—not my nails—pressed into his temples, and pulled his forehead to mine. "She stabbed me, threatened to kill everyone I love, and said she would break our contract if I helped you destroy the Door. I made a deal with you. Not her. I don't want her."

She had taken away the one thing I had always had, my last piece of armor against the world.

"She would make you her successor, the Crown's prized

dualwrought," said the Heir. "I could find a way to deal with the Door without you if you wanted that."

Forgotten I had always been, and forgotten I'd thought I would die. I didn't need her to make me important.

"I don't want that," I said. "Alistair, please. I want to help you, but I cannot work with her. She has forbidden me from trying to destroy the Door."

His eyes widened. His lips parted. He knew I had to be telling the truth.

"I understand," he said and took my hands in his. "I will have you work on creating an alternative. Destroying it shall be my burden."

She thought honesty was a drawback, but this was a gift. He'd never question what I'd say again.

I lurched forward. My headache worsened, blooming along my jaw and in my teeth. The Heir rifled through the pockets of my coat and pressed the mouth of his flask to my lips. I drank, he checked my eyes and pulse, and exhaustion crashed into me. He made sure I locked the door behind him when he left.

"I doubt we will be able to continue our research unscathed," he said through the door, "but we have a deal. Even if she breaks our contract, I will not let her hurt you or your friends from Felhollow."

That meant Basil was the only one in true danger. I'd have to save them.

My vilewright hummed against my chest, loud in my noblewright's silence. I picked at where the hole had been.

"The Crown cannot remain the Crown," I whispered.

Light flickered through the slatted window, and I jumped.

"We'll never be able to sacrifice enough to destroy the Door completely, will we?" I said aloud.

My vilewright trilled, the sensation ringing in my ears for ages.

When I rose again, it was night. Footsteps echoed up and down the hall outside.

"She doesn't care. The peers don't care if most of their country dies so long as they live well." I dipped my fingers into the bowl of red dirt. It clung to my skin like blood and congealed where the Crown had stabbed me. "I hope you're one of the Vile. They can be killed."

A single knock rattled my door.

"I'm annoyed," came Carlow's voice with its familiar bite. "I'd mock you, but we both know why you're doing this. We're going to the Door."

There came a soft scratching as if she had laid her hand against the door.

"I got stabbed," I muttered. "Why are you in a bad mood?"

"You never cared before. You know we can destroy the Door."

I threw on Julian's coat, grabbed a lamp, and opened my door, barely catching sight of Carlow stomping around the far corner down the hall.

"Can we though?" I asked.

She let out a laugh that sounded more like sobbing. "I would know."

I followed her outside. It was late, the crescent moon lurking above us like a narrowed eye. Tree branches rustled above me in the breeze and groaned as I passed. Even the earth was tired, and I rubbed my eyes on the inside of my sleeves, staring at Carlow's blurred white coat darting through the winding path through the gardens. This one was longer than my normal route, and I dragged one hand across a tree. My nail caught in the bark and snapped back. I hissed.

"I'd mock you, but..." Carlow laughed again and vanished around a bend.

I stuffed my hands into my pockets. "Ass."

Something sharp stabbed my hand.

I stopped, turning out my pockets onto the ground, and

stared at the single blue rosebud speckled with blood before me. I went to pick it up, pricking my finger on the velvety petals again, and blood spilled to the dirt. It pooled like water atop stones. I froze.

The small thorns on the stem dripped blood, none of it seeping into the earth beneath my feet.

"Carlow?" I called.

Her laugh echoed despite us being in the gardens.

I pressed my fingers against the ground, and my knuckles cracked against a floor. There was no dirt, only cold, hard stone that I could not see.

Touch was the only sense the Door could not replicate.

"Where are you leading me?" I whispered and squeezed my eyes shut.

"The Door," said the thing that was not Franziska Carlow.

I looked up.

I was in a hallway I didn't recognize. There were no windows and no lanterns. The only light was the small circle flickering from my oil lamp, the flame spluttering with my panicked breaths. My noblewright oozed against the back of my neck, the skin prickling against it. I raised my lantern and glanced up. A pair of red eyes like Carlow's blinked and vanished.

I scrambled back. My hands hit a door, fingers scraping over the wood. My heart was beating too fast, bumping so loudly that it was all I could hear, and I couldn't take my eyes off the corner. That hadn't been Carlow. It was the Door.

"I'm annoyed" had been the start of her conversation with Creek. The whole conversation had been nothing but rearranged words she'd uttered the other day.

I groaned and struggled to open the door behind me. I raised one hand to the snuffed lantern on the wall above me.

Create a light please. Take the least you need to do so.

My noblewright slithered down my arm, its unhappiness bitter in my mouth.

"Remember who feeds you," I whispered. "I cannot if the Door kills me tonight."

The lantern flared. A trail of muddy red footprints was splattered on the ground and led around the corner.

The door behind me creaked open. An arm wrapped around my waist, and a hand covered my mouth. My wrights ripped away from me, ready to fight, and I bit down hard on the hand. Whoever it was hissed.

"It's me." The Heir's voice cracked. "It's Alistair. Stop screaming or guards will come and my mother will know."

He pulled his hand from my mouth but didn't let go of me. I swallowed, the taste of his skin stuck in my throat. He wiped his hand on his trousers.

"Look," he whispered.

His arm vanished, and he set a pair of red glasses over my eyes. The footsteps leading to the Door were the same as the red granules I had been trying to destroy and writhed as if alive. I lifted the glasses up. The footprints were normal footprints. I dropped the glasses down again. I picked up the blue rose and cradled it against my chest.

"What would've happened if I followed it all the way to the Door?" I asked.

"My glasses never lie," he said, dragging me back through corridors with one arm around my waist. "It would have convinced you to open the Door. What happened?"

So his glasses showed vilewrights *and* Vile.

"It looked and sounded like Carlow, and I thought it was leading me to the laboratory. She said we could destroy the Door." I glanced over my shoulder, and the Heir's vilewright was a shadow embracing both of us. "I thought I was outside, but..."

I peeked at the blue rose in my hands. The bud was barely open, but it was undoubtedly a rose. I peeled it open. It had the same coloring as a pale-blue pansy.

"You noticed that nothing felt right," said the Heir.

I nodded. "The ground wasn't right."

Creek had grown a blue rose. He had fulfilled his curse.

"The Door wants to be opened, and it knows you now." He tightened his grip on me. "Once you get back to your room, lock the door and don't leave until I come get you in the morning."

We burst outside, and I looked up. The moon, full and bright, stared down at us. The Heir loosened his grip on me. The ground was cold against my feet, and the chill cleared my head. I pulled away enough to look at him.

He was still dressed. His greatcoat and cravat were gone, the collar of his shirt flopping open without them. A few smudges of ink and blood stained his white shirt, and his sleeves were rolled hastily up to his elbows. His boots had been replaced by black velvet slippers.

He stared at my feet. "Where are your shoes?"

"I don't know," I said. "I thought I put them on, but perhaps that was the Door as well?"

He bent down, sweeping his other arm around my knees. They buckled, and I folded into his arms. I grasped his shirt.

"You can't walk around barefoot," he muttered. "It will try this again, and you will probably want to run when it does. You can't do that with a foot full of rocks."

We spoke no more. He set me down at the door to my room, frowning at the few small cuts I did have on my feet. I returned his glasses and assured him I could heal myself. He waited on the other side of my door until I checked the lock and retreated to bed. His fading footsteps didn't echo. I bunched my blanket over my ears.

Carlow didn't come calling again.

twenty

T HE NEXT MORNING, I AWOKE WITH A PAIN IN MY
foot and Carlow's voice ringing in my ears. She was arguing with Creek, their shouts muffled by the wall, and I rolled
out of bed. Julian's coat was sticky with sweat, but I kept it
curled around me. I rubbed my hand across the wood of my
door before opening it and peered into the hall. Creek stood in
the doorway to Carlow's room, his arms crossed. A blue rosebud
was tucked into the chest pocket of his greatcoat.

"Let her work or so help me," he was saying and shaking
his head.

Carlow shrieked from inside. "Easy for you to say."

Her voice turned my stomach, and I groaned. Creek glanced
at me.

"Hold still," said a voice I didn't know. "I'm not even holding the needle yet."

"The Door baited you last night," he said, beckoning me
over. "Alive?"

"I think." I pulled the blue rose from my pocket, the petals
withered and bloody but still intact, and hid it away once he
saw. "I have you to thank for that. The thorns pricked me."

He stared at me, blue eyes endless, and smiled. "A pity you
didn't open the Door. Carlow would be free then."

"Does she know?" I asked softly. "Does she know you fulfilled the covenants of your curse?"

"I have been placing the evidence before her, but she never truly sees. I'm not supposed to leave her to face eternity alone. The idea that I will is unthinkable to her." He shuddered. "No. No one is aware, though I think the Crown suspects, and that is how I prefer it."

"Fine," I said. "When did you manage it? It's only been a week or so since you revived last? What if she kills you?"

"A week ago," said Creek quickly, his gaze darting to Carlow. "I'm not discussing this near her."

I sighed and whispered, "Fine. Keep your secrets and lies, but if she kills you, she'll never forgive herself."

Creek laughed quietly. Carlow glared at him, hands clutching the bed. Safia, the healer employed by the Heir, was leaning over Carlow's bare thigh and stitching shut a short, deep cut. Carlow threw her arm over her eyes and groaned. Creek chuckled.

"She hates needles. Her. Franziska Carlow, noblewrought and scared of nothing, is scared of needles. It's so...mortal," he said, savoring the word.

"How did she hurt herself?" I asked.

"The usual way," said Creek. "A sacrifice."

Safia leaned back in her wheelchair, black eyes bright with laughter, and patted Carlow's arm. "I'm done, you big, immortal baby."

"Will it scar?" Carlow asked, voice softer than I'd ever heard.

Safia shook her head. The green binding carved into her chest was red with fresh blood. "The stitches are only for the next day," she said. "I'll be able to heal it tomorrow, and I can make sure there's no scar." Safia glanced at me over her shoulder. "Did you need something?"

"No, just heard a commotion," I said.

"I think she prefers Carlow." Safia rolled her lips together and dodged Carlow's half-hearted swat. She slung her bag onto the back of her chair. "Unless there's another commotion, I'm due at breakfast."

Footsteps echoed down the hall. I flinched, and Creek turned. Hana and Basil hurried toward us, the guard sporting fresh bandages on her hands and arms, and Basil carried a stack of books. Hana looked anywhere but at us, keeping her strides short so as not to leave Basil behind. Basil's fingers tapped a frantic rhythm against their books. Hana stopped before us.

"Is Carlow still here?" she asked.

"Hana!" Safia's voice came out a bit breathlessly. Safia adjusted her dress and the silk scarf wrapped around her tight black curls. She didn't need to; she was easily the prettiest person out of all of us. "Did my good luck charm not work?"

Hana blushed, hand jerking to her necklace. "No. I mean, it did. I'm fine. I'm here to get Carlow, Creek, and Adler."

Safia fiddled with her silver moon bracelet, and I glanced at Hana's necklace.

"His Majesty asked me to get your thoughts on several sacrifices and replication mechanisms," said Basil, peering around Hana. "The others he wanted in the laboratory immediately."

"Well, at least I finished in time." Safia waved farewell to us and joined us in the hall. "Let's see what you have for me, Baz."

They vanished into Basil's room. The others started walking, and I grabbed Creek's arm. He glared at me, eyes slits of sky.

"He sent the only person who could die away," I whispered. "Why?"

Creek shook off my grip. "The Crown must be visiting. Why else?"

"She was mad at Carlow last time." I clenched the rose, thorns cutting through me, and nodded. "The calculations upset her."

It was only a lie by omission. The Heir had so few friends, and losing them would break him. It couldn't be me. It couldn't be Carlow. It had to be Creek.

"Do you think she would hurt Carlow?" I asked.

So questions didn't count as lies either.

"Carlow is immortal for now, but she is not immune to pain," said Creek, his blue eyes dark in the dim morning light. "The Crown could do much worse to Carlow than killing her."

"But she would be all right." I worried my lip and blinked as if keeping back tears. "She wouldn't sacrifice Carlow to the Door, would she? Could Carlow survive that?"

Creek's face snapped to me, his eyes wide, and for the first time, he looked afraid. "That would kill Carlow quite permanently."

"What do we do?"

"You? Nothing." Creek took a breath, glancing toward Carlow's retreating back, and motioned me on. "Go to the laboratory. I will handle this."

"All right," I said. "Be careful."

How many could we justify killing to save Cynlira?

"One," I said to myself, pulling the rose from my pocket and letting the wind take it, the petals wet and red.

The Crown was in the laboratory when Carlow, Creek, and I arrived. She was dressed in a gauzy white dress with green stitching, and she smiled when she saw us.

"Lovely," she said, taking me by the hand and leading me inside. "We're all here."

There were no guards, and she didn't give us time to bow. The skin along my neck prickled. My wrights twined about me, twisting around my chest and settling over my heart, and the Heir's eyes followed my vilewright behind his glasses. His fingers twitched toward me, and I took the place at his left side. Creek stood to his right, dragging Carlow by the arm and keeping her close. She pulled her goggles down to hang about her neck.

"What's bothering you, Your Excellency?" asked Creek, head bowed.

"Your face," she said. "I see it too often, and too often any news you bring me is disappointing."

He inhaled. "Apologies."

"Mother," said the Heir.

She cut him off with a look. "Alistair, you have missed every single court meeting this week, and as my heir, that is unacceptable. I didn't save you so you could disappoint me."

He sniffed and nodded.

"Your fiddling with the Door is putting my people in danger," she said. "It baited multiple court members last night, and we cannot afford to lose their support. I heard even Lorena saw it in action."

She glanced at me.

"No, Your Excellency." I rolled my answer along my tongue, testing how much I could lie, and the magic demanded more. "I did not see the Door."

Whatever phantom Carlow I had seen wasn't truly the Door.

"Oh." She clucked her tongue and ran her knuckles across my cheek. "You are so much better at this game than he is, even after the other day."

The Heir shivered.

"And, Franziska, my darling, you look nervous." The Crown stopped before Carlow and cupped Carlow's face in her hands. "Remind me again the covenants of your curse."

"The first person I love dies." Carlow lifted her chin and clasped her hands behind her back. "The second inherits my curse, and then I die."

"Tedious," said the Crown. "This would be easier if you had Creek's, but I suppose, since you can't die, this will at least be fun."

Carlow started to tremble. "Why am I to...not quite die?"

"You gave Shearwill your calculations. That is an unacceptable breach of trust and goes against my explicit orders. The people made aware of your little five-month deadline were the ones the Door lured in an attempt to open it."

Creek, hands hidden from the Crown, slipped a finger between Carlow's hands and forced them apart. He splayed his hand across her back.

"I went to Shearwill," he said and met the Crown's gaze without flinching. "You weren't taking Carlow's warnings seriously. If any of Cynlira is to be saved, the country—the whole country—needs fair warning."

The Crown hesitated, mouth open, and ran her tongue across her teeth. Her gaze slid from Carlow to Creek.

"Shearwill hates Carlow," I said. "I saw them arguing the other day, and I don't think Shearwill would ever believe Carlow, much less meet with her."

The Crown turned to me and nodded, a smile slowly spreading across her face.

"Lorena." She glided to me and hooked one arm through mine as if we were strolling. "Do you want to kill Creek or should I?"

This was what I wanted. This was what we needed. This was what had to happen for the Heir to see things through and save Cynlira.

But when I opened my mouth to say I would kill him, nothing came out.

"Consider this a learning opportunity." The Crown stood me in front of Creek and placed a knife in my hands, curling my fingers around the handle. She backed away. "Remember, Lorena—there is always someone with dirtier, meaner hands than you, so who do you want holding the knife?"

I moved without thought, jamming the blade between his ribs and directly into his heart. Carlow gasped, and the Heir stared straight ahead. Only Creek looked at me.

He smiled and winked. I pulled out the knife.

Creek dropped to the floor, blood pooling beneath him.

"That was unnecessary." The Heir's voice wavered. "On both counts."

I dropped the knife.

Save him, I prayed to my vilewright. *Save him as sacrifice for later. Don't let this be for nothing.*

It swept across him and settled over my shoulders.

"It wouldn't have been necessary if you kept your wrought under control, Alistair." The Crown picked up her knife and wiped the blood on the back of my coat. Julian's coat. "Your research is done. You have three days to organize what you have and bring it to an end. There will be no more experiments with the Door. We have five months to prepare for the final sacrifice and the opening, and we must focus on how we will protect ourselves from the Vile."

Ourselves—she was going to sacrifice a tenth of Cynlira to buy time to save herself and her peers.

"You will bind Lorena to me, and you will report to court and council meetings," she said. "If you do not establish yourself now as someone not to be questioned, then the court will eat you alive."

"I killed a whole city," he muttered. "Who doesn't fear me?"

"You cannot rule on the coattails of past victories," said the Crown, turning from all of us and walking to the door. "You must give them new reasons to fear and obey you."

With the Crown's back to her and attention elsewhere, Carlow nudged Creek with her foot. Tears pooled in her red eyes. She kicked him.

Nothing.

I stepped into the empty space at the Heir's right side. "Carlow? I'm sorry."

I was, but I was still glad I could utter the words. It wasn't a lie. I wasn't a terrible person.

"Get up," Carlow mouthed. "Get up."

"He's dead, Franziska," the Crown said, "and you should take it as a threat."

twenty-one

THE CROWN LEFT WITHOUT ANOTHER WORD. THE Heir glanced at us, eyes hidden behind his glasses, and followed her. The door shut, and Carlow sunk to her knees, choking on a scream. Her fists slammed into her table. Creek's blood was still warm on my hands.

"You asshole!" She kicked him as she had that first day I met them, but this time, he didn't move. "I can't be the only one left. I can't be."

His ribs crumbled like withered grass. I swallowed. Stay clear, my mother had always said, and focus on doing. I could panic later. The scent of blood filled my nose.

"I'm so—"

"Shut up!" Carlow kicked him again. "Del..."

I flinched, and the quick patter of my heart pounded in my ears. White specks danced before my eyes.

Take my sorrow and anxiety as sacrifice, I prayed to my noblewright. *We'll create something soon.*

I had never asked them to save sacrifices for creation and destruction later, but we would need all the help we could get to pull this off. My noblewright passed through me. The world cleared, and my attention sharpened. We had to act.

"Does he have anyone who would want to claim him?" I asked.

"Who would want him?" asked Carlow, rounding on me with bared teeth.

I held up my hands. "We should move him now."

If we didn't, he would get stiff and heavy, and if Carlow was the sort of person I thought she was, she would soon have plans for him.

"I can take care of him," I said, "unless you've got an undertaker here."

They were grieving. I wasn't. It was the least I could do.

"Carlow," I said, "do you want to say goodbye?"

"Yeah." She wiped her face and leaned her forehead against his. "Fuck you for leaving me alone here."

I found a guard to carry Creek to the healing houses. There was a small building meant for undertakers near it, the stone pool and tools far too nice to waste on the dead. Safia helped, showing me where everything was, and Basil stood watch with Carlow near the door. Neither could stand looking at Creek for long, but they couldn't leave either. Carlow came while we were draining his blood.

"You don't want to be here for this," said Safia.

Carlow sighed, pulled a small bottle of mourning wine from within the pockets of her coat, and nicked the back of her hand. The cork came free with an easy pop. Her blood vanished. The cut remained.

"My father died because he loved me, and his death passed this curse to me," she said. "Poppy died because I loved her. There is nothing in this world left that can frighten me now."

"If you're certain," I said and cut into Creek's body with trembling hands.

"He was an ass until two years ago, you know, and then after Poppy died, something changed, like a new person with his face. Too little, too late." She poured a finger of wine into the water at my feet. "The Crown likes me because I have suffered and my suffering has made me hard, but I don't want to be. She likes suffering, thinks it makes us strong."

Carlow stared down at Creek's corpse and dipped her finger into the water.

"She doesn't understand me at all. My suffering comes from fear for others, not fear for me," said Carlow. "All she sees is a suffering girl and kinship. As if the only thing the world has left us as bond is pain. It left its mark, but I'm more than that. We are more than what the world has done to us."

"I'm sorry." I did my work with my back to her, hiding the state of Creek's body with mine. "The court, the council—all the folks running Cynlira right now should—"

"Die," she whispered.

"—not be ruling over so much as a grocery list," I said. "She doesn't like us. She likes us as tools she can use."

Carlow nodded. "It's guilt, I think. She wants to have suffered to make her accomplishments seem greater, like pain is a contest and she must be the winner."

She had suffered. Then, she had taken that suffering and made the rest of us drown in our own while she flourished. So what if she wanted to save me? That still left most of the world dying and dead. The Heir's apathy would be worlds better than her violence. We could continue with the Door. If we did, the Crown would kill us. If we didn't, the Door would open.

"Do you remember?" Carlow asked. "All mortals are doors if you pry hard enough."

Wrist-deep in his chest, I froze. "You want to use Creek to make a new Door?"

Every part of his death would be used—his loss for the Heir and his body for our work.

"His noblewright was a piece of a Noble soul." She paced around the table, ignoring Safia's gestures for her not to, and peered into his corpse. "Finally, Del, you're going to be useful."

"I'll prepare him." I looked at the sparse supplies of the room. "But we'll need a way to get him to the laboratory."

"Bring him to the laboratory once you're done. I'll figure out how we can test it," said Carlow.

The Sundered Crown had threatened us all and told us

to stop our research, but Carlow had come to this so easily. I grinned.

"That's a terrible plan. No sense at all." Safia shook her head and patted Creek's cold hand. "First, test out small pieces—bone, blood, and flesh to see what works best."

"Great," muttered Carlow, "and if it works, we can drag him across the grounds, get caught, and be executed."

"Come." Safia washed her hands clean and took Carlow by the arm. "Let's give Lorena room to work."

They left me standing in the water I'd washed from Creek. I didn't mind. I was soaking in the death of their friend, dress knotted around my knees and stockings off. I had nudged Creek toward death, so it was only fair I carry him through it. I placed his heart, two ribs, and a patch of unblemished skin aside. Carlow and he had spent so long trying to create things to stop the Door.

"Maybe it was you all along," I whispered.

"Doubtful," said Creek.

I spun around. The room was empty, and Creek's mouth hadn't moved. I wiped his blood from my hands.

"Just guilt," I whispered and finished preparing him. "Rest well, Delmond Creek."

Carlow and Basil were in the laboratory when I arrived. Basil's eyes were red, and Carlow's hands shook. I set the box containing Creek on my desk. Carlow set the bowl of red dirt next to it.

"You destroy some of the granules, and we trap what's left in different versions of a lockbox made from Creek," said Carlow. "We'll see if using the body of a noblewrought keeps the granules from replicating."

Basil shuddered.

"We create the containers first," said Carlow, voice flat.

We sat in a circle on the floor, the pieces of Creek and the Door between us, and contracted our noblewrights.

From Creek's bones, Carlow made a lockbox with one side so thin we could see through it. From his flesh and blood, Basil made a small puzzle box. From his heart, I made a chest no larger than my hand that would seal shut once I closed the lid. For it, I sacrificed some of the last good memories of my mother, and Basil gave up nearly all of their blood. Carlow refused to share her sacrifice. We had to spend two hours recovering after. Our wrights whined and ached.

"Place three granules in each box," muttered Carlow. "Let's get this over with."

She placed three granules into two of the containers. I destroyed all six using Carlow's blood as sacrifice, and she passed out immediately. The grains went up in smoke as they had every time before, and Basil caught the smoke in their bowl. I locked and sealed the other two. My wrights slumped against me. My awareness of them quieted.

"That's all I can do today," I said, voice hoarse.

Basil nodded. "That's all I think we should do."

"Did it work?" mumbled Carlow, forehead pressed to the floor.

Basil turned the box over in their hands and passed it to me. "See for yourself."

I leaned so that Carlow could see inside too.

Inside the box, the black smoke of the destroyed Door pieces writhed and blustered but never reformed into granules. I peeked into my box. None had regenerated.

"Well," Carlow said, "he was finally good for something."

twenty-two

THE CROWN CAME TO MY ROOM THE NEXT DAY AT noon. She did not knock or ask to enter. She looked at the papers on my desk and my exhausted face, her expression clearly implying that I had been found wanting.

"Do you know why I like you?" she asked.

I bowed my head. "No, Your Excellency. To be honest, His Majesty and I thought you would kill me."

"See? My reputation precedes me." She glanced at me over her shoulder and smiled. "I might have if you were less interesting, but under all that bluster and fake honesty, you're as furious as me. Was Felhollow ever what you wanted?"

I was nothing like her.

I had wanted my family. I had wanted Julian and Will. I had wanted Mack. I had wanted a home.

"Yes," I said, and she looked disappointed. "I wanted to survive."

"And you were happy like that?" In the chair at my desk, her dress fluttering around her as she crossed her ankles, the wisps of her hair curling around her face, the soft slant of her mouth as her smile fell, she didn't look threatening. She gestured for me to sit on the bed. "There was nothing else you wanted from life?"

"I don't mean for this to sound like an insult," I said slowly and sat across from her. That was true enough; I didn't want it to come across as an insult. "All I ever wanted growing up was safety and someone to trust. A home. Family. You always had that. You couldn't understand."

Speaking uncomfortable truths always put people like her on the defensive. It was insulting that there was something she couldn't understand.

And she had killed her family.

She took a deep breath, the muscles of her forehead tensing. I carried on before she could speak.

"Your life was always this unreachable dream," I said and gestured around me. "This was unreachable."

"You are dualwrought," she said. "Nothing is unreachable for us."

"My mother feared what would happen to me if more than one peer wanted me. She was worried they would bind me too strictly or do something worse."

"She was right to fear." The Crown's tensions eased. "They would have bound you so tightly that every contract could have left you bleeding. They would have worked you to death by now or trained you up to assassinate me."

I would have failed, she didn't say. She couldn't be killed by the likes of me. It was the truth the same way gravity was.

My mother would've loved this, killing the Sundered Crown. She'd killed enough of us. It was only fair.

"You're allowed to want more than surviving," she said and unwound her spiraling bracelet, small joints snapping as it straightened. It unfolded into a long needle. "You have power many would try to deny you because they fear it or want it for themselves. You must stop fearing yourself. I can see it in your eyes when you sacrifice to your vilewright. Don't be afraid to take power."

I took the needle and asked, "How did you get over the fear?"

"I realized that without sacrifice, Cynlira would be torn apart by the squabbles of my peers and the council. They needed a strong figure to corral them. The people we sacrifice to the Door are hardly worthy of carrying on Cynlira's legacy if they die so easily. Do not mourn them. Rejoice in what their sacrifice is building." She held out her hand to me. "Destroy my memory of breakfast today. I ate alone and went over my correspondence. Losing it will be of no consequence. Don't be afraid."

I pushed the tip of the needle into the vein in the crook of her elbow. There was no need for violence with sacrifices. My vilewright would claim what it was owed no matter what.

Take her blood, I prayed, *and destroy the memory she spoke of.*

My vilewright glided from me to her arm, and the Crown, for the first time I had seen, shuddered. It would have been easier using something intangible for the sacrifice. She thought violence a solely physical act.

Wait. Do it slowly. Let her underestimate us.

We sat in silence, my fingers loosely gripping her wrist, and she stared. I squeezed my eyes shut and moved my lips. Pretending wasn't a lie.

Now.

Her eyes glazed over. She shook her head, using her free hand to pull a scrap of paper from her pocket.

"Good," she said, reading the note that must have listed what she ate this morning. "That was good, but we can improve it, especially the speed. Your vilewright is slow. It will learn, and you will get used to the sacrifices."

My vilewright growled deep in the pit of my stomach, and I set the needle aside. Distantly, I thought I heard Creek laugh.

"Have you stopped researching the Door like I instructed?" she asked.

"I have stopped researching the Door," I said. I hadn't

researched anything since yesterday, only experimented. She was not pedantic enough for this game.

Or perhaps so many feared her that she had never needed to consider the importance of words.

"Good." She smiled and stood, her stout frame blocking the light from the hallway. "Do I terrify you?"

"Yes," I said.

"I love the truth." She touched my chin and tilted my head up. "Alistair will need someone to look out for him once I'm gone. Will you still be here when he is the Crown?"

This was all I and every other Liran was to her—a tool to be shaped and used regardless of what we wanted.

"Yes." Though that time would come sooner than she thought. "I will be."

"Good." She said, "You will join Alistair and me in court tomorrow. Prepare yourself."

No lies—she had handed me the perfect way to trick her and everyone else.

"Of course, Your Excellency." I didn't breathe again until she was gone. "Prepare myself."

The door shut, and behind it stood Creek. The knife was still in his chest. Blood dripped down his front.

"You're not real," I said. "You're dead."

"Thanks to you." He clucked his tongue and waggled a finger at me. "Quaint little Lorena Adler, who had never been trained and had never killed before. What would your mother say if she saw you now?"

"Creek was annoying," I said and turned away to my desk, "so you're a bad manifestation of my guilty conscience."

I had dreamed about him last night too. This was exhaustion. A trick of—

He was sitting on my desk. "You wound me."

"You're the Door, aren't you?" I asked.

"Am I?" He brought his hand to his ruined chest and fluttered it over his heart, except I had cut his heart from his corpse not a day ago. "Shouldn't I be telling you to 'open the Door' or something trite then?"

"I wouldn't want to tell you how to do your job." I pushed him from my desk.

My hands shot through him and smacked the wall. Creek laughed.

"I thought she would hurt Franziska," he said, "and you used that care. So devious."

"Necessary," I whispered and stepped back. "It's necessary."

He vanished from my desk. I sat in the chair, stiff and uneasy. My stomach rebelled, and I gagged, panic sticking in my throat. I covered my eyes and breathed.

"What's your number, Lorena?" Creek asked.

"Not real. Not real." I grabbed a sheet of clean paper and quill. "You're not real. You're the Door or my guilty mind and neither—"

"Is of any consequence?"

My hands shook as I wrote.

Julian and Mack, Stay inside tomorrow. Don't worry about me or anything you hear. Don't leave unless you must. I love you both. Lorena

That was vague enough, and it was reasonable for them to worry about me being present for court. I slid it under my door for one of the palace messengers and laid my forehead against the warm wood.

"Lorena," said Creek, his mouth near my ear, "open the Door."

Someone pounded at my door. I stumbled back, crashing against my bed. Creek was gone, nothing to prove he'd ever been here, and my door rattled in the wall. They rapped another three times.

"Lorena," the Heir called, "open the door. We need to talk."

twenty-three

I TOOK A MOMENT TO COLLECT MYSELF BEFORE OPEN-ing the door. My entire plan, if I could even call it that, hinged on the Heir's state of mind. His mother had taken away what he loved the most today. He had lost his research and one of his few friends all in one fell blow.

Dusk had fallen outside. In the dark, shadows danced around flickers of moonlight. Stars stared through my barred windows like curious eyes. I opened the door a crack, and the Heir nodded to me. I prodded his shoulder. He felt real enough.

"Satisfied?" His greatcoat and gloves were gone, and his sleeves were rolled up. For the first time, I could see his red binding on his chest. "You once said my mother had to be stopped."

"Inside." I beckoned him in and shut the door. "First, you should know that Carlow, Basil, and I kept experimenting with the Door."

He tilted his head to the side. "I see."

"It didn't work completely, but it did work somewhat." I sat him on my bed and pulled the chair from my desk over so that I was across from him. "I understand if you are angry, but five months is not a lot of time, and this is progress."

"I'm not angry with you," he said softly, "but she is my mother."

I reached for him, and he flinched. My vilewright unfurled

around me like a cloak coming undone. Gently, gently, it seemed to say in the way it moved. The Heir needed coddling. He'd probably never had it before.

"She's going to bind me, Alistair, and go back on our deal. She's going to get us killed and kill all of Cynlira." I leaned slightly toward him as Julian always did when trying to coax me to bed. "You have spent years researching the Door. For what?"

He looked away from me. "What experiment did you undertake?"

"We used pieces of Creek's body to see if it could slow the replication of the Door after destroying the granules with my vilewright." I trailed off and turned away, shuffling through papers on my desk. He followed, and his fingers brushed my sleeve. I stilled that hand. "I haven't checked it since yesterday, but the smoke didn't reform into granules like it normally does. Even if it does, it might not be able to breach the box and rejoin the rest of the dirt."

"That is more than we've accomplished, and Creek would like that. I knew him my whole life, you know." He pinched the hem of my sleeve between two fingers and tugged. "She wants you to rule with me, as an adviser."

"Is that what you want, Alistair?" I turned to him. "To be remembered as the Sundered Crown's son who stood aside as she sacrificed a tenth of Cynlira and saved only her chosen few from the Vile who invaded after?"

"No," he whispered. "That's not what I want at all."

"You said once she wouldn't let the Door devour us all because the dead don't bow," I whispered. "But if it is fear and power she longs for, what greater power is there than standing atop a nation of sacrifices and staring down at the survivors?"

I took a small step forward, and he stepped back. Another step. His knees hit my bed. I pushed him down on it and knelt at his feet.

"Alistair, she made me kill him. What else will she make us do?" I asked.

He took a deep breath. "I will be a bad Crown. I do not care for politics."

"But you have me." Carefully, slowly, one word at a time, like stitching shut lips before a viewing, I said, "If you were Crown, you could assign people to care for your court responsibilities. No one would question your research with the Door. We only have five months. Imagine what you could learn in that time if you could dedicate yourself to your research? Imagine what we could create."

This close, his red gaze burned.

"My father made us watch the sacrifices. He thought it would make us harder and prepare us for the responsibilities of ruling. He didn't have trials. It was simply whoever he didn't need anymore, but back then, it demanded far fewer people. The peers who backed my mother did so because she said she would have trials." He curled his fingers around my throat, my pulse fluttering, and tilted his head to the side. His thumb stroked beneath my ear. "I have killed so many people but rarely with my hands."

I could not say that his mother killed Creek; that was too far from the truth.

"You blame your mother for Creek even though I held the knife," I said and didn't pull away. "Nothing we could sacrifice would equal taking a life. I'm sorry, Alistair."

His grip loosened. "I know. I must do it."

"I know you feel..." I stopped, his eyes narrowing behind his glasses. It wouldn't help to talk of feelings or morality. He wanted to be objective, so I had to appeal to that. "You pretend not to care, but I know you do. If you didn't, you wouldn't be so careful with your contracts. I understand that your apathy lets you be objective. Use that."

The only logical conclusion was that he had to kill his

mother tomorrow, but I had to let him get there, fully invested, on his own. It would do no good if his reign began with him distrusting me.

"If I didn't love her so, then I would have my answer." He slid to the floor, gripped my hips, and turned me around. His legs stretched out on either side of mine, and I leaned back against his chest. His left arm encircled my waist. His right hand traced the sigil of Death over my heart. "I want to understand everything."

"I know."

"No, I don't think you do." He dug his nail into the flesh beneath my collarbone. "I want to peel back the skin of the world and see how it works. I want to see the way its tendons move." He dragged his finger to the center of my chest and pressed against the sternum. "I want to break it down to its bones like you would break a corpse and study every little piece until I know how to put it together perfectly." His hand flattened. "Not knowing has left a hunger in me I cannot sate. It's a contract with no sacrifice. I can feel your panic just like I could see your disgust when you talked of using Creek's body for experiments. When we traveled to Mori, you could barely stand to look at me. You were horrified by what I did to Hila and all I did after."

"Was I?" I asked.

For what I was orchestrating now, I hardly had room to be upset.

"I can't afford to care about who I kill, or I would never stop caring," said the Heir. "I'm not like you. I don't think I care about people dying when the Door opens. I just want to understand how it works and why."

I leaned my head back against his shoulder. "How many times have you destroyed your feelings rather than deal with them?"

"If I asked you that, Lorena," he said, tracing the sigil of Death across my skin again, "could you tell me the number?"

How much had I given up that I couldn't remember? How

much did it matter if I couldn't remember? At least I, not the world, was the one breaking me down piece by piece.

"Your mother took the comfort of lies from me. She took your friend and research from you." I reached up and tugged his glasses from his face. "You don't owe her because she's your mother. Family isn't infallible."

People with good families never understood. It was unthinkable and called into question everything they'd ever known. Family loved each other. It had to be the truth.

If it wasn't, what else was a lie?

"My mother loves me," he whispered. "Even at my worst, she loves me."

"Love isn't enough, Alistair." I reached back and stroked his tangled hair.

He leaned into my hand. "Can good ends come from bad means?"

"I hope so."

"Are you sure?" His grip on me tightened. "The coattails of past victories. How long before I must demonstrate my power to them again?"

"Alistair." I was losing him, but his real name on my lips made him sigh. I threaded my fingers through the hair at the nape of his neck. "I always wondered what your contract was. I was there that day your mother paraded you through Mori."

"You were?" His breath hitched.

"Of course I was," I said and let my hand fall away. "You were the only other vilewrought I knew of who was near my age. We were the same. I wanted to see you."

"The same?" he murmured, chin bumping my crown. "The contract wasn't right, and the sacrifice wasn't enough. I slept for days and couldn't use my vilewright for months."

So what if his reasons weren't altruistic? With the right help, he could be a far better Crown than his mother. With the right push, I could get him to be better.

"Tell me," I said. "I want to understand it all."

He talked for hours. I hated how easy it was, knowing the root of that ease. Alistair Wyrslaine—it was hard to think of him as the Heir now that I knew why people called him that more than his real name—had spent so long feeling terrible that he'd used his wright to wash it all away and let him live without the threat of guilt or shame. He couldn't sacrifice his feelings as I did, but he could sacrifice something else to destroy his guilt. How monstrous we made ourselves to survive.

What monsters Cynlira made of wrought. We were forced, contractually obligated, to use our work and wrights only for the "good of the country," but it rarely benefited everyone. Only the peerage and wealthy reaped the rewards our wrights sowed. They used our wrights for their gain, all while promising us more.

"You've learned so much." I turned away to hide my disgust and pretended to be straightening my dress. "You've created so much without having a noblewright. We can stop the Door, Alistair. I understand why you're hesitant."

He wanted to be understood so badly. A lonely little boy full of thoughts and absolutely no feelings for how those ideas affected others.

Dawn crept through the window outside, and he tapped his fingers against my stomach. "We should part and get ready."

"Are you ready?" I asked, helping him up. This time, he didn't flinch when I touched him.

"Yes, but you must wear the proper attire. You're an under-taker, Lorena. You must look the part today." He touched the collar of my coat—of Julian's coat—and smiled. "She always said the reason they listened to her those first few years was because she took the crown from his still-warm corpse before their eyes."

twenty-four

I TOOK OFF JULIAN'S COAT SLOWLY. BLOOD DROPS speckled the sleeves near the wrists, dark red against the pale brown. I laid it across my bed, the wrinkled cloth leaving a smear of dust on my arms, and I changed clothes with tired hands. Each button of the greatcoat calmed my heart. Obscurity was the best armor.

Once I was dressed, I dragged a hand down my face, drew a line across my mouth, and slipped a knife into my sleeve. The old, brown coat I tucked beneath the bed.

"Adler?" Hana knocked once. "I'm coming in."

"It's lock—"

She shouldered the door open, and I stared at her. It was attractively competent.

She shrugged. "I'm His Majesty's guard for a reason. Come. I won't be late because of you. Today is already odd enough."

"How so?" I asked as we left.

"He's never used another guard. They annoy him," she said. "I know all his specifications and contracts."

"I imagine he has a lot," I said.

"The contracts require a knowledge of the sacrificed memories." She glanced at me. "My parents were guards. He knows many of my memories. That makes the sacrifices easier. A new guard is a hassle."

"Well, that makes sense," I said, because I couldn't say that it would be fine.

Court was held well within the palace grounds. The nearer we got, the more orderly the gardens grew until there were no trees. It was as if I'd walked into a different world. Glittering quarters of stained-glass windows overlooking patches of blue tulips and gold sunflowers speckled the landings dug into the side of the mountain, and the building that housed the court, where peers made and altered the laws of the land, was a great thing of pale marble inlaid with blue stones. I definitely didn't belong here.

Hana led me into a large room and pressed me against a wall near the door. "Don't move."

The courtroom was as wide as a city street and as tall as three stories. A long, low table in the shape of a half-moon carved from a single slab of pure black stone took up the center of the room. The chairs that lined it—the two hundred and something peers that made up the court—had not been set around the table but carved from the stone of the floor, making them as permanent as the peerage. There were gilded wooden chairs along the borders of the room for councilors on days when both groups met. Rich but replaceable.

As if there only being twenty-five allowed on the council wasn't hint enough.

At the front of the room was a raised platform and a dark throne inlaid with slivers of sapphires, rubies, emeralds, diamonds, and onyx. Every god who'd abandoned us was represented in those colors.

No one paid me any mind. The peers filtered in over the course of an hour, though I was sure court was supposed to have already started, and they all bent at the waist as Alistair entered. The soldiers, servants, and I dropped to our knees. Alistair didn't even look at me.

Good.

The white doors across the room opened. The Crown, sundered gold sparkling in the morning light like fire atop her head, glided into the room. Five guards flanked her.

"Alistair!" The Crown opened her arms and smiled. "At last you find it fit to grace us with your presence."

"Yes," he said, bowing to her. "I should have done this sooner."

No waiting. No hesitation.

Patience, I prayed to my vilewright. *Pass over her as if you're destroying something.*

My vilewright rose, hungry and willing. The Crown swept Alistair into a hug. He sunk into her embrace, his tall frame engulfing her.

My vilewright yanked away from me, and I stumbled. The Crown froze. Her face turned to me.

Hana grabbed my arm. "What's wrong?"

"I'm sorry," I whispered, and I was glad that I could say those words, that they were still the truth.

My knife slipped from my sleeve to my hand, and I buried it in her side, below her navel and away from most organs. She shrieked and slumped. I lowered her to the ground.

The Crown's eyes crinkled when she smiled. Alistair pulled away from her. She sunk to her knees, the front of her dress stained red. The court erupted and the peers scattered. The guards descended on Alistair, and he didn't move. Blood dripped to the white floor, the red sigil of something new. He stared down at his mother.

"Stay out of this," he said, needle spinning in his hands.

One guard didn't obey. They leapt to the Crown's side, and she grabbed their shoulder. The guard doubled over, a hole in their throat.

"No hard feelings," the Crown said, spitting out blood and turning to me. The wound in her chest was half-closed and nearly healed. "I would have done the same, but you're far too slow."

"Am I?" I asked, displaying the knife in my hand. She'd go

for me first. I was dualwrought, which meant I was the greater threat.

Her noblewright was already working. She dug her needle into her arm and gritted her teeth. My hand prickled, and the knife began to crumble. Now, her vilewright was busy, too, and I knew how long it took for them to work.

Destroy her noblewright's ability to heal her, I prayed. *Use Creek's sacrifice.*

My vilewright tore from me, and I stumbled. A life wasn't equal to a life; for a wright to kill, even indirectly, it needed far more than a single soul. There was no equal exchange, and the universe didn't use the same weights as Liran merchants. That was why wrought didn't go around killing folks every day. It was why Alistair was better poised for the killing blow.

Alistair caught my eyes and followed the path of my vile-wright. His binding had prevented him from doing what I had done, but he knew without my saying what I'd destroyed.

He buried the needle in her chest, piercing her heart, and ripped it out.

Her hand twitched, but her wrights were already busy. Even if they weren't, she couldn't heal anymore. Her needle clattered to the floor. Alistair stepped back.

Hyacinth Wyrslaine slumped to the floor, and the sun-dered crown rolled from her corpse.

The Wyrslaine guards who'd heeded Alistair's warning fell to their knees and pressed their faces to the floor. Alistair looked at me, his hands as red as mine, and gestured to the crown. One by one, the peers knelt. I walked slowly to his side and picked up the bloodied crown. He stood before the throne.

I set the crown atop his head and bowed.

"If any of you take issue with me, you should speak now," he said and nodded at the silence. "Court is adjourned for today. You will all be here tomorrow at noon. Understood?"

Agreement echoed around the room.

"Good," said Alistair, blood dripping down his face in five long streaks and cutting across his smile. "Now leave."

They were gone in an instant. Only Hana and I remained. I pulled her to her feet, and she grunted with pain.

"Let me—" I started but she shook her head.

"Did you even use this as a sacrifice?" Hana asked, pointing to her wound.

"A distraction," I said. "I can heal it."

"No!" She jerked away from me, words muffled by her clenched teeth. "Safia can heal it. I will report tomorrow morning, Your Excellency."

She limped away, clutching her side, and I took a deep breath. That was fair. Trust could be rebuilt.

"Lorena?" Alistair's voice broke.

I turned. He keened, dropped his head into his hands. His glasses shattered against the floor.

"I killed my mother," he said. "I killed my mother."

"Yes." I crouched before the throne and wrapped my arms around him, keeping him upright. "You did."

"She killed my sisters. I wanted... I thought it would feel better. Different." He leaned his head against my shoulder and whispered, "Why don't I feel better?"

"Breathe." I lowered us to the floor, limbs tangled, him half in my lap. "It's fine. You're fine."

"They won't be scared of me if they see me like this," he said, hands leaving a red trail across my coat. He'd gripped the needle so hard it had cut into his palm.

Take my ability to taste for the day, I prayed to my noblewright, *and heal his hand.*

My noblewright hummed. Gods in my veins, but he called his wright a monster.

"Who cares what they think?" I asked. "You've done what you set out to do."

"You don't understand. What you did to Creek is not equal

to this." His grip on me tightened. His nails bit into my ribs. "There aren't many people I love, and one of them is dead behind us. What use am I if I can't get over that?"

"And she taught you exactly what you did today." I traced a pale scar running through his brow. "The factory where my mother worked was owned by Northcott. There was an accident. She didn't die the first day. I cut myself so much and so deep to try and save her, and I would sit there each morning wondering why she kept getting worse no matter what I did. Do you know why my wrights and I are like this?"

His hands slid up my sides to my shoulders, my neck, my face. The sound of the world became a hum through his trembling fingers. "What does this have to do with—"

"I'm not done," I said, and he rolled his lips together. "I kept her alive for so long when it was hopeless, and I should have let her die in peace. I prolonged her pain. Half the scars I bear are from trying to save my mother's life when I shouldn't have. Do you know how much it hurts to have your skin regrown day in and day out? I can't remember her voice, but I remember her screams."

Noblewrought sacrifices didn't have to be blood, but Cynlira was designed to encourage us to hurt ourselves. It taught us, without so many words, that hurting ourselves was the only way to have power—that it was the only way we could control what happened—and then it blamed us for bleeding out. Long hours and long cuts. They were all the same.

A way to keep common folk from fighting back.

"I am good at using my wrights because I failed my mother," I said, "but we are worth more than what uses society can scavenge from our traumas."

He stared at me, eyes wide, and dropped his hands. "What now?"

Now, he buried himself in his research, and I saved Will and the rest of Cynlira.

"We figure out how to close or replace the Door for good," I said. "The sacrifices we need until then will only be people we are certain are guilty. They confessed or gave themselves up. You won't be remembered as the Red-Eyed Crown but the one who uncovered the secrets of the Vile and their Door."

He nodded and grabbed my hand, lacing our fingers together tightly. Painfully. Knuckle to knuckle and bruise to bruise. "You'll help me?"

"Trust me, Alistair. I cannot lie to you, and I don't want to." I didn't need to. Making someone feel wanted was far more effective than making up stories. "Sometimes you must destroy to create wonderful things. We can create wonderful things."

They could fear Alistair like they always had and stay in line, the way children feared the dark the first time they slept alone. I would be one star among many. I could be one good part of the dark.

"This world is broken," I said, "but we can fix it."

part two

TEETH LIKE STARS

If they love you,
they'll come back.

twenty-five

IT WAS AN HONOR TO WORK WITH THE DEAD, BUT IT took all night for me to break down Hyacinth Wyrslaine for her funeral rites. The overlapping sigils of Life and Death oozed white and green ink all night, the power of the binding leeching from her body and into the pool with her blood. Her wrights were still trying to revive her, their prickling existence twining about me like eels, and twice I stabbed her through the heart while washing her. They did not fade until I cut her heart from her chest and set it aside.

"What flowers will grow from you?" I asked her once I was done.

Creek's ghost drifted through the pool to me, no ripples or wake at his feet, and said, "None."

As dawn's harsh light crept over Mori, shading the world red, I washed my hands and left Hyacinth for whoever came for her. The city outside the palace was silent and the streets bare. Only a few soldiers, all of them in the black-and-red uniforms of the Wyrslaine family, patrolled, and there were fewer the farther from the palace grounds I wandered. The Wheels was oddly empty, and the morning market hadn't even been set up. The quiet ached.

It was unnatural. Back in Felhollow, there was never silence. Autumn would be spilled across the town this month in a wave of crinkling auburn leaves, and the houses would be golden with ears of corn hung up to dry. They'd be throwing back a single shot of shine from leaking snowdrop blooms, their hands sticky and cold, and celebrating the end of summer. Five winters I'd spent curled up with Julian and Mack before hickory fires, and I might never return again. I needed home.

I rapped at the door to the Chase quarters in Noshwright. "Julian?"

I needed home to still need me.

Footsteps shuffled toward the door. It creaked open, a pair of bright black eyes glaring at me through the crack. Mack's tired face fell.

"Where've you been?" He yanked me into his arms and shut the door with a kick. "Jules! Lore's here!"

"Only one undertaker left now the Sundered Crown's dead," I muttered and wrapped my arms around him. "You heard?"

"Course we heard," he said, locking the door. "What happened? Basil said you were there."

"Alistair killed his mother and made himself the Crown." I pulled away from Mack. "Basil said?"

"They write." He nudged me into the room and murmured, "They're a nice break from Jules. He's caught up in his father's case."

Mack nodded toward the paper-covered dining table, and a clatter came from another room. Julian always woke up slowly, stumbling about like a minute-old calf.

"How's this going?" I asked and picked up one of the pages.

"Bad." Mack sighed and twisted one of the gold coils on a loc. "Will knew he was getting arrested, and I don't like that he let you make that deal. He's hiding something. He's not here, by the way. Took off to some councilor friends soon as the word got out about the Crown."

"Thanks." I squeezed his arm.

Mack's distrust unnerved me; he'd been Julian's friend long before either knew me, and their families had been friends for decades. Will could only do so many things to break that sort of trust.

"Lore!" Julian skidded around the corner and scooped me up, crushing me against him. "What happened?"

My skin itched at the closeness. There was so much going on and so much that had touched me. Julian's grip was unbreakable, his hands gripping my ribs so tight I feared they'd bruise. I shuddered, and he pressed his mouth to mine. His teeth clacked against mine.

I kissed him quick and pulled as far away as I could. "Sorry. The last few days have been a lot."

There was too much in the world, and too much in me. The whole of me was like a rotting wound, feverish and tight and fit to burst if prodded.

"Crown's dead," he said and brought his hand up to my face. "Father said his friends saw you there?"

I nodded and tilted my head away. "Alistair killed her. I'm fine. I was there, but I'm fine."

"Alistair?" Julian tugged my hair over my shoulder and tangled his fingers in it. "Shit. You sure you're safe there?"

"As safe as I can be anywhere given the deal I made." I couldn't pull away, so I led him to one of the chairs around the table. "We need to talk about Will's case now that Alistair's the Crown."

"Course," he said and sat in the chair across from me. "Can you get him off?"

I rubbed my arms. "My contract stands, but Alistair is certainly in a more forgiving mood than his mother these days. What have you found?"

"Nothing good." Mack passed me a stack of papers. "Inconsistencies in wages, a few employees I can't find any records of outside them getting paid, and folks missing no more than a halfan a year. Adds up to thousands over the years, and he's already used most of it to buy up two of the old churches in Formet. He won't tell us why."

"None of it's treason," said Julian, fidgeting with the edge of a page.

Mack snorted. "He's not paying people what they're owed, Jules."

My chest ached. Will was supposed to be better than the other councilors. He was supposed to be fair.

"He bought that old church outside Felhollow." Mack set the papers down. "But with whose money and why?"

Felhollow had trusted him, and now Will had dragged it into this mess.

"I think," I said slowly, "Will's going to owe some money and jail time no matter what."

Julian flopped onto a chair. "It's all minor stuff though—labor violations and some iffy tax records. He shouldn't go to jail for stuff every business in Mori does. It's the only way to turn a profit."

I winced.

"Just because everyone's exploiting folks doesn't mean he has to," I said.

"If he got rich undercutting Felfolk," said Mack, "would you be all right with it?"

"He bought an old town in Ipswit. Whole place is mostly graveyard now. Why? He's sending guns to nearly every main city, and he's not bought any ammunition, only received it from friends." I flipped through a ledger detailing the exchanges. "No, he's sent some to every holding except Drail. You know why?"

"No. He doesn't know anyone down there," Julian said. "That's that Oakeshaw woman's holding, and he doesn't like her. Some disagreement between councilors and courtiers."

Dripping-Rain-of-Life was in the southwest of Cynlira, as far from Mori as you could get, and where I'd have gone if I hadn't moved to Felhollow.

"Julian, I love you and Will, but right now, I've got some disagreements with Will," I said.

"Why?" he asked. "Y'all never questioned it before."

"Maybe we should've." Mack gestured to the array of ledgers on the table. "Will's up to something, and it might not have been treason, but it's not good. I think you know that, but I can't lead you to the right answer. Neither can Lore."

Julian groaned and rubbed his face. "Look, my father told me something, but he made me swear I'd keep it to myself. It's not bad or wrong, not like you two are thinking. It's just dangerous. If this were Felhollow, I'd know I could trust you, but can I here? You're calling him 'Alistair' and working with him every day? You never wanted anything back home, but now you're amassing power like bees hoard pollen."

"Of course you can." I'd have said our relationship was built on trust, but I couldn't. I'd never let him know all of me. I didn't think I could. "I couldn't lie if I wanted to."

His brows wrinkled. "What do you mean?"

"The Sundered Crown left me a parting gift." I tapped my lips. "She caught me lying one too many times and destroyed my ability to lie. I still can't."

She had left me with only the horrible truth of knowing myself and exactly what I was willing to do.

"Shit, Lore," whispered Mack.

I nodded. "Stabbed me. Stopped me lying. Killed another wrought working with us. It all pushed Alistair over the edge."

"She do anything else?" Julian asked, looking me up and down.

"Not really." I shrugged. "I'm only around because Alistair wants another person with a vilewright nearby to study the Door. I'm on the same level as kitchen cats."

"Necessary, fed, and occasionally kicked?" Mack asked.

"Exactly," I snapped. "I don't want to be powerful. I want to be safe, and I want Felhollow to be safe. I want my friends to be safe. This isn't about power, Julian; everything I've done is about surviving. I came here to help Will and you because I love you. Because you're my family. I would hope you'd think of me as such."

I'd always been afraid of coming off as cold, but now I couldn't find it in me to care.

"You're family, but this is my father." Julian hit the table. "I hate this. I hate we're here and involved in this. I hate knowing it all. None of this would matter if my father hadn't been caught."

"He'd still have been doing bad things though," I said.

Sometimes, I looked at Julian and he was home, but other times, there was a deep, dark loss; the boy he used to be was so different from the man he was. There was nothing wrong with it. We grew. We bloomed.

The world was a garden, and we'd grown apart despite all our care and tending.

"I'm sorry." Julian took my hands in his and kissed each scar. "I really am. I wish he'd not done it."

"Done what?" I asked, stuttering.

"He committed treason," said Julian, wiping his tears on his shirt. "He hired some vilewrought girl and her friends to kill Alistair Wyrslaine, except they failed, panicked, and tried to get to Felhollow to tell him."

Mack doubled over and grumbled into his hands.

"That girl," I whispered. "Those bandits weren't bandits at all. He set them up to get them killed."

"They were going to take the money and leave even though they failed and led Alistair Wyrslaine right to him," said Julian as if that explained everything.

"How long have you known?" I asked. How long would he have let me stew in my contract with Alistair?

"Few days. Not before." Julian sniffed, his eyes red. "Took me a while to think about it. I couldn't believe he'd do this to me. To us. He stood there and let you deal with that boy. He knew he was guilty, and he let you defend him. I hated him at first, then I was sad. It is what it is."

I squeezed my eyes shut. I'd thought the same thing, screamed it, when my mother was dying. Grief left no ugly emotion unturned.

"Maybe he's right. Maybe someone should kill the Heir." Julian snorted. "The Crown. It'll get you out of that contract."

Mack, eyes wide, turned to me. "Does him dying even get you out of it?"

The vilewrought girl had failed at killing Alistair, and he'd been chasing her. He'd known about the treason from the start, even when writing up my contract. He'd known I'd never be able to save Will.

"Fuck," I said. "Alistair trapped me."

twenty-six

COURT WAS IN SESSION AND THE NEW CROWN ON full display. He stood where his mother had died, the crown still stained. Blood flaked from the gold as he spoke, the peers flinching each time he moved and it rained, and I watched it all from the back of the room with the servants. Fear would only get him so far, but the peerage was listening. The Wyrslaine guards had flocked to him. Mori had let the change in rule occur without revolting.

Once court was done, I waited in the wings. Alistair moved through the motions of conversations, but even from this far away, I could tell his expression was hollow. It only made me angrier.

I took a breath and tilted my head back to keep any tears from showing. We were too high up for even the mountains to block the light, and the stained-glass dome above me had a clear view of the sky. Red and blue, green and white, and smoky black danced across my eyes. From here, only the moon could look down on the peers.

"Lorena?" asked Alistair.

I hadn't heard him approach, and my wrights hadn't so much as shifted.

"Do they ever hold court at night?" I asked. "Did you ask your mother that once?"

"I did," he said with a low laugh. "She said it was best we

worked during the day so that the leftover Noble, banished to the worlds beyond the moon, couldn't look down on us."

I shrugged, lowering my face. His red glasses were bright smears, and I blinked. Alistair frowned.

"Lorena? Are you all right?" Alistair smiled, a soft and slightly crooked thing, as he approached and dismissed the courtiers vying for his attention. Soon enough, it was only us in the room. "I did as you wanted. No one can pay to get out of being sacrificed, and as of tomorrow, fines are the first response to safety violations in Mori factories. The second is closure and inspection."

Another way I had played right into his hands. Now Will couldn't buy his way out of dying. At least one good thing had come from my meddling with Alistair and the court—fewer children would lose their parents or themselves to accidents.

"I'm not all right at all." I hated knowing my truths. I hated having to reveal my truths to him. "You knew Willoughby Chase was guilty the moment you got to Felhollow."

Julian's apathy over his father's faults disgusted me, and I couldn't reconcile him with the boy I'd fallen in love with years ago. That Julian Chase would never have preferred not knowing his father was sowing evil, and he was reaping the benefits. Red hands were still red even if you hid them under gloves, he'd have said.

But Alistair's betrayal reached deep into the heart of me—the little, hopeful part I'd tried to bury—and ripped it out. I'd thought we had an understanding. I'd thought I understood him.

"Ah." Alistair hemmed and hawed under his breath, the light in his glasses hiding his expression. "Yes, I knew Willoughby Chase was guilty of treason when we wrote the contract."

I had thought I could be the one to drive Alistair toward a better path, lure him with understanding, but Alistair was only another boy with blood on his hands and lies on his lips. My arrogance had undone me.

"You let me write that contract knowing I was doomed to fail," I said.

"Yes," said Alistair, "and you never asked."

Hadn't I? I knew he had filled in the warrant then and there, but I couldn't remember if I had asked him outright.

"That hardly matters." The words came out in a rush, and he arched a brow. "Don't patronize me!"

My wrights loomed, and he lurched back.

"We were using each other." He ground his teeth together and studied me. "We understood that. We started from the same point of understanding."

"Don't be intentionally oblivious," I snapped. "You ensured I started with one foot in the grave. There is a difference."

"Is there?" he asked, taking one step toward me. "I ensured I had a dualwrought by my side as I took on the Door. You ensured I killed my mother and took her crown." He took another step and cocked his head to the side. "How much of that did you plan?"

I wouldn't have done any of it if I hadn't been here, but still, I had chosen this. I knew who I wanted holding the knife.

"It was foolish of me to think we had an understanding." I stepped back from him, and he did not follow. "I will work with you. I will help you. I will uphold our deal. I cannot be your friend."

What did it say about me that I had trusted him, if even a little? That I had wanted the understanding I thought we had?

"Lorena, please." He reached for me.

"Don't touch me!" I darted back. "I thought we were on even footing, but I know better now. I need time to figure out where I stand with you."

"Next to me. I want you next to me." He lowered his hands and kept them in my sight. "What can I do to make this right?"

"You've thoroughly destroyed my trust in your deals," I said, smiling when he flinched. "There is nothing you can do except wait for trust to rebuild."

He hated his vilewright; he hated that he could only destroy.

"Would you pardon Willoughby Chase?" I asked.

"If I did, would you stay?"

"Yes," I said and hated knowing that it was the truth. Mortals weren't made to know their terrible true selves. "I have nowhere else to go."

My tongue didn't curl and my throat didn't clench, and I knew myself.

He shook his head. "He wanted me dead."

"So he did." I bowed to Alistair and turned to leave. "I will see you in the laboratory, Your Excellency."

I did not see him again until that evening. The moon rose, and we descended into the depths of the palace. Basil drew in a sharp breath as we entered the cavern, and Carlow dug her nails into the binding on her chest. They paced before the Door, Creek's ghost following after Carlow and glaring at me, and I set down three pieces of Creek—bone, blood, and flesh—on the Door's boundary. His bones lasted the longest.

"It's odd," said Alistair, studying the boxes we had made of Creek. The granules had reformed this morning and worn a hole in the boxes to rejoin the others. "The Door never leaves behind the bones of the sacrifices."

"Have any been wrought?" I asked.

He had, true to his word, not approached or touched me. He treated me like Basil.

"No." He made a note. "No wrought and none cursed. Carlow is the last of her kind."

"Joy," she muttered, and Creek's ghost laid his cheek upon her scalp. "Another thing to set me apart."

"Through no fault of my own," Creek's ghost said, but only I heard him.

"We shouldn't tell anyone else." I studied the Door, remembering how easily it had tricked me that night so many days ago. The door to my mother's sickroom still creaked and warped as if it breathed.

Alistair nodded. "Agreed."

Within an hour, we learned not to touch the Door with our wrights. Basil attempted to create a small lock on the Door, and the cuts on their arms tore wider. Carlow ran to get Safia, her goggles forgotten, and I cared for Basil as best I could. I'd never learned how to ease the pain of sacrificial wounds or even if I could. Safia was the only person I knew who could, and she'd spent years studying the ways sacrifices affected healing. The Sundered Crown had never seen a reason to build a lift to the Door, but Alistair had already asked Carlow and Basil to design it. We would need healing to tackle this vile thing.

"It takes anything left near it," said Alistair, gesturing to the empty spots where Basil's blood had splattered the ground. "It's always hungry and always wants more."

Like our wrights. Like him.

"We were like cattle to the Noble and Vile. Would we take the threats of a steer seriously?" Carlow approached and adjusted my coat, straightening the collar and unbuttoning it until the lack of binding on my chest was clear. "The councilors won't take a Wallower seriously unless you look as good as they do."

I laughed. "Why should they take cattle seriously?"

twenty-seven

WITHIN EIGHT DAYS, WE KNEW THAT WHATEVER the Door was—one of the Vile, most likely—it existed like our wrights. It could affect us and the world around us even though we couldn't affect it.

"What do you see?" Carlow asked and chucked another rock at the Door. It didn't even waver as the rock sailed through it.

"The door to my mother's sickroom," I said. "She died there."

"Grim." She sipped from a mug of tea. "I see the door to your room. It was Poppy's before it was yours. She was too young to be away from home. Used to come running to Creek or me every night when the Door gave her nightmares. Next time I love someone, they'll be cursed and I'll be dead." She downed what was left in her mug and shuddered. "At least she's not cursed."

Basil grabbed Carlow's hand, lacing their fingers together when she tried to shake them off. "The door to the courtroom when I was bound. I want to rip it open and stop myself from letting anyone known I'm noblewrought."

"It's odd," said Carlow. "I know Poppy's dead, but I still want to open that door and see her."

I'd sacrificed so many things over the years to heal the folks in Felhollow—my mother's laugh, my first memory of her, and the feel of her hand against my cheek. She was a smear in my mind, a slightly blurred hodgepodge of emotions. My only clear memories of her were the ones my noblewright had never wanted. Losing them would have been a mercy, not a sacrifice.

"I only have bad memories of that room," I said. "The Door's not as smart as it thinks it is. I burned that room and the building around it. What do you think I'll do to you?"

Darkness seeped into the cracks of the wood, swallowing up the door I knew too well, until there was nothing but jagged splinters like teeth hanging before me. Carlow gasped.

"If I didn't know better, I'd say you offended it." Basil leaned closer to the Door and glanced back at me. "It can't get offended, right?"

My noblewright reared up behind me, and I rose. Our wrights were only pieces of what the Noble and Vile could do. The Door didn't need a contract or sacrifice to act.

"Of course it can," I said and licked my lips. "It's one of the Vile, and look at what it's been reduced to."

Within ten days, we had fashioned Creek's bones into a new door with a sturdy lock. His bones thrummed the same way my wrights did, a low sound that was more uneasy feeling than sound. Carlow drew up a blueprint of the mechanisms needed, and I worked the bones into it. She couldn't, because her binding to Order prevented her from working with bone, something only healers were allowed to do. Safia couldn't, because her binding to Life prevented her from doing anything with bones that would kill a person.

"It's a miracle either of you can manage to do anything," I muttered.

Carlow grunted. "I manage nothing."

"We manage fine," said Basil with a sigh, "so long as all we attempt to do is what they say to do."

They kept bridges, roads, and buildings safe—keeping folks happy with the council and court—and made beautiful homes and trinkets for those who could pay—keeping the council and court wealthy.

"I'm shocked none have argued for my binding yet," I said and settled Creek's reworked bones over the Door. A high-pitched whine pierced my ears. The Door trembled.

"They have," said Basil, glancing around the cavern and our makeshift laboratory. "His Excellency threatened to strip them of their titles and let them try to destroy the Door."

"They'll take you seriously now," Carlow said. "Good luck with that."

Within twelve days, the lift was made and Safia joined us in the cavern. She took a shallow breath when she saw the Door and wrung her gloved hands so violently the seams ripped. Hana rubbed her shoulder.

"It can't hurt you," Basil said to Safia, "so long as you don't cross the chalk line."

Hana would have said it, but Alistair had sacrificed her voice the day before, and it hadn't yet returned.

I beckoned him off to the side while the others showed Safia around. He came immediately, stayed at least one step away from me. He hadn't touched me since our argument, and he kept his hands always at his sides when nearby. He never even stood behind me.

"There is a law the council has put forth, but the majority opposes it," I said. "However, I think you should override it if they vote it down."

"What's the law?" His expression was inscrutable behind the red glasses.

"It demands noblewrought, not just healers, be in residence at munitions factories in the event of an accident and would lift some of the restrictions on their bindings."

"Consider it done," he said, waving his hand. "I will broach it during a coming meeting."

"Your Excellency!" Safia's voice echoed. "I've never seen the Door before."

Alistair turned, scowling. "Yes, that's why you're here now."

"No, I mean that it's taking the form of something no one here, including me, has seen before." Safia yanked a journal from her bag and flipped to a clean page. "It's the door to Mother's church. I've only ever heard about it. Look." She sketched a large set of stone doors with a line of Madshavi carved atop it. "The Madshavi is correct. Does it know the language, or does it use my knowledge of the language?"

"It's never duplicated languages before," said Alistair, tugging the paper from Safia. "Is this replication accurate?"

"I'll have to ask my mother," Safia said. "I've never been to In-the-Presence-of-Wrights, but it looks right."

"If it is, does that mean it's good at extrapolating information it gains from us?" asked Carlow softly.

"Or that it's seen the door?" I turned to it, exhaustion slowing me down. For days, the Door had taken up every thought and movement. It was one of the Vile, the only one left in this world, and all that was holding its fellows back. It conjured up our greatest wants to tease us into freeing the Vile. It accepted whatever we offered, devouring all without a care. "I've heard of that town before. Why have I heard of that town?"

"Ipswit?" Safia shrugged. "There's nothing much there anymore except for the church. The whole town's abandoned."

"I will have someone travel to In-the-Presence-of-Wrights and sketch the door so that we can compare." Alistair glanced at me. "And check on whatever is bothering you?"

"Nothing there but the church?" I clucked my tongue. Will had bought land in Ipswit, and I needed to know why. "Yeah, I need to know what's there."

In twelve days and one night, I had spent no time alone with the Door. I returned that night after the others left, slipping into the Door's cave with only the dim light of my hand lantern. The Vile had possessed magic we couldn't imagine, and yet the Door could do little outside this cave. Alistair's vilewright, if asked to destroy the infection in a wounded arm, would destroy the whole arm. The Door devoured whatever was offered to it.

"You're more discerning," I muttered to my vilewright, and it trilled, acknowledgment fluttering in my chest.

As a child, I'd fed my wrights when I was lonely. They had grumbled and stretched, and I had felt them there within me. Without me. The only creatures in existence to never leave me. I asked for nothing, just wanting to know they were still there. I liked to think they understood and did small things for me without a sacrifice first because of it.

The Door was like wrights in a way; maybe it could be trained like them too.

"Are you hungry?" I asked.

The Door creaked. I cut my fingertips open and pressed five bloody prints into the earth within the Door's boundaries. My blood vanished the same way it did when I sacrificed for my wrights. Pain scraped across my fingers. The dirt stuck to my hand.

"Let me go and I'll give you more blood," I said, "but if you don't, you will get nothing more from me, and I'll starve you until we have to sacrifice someone. You'll get nothing in between. I can imagine it now—a withered door too weak to change its appearance until finally we feed you again."

The dirt slipped away and settled on the ground.

"Good." I patted the earth, letting more blood drop. "What's your number? There must be an end to your hunger. If you devour all the mortals to stay shut, what will you eat after?"

Perhaps Alistair was right—the Door had opened something in me, and now the dark was spilling out—because I never would've had this thought of people as numbers before.

Footsteps echoed in the cavern. I turned, hands still red. Alistair stood in the mouth of the cave.

"This is dangerous," he said. "Especially alone."

"Wrought are never alone." I stood but didn't move. "Are you *you*, or are you the Door?"

Alistair chuckled and tossed me his glasses. I caught them, their solid weight familiar and comforting.

"Did you speak to the council yet?" I asked, rising and brushing off my knees.

He shrugged. "I will get to it tomorrow. Safia's revelations were too tempting to abandon."

Getting him to do his job was as hard as cracking a corpse's chest, but at least I knew the outcome would be good.

"It's been eating the cover and lock." Alistair touched the glasses in my hand, careful to not touch me, and gestured for me to put them on. "Creek's bones won't hold it shut."

"They already weren't. It just took some of my blood without any issue." I dropped his glasses over my eyes and gasped. "Is it always like that?"

"No," said Alistair. "This is new."

Shadowy tendrils reached out from nowhere, as if parting a curtain we couldn't see, and picked away at Creek's bones. They pulled the pieces into whatever invisible space they came from and then vanished again. The air shimmered where they all disappeared.

"Perhaps the lock only made it harder for it to accept sacrifices?" I handed Alistair his glasses and took a step over the boundary.

Alistair reached for me, fingers brushing the back of my coat. I waved him away.

"What's it doing?" I asked.

"The same thing," he said, and part of me thrilled at the catch in his voice. "A few shadows reach for you, but they're less substantial than the others."

"You couldn't eat me right now if you wanted." I tapped my toe against the dirt and backed away. "Let's see how long it takes to break down the lock."

I had ignored the notes from Julian and Will. Mack, at least, was as troubled as I was. I didn't know how to move forward when Will's guilt was guaranteed, the contract bound me to Alistair, and his treason might have been justified. If we shut the Door, at least Will would live and we'd have time to untangle the mess.

"I want to witness the next sacrifice," I said, "and see exactly what the Door can and cannot do."

twenty-eight

THE NIGHT BEFORE THE SACRIFICE, I COULDN'T sleep. We had, by Carlow's newest calculations, a little less than four months before the Door opened, give or take a few days. It was troubling, and we all figured it would open sooner unless we sacrificed a tenth of Cynlira to it. Already it was growing, and Carlow had to adjust the boundary line every day. It had broken down Creek's bones within days. We couldn't keep it shut.

I threw my arm over my eyes, the dark of my room not quite dark enough, and tried to fall asleep. These days, it was more of a chore than a guarantee.

"Lorena?" Alistair rapped on my door three times. "The Door's changing. I have to get Hana. Meet me down there as soon as you can."

It was well past midnight. A hangnail moon hung in the sky, pale and yellowed. I pulled my greatcoat tightly around myself, the chill seeping in regardless, and stalked through the gardens to the stairwell that led to the Door. Pale swallow-wort vines curled around my wrist and stuck to my sleeve. They'd grown through the wall.

Carlow's voice echoed up the stairs. I hesitated, vines tightening.

It felt like the wall leading to the Door. It was cool and hard, damp gathering at my fingertips, and when I scuffed my feet, the sound and feel of leather against stone was real. There were no doors between the Door and me, so there was no way to trick me into opening it. Creek's ghost drifted past me, a trail of blood in its wake, and paused at the bottom. He looked up at me.

"Can good ends come from bad means?" asked Creek, blue eyes unblinking.

"Are you my guilt or the Door this time?" I yanked away from the vines. "Or am I to ask Will that when I see him next?"

Alistair had set me up. Will had set me up. Julian had set me up. Was there no one who wouldn't use me to thrive?

"Open the Door," said Creek's ghost, "and find out."

I breezed through him and into the Door's caverns. "Clever. You didn't have to reuse words Alistair had already said. You're learning."

The cavern rattled as if great feet stomped above me, the utter petulance making me roll my eyes.

"You're arrogant." The Door creaked, and the charred scent of my mother's sickroom clogged my throat. "Do you think memories can't haunt you once they're sacrificed? I'm not some vilewright bound to a mortal soul. I am everywhere, with everyone, and I can see all your little secrets, my vile pet."

"Hush," I said, standing at the chalk line Carlow had drawn. "I'm not opening you."

"Maybe you're the one I want to open." Its voice was softer. The words were a familiar rasp that made my heart ache. I couldn't remember it, but I recognized it. The Door creaked again, as if laughing at my pain. "Gift me your noblewright, and I'll shut. I haven't tasted Noble in so long, Lorena."

My name in that voice stung. "Never."

My noblewright curled about me, a protective weight about my shoulders.

"Not even to save everyone?" it asked, the sickroom door stretching like a close-mouthed smile.

I shuddered, but I knew myself. My wrights were my oldest friends. They were my only friends.

They knew how selfish I could be.

"You wouldn't keep that deal anyway," I said. "I'm not trusting something hiding behind my worst fear. Show me your teeth or stop barking."

A hand I couldn't see grabbed my chin. Another grasped my shoulder. A finger, too long to be mortal, pried open my mouth, digging into the soft flesh at the back of my teeth. I flailed, but it wouldn't let go. My hands passed through the air as if there were nothing there. It opened my mouth wider. I clawed at my face. There were no hands there.

"What are you to think you could do anything to me? I am always with you wherever you go," it said in my mother's voice, walking fingertips along my teeth. "I could pry those wrights from your soul, eat my fill of the Noble, and reclaim what mortals stole from the Vile."

My wrights whined within me, unable to move with a prayer, but I couldn't think of anything we could do against the Door. I was nothing. I didn't have power like it did.

My vilewright yowled, and stillness settled over me.

"Who's hiding now," said the Door, yanking at my back teeth, "vilewrought."

But I was the legacy of those who had feasted.

Show it who we are.

I bit down hard. It dropped me, whatever I'd bitten off still in my mouth. I scrambled back, my teeth crunching through what tasted like old bone and how lightning smelled, and the Door to my mother's sickroom slammed shut. My wrights unfurled from me and hung between us. I swallowed.

"I will give you nothing," I said and wiped my mouth, licking the remnants of the Door from my fingers. "Especially not my wrights."

My noblewright cooed. I stumbled back, curling up against

the cave wall. The only evidence of what the Door had done was five holes in the shoulder of my coat and a weight in my belly. My vilewright rippled across my hands and plucked at them. It was like walking through a spider's web.

"What do you want?" I whispered. "Do you need a sacrifice?"

They had acted on their own. They had protected me.

I closed my eyes and thought of my house in autumn. Before it grew calendula orange as a hunter's moon and hydrangeas of rain blue and midnight purple, bright spots against the old brown wood. A tapestry so familiar it hurt.

My first memory of home. Take it and answer my questions honestly.

"Are you there?" I whispered. "Do you understand me?"

A cool night breeze settled over my shoulders, and the hair near my ears ruffled. A sigh. Pressure touched my chin, and I knew somehow that it was my noblewright. My vilewright touched the top of my head. They moved my head up and down in answer.

My memory of home remained.

"Why?" I asked.

Pale-pink scratches appeared on the back of my hand, blood welling along the lines.

We.

"Of course it's 'we.' I'll never leave you."

They nodded my head again.

I sniffed and rubbed my thumb across the marks. "And you'll never leave me."

I waited in the cavern and watched the Door. It didn't speak to me again or try to trick me. If anything, it looked paler. The wood of the door it was imitating was bleached by the sun, and a notch had been taken out of the top right. My wrights prowled about me and stayed alert. An unnatural awareness shuddered through me. I didn't stand till I heard Alistair's footsteps.

He walked in and paused, eyes glancing at the Door. He dropped his glasses from his forehead to his nose, looked me over, and nodded.

"Are you well?" he asked.

He still stayed away and didn't come close enough to touch me.

I beckoned him so I could check his coat. The Door could make us see and hear things that weren't real, but it couldn't change how the world felt.

"I'm fine." I rubbed his coat between my fingers and stepped back. "The Door was playing with me earlier. How long until the sacrifice?"

"Not long." He hummed and tilted his head back. "Did something happen? Your vilewright is...agitated."

"Yes," I said and ran my fingers along my lips. My stomach growled. "I don't want to talk about it."

"All right. So long as you are certain you are well." He moved as if to touch me and yanked his hand back. "Come. I'll show you where to stand."

The trial had already taken place for the sacrifice this morning. He had confessed, been determined guilty by the court's noblewrought, and then found guilty by the council. He'd no family, so a courtier and councilor had come to see the deed done, and hopefully seeing the Door would keep the court and council on Alistair's side for longer. We needed more time with the Door.

More and more, I worried it would open no matter what we offered it or what we did.

Carra Shearwill swept past me in a breeze of blue silk and perfume. Her shirt was low-cut to show off the sigil of Order carved into her chest, the cuts clean and small. It was nothing like the large, ungainly binding on Carlow's chest, and I glared at her, since Carlow wasn't here to do it. More people entered the cavern, three of them courtiers I didn't know, and each bore a different sigil on their chest. Alistair kept well away from the one with Chaos's red ink, and I peeked at the green sigil of Life carved into the white-skinned woman next to me who arrived last. Shearwill didn't bow to her, only inclined her head. This was a councilor then.

There was one with each god's sigil here—two councilors and three courtiers. With so few vilewrought and one dual-wrought, the courtier with Death's white sigil had to be the only one of his kind. Were there even any wrought still bound to him now that Hyacinth Wyrslaine was dead?

Alistair cleared his throat and raised his head, red glasses black in the flickering light. "I prefer concision. Do you have last words?"

The sacrifice shook his head. Lank hair covered his face, and the steel shackles about his wrists were a rusted red. What hypocrisy. I'd let Will escape this, and he was guilty. He'd let me bargain my life on his innocence while in the wrong. All the sacrifices now might've been ruled guilty or confessed, but who'd been killed unfairly? Who'd suffered while Will plotted? Cynlira had failed them.

"I will not draw this out," said Alistair. "Stand here."

Hana placed the man before Alistair, right at the boundary to the Door, and his feet sunk into the dirt. The Door was my mother's sickroom again. I hadn't noticed the change, but it looked as it always did. Alistair glanced at it once and drew the needle from his sleeve. Hana retreated to stand behind him.

"Feast," said Alistair.

He jammed his steel needle into the man's chest, between his ribs, and withdrew it in one smooth motion. The man gasped and flinched. Alistair pushed him toward the Door.

It opened. A shiver ran through me, clenching at the base of my spine. I had asked Alistair how he knew when the Door needed to be fed, and he said the Door let them know. It slammed shut, the old wood rattling and raining down splinters, and I gasped. A want so deep I nearly doubled over opened up within me, my wrights twisting about my hands. I clasped them behind my back.

"Not today," I whispered. I couldn't fight the Door again.

The Door shook as if something knocked on the other side, and the courtier stepped back. The leg of the sacrifice rose into the air, upending him, as if a great hand had lifted him up, and the door opened fully. The squeak of the hinges was the exact one of my mother's room. The invisible hands picked up the man and slowly pulled him through the open Door. Blood dribbled from his chest, vanishing the moment it hit the red earth.

There was no crunch. No violence. No revelation about where the Door led or how to keep it shut.

"Feast," Alistair said again, "and fasten."

"Coward," I muttered, and my wrights growled happily. "Go back to hiding."

But the Door shut with none of us the wiser.

twenty-nine

I HELD ALISTAIR BACK AFTER THE SACRIFICE WITH A
look. He sent Hana on her way with the courtier and councilor, cleaning the needle on a white handkerchief the whole
while. Red streaks crisscrossed the white and smeared against
his black gloves. They were all the better to hide the blood, and
he kept cleaning long after the needle was spotless. We all had
our tells.

"Alistair," I said, "did you think I would run?"

"I'm not completely oblivious. Of course you would have."
He scoffed and slid the needle back into its hidden holster. "But
then you gave me the perfect way to keep you. I didn't even
have to suggest the deal."

"No, I blurted it out and handed you the knife for carv-
ing." I rolled my eyes, and from the Door, I heard a squeak of
hinges that might have been laughter. "All that's left is to live
with the consequences of what we've done. Do you know why
Will Chase wanted you dead?"

"The usual reasons, I suppose." He raised one shoulder and
slowly let it fall. "Who doesn't want me dead?"

"I don't want you dead," I said. "Right now."

He chuckled. "Fair. No, I do not know the particulars of
his reasons. You will have to ask him. The vilewrought girl was
one who'd disappeared several years ago, and my mother had
a bounty out for her. She made more money for the folks she

fell in with than they would've earned turning her in. Her vile-wright was no match for mine, but I had never met another. I hadn't really met her; I'd only felt her trying to destroy me."

"So you gave chase?" I moved around him to glare at the Door.

It was my mother's sickroom door again, the cracks filled with watching pale-brown eyes.

"I did," said Alistair, following my gaze. "I wanted a vile-wrought, but instead I found you."

"And your would-be assassin," I said.

"I knew she was returning to who hired her." He inclined his head to our long worktable and placed himself between the Door and me. It was the closest we had been in over two weeks. "Willoughby Chase was the only councilor in Felhollow."

"Perhaps his treason is justifiable." I smiled as Alistair frowned. "There aren't enough sacrifices left to last us two months, much less the three Carlow predicts we'll need."

"Perhaps it is," he said evenly. "Yes, what is something you would do to solve this? Volunteers?"

I could already imagine the courtiers promising to fund whole families so long as someone volunteered.

"No, it's far too easy to make someone volunteer," I said, but the answer needed to be logical. It needed to suit Alistair's hunger for order. "Drawing lots would work so long as we ensured no one cheated."

And it would infuriate the peerage. Luck was the only thing they couldn't control.

"If we can't shut the Door or create a new one, what do we do then?" I asked.

He frowned, eyes crinkling at the corners of his glasses. "Die."

"I would hope not," I said. "Could we move everyone to consecrated ground? The Formet district could work."

"It wouldn't be large enough." He tilted his head back and

forth. "Noblewrought would be the best defense against the Vile, but not for long."

"We will try." I stood on tiptoe to stare him in the eyes. "If it comes to that, we will try."

"Agreed." He held out his hand to seal the deal and didn't flinch when I took his hand. "Or a nonbinding contract? You are passionate about these things, Lorena Adler. You won't be satisfied with only my word."

"No more contracts," I said, the warmth of him seeping into me. "Not between us."

His smile was the most honest—crooked and quick—that I'd ever seen from him.

He knew me well enough. He hadn't touched me since I'd asked. He hadn't tried to change my mind. Even now, he waited for me to set the pace of our conversation. It was refreshing.

I pulled away from him slowly. "You've kept your distance."

"You took my request seriously." He nodded toward the mouth of the cavern. "It's only fair, especially now, that I take you seriously."

Julian never took me seriously and never at my word. He didn't think I was passionate either, always pairing the word with intimacy. He thought, one day, passion would take me, I would take him, and all would be well if he just kept working at it. He'd have never left me to my own devices.

"Thank you, Alistair."

What did it say about me that I understood Alistair Wyrslaine so well and he understood me better than anyone else?

He offered me his arm, sighed when I took it, and led me away from the Door. "You were right, of course. I trapped you here. Haven't you ever wanted something so much that you'd do anything to get it?"

"Wanting I understand," I said softly as we wove our way back into the palace and toward his quarters. "Taking I don't."

People like Alistair, and even Julian, didn't understand the dangers of wanting. They already had power, Alistair by birth and Julian by his father. Cynlira dangled power and wealth before its citizens, hooked them with the promise that one day, we, too, could be like those at the top, and then used every part of us to fuel their aims. They worked people to the bone or forced bound wrought to sacrifice until there was nothing left of them and told us we might make it if we worked harder. If we sacrificed more. If we obeyed better. If we followed the rules and made them their money, all while tearing ourselves and one another down.

"Alistair." I splayed my hands between us, the scars of every sacrifice on clear display. "Do you know why I'm upset about this?"

"I lied to you," he said and drew out each word. "I took away your choice."

I nodded. I'd not thought he would know in full. "I didn't want to be bound, because I wanted to choose exactly what sacrifices I made and for whom."

People at the bottom were allowed to want but never to take.

"You asked me once if you were allowed to say no to me," said Alistair.

The powerful didn't need to carve bindings into chests to keep rebellion at bay; they only needed to keep pay low and hours long.

"You are. My word may mean little, but it's true. I do not want to be seen as one of the Vile, making tricky deals designed to ensnare the unsuspecting," he said, nodding to a pair of guards as we passed into a part of the palace where I'd never been. "I am certain that if you killed me, I would accept it." He smiled but didn't look at me. "Surely, you would have a good reason."

This part of the palace was almost entirely carved into the dark stones of the mountains with thin vents letting in fresh air and little light. He led us to a set of tall oak doors carved with the creation story of Cynlira. I touched the rippling waves of the Tongue, its waters splitting this older, neater version of Mori. Alistair pushed one of the doors open.

"Sit," he said and ushered me inside. "If you want."

I didn't. The room was long and wide, the walls lined with wooden shelves. A plush rug of red and blue cushioned my feet, and at the opposite end of the room, Alistair rustled through the drawers of a large desk. I dragged my feet through the lush threads and pressed my hips against the desk. He held out our original contract so gently he nearly dropped it.

"I understand. What do you need?"

The contract fluttered back to the desk, and Alistair pulled a pair of shears from the desk drawers. He reached out with his other hand, gloved fingers curled. I let him grasp my braid.

"Not a sacrifice," he whispered, rubbing his thumb down the braid. "Only something of yours and mine."

He snipped off the bottom of my braid and the ends of his, and the red and black strands tangled atop the contract. In one swift slice, he destroyed the contract and our hair. The smog of burnt hair stung my nose.

"Thank you," I said.

Now I could save Will, even though he was guilty.

Alistair came around to my side of the desk. "I hope that we—"

"We are good, Alistair." I laid my hand flat against his shoulder, his shudder running through me, and tugged at the uneven ends of his hair. "Needle?"

He handed it to me without question, and I pricked his thumb.

Take his blood as sacrifice, I prayed to my vilewright, *and destroy the too-long pieces of his hair. Make it even.*

My vilewright fluttered over him. He closed his eyes, and his hair evened out until it hung about his shoulders. I ran my fingers through it.

"You are the Crown of Cynlira," I said and brushed his hair from his face. "They will expect you to look the part."

"They will expect the same of you," he muttered and pulled a small brooch from his pocket. It was gold twisted into the shapes of two phoenixes devouring each other, and their eyes were a ruby and a sapphire. The knot of their bodies was so tight and the feathers so detailed, I couldn't tell how the gold-smith had woven it. He undid the pin and pulled me down by my shirt collar. "This is for voices of the Wyrslaine family—advisers, generals, peers, and the like. They will listen to you so long as you wear this."

He pinned it over my heart where my binding would be if I had one.

"Why haven't you tried to break your binding?" I asked, covering his fingers with mine.

He rolled his lips together. "It would interfere with my work. To break it, I would have to break all of them by killing the noblewrought who bound me and the court and council members who hold the bindings. For now, I am content."

"With you," he didn't say, but I could feel the words in the way he leaned against me. It was almost a pity that I would have to break this delicate bond between us to save Will. Julian would never understand.

I wasn't the same Lorena he had loved—I might never have been that Lorena—but this new one got things done.

"Fascinating." I placed one finger beneath his chin, tilting his head back till our eyes met, and smiled. "You weren't what I was looking for, but you'll do."

thirty

THE NEXT MORNING, I WOKE UP TO FAMILIAR laughter outside my door. I cracked it, expecting some trick of the Door, and found Basil and Mack eating in the doorway to Basil's room. They were a few doors down, but I could smell the jellied eels from here. Mack, locs up in a bun speckled with new silver cuffs, was eating with the look of a wolf fed turnips. Basil nibbled the filling out of a hand pie.

"Like them?" asked Basil.

"They're great." Mack poked at the eel cuts in his paper cup, and I wandered down to them.

"They're an acquired taste," I said, taking the cup from him. His fingers felt real, and the cup was definitely real. "What're you doing here? Can't be flirting. You're no good at that."

Mack opened his mouth, clucked his tongue, and looked away.

Basil grinned. "Don't worry," they said. "If Carlow had come out here, I would lose my words too."

The door to her room slammed open. Basil jumped. Carlow, wearing only a gauzy dress and the sticky remnants of sleep about her red eyes, raised a mug to Basil. Wine sloshed out of it.

"Bold to invoke me," she said, "when you know damn well I do everything out of spite."

Basil sniffed. "Is that mourning wine?"

"It is morning." She sniffed the mug. "I thought this was

my tea..." She vanished back into the room and reappeared with a different mug. "You never invite me to parties."

"You hate parties," said Basil. "And this isn't one."

"Then be quieter."

The door slammed, unnecessarily, behind her.

"That's our cue to leave." I tipped the last of Mack's eels into my mouth and tossed the cup at Carlow's door. "He's got a sweet tooth, by the way. Not much for salty things."

"I'm fixing to kill you." Mack grinned, though, and flicked my shoulder. "Met Basil this morning in the market and needed to see you. I think you should talk to Jules."

We said goodbye to Basil and left for Noshwright. Mack's stoic expression kept dropping. I looped our arms.

"What happened?" I asked quietly.

"A lot we didn't know about." Mack shook his head and sighed. "Will's all right with dying. He says he made his peace with being sacrificed the moment you left Felhollow, but Julian's not handling it well. It's a lot for him to take in on such short notice, and I don't agree with Will. It's putting a lot of things in perspective."

"Like Basil Baines," I said. "Never known you to make the first move."

Mack laughed through his nose. "They're the only good part of Mori, no offense."

"Offense taken but understandable," I said, squeezing him tightly. "People still deserve happiness even when the world's a mess."

"It's a right bigger mess than we figured. Killing Alistair wasn't all Will was up to."

I nodded. "All right. No more talking till we get to Noshwright."

We walked quickly. Mack kept his face down but his eyes up, taking in every inch of the palace grounds. I pressed close to him, worry shaking gently through me, and kept pace. Trying to assassinate Alistair and letting me sign that contract was bad enough. Will had doomed us both.

Will and Julian were waiting for us in the dining room. The table had been cleared and the ledgers organized, a map of Cynlira laid out like a tablecloth. Pins sprouted all across the country, mostly in larger cities, and a single one pierced Felhollow. Will rose when I entered, and Julian let out a strangled yelp. He threw his arms around me.

"You good?" he asked, mouth against my ear.

I swallowed, skin prickly and tight. The Door. Will. There was so much in my mind that I couldn't handle anything on my skin. It was all too much to think about.

"I'm good," I said. "I'm a little tired though. Sorry."

I hugged him quickly and pulled away, and he frowned.

"Here." Julian sat me in a chair and then dragged it next to his, dangling an arm over my shoulder. "First, my father owes you an apology."

I nodded, sweat gathering in the skin beneath his arm. "He does."

"I wronged you." Will sat on my other side, perched on the edge of the chair, and leaned over his knees. His mouth held a downward tilt. "I was greedy, and when you leapt to my defense, I led that greed override my pride and worry over you. You were always like family. I owed you more than that, and I'm sorry. I understand that the contract can't be broken. I will fulfill my part. I only ask that you hear me out."

He held out his hand, and I took it. He and Julian weren't like family—they were my family.

Or had been.

He clapped his other hand over mine, holding me tight, and his smooth skin was clammy against my rough scars. "It means a lot that you're here, and I think Mack could use someone like you to convince him. You're exactly what we need, Lorena."

I was always what someone needed.

"You're working on the Door with His Excellency," said Will in a tone I hadn't heard since Julian was eight and stole a whole pie from Mack's mother. "What do you know about it?"

"You know I am, but you think you know something I don't," I said slowly. "The Door will open soon, the Vile will be unleashed, and Cynlira will be overrun."

No one flinched at the news.

"I know how you should know that, but Shearwill didn't have Carlow's numbers until recently," I said. "You wouldn't have known it was opening so soon when you tried to have Alistair Wyrslaine killed."

"No, I do not know because of Carra's noblewrought." Will leaned back in his chair, crossing his arms like this was a normal conversation. "The council has been aware of the Door's weakening for a while now, and Carra's numbers only bolster our cause. I and most of the council have been preparing for the day the Door opens. We have a plan for the end of the world, but His Excellency's research threatens that plan. He cannot continue.

"We have all," Will said, "acquired the necessary resources for survival when cut off from Liran farmland, an acceptable number of noblewrought given that twelve of my friends control their bindings, and enough consecrated land to support us without Vile intervention. Old churches are, thankfully, quite cheap."

I shrugged off Julian's arm and pulled one of the ledgers to me, lines upon lines of gun sales and land purchases averaging out to a nice little amount of gold tiens. I'd never even seen one. I tapped the column dedicated to listing Will's last purchase, an old church in Formet. "There's not enough room in Formet for everyone, and there aren't enough churches across Cynlira for the people not in Mori."

"We don't entirely know how we'll do it yet," said Julian.

"Put your mettle to it," I said and shrugged. "I'm sure you'll..."

Hyacinth Wyrslaine's magic made me choke on "figure something out," and I smacked the table.

Will raised one brow. "Lorena?"

"The Sundered Crown destroyed my ability to lie before she died, and it cuts off sarcasm too." I rubbed my throat. "Will, you can't leave most of Cynlira to die."

"Did she really?" asked Will, fingers tapping against his thigh and smiling. "We heard rumors of you, but most of them were outlandish. That could be useful though."

"Fine. Fine." I flipped the papers before me over, chest tight. My eyes stung. "That's what the vilewrought was for then? Why you hired her to kill Alistair?"

"Yes," Will said, "and that is why I let you make that deal. It bought me time to tell Julian and prepare him to take over for me once I am sacrificed. The peerage had its chance to rule. It is our turn now."

"So for years, the council has been buying land the Vile can't cross, hoarding food and arms, and collecting wrought so that they can hunker down when the Door opens? And it will, because you need it to open, but only on yours terms." I covered my mouth with a hand. "You'll let the rest of Cynlira die? The peers? The people?"

Will glanced at Julian over my shoulder. "We have determined which towns will be the most useful in the coming years. They, like Felhollow, will be protected. Of course, anyone outside of those havens who survives will be a boon to us. It will be an honor to lead them."

They weren't creating a better world for their kids to inherit; they were creating a world for them and their kids to rule.

"Cynlira is dying." Julian pressed his hand to the small of my back, but the comforting gesture made me flinch. "Even if you found some way to shut the Door, we'd still be stuck here with the peerage and dwindling resources, cut off from the rest of the world. If you mess up, the Door opens, and none of us are ready."

"And the Vile will cull the population," said Will. "Most peers will be in Mori, and the Vile will emerge here first. We'll be left with few enough people for our resources to support and only the ones useful enough to survive the Vile and new world."

"What do you think?" Julian asked.

"I think the people who can afford to prepare for the end of the world like this could have afforded to fix it."

Julian reacted as if I'd slapped him. Across the table, so that only I could see, Mack raised both of his hands so that only his first and last fingers were up, like a bull's horns. *Bullshit.* I nodded.

"Fix is a strong word." Will turned to me, hands on his knees, and leaned forward. "There's a lot wrong in Cynlira, from the peerage to the people, and no amount of money can fix that. This is the sacrifice we are willing to make to save Cynlira."

Vilewrought were kin to sacrifice. I knew it better than I knew myself, and this wasn't it.

"How brave of you," I muttered. "I've heard enough."

"I haven't," said Mack. His gaze cut to Julian. A trembling tension gripped his body, shaking his leg under the table and his fingers above it. "How many people can your safe havens support and for how long?"

"About twenty thousand," said Will. "Our families, a few towns, soldiers, noblewrought, and other necessities can survive on what we've got for about a decade if there are no issues. After that, we either fight back against the Vile or cut a deal. They get part of Cynlira; we get the other part."

"So more people could survive for five years?" I asked.

"Lore." Julian groaned and pulled away from me. "In the grand scheme of things, what are their lives if they only survive five more years?"

"The scheme of things!" I surged to my feet. "If I'd never left the Wallows, you'd be killing me. You're killing folks not lucky enough to be born to rich parents. You're killing folks like

Mack or most of Felhollow. If you weren't from there, you'd be killing all our friends."

Julian grabbed my wrist. "You're not still in the Wallows."

"That's not the point," I said. "You're spitting in the face of all those you're willing to sacrifice without their knowledge."

"Sacrifice?" He snorted. "Like we've not heard what you've been doing? How many have you killed for that boy, and what makes that different from this?"

My memories of my mother were an empty room and a door with nothing behind it. No voice. No face. No tender hands. I had given it all up to save her and then to save the dying folks of Felhollow. I had given up everything for Will. This was my repayment?

"I've sacrificed worse things than you can imagine," I hissed.

Creek's blood had been so warm on my hands, and even now I could feel the heat of it burning in me. A lit coal that I could never put out.

He scoffed. "Like what? Your desire?"

I flinched. The words burned worse than any wound. "Even now, when I ask what the worst thing you think has happened to me is, you make it about you."

"Lore—"

"Cynlira may deserve better than Alistair Wyrslaine," I said, "but it deserves better than this. Will, you've got barely any time left before your trial. Is this really what you want to do with it?"

"I'll see Lorena out," Will said and stood. He took my arm before I could protest and herded me to the door. "I have no qualms with how I have spent my remaining days, and I am willing to die to ensure this plan goes through."

I ripped myself away from him. "Felhollow know about this? Old Ivy? Kara? They all right with killing everyone in Cynlira? They know that those bandits who killed Rylan weren't even bandits?"

Will's hand tightened around my arm. "Felhollow will understand once the time comes."

"Felhollow will be horrified," I said, "and even Julian will see you as a monster once he isn't in grief's grip."

"Julian's a smart lad. He knows what needs to be done, and he'll do it." Will clucked his tongue and shook his head. "You can protest it all you want, but the Chase family built that town. You were only visiting."

I jerked, and he slapped his other hand over my mouth.

"Killing Alistair Wyrslaine might be illegal, but it's not wrong," he hissed. The meat of Will's palm, salted with sweat, covered my mouth. Creek's hollow blue eyes stared over his shoulder. "I'm willing to bear those deaths to make Cynlira great again. Sacrifices must be made. What are you willing to sacrifice?"

I'd sacrificed my body and mind for Felhollow, each memory of my mother yanked out of me like a tooth. Even now, I could feel the holes left by my noblewright. I'd killed Delmond Creek. I'd killed Hyacinth Wyrslaine.

"There is always someone with dirtier, meaner hands," whispered Creek's ghost. "Who do you want opening the Door?"

The knife hadn't always been in my hand, but it had always been my knife.

I stopped struggling.

"I would've run if Julian wouldn't have killed me for getting you killed by that damned contract." Will removed his hand. "I know this is a lot, Lorena, but you are like family. We would like your help. It will be easier for the council to take control of the wrought and schedule the date of the Door opening with Alistair Wyrslaine gone."

The words I meant to say stuck to my tongue. I couldn't let Alistair die. I couldn't let Will open the Door. But drawing attention to Will—even going through with the trial—might reveal his plot, and when he was found guilty, the Crown would possess his property. The peers would use it and leave the people to fend for themselves, just like Will. There had to be a way to remove the council and court before it all came to a head.

"I need time," I said finally, each word clawing through my throat as if the magic knew I wasn't lying outright but wasn't being honest. "Alistair said he wouldn't pardon you." He had once, but my breath caught anyway. "I need a few days to digest this. Your trial's coming up. Give me until then. Trust me. Please."

"Of course." His eyes crinkled. "I have to, don't I?"

"Oh." I smiled, the expression tight and false. The taste of his hand still burned in my mouth. "Of course you do."

thirty-one

WILL'S THREAT HURT, BUT JULIAN'S MISUNDER-standing hurt worse. It was deliberate. It had to be.

Julian had been with me in Felhollow every step of the way. He knew how often I healed people, and he saw how pained it left me. Every cut, every missing memory—he had been there for them. Life and death weren't an equivalent exchange. I couldn't sacrifice a finger to create a finger. Wrights, noble or vile, didn't work like that.

To alter the course of a life, the sacrifice had to cost more than the life taken or saved, or the wrought died.

I had told Julian that often enough during one dark day when I couldn't save someone and was drowning in grief. He had hushed me and sung, rocking me like a child. He had comforted me.

But had he even been listening or just going through the motions?

The weight of his arm was still around my shoulders, sweat sticking my shirt to me. He certainly wasn't listening to me now.

I couldn't let Will's plan come to fruition. The councilors had to be stopped, but I needed their supplies. Their havens could save hundreds more.

I needed to get the havens into my hands.

"Without lying," I said to the empty hallway outside my room. "Three days before I talk to Will again. That's plenty of time."

Creek's ghost laughed and echoed. "Easier to open the Door."

"Shut up. Is everyone I've wronged going to haunt me?"

"Oh no," he said and picked his teeth with his nails. "I'm singular. A crown among crowns."

"A vile one maybe." I winced at his too-loud laughter and shoved open my door.

Alistair slouched at my desk, long legs thrown over the corner of it, and read a book balanced atop his knees. He didn't react to Creek at all.

"Lorena," said Alistair, glancing at me over his shoulder. "You're angry."

"Don't worry. I'm not angry at you."

He lifted his legs from my desk and asked, "Do you want to talk about it?"

"No." I sat on my bed. "I definitely do not."

If he knew, he'd kill them all or something equally unnecessary. Creek's laughter vanished into Carlow's room, and I peeked at Alistair's work. He only had eyes for the Door; it made moving around him easy.

"Good," he said. "If it's about Willoughby Chase, I suppose I could pardon him."

Will wouldn't even be sacrificed until right before the Door opened, and even then, if they were smart, they'd have someone open it early. It would be easier to prepare for the end of the world if they knew exactly when it was.

"I don't want to talk about him." I grabbed his journal and quill.

"Wait!" He reached for my wrist and hesitated. "Not that quill. Not that ink."

It was the water-thinned blue ink that he had used for our contract.

"Why?" I asked and handed it back to him. "What's different about this ink?"

"Everything," said Alistair, tapping the leftover ink back into the pot. He'd forgone gloves tonight, and his hands were mottled, bruise-like, with different inks. "My sister made this for me."

"I'm sorry." I rested my fingers against his shoulder.

He leaned into my hand, humming as I carded my fingers through his hair. "I use it for important things—contracts, court signings, and the like."

"That's nice," I said. I tugged at the knot of hair. "Did you sign the new law on regulations and fines yet?"

He hummed noncommittally and scratched his binding.

I ran my fingers through his hair again, catching the knot more sharply.

"The fines will make them take notice," he said, "but what does it matter if we can't shut the Door?"

Everyone was going to die. When didn't matter. As long as I could make their time before death better, I owed it to them to try.

"It'll matter a lot to anyone waiting on their employer to pay for their healing or funeral plot." I picked apart the tangle in his hair and set the smooth strands aside. "Northcott paid the Crown fifty tiens for breaking the laws when his munitions factory caught fire, and a month later, it caught fire again. It took days for my mother to die. He paid me four halfans."

"That's not enough for a healer," he murmured.

"Or a funeral plot," I said. "Cheaper, though, than keeping the factory within regulation."

"Come with me and speak on it for the next meeting." He tilted his head back to stare at me. "If your mother hadn't died, perhaps I would have met you sooner. Imagine what we could have done with that time."

Terrible things, probably.

"But you'll push it through?" I asked. "Make it law?"

"Does it concern wrought?" asked Alistair.

Workers and wrought: we were all the same, and we had

to recognize it. Wrought were forced, bound by blood and ink, to use our wrights only for the "good of Cynlira," but what we really did rarely benefited everyone. Only the peers and wealthy reaped the rewards our wrights sowed.

"I personally find it very concerning." I settled my hands on his shoulders. "Please, Alistair?"

"Fine," he said with a bark of laughter. "We could bind them to agree with your wrights, you know? My mother always wanted to do it, but since the councilors and courtiers controlled her wrights, she couldn't. She only tried once, and she nearly bled out. You, though, are unfettered."

I sat back on my bed. "Are you disappointed that I don't do things like that? Use my wrights to do everything?"

He sat next to me, right thigh to my left, and shook his head. "You do what you think is right. You know who you are, and you know what you want. My father—" He hesitated and took the glasses from his eyes. "My father had many rules, especially for my mother and me. We had to follow them, and then one day, my mother didn't. She broke the rules and took his crown. I still follow some of them. I'm not as strong as you. I am sand beneath waves, but you are a cliff edge—eternal and unyielding. You will be here long after the rest of us are gone, and you won't be drowning in regrets."

I was haunted by regrets, but I was used to them too. Creek was an old friend now.

"This monster in my veins," he said, "has given me regrets enough for a dozen lives. I fail constantly. It is unbearable."

"Sometimes failure is the only option." I reached up and brushed his hair behind his ears, tracing the little indents from his glasses. "Sometimes we fail even when we do everything right. Sometimes there are no answers."

He shook his head. "No, the world has rules. The Noble knew them and the Vile broke them. If we can figure out those rules, we can do anything."

"Alistair." I sighed. "What if, like Creek, nothing we do is ever enough? It's one of the Vile. It doesn't have to obey the rules."

"I refuse to accept failure so easily," he said. "This monster in me will be good for something."

"Maybe it's only good at bad things because monster is all you've ever called it."

My vilewright trilled, its agreement shivering through my veins.

Gray eyes full moons against the dark shadows around his eyes, Alistair stared at me and laughed. The sound died out quickly. "It's not of this world. It's a force of nature."

"It is of this world though," I said. "It's like the Door—here but not completely. It affects us unseen."

The Door's hands had been harder to see than Will's but no less real.

"It can affect us even when we're not within its boundaries." I touched my lips and tasted its red, red dirt. "It showed Safia a door she had never seen."

"But it can't affect us," said Alistair, holding up his fingers and casting the shadow of a dog on the wall. "Outside its boundary, it can only lure us. Whatever world it occupies, it can only truly get through to us in that cavern."

I brought my hand up to my shoulder. The holes in my coat from the Door were oddly spaced and burned around the edges, the threads eaten away by whatever its body was made of. It had touched me, and I hadn't been able to touch it. At least not until it had shoved its fingers inside me. I poked a finger though a hole, nail digging into my skin. My other fingers pressed painlessly against my coat.

"We are always with you," I said. "We are always watching you."

Alistair touched my hand. "Lorena?"

"It's not a Door. It's a hole or patch or hem, but it's not a Door. It's where their world is connected to ours."

"Lorena," he said, "you're not making sense."

"Here." I brought his hand to my shoulder and aligned his fingers with the holes. "Imagine the surviving Vile weren't banished anywhere, and instead the world was wrapped in cloth. Our world was separated from theirs." I stuck my hand beneath a lower, whole section of coat, wiggling my fingers, and his mouth opened. "The Door is a weakening patch connecting our side of the cloth to theirs."

Alistair pushed his fingers through the holes and gripped my shoulder. A small noise escaped his throat.

"The Vile didn't go anywhere," I said. "The Door isn't a door. That's just how we perceive it, or the only way our mortal minds can perceive it. How it wants us to perceive it? It's a threadbare part of the cloth threatening to unravel completely."

I pushed my fingers against my coat, and he laid his free hand across the fabric. Even through the cloth, I could feel him tremble.

"Our vilewrights are bound to us, like buttons, so they can interact with us without being seen."

Alistair nodded. "The Vile, not attached, cannot. Of course, this was always their world before it was ours. The banishment of the Noble and Vile just kept them from interfering with us."

I grabbed his hand, drew a circle on his palm, and said, "The world."

I drew another circle around it, and he inhaled.

"The fabric," he said.

"And the Door." I drew a single line through the top of both circles, pinning the outer one to the inner like one would a brooch to a coat. "With the Vile outside it."

Nowhere in Cynlira would be safe when the Door opened. The Vile wouldn't spill out of Mori; they would simply appear. Everywhere. All at once.

If Will went through with his plans, they would fail. There

would be no time to flee to the havens once word got out the Door was open.

If I was right.

"We need to verify this," I said. "Let's start testing now."

Alistair took my face in both his hands and laid his forehead against mine. His lips skimmed my nose. "I knew we would do great things."

thirty-two

WE COULD ONLY DO SO MUCH IN THE FACE OF such intangible, untestable knowledge. The Door was a Vile, we had already known that, but to consider that the Vile were with us at all times and only separated by a thin membrane unknown to this world was something else entirely. Alistair was infatuated with the idea, but I could not think of any way to test it. The fact that it ruined part of Will's plan, though, was enough. I had to find a way to use it.

Basil, Carlow, and I had left Alistair in the cavern muttering over a contract. I blinked into the midmorning sun, unable to believe we had spent all day and night down there, and Basil groaned. Carlow paced the garden path.

"It's a negative," Carlow said. She spun around, her goggles smacking against her chest. The glass caught the light. "We can't prove a negative."

In the reflection of her goggles stood three figures.

I spun. There was no one behind Basil and me.

"What's wrong?" Basil asked, elbowing my side.

"I don't know," I said. "Carlow, your goggles magic at all? Can I see them?"

"They're only glass." She pulled them over her head and held them out. "Won't shatter when hit, only crack."

I held them up to the light. In my own reflection, the black of my eye, reached a finger, and I knew it was the Door's. I tossed Carlow's goggles back to her.

"The Door makes us all see things," she said. "I see Creek constantly."

I nodded. "I think it's angry at me."

"Odd," said Carlow. "Creek's never angry with me these days. It's how I know it's not him."

The chime of a great bell racked the garden. Basil grabbed my hand, their fingers lacing through mine. Carlow looked toward the city.

"Fire," she said. "That's the bell for a fire in the city."

I froze. I'd heard it in the days before my mother died. I'd heard it, still echoing, as she lay burned and barely breathing in her bed. I'd dreamed of it every day I couldn't heal her enough.

"We have to help," I said and choked. "We have to."

I ran, Basil at my heels. We tasted it first, acrid smoke too dispersed to see but too bitter to ignore. It boiled and thickened over the city, a gray-black fog sticking to everything, and the stench of burning flesh and gunpowder, urine and sulfur, spilled through the streets. I led Basil through the familiar listing lanes, and folks ran every which way, crying for water and healers. The buildings were too close. Even ones blocks from the fire smoked with drifting cinders. The smoke was thick as water by the time we made it to the Wallows.

The fire was in the first building of a munitions factory. The only exit was overrun. A noblewrought kid far too young for the job they'd been given was trying to keep the front doorway from collapsing.

Basil dove into the crowd and yanked the noblewrought aside before they could finish their contract. They shoved the kid to me. Basil's lips moved, and they brought their shaking hands together. Stones rose from the ground at their feet and bolstered the doorway. The dirt beneath them sunk.

"They tell you anything?" I asked the kid, dragging them away.

"To use stone. There's plenty in the ground, but I don't know how to do that." The noblewrought kid coughed, and the sigil to Life on their chest spurted blood. "None of my contracts can fix this. I don't know how to use stone."

I wiped their face off with my coat. "You work in there?"

"Yeah," they said, "but I just started. I don't know how—"

"It's fine. Listen—have you heard an explosion?"

They shook their head.

"Do you know which building stores the loaded shells?" I asked, glancing at Basil. They were almost lost behind the wall of people and smoke. "Or the gunpowder?"

"It's around back," they whispered. "It's close."

Of course it was. Everything in the Wallows was crowded. That was why the factories and a canal fed by the Tongue separated it from Norwel district.

"Go help any healers you find." I shoved the kid back. "Basil?"

"Lore! Here!" They waved at me over the heads of the crowd. Their eyes were bloodshot, and the binding at their chest wept ink and blood. "I can maybe keep the building from collapsing, but I can't use oxygen in my contracts. It's not allowed."

Of course. Better to disallow all noblewrought from creating it lest one bound to Life created a bubble in a vein. These bindings were a scourge. Without them, the noblewrought could have stopped the fire completely.

But no—these lives were necessary sacrifices to ensure no wrought ever harmed anyone.

"Basil," I shouted. "What makes gunpowder work?"

They swayed. "Saltpeter. It creates oxygen when hot, and—"

Noblewrought had created the gunpowder used these days, and water wouldn't render it harmless. Oxygen kept the fire alive, but destroying it would leave everyone breathless. The sacrifice for that much destruction would be too large anyway.

Carlow's sharp voice cut through the screams. "Move! I have an idea."

Basil and I turned. Carlow rolled a metal barrel toward the fire, soldiers and healers trying to stop her. She pushed them off and kicked the barrel onward, a white crystalline powder leaking from one end. Basil hissed.

"Did you rob a soap maker?" I screamed.

"Yes!" Carlow, binding bleeding freely, laughed. "How much ammonia and sulfur do you think is in there?"

"What?" Basil grabbed her arm. "You can't."

"At least this curse is good for something," said Carlow.

She closed her eyes, and the power from her noblewrought rippled over me. My wrights whined, and Basil winced. The powder Carlow had brought with her vanished, her noblewright taking it for whatever she was creating, and a pale-yellow snow settled over the front half of the building. It flowed when it hit the flames, sinking into every burning crack.

"Gods," I muttered. "Carlow, what did you—"

She laughed and collapsed.

"We're not allowed to do major chemical alterations." Basil wrapped one arm around Carlow and tried to pull her away. "Her binding killed her."

"All the binders, those councilors and courtiers, should burn." I grabbed Carlow's legs and helped carry her to the gathering of healers a block away. "The back's still burning. We have to stop it before it hits the loaded shells."

Basil blanched. "Shit."

I scanned the crowd. There had to be someone here who could help, someone who could do anything. I needed a sacrifice, more than blood or memories, to destroy the fire or its oxygen. Because of their bindings, the wrought couldn't do anything. The wealthy had ensured the common folk of Cynlira could never save themselves.

Basil, red hair black with ash and cheeks pink with shining

burns, dragged another survivor from the wreckage. They brushed the woman's brittle hair from her face and listened to her lungs. Their eyes said what they couldn't.

I approached slowly, bile rising in me.

"I'm sorry," Basil was saying. "I can't heal this, but one of Safia's teachers might be able to help."

It was a kind might. Half the woman's chest had burned away.

"I'll get one of the healers." Basil patted her unburned hand. "They can take the pain away."

"Wait," I said and knelt next to the woman. "I can do it."

"Thank you," said Basil, darting off to help elsewhere.

I took the woman's uninjured hand. Her eyes rolled to me, the question in them obvious.

"I'm not a healer, but I'm not bound either, so I can make sure nothing hurts you," I said. "One of the healers might be able to help, but the sacrifice required is probably more than their binding allows. I know I'd have to near kill myself to do it."

She dragged her trembling fingers down the back of my hand. Five jagged lines. An understanding.

"I can keep the shells from exploding and put the fire out, but it requires a sacrifice. One I won't ask for. I can guarantee it will work, though, and I've seen what the healers can and can't do. My mother died in a fire like this, Northcott's years ago, but she held on for days. It wasn't worth it. It was painful. She told me not to heal her, and I should've listened."

She laced her fingers with mine.

"I need to know where the shells are," I said. "Do you understand what I'm saying?"

She nodded, pulled away, and raised her hand to point to a large shed with locked doors off to the side of the factory. It was unmarked and wedged between two identical buildings.

"Thank you," I whispered.

Destroy her sense of pain. Destroy the oxygen near the fire until it dies.

My vilewright, hungry and frantic, swept toward the flames. They went out all at once, as if a single breath had snuffed them, and I groaned. My vilewright returned, carrying the scent of blood and knee-buckling exhaustion to me. I bowed over the woman.

Her finger dug into my arm.

"I wanted you to see it," I said and forced myself up. "It's your doing. You saved them."

She stared up at me with wide eyes, and I couldn't help but see my mother in them. I'd never been able to begin fresh like Northcott, who'd paid for his crimes with paltry fines. I'd never recovered. So many hadn't. Grief never healed. It scarred.

Fines were never enough.

"Are you ready?" I cupped her face in trembling hands. "Anything you need me to know? Anything to tell your loved ones?"

She touched her heart and dragged her fingers down my face, leaving five broken lines of blood and ash. She cut a sixth line across them.

"I'll be quick," I said and pinched her cheek. "This hurt?"

She shook her head slowly, and I twisted her neck just so, snapping her neck below the stem. I knew death far too well.

Take her as sacrifice.

The woman exhaled once, and I stayed with her long after my vilewright passed through her. Wallowers moved around me, racing into the building despite the pockets of flame still smoldering. I drew Death's sigil across the woman's face and winced at the pounding ache in my head. My vilewright grumbled.

Sacrifices were never enough.

Create oxygen for the survivors as quickly as you can, I prayed, *and take my voice, my wakefulness, my sleep. Take something that won't kill me and let them live.*

My noblewright engulfed me, and my breaths quickened. My chest tightened. It wasn't enough.

My mother. That last day before the accident when she called me to supper. Take my last memory of her.

My noblewright trilled and ripped away. Screams and sobs echoed across the wreckage. The skeleton of the building cracked.

I was a child again, standing in the ashes of my mother's factory and dragging her home to save. The Wallows never changed. Cynlira never changed. It would always demand we save ourselves through suffering.

I'd tried to get Alistair to make the councilors and courtiers see reason, but I would never be able to. They were beyond it. They were above it.

"I can't," I said and choked. "No one can fix Cynlira."

Nothing would ever be enough.

thirty-three

I AWOKE IN A BED, SWADDLED IN BLANKETS AND CON-
fusion. A bitter taste stuck to every nook of my mouth, and
fingers curled around my ankle. My hands stuck to my clothes,
peeling away slowly. Everything hurt.

"You shouldn't sit up," said Alistair from near my feet. The
fingers on my ankle tightened.

I sat up and swallowed back the nausea. "You shouldn't
have put off signing the safety regulations law."

I lunged, pinning him to the bed. The ashes of the dead and
dying and the knowledge of how little they were worth to the
people meant to represent them clung to my skin, and they
left ghastly smears along his skin and clothes. Alistair's hands
flexed near my sides.

"I told you to deal with the safety regulations," I said. "You
didn't. I'm done. Why keep me here if you don't listen to me?"

It wasn't enough to not be bad; a person had to be actively
good. They had to try to do good. Apathy was as bad as villainy,
and it would destroy this world. I'd been wrong.

"I shouldn't have stayed," I said and let him go. I hadn't
thought I'd be able to say those words. "I thought you wanted
me here. You clearly don't."

His eyes widened. He clutched my shirt, knuckles against
my ribs. "No, no, no, no. What do you mean?"

"Will's guilty. We have no contract. You don't take what I say seriously." I shook his grip from me. "I've no reason to stay."

"We'll write a new one." Alistair tumbled off the bed after me, and his fingers tangled in my filthy shirt. "It wasn't about the Door. It wasn't important."

"It was important to me."

"I'll fix it," he said. "Please, Lorena. I'll pardon Will. I'll talk to the court and council. I'll put you in charge of them. Whatever you say, I'll do. Just stay."

Oh, now that I was threatening to leave, he could do it? How little he valued what I needed, but how perfect for me.

"In charge of the council?" I asked, letting his arms wrap around my waist. "You'll sign what I set in front of you? No more forgetting?"

Will's plan depended on Alistair not noticing the councilors prepping for the end of the world, and my new plan hinged on Alistair leaving it up to me. I needed those safe havens.

The Lirans cast aside by their leaders deserved them.

"No more," said Alistair, his mouth pressed to the crown of my head. "With you, I have learned more about the Door in weeks than I have in years. You understand it like I do. You understand the Vile."

"I thought I did," I murmured and touched his hands. "I think I've been wrong about a lot of things."

Apathy wasn't better than disdain. I couldn't fix Cynlira by moving the peers and manipulating Alistair. Cynlira had made them what they were today and taught them to think as they did, relegating people to profits. The problem with Cynlira wasn't its people or the Door. It was Cynlira itself.

This country was a machine using us all until we broke. The peerage pulling the levers profited, and the council, little more than levers themselves, stayed well-oiled and conditioned so they could keep working us to death. Alistair was no more than a golden cog, and he could be replaced. Any peer taken out would be. The factory would be rebuilt within a month.

The machine that was Cynlira had to be destroyed. There were too many bad pieces in an already terrible system.

"Help me get dressed," I said. "We're going to care for the dead."

Blood stained the front of my dress. Alistair brought me a wet cloth, turning away as I washed. I didn't even know the woman's name, the one I'd sacrificed, and it didn't matter. The anger that had always been in me, smoldering ever since my mother's life had faded, would never burn out. There was always another factory. There was always a necessary sacrifice.

"Did you think to ask how many died?" I rubbed the smooth skin of my chest and slipped into a clean dress, doing up the buttons in the front. My noblewright was quiet and still against my back. "Alistair?"

"No," he said softly. "I didn't."

I touched his shoulder, and he helped me into my coat.

"Do you know the name of the vilewright Will hired to kill you?" I asked.

He shook his head. "I am a monster, Lorena. Do you really need more evidence of that?"

"I didn't ask her either." I handed him my second greatcoat. "Wear this."

We left the palace grounds with no guards save for Hana and walked across Mori to the Wallows. Alistair didn't look like His Excellency without a carriage, soldiers, or white greatcoat stamped with Chaos's sigil. No one paid us much mind.

The talk of the fire was too interesting anyway.

By the time we reached the Wallows, the building had been reinforced, and noblewrought were searching the wreckage. The healers had set up a small tent in a nearby building. Safia spotted Hana right away.

"Nineteen dead," she said, bandaged hands clutched in her lap. "If you've got time, we could use you."

"How much help do you need?" I asked.

Safia startled, seeing Alistair and me for the first time. She bowed her head. "A healer. I'm still in training, and the factory's healer had only just started. The healing houses from here to the Works are overrun."

I glanced at Alistair.

"Hana," he said, "acquire every available noblewrought bound to Life in Mori. I don't care how trained they are. Get them here."

"Right away," she stuttered. "Your Excellency."

"Where are the dead?" I asked and tapped my coat. "We'll take care of them."

Safia pointed to a small, run-down church barely across the watery border with Formet. We made our way there, waving once to Basil and Mack helping a group repair homes near the factory, and I claimed a small table at the back of the room. Alistair frowned when I rolled up his trousers. He didn't complain about washing the corpses clean though.

I pulled back the canvas covering an unidentified corpse—burned flesh, black lips, damaged lungs. I propped them up and pierced two veins with hollow needles. Their blood was still warm.

I watched Alistair while I waited. He was washing a child no older than ten and listening—it was clear from his face that each sound was flowing in one ear and out the other—to their father sob.

I pulled the canvas from the second corpse. Franziska Carlow, very much alive, blinked up at me.

"Adler," said Carlow. "How many dead?"

I dropped the canvas back over her.

She growled, sat up, and vomited in her lap.

"Eighteen now that we're not counting you." I pushed her

shirt aside and studied her binding. Her white ribs peeked out behind the raw flesh. "How are you feeling?"

"Like Shearwill killed me for saving lives." Carlow shimmied out of her coat and dress, leaving them in a sopping puddle in the funeral rites pool, and I wrapped her in my coat. "Where's Baines?"

"Either still helping with repairs or resting," I said and took her by the arm. "Alistair, I'm taking Carlow to the healers. Will you be all right here?"

He nodded and brushed the last of the ash from the child's hair. "Go."

Carlow stared at him like she'd never seen him before and didn't even think to pull away from me.

"Come on." I wrapped one arm around Carlow to keep us both standing. "I need to talk to y'all anyway."

We made it to the healer's house without falling down. Mack was sitting against a wall in the back, his dark skin ashy. Basil was lying on the floor, their head in his lap, and staring at the ceiling. I dropped Carlow next to Basil and collapsed near Mack. He grabbed my hand.

"We're not doing it, right?" he asked.

"No, we're not, and we're not letting them do it either." I laid my cheek against his shoulder. "You still staying at Noshwright?"

"For now," he said. "Doesn't feel very welcoming though."

Safia, doubled over in her chair, motioned for Hana to help her over, and I waited for them.

"The factory's healer nearly killed themself trying to save people," said Safia, not even lifting her head. "They'll be touch and go for a day."

"Leave them to the others," Hana said and rubbed her back. "You're half-dead too."

"You all awake enough for a chat?" I asked. "I'll make it quick."

Basil cracked one eye open. "Very quick."

"Willoughby Chase, the man I came here for, was attempting to assassinate Alistair to prevent him from closing the Door. The council wants it opened," I whispered. "They've been hoarding everything they need for survival and buying up old churches to live in once the Vile are here."

Safia groaned into her arms, and Carlow punched the wall.

"They can't possibly have enough space for everyone," she said. "The population of Mori alone..."

"They're not planning on saving everyone," Mack said. "They're planning on saving themselves."

"They're no better than the peers." Safia lifted her head, the dark coils of her hair a veil, and sobbed. "We're bound to them. They'll make us help them, won't they?"

"That's their plan, yes." I swallowed, throat dry, the full weight of the last few days sitting in my chest, and took a deep breath. It tasted of blood and burnt flesh. "But I have another, and I would like all of you to trust me. Prepare yourselves for the Door opening. Trust me to deal with the council. Please."

"You can't lie to us." Carlow laughed. "Of course we trust you."

It was laughable—the court and council could've prevented this all with their money and resources, but instead they had opted to save themselves and their power every single time. If they had put their minds to it, they could've saved everyone. They could've been heroes, but they wouldn't have been rich. They would rather kill everyone than give up even a pinch of power.

"If the Sundered Crown hadn't taken my ability to lie," I said, "none of this might've happened."

Carlow laughed until she passed out, and the rest of us quieted after that. Hana snored softly, her head in Safia's lap. My vilewright was little more than a soft pressure against my chest. I was nodding off when Alistair found us.

"What now?" he asked and knelt at my feet. "What do you need?"

The property of the councilors in my control, but there was only one way to do that without killing them all.

The wrought unbound from the councilors and courtiers and free to use their wrights however they pleased, but only killing the twenty-five would do that.

The necessary sacrifice to save most of Cynlira after the Door opened.

But fear kept me from speaking it. The Sundered Crown's magic would force me to face how many I was willing to kill.

I had always been a graveyard so no one else needed to be.

"Only three things, small things in the grand scheme of it all," I said. "Trust me."

thirty-four

Y THREE DAYS WERE UP. WILL'S TRIAL WAS
tomorrow. A taut, tearing soreness lingered in my
shoulders and arms, exhaustion slowing my steps. I stumbled
around my room and shook out my bed, looking for Julian's
coat. Creek's ghost watched from the desk.

"I could help if I knew what you were looking for?" he said,
a poppy blooming blood red from the wound on his chest.

I kicked my bed. "You're a figment of my guilt. You only
know what I know."

"And it's so little." He sighed and flicked a leaf at me. "Go to
the very bottom."

I lowered myself to the floor and stared under the bed.
Nothing.

"Go back as far as you can," he said, "and open the door."

I reached beneath it. My fingers collided with the wall, and
a slat of wood fell aside. Dried flowers and spiders tumbled out.
I ripped my hand away.

"Where's my coat, you ass?" I asked, but Creek's ghost was
gone.

A knock at the door nearly interrupted my tirade. I'd have
to go to Noshwright without the coat.

"Come in!"

"I need to talk to you." Hana Worth, her uniform fresh and

her bandages clean, shut the door behind her and leaned against it. "You going to kill Alistair to save Will?"

I snorted. "No."

She hadn't been specific enough, and that was hardly my fault.

"You want to elaborate then?" she asked. "You're up to something. He made you the representative of the Crown in charge of council matters this morning."

Perfect timing.

"You've caught me in the middle of plotting his death." I held out my arms for shackling and slumped. Magic pricked my tongue. "I'm going to make sure the council attempts to assassinate him."

Her eyes narrowed.

"I'll answer your question if you answer one of mine," I said and dropped my hands at her raised brow. "Why are you his sacrificial guard?"

"Because I've met the rest of the court, and he's better than who'd inherit it," she said. "Why didn't you save Willoughby Chase?"

"I don't want to." I laughed. "Don't worry. The council won't kill Alistair."

Perhaps the truth *was* freeing.

"I was never worried for him." Hana grinned, crooked and thin. "You said 'attempt.'"

I left for Noshwright without another word, praying Mack was there. This was dangerous, the riskiest thing I'd done since fleeing Mori with no clue where to go. Mack was one of the only people I trusted to understand what I was doing and why. I nearly cried when I knocked on the door and he answered.

"I have an idea," I said, hugging him close. "Trust me. Please."

"Always," he said. "It's killing me Julian's going for it, but with Will's trial, he thinks this is the Chase legacy. This!"

Inside Will's quarters were half the council. Lankin Northcott sat on Will's right, the sigil on his chest bared. Julian sat on Will's other side, and he rose to greet me, shaking off his father's hand. I let him embrace me and rubbed his arm. He patted a stool behind his chair.

"Willoughby," drawled Northcott, "is this not the girl working for His Excellency?"

I swallowed my pride and bowed my head to him. "Isn't that why you need me? I can help you kill him, or you can try again without my help."

One of the other councilors looked me up and down. "You're the girl the Sundered Crown recruited, aren't you?"

"She didn't recruit me." I unbuttoned my waistcoat and then my shirt, tugging them aside to show off the empty stretch of skin over my heart. "I'm dualwrought. I agreed to work for Alistair Wyrslaine in exchange for Will getting a fair trial."

"Unbound?" Northcott licked his lips, fingers brushing his sigil, and he listed toward me. "The Sundered Crown certainly kept that fact to herself."

"Understandable," said a councilor I didn't know, "but unbound wrought are rare and unpredictable."

"As well as untrained," Northcott said.

I nodded, grinding my teeth to keep my smile up, and refastened my clothes.

"She's been a friend of the family for near a decade and came here for me. Hear her out," Will said.

"Thanks," I said in the most Felfolk accent I could. People always underestimated country drawls, and it was part of why Will could get away with so much. "I can't lie. Falsities can't get past my teeth without snapping my mouth shut, because the Sundered Crown didn't want me lying to her, but I'm unbound and can do more than any wrought you've ever hired to kill Alistair. I just have one question before we start."

Julian smiled consolingly, his hand on my knee. "Course."

"Are you certain that you can't save more people?" I asked. It was only fair I give them a chance.

"My dear girl, we have spent our lives studying economics and running businesses. These plans have been in the making for the last twelve years," said the councilor across from Northcott. "Ten years is the optimal amount of time to pass before we retake the land. It will ensure that enough die so as to allow us to rule but not so many that the nation crumbles."

"Once the Door opens, we wouldn't even have time to move everyone," said Julian with a shrug.

They would have no time. When the Door opened, the Vile would be suddenly standing next to them.

"I had to be sure." I shrugged. What a terrible answer to mass murder. "All right. First order of business: you should kill Alistair at your trial."

Will's brows rose to his hairline. "You think you can keep me alive?"

"I think I can keep you from being sacrificed to the Door," I said. "I won't promise survival to anyone."

"All of us will be there," said Northcott.

I inclined my head to him. "You'll outnumber him and any soldiers. I'll take care of any bullets."

They didn't even bother asking me whose.

"And how do we kill him?" Julian asked. "Will you do it?"

"No. You're going to shoot him."

Julian sucked in a breath, and Northcott laughed. Lying wasn't necessary; the silence that followed my statement told them what they wanted to hear.

"He killed the Sundered Crown with a needle when a knight couldn't even do it with a sword," said Will, his eyes narrowed at me. "How will this time be any different?"

"That's the problem with assassinations—you think too singularly," I said. "Alistair Wyrslaine is only one person. Like his mother, his vilewright can only do so much at once. If you all shoot at him, he can't stop every bullet on his own. Wrights take time to work. Do you remember how long the Sundered Crown was down when Beatrice wounded her?"

All of it was the truth, but not all of it was honest. Alistair was so desperate to be understood that I knew every vulnerability of his vilewright. My own hummed unhappily.

Northcott nodded. "We thought she was dead, and then she wasn't."

"It took so long because her wrights took that long to work. Alistair cannot stop every bullet alone." I nudged Julian with my foot. "Alistair will die. Will won't be sacrificed to the Door."

Not a single one of them asked me to specify what I meant.

"Kill the Crown, save my father, and open the Door on our own terms?" Julian glanced at Will. "I'm willing."

"The contract I signed with him forbade us from hurting each other. All I can provide is information and an opening. I will distract him. You shoot at him then," I said and tapped Julian's knee. It was all true. The contract had forbidden us from hurting each other—until Alistair destroyed it. "Use your crossbow if you can get it in. He would have to use a different contract for it. I'm assuming you have a way to get your weapons into the courtroom?"

"Simple," said Northcott. "The majority of the soldiers are already ours."

Were they loyal to this plan, or were they loyal to their job? A web to untangle after.

"I admit," said Will, "this is preferable to dying."

"Alistair will not pardon you," I said. My tongue burned. It wasn't a lie, but it wasn't the full truth.

Will smirked. "Did you ask?"

"I did," I said, "and he refused."

That conversation felt like decades ago, but it served me well now.

Northcott chuckled and patted his knee. "You've no need for a pardon if this succeeds."

"True," said Will. "You won't stop our assassination?"

"No." I smiled, wide and true. "If you're done trying to catch me with the truth, we have a deal."

We still had time until the Door opened, but it would be better if I knew when exactly it would open. But first, I needed access to every councilor's safe havens and supplies. Letting Will go to his death with a guilty verdict would have gotten me only his. If tomorrow went well, I—as the representative of the Crown in charge of council matters—would own the property of every councilor found guilty of treason.

"Tomorrow," said Will and held out his hand. "We lead the way for a new, better Cynlira with your help."

I took it, and all I could remember was the feel of it against my teeth. "I will lead Alistair Wyrslaine to his death."

thirty-five

I SPENT THE EVENING IN THE CAVES WITH ALISTAIR, knees pressed together and fingers slick with ink, going over every test, contract, and history involving the Door. We both knew it was pointless, but he couldn't give up. He so desperately wanted to be special.

"Every text says the same thing—the only way to entice a Vile into a deal is to offer up lives in some form or fashion." I tugged the book from his hands and closed it. "It's one of the Vile, Alistair. You may be the cleverest boy in the world, but you're still only a mortal playing with immortal things."

"Drawing lots is the most logical route." He glanced at me, relaxing at my smile. "Those with skills unnecessary for the survival of Cynlira would submit their names, and the sacrifices would be randomly selected. What would we do if all our healers were part of the sacrificed? No, it would have to be based on skill, and then those within the draw would have an equal chance of survival."

I sighed. I should have known not to hope by now.

"You're disappointed," he said.

I said nothing, and he had his answer.

"I understand how you reached that conclusion," I said, "but surely you know that those with the money and time to master the skills would be exempt from the lots. It wouldn't be fair at all."

"You've been disappointed quite a bit lately." He angled away from me. "Why stay?"

I grabbed his chair and turned him back to me. "For ages, people thought bad smells caused illnesses."

"Yes?" His brows arched over his glasses. He had removed his coat, but the glasses never came off down here. "What does that have to do with anything?"

"Their logic was sound, but they were still wrong."

"Oh." He sneered and snapped his tongue against the back of his teeth. "My logic can't be infallible because I am fallible. That's an excuse."

I shrugged. "Whoever defines worth will define who survives, and that definition is not fixed."

He stared at me, tired eyes hooded and heavy, and held out his hand. "I don't want to kill that many people anyway. I want to create a better solution."

He wanted to outsmart the Door, but I laced our fingers.

"I know," I said. "You created a new way to sacrifice when you were a child. Surely, you have some ideas about this you aren't sharing?"

Using intangible sacrifices wasn't his creation, but considering what was coming, it was only fair I treat him nicely.

"They're untested." His lips crooked up, and he tugged me closer. "But I have a few."

He spoke endlessly. It was as if we were back in that carriage weeks ago, our contract unwritten and no words existing between us. Except this time, I understood all of what he said, and he caught himself, backtracking to explain academic references I didn't know. He never made it my fault for not knowing things. There was a tenderness in trusting another person to understand the threads of your thoughts.

For all of Alistair's flaws, he did respect me. It was everyone he didn't I worried for.

"You know," I said, uncrossing my legs. I had taken a seat

on the desk halfway through his latest ramble, and my knees were even with his chest. "Undertakers were all vilewrought back in the old days because deaths were a necessary sacrifice for life. People thought dying meant someone else could live."

"That never made sense to me." He stifled a yawn and turned so that my feet were in his lap. His fingers picked at my laces. "We know sacrifices aren't equivalent. You can't trade a life for a life."

"Because we like explaining things," I said and tapped his nose. "As hard as you pretend otherwise, you are very mortal."

"I could hardly pretend to be immortal." He cracked his neck and rolled his shoulders back, skin thin as his fancy paper stretching across the blue veins of his throat. How fragile we were. "You should sleep."

"So should you." I plucked his glasses from his face and dropped them on mine. "Will you? Will he?"

His vilewright, always so shy, peeked over his shoulder.

"I want to keep reading." His fingers tightened around my ankle. "If I sleep, I'll have to prepare for tomorrow. It's so tedious."

"What if I help?" Tomorrow, everything would change, especially between us, and it was only fair that I give him what he wanted tonight. Everything would come to fruition or fall to rot. "We can talk. Believe it or not, I like talking to you."

He didn't treat me like I was only Lorena Adler, undertaker and outsider. Carlow and Basil were wonderful, but even they talked over me sometimes when discussing magic. It would have been easy to love Alistair. I wanted to love him, but what he had done and what he had allowed to be done tainted all the soft affection between us. So many people were valuing me for my wrights. It was nice to feel like he valued me.

"Considering what my mother did, I have to believe you." He stood and helped me from the table. "Do you want... Well, we would have to go to my quarters."

I pulled my legs from his lap and slipped from the desk. "I would like to judge how our Vilewrought Crown lives."

No one had settled on a moniker for him yet.

He flushed. The halls were dim and empty, a few servants flitting about. Hana, a constant shadow behind us, walked silently, and Alistair carried on our conversation in a whisper as he led me toward the same wing as his study. His quarters were at the end of a high hall hung with portraits, their eyes a weight at the back of my neck. Alistair opened the door and ushered me inside. A painted Sundered Crown glared down at us. Hana stayed in the hall.

Crowns lived like the rest of us, only bigger and gilded. The room had an entry hall like a house would have had, and Alistair left his shoes and coat in a pile by the door. A shelf with telescopes, withies, books, swan-feather quills, statues, and two stuffed rabbits loomed over one wall. There wasn't a speck of dust anywhere, and everything had its own place. It was more museum than home.

"I can have a chair—"

"Alistair," I said quickly, staring at him over my shoulder. "Really?"

It was hard to be scared of this barefoot boy wringing his hands at the impropriety of it all.

"You always treat my furniture like chairs, so I'm going to repay the favor," I said.

Chairs were too confined and rigid. I wanted grounding and sprawling freedom. I wanted to be able to enjoy being understood so well by someone without any of the expectations that went with it. Intimacy without expectations was a luxury. "Unless it bothers you?" I raised one brow like he always did. "Or you had other plans, in which case I'll be leaving."

"No, thank you," he said and wrinkled his nose. "The last time I had other plans was two years ago, and he's half the country away, thank you very much."

He grabbed my hand and pulled me through a series of rooms, each more ornate than the last, and laughed when my eyes went wide at the walls lined not with tapestries and portraits but hand-scrawled notes and maps.

"You can read them later," he said.

His bed was the only furniture in the final room. I sat on the edge, pulling a book from beneath a quilt. He stared at me as if he had never seen me before.

"No shoes on the bed," he muttered and tugged off my boots. "I need to shave, wash my face, and go over my notes for tomorrow."

"I can help with some of that." I followed him into a small washroom with an extravagant copper tub, cushioned bench, and wide mirror. "Sit."

"Really?" he asked but sat.

"Really." I dampened a cloth and found his shaving tackle. "Do you trust me?"

"Of course," he said, "but have you done this before?"

I laid my empty hand against his cheek and tilted his head back till his neck was arched and bare. "Only to the dead."

He laughed.

I pressed both of my hands into his cheeks to warm his skin. He shuddered, pink pooling along his cheekbones and tips of his ears. I tapped his nose and gently ran my fingers in two circles up his nose and along his brows. I pulled away, and his face moved with my hands.

"Still," I said and moved his head back till his crown was against my stomach. I spread the lather across his cheeks.

He closed his eyes. "What was your first contract?"

"My mother got hurt." I ran my thumb across his mouth and flicked the soap away. "I wanted to heal her. Only managed to stop the bleeding, but I was thrilled."

"I did the same thing," he said. "Different reasons, of course. It was against the rules to use wrights without permission on the grounds then, and my mother seemed so smart. I didn't want to fail when I showed her."

"Alistair." I picked up the blade. "Why were rules so important?"

"My mother made up most of them," he said softly. "It was like a game when we were children, but after everything, I realized it was to make sure my father didn't get angry at us."

"She was protecting you." I swept the blade down his cheek, and the scrape of metal against skin echoed in the silence. "Alistair, what I did—"

"You were right. She was dangerous in the worst ways." He opened one eye. "Can we not talk about this?"

"Of course."

His eyes fluttered shut. I worked in long, steady strokes. Layers of soap peeled away from his cheeks, and softly, I touched his jaw. The skin of his neck pulled taut, and he gripped his thighs. Here, too, I went slow, fingers bracing his chin as the blade slipped down his throat. He never flinched, and I never nicked him. I checked my job with the back of my empty hand.

"Why did you never use your wrights?" he asked, one of his hands reaching back to touch me.

I set aside the blade and cleaned his face. "My mother was afraid the Sundered Crown would find me. I wanted to be invisible. I wanted a life that wasn't about what I could do for other people."

"That sounds nice," he whispered. He grabbed my hand, led me to the bed, and set me on its edge. "We should talk. Not about the Door. Just about us."

"You have things to do," I said, one hand still in his. "Doors to investigate and people to sacrifice."

He folded himself at my feet, his cheek pressed against my knee. "Do you ever think about killing me like we did my mother?"

We—such a simple little word.

"No," I said and pulled him onto the bed next to me. "It would be a waste."

He wrapped one arm around me and laid his head on my chest. "Sometimes I think the same thing about you. What else are you thinking, Lorena Adler? Tell me everything."

"Fine, but I want to hear about you."

"Hardly an equivalent trade," he muttered, but he couldn't hide his shiver. "Do you think I'm a bad person?"

"Yes." I threaded my fingers through his hair. "I do."

He sighed. "You're probably right."

thirty-six

THE MORNING OF WILL'S TRIAL DAWNED RED AND bright. The color bled through the thin vents in the top corner of the room, creeping along the bed until I pried myself from Alistair's sleeping grip. We had turned in our sleep. His head was nestled against my calf, and mine was pressed against the arc of his foot. Not once in the night had he expected more.

"Don't leave," he mumbled. The warmth of his breath against my thigh shuddered up my spine.

I tugged his toe. "We have to get ready."

I left him to get dressed, the soft rustle of the palace coming alive only adding to my anxiety. So many people. So many potential deaths.

This would go right. This had to go right.

When I entered the courtroom, there in the seat beside Will was Julian. Will was bent to speak softly in Julian's ear, and Julian's gaze swept over me. All twenty-five councilors were present, and as I made my way to Julian, I counted each councilor with a sigil displayed on their chest. All twelve were here, and I sat next to Julian with a soft smile. The soldiers around the room weren't in Wyrslaine red and black. I touched his arm.

"How are you?" I asked him, not looking at Will.

If Will and the councilors believed in their purpose enough to kill for it, then they could die for it. They could be the sacrifices for once.

"Good," said Julian. He grabbed my hand and squeezed, smiling as if the last few weeks hadn't happened at all. "I miss you. I miss us. I feel like I'm not myself."

I didn't feel like myself either, but this was necessary for all of us and not just some of us.

"Me too." We'd been such good friends, and the Julian sitting next to me now wasn't the Julian I had loved at all. Cynlira had changed him.

Or me. This plan had opened him up and showed me the darkness in him, and now it was all I could see. My best friend was gone. The boy I'd loved was gone.

Cynlira stripped us of control till we broke ourselves down piece by piece, sacrifice by sacrifice, workday by workday, to feel even a little in control. The world depended on our self-sacrifice and harm. As long as we were struggling against each new loss of some part of ourselves, we weren't fighting against Cynlira. As long as we weren't working together, we couldn't fight.

It couldn't continue. We didn't deserve this pain.

"We're so close that I can taste it," whispered Julian.

The world had taught us to swallow our honor and eat each other to survive, but it was always the rich and powerful who dined on us. The fruits of our labors were always theirs first. It was always Will Chase and his ilk feasting, telling us that if we were very, very good, one day we might be allowed a taste. They pitted us against each other so that we didn't turn our teeth on them. They made us think we needed them and the scraps they threw us. We didn't.

"Me too," I said and kissed his cheek. "Goodbye, Julian."

But he only had eyes for his father.

I took a spot behind Northcott. Alistair entered a short while later. He wore his crown atop tangled hair, the binding over his heart oozing slightly. He must've started working after I left, only remembering this with enough time to don the marks of his station and not clean clothes, and he scowled through the introductions. He straightened his glasses constantly during the opening talks, his mind wandering. I didn't understand how those who lived here feared him.

He was so easy to read.

Create a bar through the two doors, keeping them locked and shut, and take my doubt.

It was best to go into this clear-eyed and certain. And, of course, there could be no interruptions or escapees.

"Willoughby Chase," said Alistair from his seat before the full council, "how do you plead?"

I slipped the penknife from my pocket and shifted toward Northcott. He'd a six-shooter in his lap.

"Guilty," said Will, rising to his feet.

Destroy as many bullets in this room as you can once they're fired, but do not destroy Julian's shot.

I jammed the knife into Northcott's throat, slicing through the arteries of his neck, and let out a low, long-held breath.

Take him as sacrifice.

Shots rang out, the sound echoing in the large stone room. Smoke slithered up my nose, and I coughed. The council had gone overboard.

Please.

A breeze from my noblewright ripped the smoke away from me, and I dragged in a ragged breath. I blinked the grit from my eyes.

Alistair still sat at the head of the table. The left eye of his glasses was shattered, red scattered across the table. One hand covered the crossbow bolt buried in his chest, blood splattered against his pale face, and a hush fell over the room. The other had jammed his needle through the muscle of Hana's thigh, and she stumbled, yanking free. The needle clattered to the floor.

Julian stood. "Is he?"

Hana stared at the soldiers, each of their rifles on Alistair. It was hard to blame them; we all made sacrifices for survival. She placed her pistol on the ground. Alistair slumped.

"Well, shit. You were right, Lore," said Julian, turning to me. "What happened to Northcott?"

"It happens occasionally." I took Northcott's gun, my limbs shaky from the sacrifice. I saved Alistair's life, and Northcott's death had barely been enough. "Necessary sacrifice."

One of the councilors, oblivious to Will's slow look from me to Alistair, approached the throne and prodded Alistair with his pistol. He cocked the hammer. "He's only vilewrought, but—"

Alistair ripped the bolt from his chest, plunged it into the councilor's side, and lurched from the chair. The councilors shrieked, more shots ringing out. In the panic, I took careful aim and fired six times. My bullets hit three of the councilors.

Take them as sacrifice, I prayed.

Will swiveled his gun to me and fired.

The hit never came. My vilewright thrummed around me, waiting for the rest of the prayer. Alistair stood unsteadily across the room, and he spun the crossbow bolt like his needle. He nodded to me and then Will's now empty hand.

"That was remarkably uncalled for," said Alistair, spinning the bolt in his fingers as he did his needle. Blood poured from the wound in his chest. "Are you going to shoot Lorena and me again, or will you let me arrest you all?"

I'd not expected such restraint.

And Julian, hand shaking, turned to me with his crossbow loaded for a second shot.

I froze.

"Move your arm, Chase," said Alistair, viciously quiet. "Now."

Julian's jaw tensed. His hand shook, but he didn't move.

"It's fine," I said and nearly cried, because how could it be? "This does hurt more than Will trying to shoot me though."

"You lied," said Julian.

"No, I didn't." I stood and let Northcott's pistol fall. "I told you the truth, but it wasn't the one you wanted to hear."

He shook his head. "Who are you?"

Seven years, and all of it destroyed so quickly. I'd met them my first day in Felhollow, Julian bundled up in Will's too-big coat, and both of them had turned to the small, bedraggled girl I once was with blackberry juice stains on their hands and lips. They'd offered me some without question. They'd taken me home.

"Oh, Jules, I don't think you ever knew me."

Alistair's hands flexed, and a terrible taste filled my mouth, the brimstone and ash taste of a vilewright working something big.

Take my first memories of meeting Will and Julian, I prayed, *and create a garden from the bow. Make it unusable. Make it beautiful.*

My noblewright unfurled from me. A release, like the pop of a baby tooth from its home, shivered through me. Spring green vines burst from the wood of Julian's crossbow and twined around his wrist. He startled and dropped it. The writhing plants clung to him.

"Would anyone else like to shoot me?" Alistair asked, picking up Hana's pistol. "I'm not above killing everyone in this room."

The soldiers knew the fight was lost. They dropped their guns, knees clacking against the stone floor. The councilors nearest the door lunged for it, and Alistair fired. Several more aimed at Alistair. I didn't bother with those bullets.

Alistair sacrificed a councilor aiming at him, and the bullets were destroyed in a smattering of metal shavings.

Will grabbed Julian's arm and tucked him to the ground, a tangle of flowers and thorns knotted around Julian's hand. Finally, the rest of the councilors gave up. I paced the room and checked the dead. Five of the fallen bore the wrought bindings.

Destroy the hearts of the final three who control the wrought.
Use the ones I killed earlier as sacrifice.

My vilewright reared, the rumble of its howl escaping me as a sigh, and even Alistair looked up. The three remaining councilors died.

Feast on my enemies, old magic mine, I prayed and laughed. It wasn't enough. Pain ached so deep in my bones I was sure it would never leave me. The sacrifices were never enough.

"Lorena?" Alistair groaned and grasped his chest. A red rash like blood poisoning ran up his arms.

Magic, even with sacrifice, reaped.

I stumbled and caught the table edge. My vilewright weighed more than it ever had, a mountain of corpses upon my back, and I looked up at Alistair. My vision doubled and blurred. I opened my mouth. Nothing.

He leapt over the table to me and stumbled, catching himself by grabbing my collar. We flailed backward until my back hit the wall. He pinned me there, thigh between my legs and knuckles against my throat, and I brought my hands up to his chest. If he were going to kill me, he'd have used his vilewright. He'd think that more personal.

"Hana," he said as if we weren't the only ones standing in a bloodbath, "fetch some of our soldiers and arrest everyone breathing."

"You'll have to destroy the lock," I muttered. "My noblewright jammed it."

Alistair sighed and dug his nails into my arm until I bled. A sickening crack echoed from the doors. Hana shouldered them open.

"So," said Alistair, "did you want them all dead or arrested?"

"Arrested," I said and wiped the blood from his face. I slid a piece of broken glass from his skin and cut my hand. "They were plotting treason, a sacrificial offense."

"You could've asked," he said. "I could have had them

arrested with no questions or bloodshed. Honestly, if you wanted, I could've kept the bloodshed too."

The bloodshed, however terrible, was another necessary notch on my soul.

"I could've asked, yes, but I didn't because I knew you would do it without question," I said and tried to continue, but Hyacinth Wyrslaine's magic stopped me.

I couldn't create a better world not beholden to power by abusing power, I wanted to say, but that wasn't true. I could have. I didn't want to.

Create new flesh to heal the wound in his chest enough to stop the bleeding. Take any more blood you need.

"Let me have one part of me that is still better than them," I whispered. "Arresting them they couldn't have avoided. Everyone here today chose to be. They had their chance to walk away. They didn't."

He glanced at Northcott. "Even him?"

He was dead, but I felt no better for it.

"You understand, don't you?" I asked.

His fingers spread out across my chest, covering the skin where a binding would've been, and the warmth was enough of a sear to brand me. His thumb traced the edge of my collarbone. It stopped on the fragile hollow of my throat. "Did you mean for the assassination to fail, or were you taking everyone you hate out at once?"

His wound stopped bleeding, and my blood sunk into my noblewright. Behind him, soldiers poured into the room. Hana sat near the door.

"Yes, I meant for the assassination to fail, though it got a bit messier than I intended." My voice wavered. Black peppered the edges of my sight. "Alistair, I will never kill you."

His hand stayed flush against me. "Will you have someone else do it?"

I blinked and slumped as if nearer to fainting than I really was. "I don't want you to die."

262

He pressed his cheek to mine. His lips brushed my ear.

"That wasn't an answer," he whispered. "I didn't kill him, but he seemed happy enough to kill you. Remember that."

For all our faults, we had an understanding.

"Thank you." I shuddered and felt the creep of his smile against my neck. I glanced down at the warmth where his hands held me. "The dead and arrested have to turn over all their property to the Crown. I'll begin sorting through it today. I can tell you who I know was in on it, and we can go from there."

Their safe havens, their soldiers, their resources—they were all mine.

"What are you doing?" he asked.

Cynlira was broken. Alistair couldn't fix it. Julian couldn't fix it. I couldn't fix it.

"Creating something new."

thirty-seven

I SLEPT POORLY. BASIL AND MACK WERE THERE WHEN I woke up, their heads bowed over Mack's dismantled crossbow. The rotund noblewrought was wrapped in a thick quilt and picking at the mechanism that reloaded the bolts, and Mack was staring at Basil's focused expression with a little half smile. I stayed still and quiet, too tired to ruin this moment. They both deserved it.

"You're staring," Mack said and tickled my foot.

I jerked away from him. "You're staring."

"How do you feel?" asked Basil quickly. "You had quite the day."

"Quite," mumbled Mack. "Don't encourage her."

"You did," said Basil. "You're lucky you're not bound. That would've killed you."

Their own binding was half visible beneath the slightly open buttons of their dress, and blue ink leaked from the lines of the sigil. But some of the lines looked like little more than normal scars.

"I suppose half the people controlling your bindings are dead now," I said slowly. "Can you tell?"

"I suppose," said Basil, nicking their finger. "It's hardly noticeable."

One of the small cuts on my hand healed. The sigil on their chest oozed more blue ink, so unlike Safia's green, like an infection draining pus. They'd both be free soon.

I smiled, sat up, and winced. My shoulder ached as if

something had been sitting on it while I slept. "Mack, where are Julian and Will?"

"Alive." Mack helped me up and held a cup of water to my lips. "Julian's pissed as a possum and refusing to talk to anyone. The surviving councilors were arrested. His Excellency passed out right after bringing you here, so the peers've been dealing with it. They're thrilled about selecting new folks to hold the bindings and possibly doing away with the council altogether."

Perfect—I needed them all here, distracted and vulnerable.

I took the cup, my hand shaking. "How long's it been?"

"Two days," said Basil. "Door had a fit too. Starting splintering till we sacrificed someone early. We're up to two to three people per week."

"And out of folks who plead guilty," Mack said.

It would be soon, sooner than the eight weeks we still had. Either we killed more or it opened forever. I had to finish this first.

But even then, we'd need at least four sacrifices to keep it shut those eight long weeks.

"I need to see Julian," I said and threw back the blankets. I was in the same clothes, excepting my shoes, and Mack pushed me back. "No, no. I don't care about whatever you're about to say. I need to talk to Julian."

Basil bid goodbye to Mack. He filled me in on what had happened after Alistair and I passed out as he helped me dress. I was weak, my wrights' reaping had left me quivering, and he helped me to the lift down into the cells and lab. Safia's nervous laughter and Hana's gruff voice carried up the shaft. I turned away from the tunnel leading to the lab. The cells off to the right were dark. I peered into the first one.

A hand shot out from between the bars. Bruised fingers tightened around my throat.

"You vile girl," hissed Will. He was filthier than I'd ever seen him, and long, pale strips lined his skin where he had clawed the dirt from his face. "What did you do?"

"What I had to," I said. "There is always a meaner, dirtier hand willing to hold the knife, and I realized that I would rather hold the knife that killed Cynlira."

He dropped me and backed away. "You said you wouldn't sacrifice me to the Door. So what's your play, Lorena? Going to toss Julian through it? Make me watch?"

"Don't be dramatic. I'm too angry you dragged Julian into this to come up with such petty plans," I said. "I shouldn't be surprised. We're all animals, even you—protect your own or devour them to survive. Oh, but you probably never had to live with mice. They do that, you know. They'll eat their young, sometimes not even to survive. Just because."

They could have saved Cynlira, but instead, they were devouring it.

"I was prepared to die," he said. "You are—"

"Not interested." I turned away and called out, "Julian!"

"Lorena?" came Julian's soft voice. He didn't sound mad, only tired. A pale hand reached from a cell at the end. He crooked his finger, beckoning. "What did you do?"

"I picked the less vile of two vile options," I said.

"We made a deal." He lingered in the dark beyond my sight. "We would've saved people."

"Only the wealthy who could afford to help. That none of you would even bargain to save more disgusts me." I grasped the bars and pressed my face to them. "So I did what I had to do for Cynlira."

"So you killed us?" he asked. "So you betrayed us? All our years for nothing. For some monster in a crown."

"You were going to shoot me."

He fell back against the cell wall, head shaking. "Would it have even hurt you? If I sundered you in two, would you even notice?"

"I would very much," I said, "though probably not in the way you're thinking."

The unease in the taut pull of his arms as he crossed them and the furious rasp of his voice hurt far worse than a bullet would.

"You betrayed us," he said.

"You betrayed Cynlira first."

"Since when do you care about Cynlira and your nation? You never cared about anything, and now you're so passionate, you're killing friends left and right!" He sneered. "Folks would've been fine if they tried. It's not like we're shooting them in the knee and then letting them have at it. The strong would've kept walking."

In Felhollow, no one gave kids younger than five shoes. It was partly to build callouses and make the kids strong and partly a holdover from worse days. The strong walked on. The weak died.

"No," I said, "the folks rich enough to afford a healer after a nail goes through their foot or a wheelchair or paved paths survive. The ones who can't afford any of that suffer. The ones society discounts are the ones who suffer under their rulers first, long before people with even a modicum of power notice."

"Oh," he said, "you'll be a fine ruler then."

"Curse ruling!" I hissed. "I want to save people."

"Really?" he asked. "Or do you want to be the hero?"

I shook my head, disgust crawling over me, and my wrights curled around my shoulders as they sensed my unease. Julian leapt to his feet and paced.

He looked me over, mouth curling up and nostrils flaring. "What? No coat? No brooch? Just little Lorena Adler pretending she doesn't have power and trying to tell me she's right?"

"Julian..."

"You've always had power." He jerked me close and grabbed a strand of my hair, twisting the pale red about his fingers. "Maybe this was a warning—here she is, this necessary Chaos, last remnant of the Vile."

I pulled away from him, hair ripping.

"I didn't do this for power," I whispered. "I never wanted power. You know that."

"You have always had more power than us," said Julian. "Power always corrupts, especially yours."

"Power reveals." Tears welled up behind my eyes, hot and painful, and I smacked the bars. "Those you loved gained power and misused it, but I am not them. I showed you who I was over and over and over again—with each cut to heal your sorry ass, I showed you—and I lied to keep myself safe. You keep holding that over me. Do not make me the monster while you thrived from my work!"

"Yeah, I bet your power's been really revealing," Julian said, voice a low rasp.

I reared back, growling. Like an animal.

His jaw tensed.

"Really? Me having sex with him is the worst thing you can imagine?" I laughed even though it hurt. "I always wondered if we were only friends because you were hoping I would change. Was I a prize, Julian? Or were you so insulted I didn't want you that it became an obsession?"

"What do you want, Lorena Adler?" the Sundered Crown had asked all those weeks ago, but wanting wasn't the problem. Not wanting, this lack, was the problem. People could forgive discretions that came from wanting because everyone wanted something, but the moment I didn't and it interfered with what they wanted, I was unnatural.

I wasn't. I wasn't unnatural or lacking or cold. I wasn't missing out. I had tried so hard to separate myself from everyone else, to make myself unappealing so as not to disappoint, and I was wrong. It was his problem to deal with.

I was simply someone who didn't desire him the way he wanted, and he couldn't deal with it.

"My existence isn't about you," I hissed, "and I am done justifying my life to people who don't even think I'm a person, because if you did, you would have respected me when I told you who I was and every day when I showed you."

"You soaked yourself in death every day," said Julian. "Who'd want to touch you after that except another monster?"

I staggered. "Another?"

But he wasn't wrong. I'd built walls of lies and kept everyone at a distance. It was easier to deal with the loneliness when no one wanted to touch me because I was an undertaker, not because they knew I wouldn't want to sleep with them.

"You were always drawn to death, so lifeless, I shouldn't be surprised you took to killing," he said with a sneer. "Those folks you killed were good people."

Maybe I was drawn to death because most weren't, because they found it distasteful, and because they wouldn't expect anything of me so long as I was death's. Death was a shield between me and what I'd no interest in. Being an undertaker had spared me justifying my existence and disinterest.

"They'd killed people and were happy to let more die," I said, voice breaking. "Your father has killed far more people than I have, and you were happy to kill more."

"What?" he asked.

"My mother, every factory accident, every person worked to the bone and given nothing in return," I said.

"That's not his fault." Julian shook his head and paced. "Lore, you can't save everyone. It's childish to think you can. Hard decisions must be made."

"I am making one," I said. "We can save as many people as your plan would've killed."

"For what?" He laughed, high and chilling. "They'll mess it up again."

We had grown apart, and I couldn't stand this boy calling for a culling. I knew him. I could trace the threads of the Julian I remembered as a child to this person before me. I didn't want to, but I could. I hated it. Him.

And I had no more qualms about what I had planned for him.

I tilted my chin up. "The Door stays shut until it can't anymore. The next sacrifice will come soon, and then we have two weeks. Our next experiment to shut it for good will be the day before. Then the conspirators go to trial and are set to be sacrificed as we figure out what to do. That's you and your father and all his terrible friends. It's so hungry now, I give it a month before it devours you all instead of waiting all eight weeks."

Not a lie. That was supposed to happen. Julian wanted to give his father the legacy he thought his father deserved, so I would give him an opening. All he needed was a nudge.

"After that," I said, "your father will be remembered as the man who wanted to open the Door and kill Cynlira to save himself. The Chase legacy."

Julian wouldn't be able to stand that. He would try to open the Door before our final experiment. We had thirteen days to get everyone in Cynlira safe. I had to free the wrought from their bounds as soon as possible.

His green eyes flickered in the lantern light. I could practically see the plan settle in his mind. He had to prove me wrong.

It hurt that I knew him so well and he knew me so little.

"At least my legacy will be my own," he said. "Yours isn't really yours."

I tightened my grip on the old bars until the rust bit into my skin. "That's how I know you never really understood me."

Take my memory of his face, the looks of loss and horror, and create a signal for me to see when he tries to escape this cell.

It would be easier if I didn't remember how much this hurt.

"I never wanted a legacy, Julian. I only wanted a happy life, and if I can't have that, I'll die trying to make sure everyone else gets it."

thirty-eight

Y OU'RE SUPPOSED TO BE RESTING," SAID BASIL,
frowning as I entered the caverns.

"There's no time." I stacked up all my notes about the Door,
ignoring its creaking laughter. "Do you know when the court is
meeting to select who will get the bindings?"

They shook their head. "Tomorrow? They don't like leaving
it up to chance. Carlow's already tried to break hers and died
once today."

I stripped useless page after useless page in my journal.
None of it mattered, these years of experiments by Alistair
or the few I had taken part in. I had stripped Creek's bones
and treated his corpse like it was no different from Carlow's
mechanical horse. The Door was one of the Vile, the Vile
were everywhere and waiting to pounce once the Door was
opened—or lifted or unanchored or however it did what it did
was undone—and the only way to deal with the Vile was to
offer them lives in exchange for letting some live. Just like
Will Chase.

Laughter trickled out of me, quiet and slow, and Basil
slammed their book shut.

"There's no point in wallowing," they said, picking at the
binding where the surviving thirteen courtiers still controlled
every contract they did. "We can't lock the Door or destroy
it and create a new one, and you've already set something in

motion. It's sloppy, but it seems to be working. What's next? The surviving thirteen courtiers?"

I stared at Basil, and they cocked their head to the side.

"I'm optimistic," they said. "You people always mistake cynicism for shrewdness, but Carlow's the least shrewd person I know."

"I'm sorry," I whispered. "You're all involved in this too. There was little reason for me to be so secretive for so long."

I'd forgotten—Basil was the youngest of Alistair's noble-wrought, but he still only took the best.

"The councilors have been plotting to let the Door open for over a decade, so they wanted to kill Alistair in case he did figure out how to close it," I said. "Then they were going to put their plan into motion while the peerage fought over who was Crown next. They've been hoarding resources and consecrated ground to protect themselves from the Vile."

Basil stiffened. "But only enough for them."

"They were going to let the Vile do as they wanted with Cynlira and then start helping the survivors as some sort of belated saviors, so I told them I would help them attempt to assassinate Alistair."

"And they believed you." Basil's fingers clenched and unclenched against their chest. "You can't lie. Of course they believed you, and now the Crown not only owns their properties but all the ledgers detailing exactly what they have and where."

Most wrought came from common families. If Basil, if everyone else weren't bound to court and council, they could do far beyond what they did now. Some, undoubtedly, would side with the court and council. There would always be people who sought power and tried to gain it by tearing others down, but there would also always be good people. We could be stronger than we were now.

"We're stronger together," I said. "They bind wrought as

children to keep us isolated and controlled, but imagine what we could do if all of us worked together instead of on single contracts."

"What about the noblewrought who bound you?" I asked.

"They were like us once," came Safia's voice at the door. She moved toward us slowly, clearly having a bad pain day made worse by the demands of her binding, and green ink stained her dress. "But they decided they had survived it and put up with it, so we should too. Never mind that the bindings have gotten more vicious and more restrictive over time."

Safia laughed, but there were tears in her eyes. Behind her, Carlow slipped inside the cavern.

"Do you know how many people I've had to let die because the court didn't want to waste me on them?" Safia asked.

"I'm sorry," I said.

"Shut up," said Carlow, goggles hiding her face. "You don't understand it."

We all came together, the four of us, before the Door. It wasn't frightening with the future so close.

"I made it all the way to ten before they bound me. I remember being free," whispered Carlow, fingers tearing into the earth. "There wasn't a lock that could keep me out. There wasn't a space I couldn't make my own. There wasn't a home I couldn't fix. I did more with my noblewright when I was five than I do now, but Vale Shad was too small a town for a noble-wrought. That was what the Sundered Crown said. I looked up one day and she was there, Creek at her side. She wasn't gentle when she bound me. She said it would make me stronger."

"The Shearwill family's run Ipswit for centuries," Safia said. "I was thrilled when they found me. The world's not made for me, and it reminds of that at every turn. The Shearwill family points out every expense, every change, they made for me as if I should be grateful for it. Like they're doing me a favor. Like I don't know they only do those things for me and not the other thousands who could use them because I'm useful. Use," Safia spat and covered her mouth with her hands. "I was always a ledger to them—costs and gains, and then suddenly I was noble-wrought and worth investing in. The Sundered Crown too. His Excellency. The lifts, the streets, and all the little changes he's made are only there because one of us made ourselves useful to him. There's no reason for healers to cost more than the price of the sacrifice and supplies. The Shearwill family could pay for every person in Mori to be cared for and still only cut into a pinch of their wealth. Adjusting the world so that I could live in it was only feasible once I started earning money for them. They shaped my life twice over."

Her fingers touched her chest and came back bloody.

"They make us ledgers," she whispered and held out her scarred arms. "They teach us to hurt ourselves, and the only way to survive is to hurt ourselves more, and then they're angry when we flinch. You understand enough, Lorena, but you can't understand this like I do. If I weren't wrought, I know exactly what I would be worth to them."

"They teach us with these little blades." Carlow laughed. Dried rings of salt stained the lenses of her goggles. "So clean as if it made the act cleaner, but it's the first thing they teach us as children. Alistair Wyrslaine and his mother were the only peers to be wrought in forty years, and they didn't learn by cutting themselves. Even the Sundered Crown was taught how to sacrifice to her vilewright first."

Of course those born with power were taught to use others first.

"Look at what he did in Hila." Safia sniffed and rubbed her arms. "We're sacrifices first no matter how useful we make ourselves. We will never be useful enough to prove our worth for them."

"Why bother?" muttered Basil. "But what can we do? We cannot survive without work, and we cannot survive working."

"The looms are easier to work when you've got small hands. They couldn't swap them out, but why bother spending money on new ones when the current ones only kill a few kids per year," I said and held up my hands. Sometimes I could still remember the steps, so familiar I could have done them in my sleep. "They'd tear off a finger, hand, or scalp if you were unlucky. Easier to have children do it. Smaller hands and smaller chance of us talking back. Who would've come to my defense?"

Low wages, desperation, and the promise of more were as binding as any sigil carved into a chest.

Basil laughed. "I cried, but then they taught me not to."

"Me too," Safia said. She took their hand.

"It's addicting, that first sacrifice." I drew a nail down my arm. "It's our first and only taste of true control, but it's not sustainable."

Cynlira encouraged us to pare ourselves down till it reaped every benefit from our scarred corpses and gave us nothing but a false, fleeting taste of power. I had always used my wrights. What was I if not wrought?

Creek's ghost, a warm breath against my ear, whispered, "You are a graveyard. You are a garden. Great things may grow from you yet."

"We deserve better," said Safia. "They won't offer us better, but we deserve it."

"We should take it," Carlow said, "but I'm so tired."

"It will take longer to break this habit than it will to rebuild Cynlira." Safia closed her eyes and tilted her head back. "But once the court and council are gone, once the peerage is no more, once our worth isn't based on birth or use, and once our bindings are gone for good, for the first time, we will be in control."

Basil smiled. "There's no reason sacrifices have to be physical. We can change that, and the wrought after us won't have to feel like this."

I pushed into the dirt, nails thick with ruddy mud, and reached past the boundary. Every hole I dug refilled. Every wound healed. The Door creaked. "They turned citizens into pieces, all of us, to be used until we can't be used anymore. They divide us, workers and wrought, noblewrought and vilewrought, small town and city folk. They divide us until we are too small to bargain and can only beg."

"Whatever happens," said Safia, "we have to be together."

From beneath the crack at the bottom of the Door came a pale hand, and it reached and reached and reached for the handle to open the Door.

"They think we'll try to rule them," I said.

"Curse ruling." Carlow threw a rock at the Door, and the stone sunk into the wood like a blade through flesh, vanishing with a soft squelch. "I want to choose again. The contracts I take. The pain I suffer. The sacrifices I make. I want to be in charge of myself."

Safia let out a soft sigh. "What would that be like?"

"Wonderful," said Basil. "Wonderful."

"When the Door opens, I hope all the other wrought are as brave as you all." I rose and brushed off my knees. "I hope I am."

Some of us weren't fit to rule, and I knew what I had to do when the time came.

"What do you need us to do?" Basil asked.

"The bindings aren't like normal magic, right? What noblewrought create and what vilewrought destroy persist beyond their deaths. The bindings are more like contracts. They can be nullified by vilewrought destruction or death." I held out my hand to Carlow and helped her up. "Is there anything that needs to be done to end the binding specifically?"

"No," said Carlow, pulling back her shirt. A third of the ink in her chest was peeling away with her skin. "Death of either party is sufficient."

"Unless you're immortal," Safia said and swatted Carlow's arm softly. "Stop dying, by the way."

"It's hardly dying when I know I'll be back," said Carlow. "I've no desire to leave you all alone. You'd be dead in a day without me. It's just nice to be in control."

I sighed, Carlow's words comforting. I worried, sometimes, that she hoped each death would be the last.

"We all need to find better ways to feel in control," I muttered.

Basil snorted. "Easier said than done but noted."

"We have eight weeks until the Door opens, but I think we should prepare to have as many people in the council's safe havens in two weeks. That way, we control when it happens," I said. "Help me find the council's safe havens and consecrated grounds. We'll have to get the word out quickly."

"The council's what?" Safia gritted her teeth. "Never mind. I don't want to be angrier now."

I rose, ignoring the way the dirt of the Door clung to me and pulled me toward it. "I have some of Will Chase's ledgers and his map with some of the safe havens on it. What we need to figure out is how many folks we can house, feed, and protect from the Vile in each place."

Will had two in Ipswit, a church in Formet where he obviously meant to live, and the church in Felhollow. He'd also bought dirt from an old building too old to be used, and each of us made a list of the lands, relics, munitions stockpiles, and rations that we found. Carlow, who'd traveled the most, mapped out the quickest routes between them and nearby towns.

"There won't be enough food," Safia muttered. "They based their numbers on minimums. People don't function optimally like that. They would've had to expend more to deal with malnutrition and illnesses."

"We'll need to find a way to keep farms working and safe," I said. "Soldiers and noblewrought only solve part of that. They can't be everywhere at once."

"And we don't know if we can hold our own against the Vile," said Basil.

We needed a guarantee of safety from the Vile. We needed something to offer them so they wouldn't go after the people of Cynlira, and I'd an idea about who I could offer them.

"I'll deal with the Vile," I said.

"I don't want to allude to mass murder, but you're going to deal with our bindings, aren't you?" Carlow sucked on the end of a quill. "Unbound, I can solve some of our travel time issues. Mori's palace is built to house seven hundred peers. It might contain the Door, but I think we can fortify it. If not, that's still plenty of supplies. Do you really think you can deal with the Vile?"

Carlow glanced at the Door, and I nodded.

"How?" Safia asked.

"I have a few hundred ideas," I said.

"Seven hundred and twenty-three ideas, I'd imagine," muttered Basil.

The idea had taken root days ago, but now it was in full bloom—good things from terrible sacrifices.

"I got your message, Baz. What do you—" Hana skidded into the cave and stopped. "What is this?"

"Oh good." Safia beckoned a confused Hana over and pointed to a line about rations in the ledger she'd been reading. "How many soldiers does the Wyrslaine house employ, and how much do you eat?"

"What?" Hana's mouth twisted. "Why? You overthrowing us?"

"If the Door opened and the peerage ordered their soldiers to protect only their families, would they obey?" I asked. "Or would they protect Cynlira?"

Her face fell slack. "You're talking treason."

"What's treason in the face of a world full of Vile?" Carlow jammed a pin into her small map and cracked her knuckles. "When the Door opens, are you with your court or your people?"

"Folks have families," said Hana. "Friends. A lot would follow orders at first, but if the Vile get out, it'll be chaos."

"But if you could protect Cynlira at the cost of your orders, maybe your courtier, would you do it?" I asked.

"Of course," she said, and Safia laced their fingers together. Hana stared down at her. "You'll need to talk to the others. I'm only Alistair's guard."

"The day after tomorrow, can you get me a meeting with whomever you think I should talk to?" I asked. "And the noble-wrought and anyone else you all think we need to bring in. When the Door opens, the soldiers in each holding will have to get who they can to safer areas and protect those who can't leave their homes. We need to make sure we can get the word to the other holdings fast enough and they'll listen."

It was time for Cynlira to survive without sacrificing its people.

thirty-nine

THE MORNING BEFORE COURT MET TO ELECT THE new twelve for the wrought bindings, I woke up at dawn. Creek's ghost stepped through the door to Carlow's room as I left mine, and he followed me to the old laboratory. His desk was as he'd left it: a mess.

"I don't remember where you tossed it," I said. "Want to be helpful, guilty conscience?"

"Not particularly." He lounged across Carlow's desk, flicking scraps of paper at the spare stool. "Murdering more people today, Lorena dear?"

"Hopefully they'll be quieter than you." I suddenly understood Carlow better than I ever had and turned to him. "Aren't you supposed to talk me out of it?"

"Kill them all. Open the Door. You monster." He raised his hands, and even though his eyes were a solid sea of blue, I could tell he was rolling them. "I've never been helpful before. Why would I start now?"

I glanced back at him and dumped out the contents of a drawer onto the floor.

"You're the one who will have to clean that up," he said and laughed.

He flicked another scrap, and the stool tipped over, rolling toward me.

"Fine!" Creek's ghost threw up his hands. "Bottom drawer in the metal lockbox. The lock isn't engaged."

I reached into the bottom drawer, pulled out the box, and opened it. A dozen vials ranging from *minorative* to *do not ingest* to an unlabeled vial of a white powder that looked like crystals. An old, brown coat was wadded up at the very bottom of the box. "Did I know where you stored this?"

"You know so little, so I couldn't say," said Creek.

It was the same vial he had showed me so long ago, but when I turned to his ghost, it was gone. I tucked it into my coat and returned to my room. The rest of the morning, I spent getting dressed.

A freshly laundered dress of pale blue had been delivered to my room while I was gone. Alistair's meaning was clear—I was his voice and had to look the part. I dressed as carefully as I could, letting the gauzy overdress drape so that it didn't cover my chest. The Wyrslaine pin pulled at the fabric, tearing it. I slipped the vial and a knife into my pocket.

"There's always a meaner hand," I said and took a breath. "Always."

The courtroom had been scrubbed clean over these last few days. I stepped into the large room, sunlight streaming across the floor, and rubbed my eyes. The wooden chairs of the councilors had been removed, and a noblewrought had repaired the bullet holes in the throne and walls. This time, a pair of Wyrslaine soldiers ensured that no guns were snuck inside. Alistair did not come.

Carlow appeared as all the courtiers were taking their seats. "If they decide on who they want to hold the new bindings, I'm to do it, since I can do them all at once."

"Will it kill you?" I asked softly.

She nodded.

Of course it would.

The courtiers settled at their leisure. Several had a soldier accompanying them, making the room a sea of green, blue, and black uniforms. Not a single Wyrslaine soldier was in the room, and the servants left drinks and small finger foods on the table before leaving again. Carlow stood with me near the doors, twisting the strap of her satchel, and I counted the courtiers. Not all of them would be here, and that was ideal. I needed some of them to survive.

The only ones I needed here were the thirteen with the wrought bindings, and they were spread out across the table.

"Are all thirteen here?" I asked Carlow. "I only see nine."

Carlow used me for leverage to look around and pointed out the other four. I nodded.

Good. Eleven of them were drinking.

Take my good memories of Julian, I prayed, *and re-create the poison in those eleven cups.*

My noblewright whined, a chill creeping across my chest, and the weight in my pocket eased. It peeled away from me slowly, like taking off a coat. Carlow shifted.

"Follow my lead," I muttered.

"Only today."

Once no more people seemed to be entering or leaving, I stepped to the front of the room and bowed, waiting for the courtiers to quiet. They took their sweet time.

"Thank you all for coming today," I said and rose slightly, keeping my chin down. Best I not look too sure of myself. "His Excellency is currently dealing with the councilors responsible for the recent assassination attempt and has asked me to assist in selecting the replacement binders. Are there any interested in taking over the contracts?"

There were thirty courtiers and twenty-three soldiers, and not one of them looked at me with bored interest or disdain. Carra Shearwill and several of the other courtiers bearing sigils sipped their drinks. One poured a fresh cup.

"Will they be permanent?" asked a tall man next to Carra

Shearwill, the high collar of his sea-green coat brushing his jaw. "Given the council's sedition, will it be revived and the bindings replaced once new councilors are selected?"

Was it a lie if I honestly didn't know what would happen?

"No," I said and only choked slightly. "The bindings are permanent. His Excellency is quite put out by the council."

The courtier on his second cup, Art Carmyth, wiped the sweat from his brow. He owned another of the factories in the Wallows, and poison was far quicker than burning to death or losing fingers to the looms.

"Carlow." Shearwill beckoned her over. "Try to create something not allowed. Art wants to know what happens."

I narrowed my eyes. Carlow didn't even blink.

"Of course, Your Grace."

Carlow's death was a spectacle. The tension eased out of the room, slipping away with each spurt of her blood. Shearwill pointed out how Carlow's sigil bled to the other courtiers and compared it to her dainty scar. Her fingers plucked at her violet dress, letting them all see how hers didn't bleed at all.

"It twinges a bit," she said, rubbing her chest. Sweat darkened the neckline. "It's hardly an imposition and does allow you to ensure your own contracts are conducted efficiently."

Carlow revived with a groan and crawled to her feet.

A willowy courtier in sunset orange patted her head as if she were a dog doing tricks.

The courtiers all dressed the same—brightly colored and vibrant, like flowers warning off predators. They were still the richest and most deadly people in Mori, their clothes seemed to say. Bite them, and they'd bite back.

I approached slowly. Carlow reached for me, letting me wrap one arm around her and heft her to her feet. I slipped the knife from my pocket, using her body to hide it from view, and helped her toward an end of the table near one of the thirteen courtiers. No one paid much attention to us. They argued among themselves about inheritances and which families had never participated in the bindings. The ones I had poisoned were all showing signs of it now, Creek's creation faster than anything natural. Carlow slumped against me.

"I saw Del," she whispered. "I've never seen anything before."

Take the lives of the poisoned courtiers as sacrifice.

"What about you?" called a stout courtier in the back. He gestured at me. "When will you be bound?"

"Not today," I said. "His Excellency needs me for his research."

The room quieted.

Shearwill leaned forward, her lips pale. "How were you able to evade us for so long? You are from Felled-Noble-in-the-Hollow, yes? His Excellency has been very reticent in regard to you, and his mother was much the same. You are vilewrought?"

Destroy the hearts of the other four courtiers.

"I'm from the Wallows, actually," I said, "and I'm dualwrought."

The four I hadn't poisoned dropped, heads cracking against the table and bodies crumbling to the floor. The soldiers drew their swords and knives, and none were close enough to reach me. A few sprinted out the door. The courtiers panicked.

The one near us pulled a dagger on Carlow, the tip skimming her throat.

"That would be a mistake," she said, taking the dagger by the blade and ripping it from his hands.

Behind her, Shearwill and the others I had poisoned struggled to breathe. The courtiers fled as quickly as they could and left me to their soldiers. I held up my knife, and they all hesitated. Carlow grinned.

"The court and council are done for, and they deserved it. The Door's opening, and they were content to let us all be sacrificed to sate it and save themselves," I said. "In ten minutes, all the wrought will be unbound. You may leave, or you can stay and help us figure out how to save Cynlira."

The one nearest to me eyed the writhing courtier at their feet and sighed. They sheathed their sword.

"Should we stop the courtiers?" Carlow asked.

"Let them run," I said. "I have other plans for them."

forty

I T TOOK CARLOW FIVE MINUTES AFTER THE LAST OF the thirteen courtiers died to give in to temptation. She tried to break her curse, her noblewrought howling so much I felt it in my bones. The scar on her chest was red and raw, the ink a stain on her shirt but gone from her skin, and I had to drag her from the room. She passed out in the doorway, and a soldier in Wyrslaine black took her from me. They flanked me as if I were Alistair. I had them help the soldiers I'd talked to while Carlow was passed out.

They were, for the most part, amenable to helping once they heard about the Door and the council's plans.

The rest of the peers in Mori fled, leaving the city in a rush of carriages and soldiers and leaving the palace a mess. Servants had been left behind, and soldiers didn't know where their peers had gone. I ran as fast as my aching legs would let me to find Alistair. Hana found me first.

"He did something," she whispered, pulling me through the crowded halls toward the wing where he lived. "It went wrong."

That was one drawback I hadn't foreseen—wrought doing what they'd always dreamed of once their bindings were gone. Alistair was on the floor of a room blanketed in dust, two worn rabbits made of soft wool before him. The only marks in the dust were his footsteps and the lines where he'd raked his hands across the stone. I stayed in the doorway.

"Alistair?"

"It didn't work," he said, voice hoarse.

The two beds in the room were for children.

"Your sisters are dead." I stepped forward slowly and touched his back. "I'm sorry. I don't think any wrought could bring them back."

Bowed over his knees, hands pressed into his eyes, face nearly to the floor, he cried. Blood dripped between his fingers. "Nothing's enough. Nothing is ever enough."

I sat beside him and stroked his hair. He fell against my shoulder. Tears and blood pooled in the nook of my collar, and after a while, he shuddered and mopped up the mess with his sleeve. I shushed his apology.

"How many people did you kill this time?" he asked.

"Thirteen," I said. "Only the ones who controlled the bindings."

He laughed low and rough.

"You know, we're the same now." I touched the scar over his heart. It was still pink and stained, but his flesh had rejected the ink. "We are not bound."

He cupped my face with one hand. "I dreamed, in those first few days, of opening you up like I might the Door, and I always woke up worrying about what monsters of yours I'd unleashed."

"You didn't unleash anything," I said and kissed his cheek. "My monsters were already here."

The peerage and the council had been here for far too long.

It took four hours to gather everyone we needed. Safia slept through most of the four hours, her eyes still bloodshot and heavy when we finally met. Free of her bindings, she had tried to heal too many people her contract had forced her to turn away, and Hana had been frantic between Alistair and her. Only Basil hadn't overextended themself.

"We'll be doing enough of that soon enough," they said, pacing the length of the room I'd chosen.

It wasn't as big as the courtroom, which was so large it felt imposing, but all the older wrought and soldiers could fit. I'd pinned a map of Cynlira to the long table, and Carlow marked everything we had found from the councilors' records so far. Mack sat on a chair next to Basil, reading over Will's notes on Felhollow.

We waited, our soft conversations barely filling the room. People began to filter in, ones I didn't know and some I recognized from the palace grounds. Hana led a group of soldiers I'd only seen in passing. Many were older, grizzled by age and the Sundered Crown's rule. They knew what they were doing far more than I did.

And many had watched me kill more people in the last week than they'd ever seen killed at all.

"Lorena." Carlow nodded to me and pulled a pair of red glasses from her coat. "These are for you."

"What?" I took them and studied the lenses under the light. They looked as if oil slid through water beneath the glass. "Did he say why?"

She shrugged. "I'm only the messenger."

Once the room was full and the two hours up, I put on the glasses. They were heavy on my face, a bloody badge better than any brooch Alistair could give me, and stood. The crowd quieted and shifted. Odd shadows too pale to be wrights moved between them and vanished when I peeked over the lenses. One breezed past a curtain, ruffling it. The Door *was* weak.

And the Vile were waiting.

"The Door will be open in ten days," I said and waited for the exclamations and grumbling to die down. "Unless you all want to feed a tenth of the population to it and then who knows how many after that, it's inevitable. We must prepare for the worst."

One of the soldiers—I'd never learned ranks, but this one wore the black coat of the Wyrslaine personal army with enough of the color-coded stripes on their sleeves to be a captain surely—crossed their arms over their chest. "Where is His Excellency?"

"He believes he can shut the Door," I said. It wasn't a lie. He did. He was down there, poring over options now that his binding was gone. Mori had plenty of corpses to use as locks now. "Maybe he's right, but I think it would be safer to not depend on hope. However, we can't save Cynlira alone."

"The council and the peers today," he said, glancing from me to Carlow. "You have unbound the noblewrought and His Excellency, and you are trusting the armies bound to each peer for decades to follow you after such a display? To turn away from the people they have been trained their whole lives to obey? To abandon their livelihoods when that money is needed most? And all for a girl who came out of nowhere and killed half the council and court?"

One of the others, coat the brown and green of a house I didn't know, nodded. I grasped the table before me.

"The council was going to abandon us all to the Vile after they opened the Door and use their hired armies—all of you—as fodder. Your homes, your families, and your friends meant nothing to them," I said. "The Vile might be the ones to kill us, but it was the council that served us up."

"And if the Door doesn't open and our employers find out, there will be retribution," said another soldier, this one in the pale blue of one of the coastal families. "They'll hang us for even considering it."

"I'm not asking you to kill them—"

"Gods know you've done that already," muttered someone.

"—but I am asking you to consider what you would do if your employer asked you to abandon your hometown to the Vile and protect them instead," I said and raised my head. "Ten days. That's all the time we have to get the majority of Cynlira to somewhere safe. Now, you can all try to drag me before the court for treason, or you can listen to us explain where the safest places from the Vile are and how to make sure our people aren't all dead and devoured in ten days."

"How do you know what places are safe?" the older Wyrslaine soldier asked.

"The council had it all planned out," I said. "Their plan was to let everyone else fight the Vile while they were safe in their havens, and once the Vile were worn out and the peerage dead, they were going to emerge victorious."

Mack snorted. "Not that they were going to tell anyone that they'd opened the Door on purpose. Willoughby Chase figured you'd all work for them once your hometowns were gone."

"We would have nothing else to fight more," said the Wyrslaine guard, grinding their teeth. "Show me."

Every other soldier in the room deferred to them. I showed them the map and pointed out the havens. They were near major cities, utterly useless for rebuilding given their lack of land, but they'd wells and enough food and weapons stockpiled. I'd flagged roads, wells, and farmlands too.

"I've seen this before," said the soldier in green. "Pierce was looking into land there and took some people to fortify the area."

Pierce Burnwell was one of the many councilors we'd arrested with Will and Julian.

"So you got the council to commit treason so you could legally have access to all this?" said the Wyrslaine guard. They chuckled. "Could've just had us seize it all."

"Too slow," I said. "The journals and ledgers were hidden or coded, and I got them all to show me outright where most of this was when I agreed to help them. They were depending on all of you to do as you were told since they would've paid you."

"Too much like something they would have done?" they asked, blue eyes narrowed at me. Their wrinkles deepened as they smiled. "Some would've done as they were told—it's hard to disobey the people who've held your life in their hands for years—but at least now they won't have to find out if they would've."

I adjusted my red glasses and nodded. "Knowing the worst part of yourself isn't for everyone."

"True," they said softly and turned back to the map. "The Vile can't cross consecrated ground, can they?"

"That's what all the stories say," said a servant. "Port Altiver's good. It's built over a graveyard."

"My partner's family lives there," said the Wyrslaine guard. "I'll get in touch."

Carlow flagged it. "That's not enough."

Her voice was still raspy and hoarse from her attempt to break her curse.

"It's more than we would've had," I said and glanced at her.

The air to her left was a haze, as if she'd a vilewright. I stared, and the shade shifted behind her. It was too tall, too thin, and too substantial to be a vilewright. I shuddered.

"What do we need to do?" someone asked.

"We need to make sure that the people without have wrought and soldiers to keep them as safe as they can be," I said, sliding through the crowd to point out areas. There were flickers, blurs, as if there weren't vilewrights but something else lurking in the world that not even these glasses could let me see. "And I bet folks know their areas better than we do. Any places where Noble walked or ministers worshiped the gods should work. A lot of the local ones aren't on maps, but they'll know where those areas are.

"We'll need to send out instructions to the soldiers and wrought in the areas to let them know what's happening," I said. "Anyone who can should start doing that now. The sooner people know, the better. After that, we need to get the supplies spread out. Carlow, Basil—can you help?"

"I can get messages to anyone instantly so long as I have time to rest, I think," said Basil.

"When the Door opens, the peerage will die almost imme-diately," I said. "We should warn some people about that too. Every town's got a council. They should be able to lead so long as we provide them with fair warning, supplies, and protection."

"How do you know the peerage will die?" asked the soldier in green.

The Wyrslaine soldier glanced at me and elbowed him. "Not your concern. Get some paper, and we'll start drafting warnings."

Everyone in the room deferred to them and got to work.

"Don't worry," Hana whispered, leaning down to my ear. "Roth's been around longer than most, and they trained half the people in Cynlira, even if they're serving others. Folks will listen to them."

Good. I didn't want them to obey me out of fear or lead them into this new world. People would need a leader, and it couldn't be me.

Carlow cleared her throat. "I'll be more helpful with repairs and construction once we know where we need to be."

I glanced at her and froze. To her left was Creek's ghost, but he wasn't right. Vines held his rotting corpse together, and his skin sloughed off like dandelion fluff. Beneath it was nothing, only a vast dark where stars glittered gold and white like broken teeth.

I pulled the red glasses off, and his ghost, looking as Creek always had in life, was there. I put them on. Creek cocked his head to the side.

"Lorena?" Basil said, nudging me. "What's wrong?"

Creek's eyes, blue and cursed in life, were the same Vile red as Carlow's now.

"Nothing. Sorry." I pushed the glasses to the top of my head. A vine of shadow curled around Carlow's throat. She didn't seem to notice. "I think the Door is messing with me."

"Then open it." Creek's ghost smiled. "What's opening the Door compared to what you've done?"

"Oh yes," said Basil, sighing. "It won't let me sleep of late."

"It's angry we're not scared of it," Carlow said, her voice no longer a rough rasp and the cuts of her bindings nothing more than white scars. "No reason to fear the inevitable."

I took off the glasses and whispered, "Was it inevitable?"

But Creek's ghost was gone.

forty-one

THE NEXT FEW DAYS WERE FULL OF PLANNING. Basil, Mack, Safia, and Carlow joined me, each of us avoiding Alistair. Not that he would've noticed; he was holed up with the Door, desperate to understand it now that his binding didn't restrict his vilewright, and he sacrificed one of Will's companions to it with a smile. The only one of us he spoke to was Hana, and that was only when he needed a sacrifice.

He did notice the unrest caused by killing the courtiers in charge of the bindings. The surviving courtiers could ruin my plans if they looked too hard at the recent movements of their soldiers and people. However, they were concerned about Alistair attempting to take over their holdings.

Most had retreated to their lands in preparation for a war that wouldn't come.

"Wrought can't last longer without food," I said, scratching through one of the notes from Safia. "We can sacrifice our feeling of hunger but not our actual hunger, and the contract leaves us tired. I could never do it longer than five days."

"Gods," muttered Safia. "At some point, we need to discuss your childhood."

"Do we?" I asked.

My life spent worried about money and where my next meal would come from was finally paying off, and I'd taken to poring over the ledgers detailing the food stored away by the

Crown in case of tragedy at all hours. Alistair had at least left his mother's last decrees alone. There was enough in the stores for all of Mori. The city would be fine so long as we could shelter everyone.

Today, five days away from the opening of the Door, we were fortifying the buildings of Formet district. Every single part of it was consecrated, and before we'd started, only one-fifth of the city would've fit in it.

Basil groaned. "Have you ever had sea foam candy? I'd do anything for that right now."

"With the pecans!" someone shouted from around the corner. "Can we make some?"

"Later," I shouted back. "Focus."

The freed noblewrought had coalesced around the palace. Many had been working in Mori already, most as healers for the city's populace but several as builders in charge of keeping everything standing. Those noblewrought bound to Order like Carlow and Basil, though, had been trained well in how to make the city more accessible and useful for Cynlira. Free of their bindings, they could do whatever work they pleased now, even if it didn't pay. I'd helped one refortify the Wallows' buildings against flooding this morning. The rest had started constructing barriers around the safe havens. One was focusing on cold cellars, wells, and water pumps.

"Don't go too high," said Carlow, face covered by a book so old the cover was hand-stitched and the pages parchment. "Once you hit three floors, the consecrated earth has to be in the floors of the higher levels. The farther you get from it, the less power it has."

I didn't wear my red glasses around her. Most of the time, Creek's ghost, uninjured, trailed after her. Sometimes, though, I saw Creek's corpse staring back at me from her cursed eyes.

I didn't sleep. The courtiers and councilors were always there in my dreams, waiting for me in the dark.

"Noted," said Basil. "It would take longer to build with stories, regardless. We don't have time for that."

Safia nodded. "It's better to keep it a single story. We can make bunks, but hoists will be hard to construct quickly and stories harder to heat come winter. Definitely no stairs. Too hard to traverse."

"Good point," Basil said. "Single stories are easier to map too. We can lay tactile pavers to make sure people know the way in."

"This is better than nothing," I said, still focused on the ledgers before me.

Carlow exhaled loudly. "We can't protect everyone."

We couldn't, not with the safe havens, but I could with all I had left.

"Is that why you're not telling the noble houses?" Basil asked. "You think they'll do the same thing as the council?"

"I think their involvement in our planning is irrelevant," I said. "But yes, I imagine they would do the same as the council."

"They have churches and graveyards, private plots of land none of us are allowed to even look at," said Carlow.

I glanced at the inked-out spots on the large map Basil had pinned to the wall of our old lab. "Yes, we should use those places too."

"Will they let us?" Basil asked.

I rolled my lips together, the lie stuck in my mouth. They wouldn't have, but their opinions wouldn't matter. Many were anxious, fleeing to their holdings to escape Alistair and ready their armies. Carlow glanced up.

"What they want doesn't matter," I said. "Have you heard from out west? Any more wrought running around?"

"Two," said Basil, smiling. "Both noblewrought."

A dozen or so who'd been in hiding, living quiet lives outside Mori, had come forward to help the soldiers and wrought stationed in their towns once the messages reached the smaller towns. For so long, Cynlira's common enemy to unite us had been each other. Vile were an easier target.

There were no other vilewrought. At least none that had come forward yet.

"Felhollow's taken care of then," I said, setting the letter from Kara aside and smiling at Mack. Old Ivy still wasn't talking to me, but she'd live. I could stand silence so long as they all survived. "Between the church, graveyard, and soldiers, everyone there should be all right."

Felhollow's graveyard was larger than its smallest farm. No Felfolk would suffer Vile.

"What about Julian?" Mack asked. He'd been quiet with me, staring any time I spoke of the councilors and courtiers.

"Julian?" I hesitated so as not to sneer. That boy's very name made my skin burn. I had no good memories of him, only fury and pain. My noblewright whimpered. "He's still holding true to his path. I'll talk to him one last time, but I don't think he'll listen. He listen to you?"

Mack shook his head. We'd visited Julian together yesterday, and he'd refused to speak with me. Will hadn't.

Will had a lot of words for me.

"I'll try once more," I said and sighed. "He's said a lot of terrible things these last few days, but I know you love him."

Mack shot me an odd look. "You do too. Or you did. I imagine he's said some choice things to you."

"He did," I said, hardly listening. I couldn't remember a good memory with Julian Chase. There were no laughs or smiles, no late-night talks. I knew why—so many of my memories with my mother were stained by the same odd *lack*. "I have to go."

I crept into the caves near the Door. Alistair was hard at work trying to shut it still, the clatter of bone against bone and swish of steel sliding over Hana's flesh echoing through the area. The dim light flickered, and the other prisoners didn't notice me. Julian didn't either.

He was mottled like an apple left on the ground too long. I grasped the bars.

"Julian?" I whispered.

"Who have you murdered now?" He lifted his head, the eight lines he'd carved into the wall above his head like a crown.

"Are you still set on murdering over half of Cynlira?" I asked. "Or have you reconsidered what you want your legacy to be?"

He only laughed.

"Did I love you once?" I asked softly.

He collapsed at the back of the cell. "I don't know. I don't know."

I nodded.

"We were going to be married one day," he whispered, "but I didn't know you were vilewrought, and then the warrant showed up for my father."

Yes, my lies were far greater a slight than his father's crimes.

"I must have loved you." I closed my eyes and tried to imagine it. "I came here instead of letting them take Will."

"I like to think you did," Julian whispered.

I peeked at him, taking in the tension of his arms and twitch in his calves. "If we left today and saved the councilors, would you still want to marry me?"

He launched himself at me. His hands smacked against the bars, and I stepped back. His fingers barely brushed my chest, and I jumped, knocking my penknife from my pocket. I stared straight at him and pretended not to notice. My noblewright whined.

"You betrayed me," he said. "I would've given you everything. I was saving us. They'll only weigh you down."

"Then I'll bear it, because I am a part of Cynlira and should gladly support my people," I said. "We shouldn't be measured by usefulness. There are thousands of Julians out there right now. Success is always an indicator of pure self-sufficiency. You're not special, I'm not special, and you're certainly not special enough to decide who lives and who dies. I'm done being quiet and unassuming. It's what the council and court and crown always wanted, and I refuse to give them what they want now."

He shook his head, an odd crook to it. "Lorena, how will they rule?"

"You're obsessed with ruling. It doesn't matter."

"You then," he said and laughed again.

"Five days before the Chase legacy dies," I said and left. "I'm glad I gave up half my memories of you."

It meant this hurt far less.

forty-two

I VISITED JULIAN ONCE MORE. THE DAY BEFORE I hoped he would open the Door went like any other, the morning a dash to ensure everything was prepared for the appearance of the Vile. The royal palace had a large church that had fallen into disuse after the gods left, and Carlow and Basil had claimed the attic with the bells, moving our things into it yesterday. We were utterly alone up there, and it was comforting to see Mori splayed out beneath us in its entirety. The new constructions around Formet loomed, taller than we'd planned but strong. Mori's population had barely questioned it.

Basil still worried about getting them all into Formet in time after the Door opened, but Carlow took my assurances that they would be safe with a side-eyed glare and a scoff. No matter what Basil said, she was shrewd.

"Julian?" I called into his cell.

Carlow had been the only one to ask why we didn't just throw the councilors in the cells to the Door now and buy a few more days. I'd not answered her.

"Julian," I said again and stepped closer. The penknife was gone.

Julian was curled up against the far wall of the cell, his shirt pulled over his head, and he didn't answer. Above him were twelve gouges in the stone.

Good.

Footsteps shuffled behind me. "Leave him be."

"What are you still doing here?" I asked, retreating from the cells and joining Alistair.

"Working." Alistair, hair tangled in a knot at the nape of his neck and glasses drifting down his nose, shook his head at me. His heart fluttered in the curves of his pale neck. "I've been known to do it on occasion."

He would have been such a good noblewrought with how often he sacrificed himself for his work.

"I've never heard such a vicious rumor," I said, following him to the cave with the Door. "Come here."

He let me tug him down to my level and shivered when I pressed my lips to his forehead.

"You need to sleep or you'll work yourself sick." My fingers kept hold of his sleeve. "Let's go to your room."

"Lorena, it's barely dusk." He straightened up, and his spine creaked so loud I jumped.

The Door, still appearing like the door to my mother's sickroom, opened with a gust and slammed shut. Alistair tilted his head, studying it. I sat on the table he'd dragged in here.

"I think it's playing me," he said. "Look."

His lips moved with a contract, and a single splinter fell from the Door. A small pain needled my hand, ripening with each breath. I hissed. The nails vanished from my left hand. Blood dripped across the table.

"You could have warned me," I mumbled, inspecting the bumpy skin where my nails used to be. "I don't have enough nails for how big the Door is."

Alistair hummed and wrote in his journal. "It's still there."

The splinter was still sitting atop the red dirt.

"It didn't last that long with anyone else," he said. "What's different about you?"

I shrugged. "Perhaps the surprise mattered."

"No, I didn't warn Carlow either."

It was hard to reconcile this boy with the one who'd stroked my jaw with a swan-feather quill.

Finally, the splinter sunk into the dirt, and the crack in the Door was healed. Alistair closed his book and leaned against me.

"I considered it, opening the Door," he whispered. "I could be the villain if it freed us from this uncertainty."

"I'm not here to be your conscience," I said softly, "but you're not opening the Door."

"I know. I simply want us to always understand each other." He took the lapels of my coat in his hands. "You rarely wear this these days. Did you wear it for me?"

I felt too close to Death these days to bother with the formality.

"You rarely wear yours." I laughed and touched his bare collar. "What does it matter?"

"Why did you stop?" he asked, one hand sliding across my ribs and up to the brooch pinned to my chest. "I want to understand."

"I was the undertaker in Felhollow because it was needed and respected," I whispered. "I feared they wouldn't want me if I weren't needed. I feared that if I didn't take a job they found distasteful, they'd expect more of me than I was willing to give. So long as they needed me, they didn't push my boundaries."

He licked his lips, gaze on the path of his fingers along my shoulder. He curled a strand of hair around his finger. "My mother wouldn't have saved me if I weren't vilewrought. She would've let my father kill me."

He said it with such certainty—he knew she would have, and he knew I would understand that pain of being half-loved and misunderstood by a parent—that my breath caught in my throat. I wanted to live in the quiet comfort of sitting next to someone who knew exactly what I was thinking and why, slip between the sheets of my bed and settle in with someone who

understood why I put my work before myself. I wanted familiarity and understanding, talks so long my throat grew sore and
my heart grew full. I wanted a life without complication.

And in less than a day, I would ruin this.

"We should rest." I slipped from the table. "Your room?"

He let me lead and didn't let go of my hand. No shadows followed us, and we met no one but Wyrslaine soldiers in the halls.
Alistair's room was warm and stuffy, the air still, and despite the
servants who must have kept it neat, he raced through ahead of
me to open one of the slits in the ceiling. There were no windows in his rooms.

I toed off my shoes. Alistair sat on his bed, elbows on his
knees and chin in his hands. His eyes followed my hands as they
undid the buttons of my coat and let it fall to the floor. He beckoned, and I went to him. His hands grasped my hips, turned
me around, and tugged me until my back was flush against his
chest. I pulled the blankets over our legs.

"You've been avoiding me," he said softly and twisted a
strand of hair at my temple around one finger. "Why?"

The pressure in my head faded, but I couldn't think fast
enough of what to say, since I couldn't lie.

"Oh, Lorena Adler," he whispered, the words rumbling in
his chest and into me, "what are you up to?"

He dragged one finger down the center line of my scalp and
split my hair into two even sections. I shuddered again.

"No answer?" he asked.

I leaned my head against his right shoulder and stared up at
him. "Why are you curious?"

"Curiosity's sake," he said and wrapped his arms around me.
He brought my hair over my shoulder, retangling his fingers in
the ends, and rested his right cheek against my left. "You've
been busy. Is it too much to assume I want to discuss whatever
project is keeping you busy?"

"Yes," I said and gasped when he pulled hard on my hair

again. "I believe you miss me. I don't believe that's why you're asking."

I tilted my head slightly and watched his long fingers deftly braid my hair. The gentle movement prickled across my scalp.

"Do you trust me?" I whispered. "Do you trust me enough for me not to answer?"

"Of course." One of his hands dropped to my waist. "It's nothing that will kill you, is it?"

I arched and kissed him, praying he couldn't taste the lie I couldn't say. His nose bumped my chin, and I pulled away to face him. He gripped my waist, his other hand sliding up my neck to the side of my face. I kissed him again.

Alistair stilled. His lashes fluttered shut against my face, a soft breath escaping his nose. His lips moved against mine, opening slightly, and I pressed against him. He kissed me back far harder. His nails dug into my skin. His teeth nipped my bottom lip.

The shock shivered down my spine and twisted in the pit of my stomach. Alistair spun us and shoved, pinning me to the bed.

"I wonder," he whispered against my throat, "what I would gain from devouring you."

"It would be a loss." I slotted my knee into the curve of his hip and flipped us. "You don't understand power like I do."

"Lore." He gasped, not fighting my hold at all. "Do you actually want to do this, or are you being nice?"

The waver in his voice drew away all the worries and thoughts trapped in my head. This was now, not tomorrow, and I understood him perfectly. He knew the little pieces of me that ached to be spoken but couldn't be. We wouldn't be all right, and it raged in me. Terrible. Monstrous.

Finally, I had a home, and I was tearing it down.

"I am not being nice," I said and let go of his wrists. "Though I can't say I want more than this."

"Fair enough." He chuckled and threaded his fingers through my hair again. "What do you want?"

"I want you to enjoy tonight. I want to enjoy tonight."

He rolled us onto our sides and tucked his face into my neck, lips trailing from collar to ear. I sighed, and he traced the curves of my ear with the tip of his nose. His tongue tasted my neck.

"You never struck me as someone who likes to be touched," he said and kissed my cheek.

"I love being touched. I don't like the expectations that come with it." I curled up closer to him, hands slipping beneath his shirt. "What does both of us enjoying tonight look like?"

"Sleep here," he said and fell onto his back, "and answer one question for me."

I walked my fingers along his ribs and nodded.

"Do you love me?" he asked, voice devoid of feeling.

"No," I said and flattened my hand against his side. "You're uncaring and singular, and as much as I love how you have always respected and understood me, I know you wouldn't extend the same respect to someone you didn't find useful. I can't love you as you are. To love you would be to hate most of Cynlira."

He reached out one hand, a warm breeze like a breath rolled over me, and the lanterns in his room flickered out. I yawned against his chest.

"I'm not upset," he said and kissed me gently. "Stop looking at me like I'll break and rest. It's not as if I can hate you for not loving me when you barely love yourself."

"You sacrificed my wakefulness," I muttered.

"Never what I've called it but yes." He sat up, dragging the blankets out from under us, and tucked me in. His bare feet brushed mine. "I just wanted to make sure you still couldn't lie."

I didn't want to love Alistair. I wanted to devour him and stifle this odd hunger knowing him had awoken within me. No one else would ever understand.

"I could have," I said, and the act of his toes curling against mine was suddenly softer and sweeter than everything that had come before. "I never lied. I do understand why you do the things you do. I get it perfectly, but I still think it's terrible. You're the only one who's noticed me. The real me. I am making terrible choices, and you're the only one who understands them."

He would be the only one who understood when tomorrow came. I was sure of it.

forty-three

THE MORNING DAWNED DARK, AN ODD HUM RAT-
tling in my teeth. Alistair was curled up in a ball, his back
pressed into me, and I eased out from under the blanket. He
grumbled and burrowed deeper under the blankets. My noblewright, its presence today an insistent thrum, created five deep
lines of blue across the back of my hand. I touched one, and
they faded.

I'd asked my noblewright to create a sign when Julian made
his move, and this must have been it.

"Alistair!" I shook him awake.

He grabbed my arm painfully tight, opened his bloodshot
eyes, and let go. "Lorena? What—"

"Julian escaped and is trying to open the Door," I said and
threw back the blankets atop him. "Come on."

I stumbled out of bed, yanking the curtain aside. I crawled
out after him. My crinkled clothes were twisted and confining.

Alistair knotted his hair back with a leather tie. He grabbed
a dagger from his bedside. "How do you—"

"Trust me!" I pulled on the red glasses he'd given me and
tossed him his. "Come on."

Create my thoughts in Hana's ears, I prayed. *Take my panic,
please, but leave the fear.*

"It's time, Hana. Don't let any of the peers know. Have the
noblewrought send word to the others."

It was only right to be afraid of this.

We raced down to the Door. The stairs were dim and slick with condensation, our feet slipping over the stones. Alistair burst through the tunnel before me and ran straight for the Door. I sprinted to the cells. Julian's was empty, the hinges of the door removed. Will, free, was in the middle of the hall. The rest of the surviving councilors were gone.

"Ah," he said, running a shaking hand through his hair. "Of course you know."

"Let me guess," I said, squaring myself between him and the exit. "You're all running free to alert your conspirators so you can make a last-ditch effort to save only yourselves?"

"You are eerily informed," Julian's father muttered.

"And you're letting Julian open the Door?" I asked. "Or are you going down together in some sort of self-righteous glory?"

"Julian," said Will slowly, "knows what needs to be done, and we imagine the Vile are not opposed to making a deal with us."

They had no idea what sacrifice meant and would never offer enough.

"It hardly matters," Will said. "You are also too late. We got word out already. Our people in Mori will be safe within the hour, and messengers will spread from here."

"So people, like the soldiers carrying those messages, will know you opened the Door?" I smiled, mouth stretching painfully, and his eyes widened in fear. "Most of Cynlira will know that the council that was meant to represent them opened the Door and let the Vile in, content to retreat to havens while people suffered?"

"What does it matter if they know?" he asked and hesitated. "How will they know of the safe havens?"

"Because they were the Crown's property—my property— the moment you were arrested, and I've been moving folks into them since your trial."

"What have you done?"

"The Door isn't really a Door," I said, stepping toward him. "It's more like a veil. The Vile won't spill from it. The veil over our world will be lifted, and suddenly, we will be able to see them and they will be able to see us. They'll appear in Mori and Drail and Felhollow at the same time, and eventually, everyone will know this was your fault. You spread the word. You're the villains this time around."

He laughed, head in his hands, and said, "You know we only kept you around because Old Ivy wanted a healer for Felhollow? She should've let me gift you to the Crown. Least the gold we'd have gotten would've done some good."

My wrights, so wrong, so warm, so weighted on my back, curled around my shoulders like the family I didn't have.

"I'm tired of hearing your voice," I said, "and all the unsurprising terrible things you say."

His words. Feast.

My vilewright unfurled from me, peeling from my skin, and Will gagged.

"It's your arrogance that got you stopped. Know that."

He mumbled and blood poured from his mouth. My vilewright tittered, its laughter settling over me like searing noonday sun. I grabbed Will's arm and dragged him to the cave with the Door.

Alistair stood in the entrance. He glanced back, his red gaze falling to Will.

"Ignore him. He'll be dead soon enough," I said. "Julian can't know that the Vile will appear all over Cynlira when he opens the Door. He needs to think that the councilors are still safe and that opening the Door will fulfill their plan."

"If he opens it, you mean?" Alistair asked.

Will tried to pull away, and Alistair laid the dagger against his neck.

"No," I said and stepped into the cave. "I don't."

Julian, white skin streaked red, stood at the cusp of the Door's territory where blood and bone dust stained the dirt. Dangling in his hands were my penknife and a small blade carved from the rock shards of his cell. He stared at the Door, head cocked slightly.

"Hello, Lore," he said softly, with such tenderness and familiarity it made my skin burn. He didn't know me. He didn't have a right to that name. "I hoped you would come."

Hold Will. My blood.

My noblewright created two loops of flowing red about his hands, holding him to the ground. The liquid shifted and hardened to iron. I leaned over Will's shoulders and turned his head to the Door.

It was only fair he witness what he had wanted for so long.

"So," I said, stepping into the cavern's mouth. "You want this to be your legacy?"

"I'm comfortable with dying," Julian said, back still to me. "Will and I got the word out, so our people will be safe. Cynlira was dying anyway. At least this way, some of us live and can rebuild eventually, and they'll know it was because of my father and me."

He glanced over his shoulder, green eyes beacons above the half-moons of his exhaustion. Behind him, the Door opened an inch. My mother's amber eyes glowed in the crack. Her hand, burned and weeping, scratched at the jamb. Will shrieked. Julian didn't notice at all.

"And I think the Vile will be happy to leave the two of us alone when I offer them you and that boy." Julian's gaze fell on Alistair. "And you know, if I die today, I'm fairly all right so long as I take you with me."

"Lorena," said what might have been a voice if not for the odd creaking between the words. Doors opening. Teeth clenching too tight. "Darling, please. Let me out."

"Shut up," I said, stepping toward it. "You're not—"

Pain lanced through my throat. Alistair screamed. Footsteps thundered toward me, then stopped. An arm hooked around my waist, Julian's arm, and hoisted me up. I grasped my neck. My fingers slipped through the long cut across my throat. Blood dripped between my hands. It abandoned me with each heartbeat. Faster. Faster.

Please, I prayed, but I didn't know the parts of the throat like healers did. They were never part of funeral rites. My noblewright whined, high and piercing, and Alistair screamed again.

I fell. Julian wiped my penknife on his shirt, blood smearing across his chest. I gagged, trying to think of a way to heal the wound, to close the hole, but nothing came. Spots crowded my vision. Julian pushed me toward the Door.

"Goodbye, Lore."

Alistair tackled him. They rolled in the dirt, weapons forgotten. Alistair punched Julian in the face, and Julian rammed a knee in Alistair's stomach, doubling him over. Julian shoved Alistair aside and flailed out with the knife. It cut Alistair's cheek. He hissed.

Behind them, Will struggled against his bonds. I crawled toward him.

Re-create my damaged flesh.

My noblewright growled and fought, the vagueness tearing it in two.

Use Will's throat.

Will Chase gasped and choked, and pain gnawed at the edges of my wound. My splintered bones snapped into place, and Will collapsed over his knees. Veins and muscle healed so fast it hurt. I clawed at my throat. I vomited blood and breathed.

"Lorena?" Alistair asked. "What is your plan?"

He had Julian pinned to the ground, one knee on his chest and his knife to Julian's throat. His gaze dropped to my throat. He smiled.

Julian jammed his knife deep into Alistair's chest. Alistair looked down, glasses slipping from his face. He touched the knife protruding from the scars where his binding once was, and Julian shoved him off. Alistair crumpled, his vilewright writhing in the red glare of my glasses.

"I'm sorry," I whispered, "but this is my plan."

Alistair's head lolled to me, eyes wide, and he laughed. Blood speckled his tongue. The words bubbled and popped in his throat. "I know, but how are you getting out of here?"

I brought my bloody hand to my face and drew my fingers down it. Alistair choked and shook his head. I traced a red line over my mouth.

Then, slowly, he dipped his hand into the wound of his body and smeared Death's sigil across his face. A hand reaching from an open grave. An invitation. An understanding.

I was a graveyard so Cynlira wouldn't be.

"Look at you. Different scar, same crown." Julian shook his head, tears washing the blood from his face, and brandished his knife at me. His eyes never left Will's corpse. "You really think those folks up there are worth this?"

Cynlira was broken because it had been built on coins and costs, and we'd one last price to pay.

"You child," I said. "Why is everything about worth with you? People aren't worth saving because they're worth something. They're worth it because they're people!"

"It's not my fault they're not prepared!" He froze, hand fisted at his side. "You're the one who changed. We made a deal with you, and you went back on it!"

"Your father was a councilor. He was supposed to protect Cynlira. They all were, and they didn't. If any deal was broken, it was the one they made with the people they represented."

"You're punishing people for succeeding," he said and took another step back. Three steps to the Door. "What are you going to do? Stop me, Lore? Kill me?"

I opened my mouth to answer—truthfully because I had

not left—and a breathy laugh stopped me. Julian and I turned to the Door. It began to open.

"You can have them!" Julian gestured to me. "I'll open you if you take them and let me leave."

"That's not how it works. A life isn't equal to just any life. It's the intention. You have to make the sacrifice matter."

The Door rattled. Whispers leaked through the cracks.

All the lives we've taken—the councilors and the courtiers, Alistair and Julian—and the peers who will die soon enough. Take them. Use them. Destroy the Vile's ability to deny my request.

"You never understood self-sacrifice," I said and touched the Door. "Let me teach you."

Take me, and create a contract between the Vile and all of Cynlira.

"Do you really think that fragment of a Noble can bind us?" asked the Door in my mother's voice.

Julian stumbled back, whimpering.

"No," I said, "but I think you'll want to take my deal, because you may be immortal, but we know what to do with immortal overlords these days."

Whispers built up in the dark behind it. Voices howling, overlapping one another as if scrambling to be heard, until finally a sound like a boot crushing a beetle echoed through the cave. The Door opened another sliver.

"You can have the peerage. You can have all of them except the children, and the wrought won't try to stop you." My voice wavered. "But you can only have them if you agree to leave the rest of Cynlira's people alone for a decade. No deaths. No tricks. No Vile can kill a mortal not part of the peerage. If you disagree, there are hundreds of wrought unbound and ready to fight. They can make your newfound freedom very uncomfortable."

"Deal," it said in a dozen voices. "Done."

And I opened the Door.

forty-four

I FELL THROUGH IT FACE-FIRST BUT LANDED ON MY back. There was no light, only pinpricks of white high above me like distant stars. The dirt rippled beneath me, like water around footsteps, and Julian's shrieks grew distant as he ran. A pair of hands grabbed my ankles and dragged me away. The dark shrunk, and the stars drew nearer and sharper. I was yanked back through the Door with a groan.

Not the night but a mouth. Not stars but teeth.

Alistair pulled me into his lap, each breath a softer and softer gurgle, and turned my head toward the cavern's entrance.

Julian stood waist-deep in the dirt. Blood welled wherever the earth touched him, and he tried to turn to me. Alistair's arms slackened and fell away. His last breath rattled in his throat. I kept his hand in mine.

"Lorena?" called Julian.

He sunk to his chest with a jerk and screamed.

"I'm sorry, Jules," I said and sobbed because I could remember loving him enough to use the pet name but not why I had loved him once. My hands were red with the death of a boy I could only remember in pieces and the death of one I had pieced together too late. "I'm sorry."

"Lore?" he whispered. "You remember when we met? The blackberries?"

"I only remember the thorns."

His last breath left him with a gasp. I slumped.

What were we if not the pieces of loved ones we had lost? A habit here, a keepsake there, and a last sentence lingering in our ears. Every part loved and returned to the earth in us. I was death.

"Don't be melodramatic," said a familiar voice. "I've met Death, and you're nothing like them."

I raised my head. Creek sat cross-legged before me, flowers blooming and worms writhing beneath him. Vines grew from the dirt and into him, twining between feathery tendons and muddy veins, and the gills of a mushroom rippled on the sides of his neck. He cracked his knuckles, and the joints snapped like tinder.

His eyes were Vile red.

"Little Lorena Adler played such a long game," he said, and his laugh was the sound of rustling leaves.

I swallowed. "I opened the Door."

"Yes," he said, picking at his nails, "and it took you utter ages."

"Were you the Door the whole time?" I asked.

"The thing you call the Door is the weakest of the Vile. That's why we made it the Door." He snorted and shook out his hair. "I am one of the Vile Crowns and have dominion over the chaotic aspects of life. You could not devour me so easily and are very lucky I like you."

"Why—" My voice broke. Pain seared my throat, my chest. An ache pounded behind my eyes.

Dead. Dead. Dead.

So many dead by me.

"I'm a sacrifice," I said and choked. "I'm supposed to die. I'm ready to die."

"Not all sacrifices make us bleed. Your sacrifice, the one that binds us Vile to your deal, is living." He stood, so much taller than Creek had been, and patted my shoulder with a hand too light to be flesh and blood. "Not all the Vile will obey it, of course, but you're only mortal. Getting most of us was the best you could do. You're going to live with yourself for a long, long time and help Cynlira recover. Or doom it. We're not particular."

"Why are you telling me this?"

"We had fun, didn't we?" He walked from the cavern, life blooming in his wake. "We owe debts, Lorena, and now our payments begin. Once you're home, I'll bring you a gift."

I screamed till I couldn't.

The sacrifice wasn't my death. It was me living with these deaths and facing the folks whose loved ones I'd gotten killed.

Maybe they'd kill me.

I crawled toward the mouth of the cave. Moss and mushrooms speckled Julian's body, but Alistair was untouched. I collapsed atop his chest, and set his glasses over his eyes. His shattered red gaze followed me from the cave.

He had understood. He had probably even guessed I'd have to live with this.

Shadows and sounds followed me, a whispering like wind or waves or rustling leaves. Bruises bloomed on my knees and elbows, and by the time I reached the top of the stairs, screams echoed down the halls. The peers, the ones I'd sacrificed, were still dying, and my wrights were still gone, enacting my will. I struggled toward the sounds of steel and stone clashing. An immortal howl shook the halls. I peeked around the corner.

Hana, face and chest splattered with blood, swept her sword in an arc through a smear of fog hovering in the hall. It split and fell, splashing against the ground. Blood oozed from the stormy flesh.

Four more Vile watched from the rafters and opened doors. A rattling thing with an empty chest dripping stomach acid to the floor drew in last breaths despite its missing lungs, but it didn't lunge and try to devour Hana or the people she was protecting. A small beast whose ribs were a cage rocked back and forth, and the severed foot and dying rat trapped in its chest squished together. That Vile hadn't lied; my contract had mostly worked. Hana beckoned the people behind her down the hall.

I tried to call out, but my voice was gone, dead as I had meant to be. I rapped on the floor. Hana spun, sword raised.

"Lorena!" She raced to me and held me up with one strong arm around my middle. "Shit. Shit. Shit. Are you dying? Where's His Excellency?"

I shook my head and touched my throat. My arms hurt with even that little movement. We wove our way through the halls of the palace to the large church at the center of the grounds, and the nearer we got, the thicker grew the crowd of spawn not attacking but simply watching. We couldn't and wouldn't need to live exclusively in the church, but for now, I needed to help with what I could.

Mack and Basil, worse for wear, were at the gate leading into the church grounds. Mack scooped me up in both arms and carried me the rest of the way. Basil fluttered about him.

"Julian?" Mack asked.

I shook my head.

Basil touched Mack's arm. "I'll get Safia."

"No," I said. "I'll live. Did it work?"

"Most folks are safe," said Hana, rubbing her face. "A lot of Vile are just watching us, but the peers who were still in the palace..."

I tapped Mack's shoulder till he set me down.

He sat in the dirt next to me, hand tight around my wrist. "What did you do?"

"I made a deal," I whispered, "but apparently my sacrifice to seal it is living with what I've done."

I sobbed, and he wiped my face.

The peerage and council were dead. Cynlira had no ruling

bodies. Vile walked this world again. We'd have to rebuild completely, but we needed a new system not beholden to birthrights or costs.

"Lorena!" Safia, cheeks streaked with ash, came to a stop on the stone path I'd sat on, and she reached for Hana. A fresh cut on her arm had the bloodless look of a sacrifice. "Something's coming. No heartbeat."

"I feel it," said Basil. "My noblewright's cowering. It's never cowered before."

We made our way to the church gate. Safia stayed on the stone path some steps back. Hana reloaded a six-shooter, and I pointed to the Vile who watched us without attacking. A path of white asters spiraled up from the grass. The Vile backed away from it.

From around the bend came a line of children, each in the same plain dress of a Wallows orphanage, and none strayed from the path. The one in the lead carried a handful of green mums.

They sped up as they saw us. Basil and I darted forward, opening the gate. The first girl stumbled to a stop on wobbly legs, and Mack picked her up. She couldn't have been older than four.

"We got lost," she said, sniffing, "but Fran came back for us."

Basil groaned. "Carlow was reinforcing some bridges over the Tongue so people could make it to Formet."

"You must be very brave and smart to have gotten all the way here," said Mack. He gestured to some cuts on her feet, and Basil healed them while the girl was distracted. "What happened?"

Hana and I herded the rest of the kids in the gate, and Safia started fussing over them.

"We were alone," she said. "Then we weren't."

The Door opening.

"Fran made us close our eyes," said another kid, his brown skin stained with blood that wasn't his.

"This plan was shit," called Carlow from the edge of the

grounds, and the older kid next to her covered a nearby child's ears. "We nearly scared the whole city to death with a bunch of Vile showing up and just *watching*."

"Well," said Hana, looking at Safia, "Carlow definitely has blood, I hope, so what did you feel?"

"Last I checked," said Carlow, nudging the last of the kids ahead, "I had blood."

She turned to shut the gate and froze. A vine of blue roses knotted around the metal, and ambling down the path, a child on his hip, came the Vile Crown wearing Creek's skin.

"You missed one," he said and stopped at the boundary to the church. "Hello again, Franziska."

Carlow stumbled back. "You're dead."

"I can't die," said the Vile Crown. "Delmond Creek, though, has been dead for about two years."

He set the kid on the ground, patted their head, and pushed them toward the gate. Carlow opened the gate, hiding them behind her. Basil grabbed them, and I tried to pull Carlow back. She shook me off.

"This will be easier if you invite me inside." The Vile Crown's red eyes swept over the consecrated grounds. "Please?"

None of us spoke, and he scoffed.

The Vile Crown stepped over the boundary of the church grounds. The flesh of his foot bubbled, skin peeling away like petals in a breeze. His blood streamed upward in scarlet rivers, and antlers covered in mossy green velvet burst from his scalp, his blond hair falling away in clumps. Dark brown strands ruffling like willow branches replaced it. Swallowwort bloomed in the wounds left by the consecrated earth.

Mack fired one shot. The wooden bolt sprouted wings and fluttered away.

"Not your gift, Lorena Adler, but one that is long overdue," said the Vile Crown. "My little thorn, Franziska Carlow. The curse wasn't meant for you."

Carlow grabbed a knife from a pocket and pressed it to her arm. Vines curled around her feet, upending her. Basil and Safia moved to help, and I grabbed them. The vines dropped Carlow into the Vile Crown's outstretched arms.

"Wait," I whispered. "He said it's a gift."

"Franziska," he said slowly, letting her struggle and stab him, "there's only one way to remove your curse. Do you understand?"

She stilled. "There's always only one way out."

He plunged his hand into her chest, sternum cracking so loud it rang. Safia sobbed. Hana threw her short sword, and the blade sunk hilt-deep into the Vile Crown's chest. He didn't even wince.

"Very rude of you," the Vile Crown muttered. "We were friends for so long, and that's how you greet me?"

He laid Carlow, the wound in her chest a yawning dark too deep to be natural, on the consecrated dirt. Roses bloomed around her.

"The most boring flower." I shuddered. "You were possessing Delmond Creek the whole time."

"When he fulfilled his curse and died, he had no more need for this body. Possessing it was the only way to enter this world until the Door opened." He chuckled. "I had been watching, of course. This curse should have died out decades ago. It was meant to punish the original recipient, not torture loved ones far removed from her actions."

"What?" Basil covered their mouth with a hand. "Oh no, no, how—"

"You may call me Creek if you wish, but I am the Vile Crown of Strangling Vines and much prefer Vines," he said.

A poppy blossomed on the left side of his chest, and he plucked it free. Hands far gentler than I'd expected tucked it into Carlow's empty chest. She breathed again.

"Franziska?" he murmured.

She sobbed and scrambled away from him, tumbling into our open arms. Vines winced. Basil cupped her face in their hands while Safia checked her over.

"It's fine," Basil said. "You're fine."

And Carlow blinked at them, irises a bright fawn brown against bloodshot whites. Basil swallowed.

"Carlow?" I said gently and knelt next to her. "How do you feel?"

"Terrible." She glanced from me to Vines. "You were in Creek. You were Creek?"

"I was." Vines drew back, his hands clasped behind his back. "I removed your curse. I'm sorry it didn't involve killing me, but you may try if you like."

"The heart is a garden," she whispered and touched the corners of her eyes as if she could feel the difference. "I wouldn't like to try. I'd like to succeed."

"Of course you would, you insufferable overachiever," said Vines. "I will give you whatever future you desire, my corpse included. Now go. Plan your decade and know you have my help."

We made our way into the church. He lingered at the edge of the grounds, a sentry among the Vile watching us with open, waiting mouths.

One by one, we came to watch the end of the world beyond these grounds. A fog had crept about the spawn keeping watch, their hungry eyes like flickering candles in the dark. My wrights were still quiet, their lack of presence an ache in my bones. I'd been awake for far too long. Exhaustion and grief had taken everything from me. Too tired to stop. Too tired to sleep.

Every now and then, new faces would appear beyond the gate. The survivors from the palace—the children of the peers—found us with tear-streaked faces and bloody hands. I stayed awake for them and greeted each one. This was the cost of what I'd done.

Me facing what I'd done. I could never hide from who I was again.

"What do we do now?" Basil asked, plucking strands of fog from the swarm around us. It writhed between their fingers. Another Vile. Another thing that wanted us dead. "What are you supposed to do when the world ends?"

I tilted my head back to the empty sky. The ever-full moon, the Door holding back the Noble, was bright above us. The Vile avoided its light. Chaos couldn't be wrought within its sight.

"We begin anew."

The moon blinked.

acknowledgments

What We Devour is somehow my fifth book, and I am so glad to have shared this journey with so many incredible people. Thank you for believing in this weird little book. I will always be grateful.

Rachel Brooks made my career. She is a wonderful agent, and I'm so glad to be part of the BookEnds Literary Agency family. Thank you for liking my pitch all those years ago.

I could never thank Annie Berger enough for all that she's done. With her effort and guidance, Lorena's story became so much better than I could ever have hoped. You are an amazing editor. I couldn't have done this without you.

Sourcebooks, you have been a wonderful home. Cassie Gutman, Ashlyn Keil, Lizzie Lewandowski, and everyone else who had a hand in *What We Devour*, thank you. Your dedication and work made this book what it is today. I cannot put into words how thankful I am to every member of the Sourcebooks team. Thank you all.

Kerbie Addis knows what she did. She knows.

So hear me out: Rosiee, I know I always open our chats with this, and thank you for letting me message you at ungodly hours about book ideas.

Brent, thank you. I could not ask for a better partner.

And most importantly, thank you readers, reviewers, booksellers, librarians, and bloggers. No matter if you've been on this journey with me for four years or four days, thank you for making this possible. I hope you love these terrible nerds as much as I do and that their story brings you joy.

Thank you.

And remember—feast.

TURN THE PAGE TO READ AN EXCERPT

FROM LINSEY MILLER'S EPIC FANTASY

BELLE RÉVOLTE

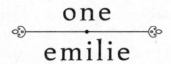

one
emilie

MY MOTHER DID NOT SHACKLE ME DESPITE MY LAST escape attempt. It didn't matter—the corset, layers of satin and silk, and summer heat were chains enough. I was certain I would be the first young noble lady of Demeine to arrive at finishing school under the watchful eyes of two armed guards. My mother made it seem so innocuous, talking of nothing but her perfect days looking down upon the quaint town of Bosquet while learning the correct topics of conversation, the exact ways to divine tomorrow's weather, and wonderful illusions to cover up everything from blood stains to whole castles. The illusionary arts, the first and simplest branch of the midnight arts, were my mother's specialty, something the perfect daughter should have appreciated. I had neither aptitude nor interest in illusions.

Illusions were, as far as I could tell, nothing but lies. My mother was a wonderful liar.

"I love you," she said, her expression that emotionless calm all ladies of Demeine were expected to possess, "but I am growing weary of your rebellion."

I peeked out the window. We had been traveling for days, bundled up in the carriage and only stopping to swap horses. It was the carriage Mother usually took to court: wonderfully impressive on the outside, with gold and silver gilding running through the ocean colors of our family's crest on the door, and frustratingly practical on the inside. I had been staring at the same black velvet and single lamp since we left. No amount of fiddling with the lock while she slept had freed me yet.

"Let us rejoice, then, that your education means no one will notice I exhaust you." I tapped the thin skin beneath my eyes where she had hidden my dark circles as she hid hers every day. "You said you would let me study the noonday arts. Mademoiselle Gardinier's school does not teach the noonday arts."

The ability to channel magic was rare, and it was rarer still for it to run so steadily in a family. Traditionally, noble sons with the ability studied the noonday arts and either specialized in the fighting or healing arts. They became chevaliers or physicians. They changed the world by sword or by scalpel.

Noble girls didn't change the world.

"I said I would let you study them, not that I would allow you to partake in such powerful magic, especially after that abomination you used on poor Edouard. You could have killed him." She folded her hands in her lap, the tight sleeves of her silver overdress rustling together like moth wings. "You are a daughter of Demeine. You will learn the midnight arts, you will—somehow—impress some-one well enough for them to marry you, you will have children, you will serve our people as the midnight artist and comtesse they need, and one day, you will understand why I made you do all of this."

Edouard, one of our guards, had caught me during my last escape attempt and laughed when I had explained my plan to join the university as a boy. Even common boys were allowed to be physicians if they were good enough and could pay the tuition.

"Being a boy's not that easy," he had said, angry for the first time since I could remember. "I would know. And you'd be doing it for selfish reasons. You don't understand. Listen to me, Emilie…"

When it was clear he wasn't going to let me go, I had knocked him out by altering his body alchemistry with my *abominable* noonday arts.

I tugged at the high collar of my dress, sweat pooling in every wrinkle, and scowled. "I could better serve our people as a physician."

"The noonday arts would wear your body out in pursuit of such a dream, to the point of death or infertility." She slapped my hand away from my collar. "Be reasonable, and perhaps you will learn you enjoy the midnight arts and the life you are supposed to lead."

My mother was always reasonable, as a good lady of Demeine should be, and unlike me, she never wore her emotions on her face.

"This will be good for you," she said. "Marais was too rural for you to make friends of the appropriate station. You will need allies at court."

"Yes, I cannot wait to meet them."

"I see sincerity was another of my lessons you neglected." She leaned across the carriage, fingers skimming my cheek, and recoiled when I flinched. "You are not a child any longer. You are sixteen, and soon you will be old enough to inherit your father's responsibilities along with the title you disregard. I remember when that was not even a possibility. You have so many more opportunities than girls in the past, than other girls now, and it is insult to refuse them."

I was an insult to our name, and my very dreams, to be a physician and study the noonday arts, to channel the magic of Lord Sun through my veins and save the dying, were the worst insult of all. I wanted the wrong things. I wanted too much.

"Noonday artists change the world, whether through the fighting or healing arts. That is a responsibility that comes with power you cannot comprehend. You are young. You will learn."

Demeine was blessed with two types of power: the noonday and the midnight arts. Each drew power from Lord Sun or his Mistress Moon, but Lord Sun was far stronger and even more fickle. The fighting and healing arts were used to change the physical world, and as such, required immense amounts of power. Such magic wore the mortal body down bit by bit until the ability to channel faded or the artist died.

Noble girls could not be allowed to handle such corruptive power.

There was nothing to learn. I comprehended the fact that I was a body, not a person, quite well.

"'I will learn,'" I said, the small nothing town of Bosquet rushing past our carriage window. "Is that a command or an attempt at reassurance?"

"Please, Emilie, we both know you are incapable of following even the simplest of orders." She twisted her first two fingers, broke the illusion hiding her fan in her lap, and flicked it open. "I prayed to Mistress Moon to console my grief at having to be apart from you, and she sent me a vision of you happy and content at court. You will be fine."

Mistress Moon's magic and the lesser power required for the midnight arts—illusions, scrying, and divination—wore the body down much more slowly but required excessive self-control. It was a safer, slower burn, but midnight artists couldn't change the world. They only observed it, or, if they were good, changed how others observed it.

Perhaps Demeine was as it was, ruled by a court on the cusp of rightly losing control, because we let no one new change it.

I had to change the world. I had to prove to my mother that the whole of my being wasn't wrong, that I wasn't a disappointment.

"Maybe you saw a future where I became a physician," I said.

The gods could take the time to answer her prayers but not mine. How paradigmatic. Divination was guesswork, hardly quantifiable. A diviner could see a dozen different futures, and none might come to pass. If a midnight artist even could divine. Many never mastered the skill.

"Though, admittedly, you appeared to have taken none of my clothing advice in my divination; you were not wearing a physician's coat," she said. "You stand at the edge of a great future."

"Whose?" I lifted a silver chain, worth more than all of Bosquet, from my chest. The layers, the jewelry—I couldn't breathe much less move for fear of drowning in silver and sweat. No wonder we were expected to be silent and still. Even this left me light-headed.

Oxygen deprivation.

"All power has a cost," she said as the carriage slowed to a stop, "and you were born with power—your title, your wealth, your magic. This is your cost, Emilie des Marais, and it is your duty to pay it. Power demands sacrifice."

"This isn't fair."

She laughed, the apathetic mask she kept up at all times slipping. "Really? There will be girls at school who lack your name, your money, and your magic, and they will not treat you as kindly as I have. You are arrogant and stubborn. Mind your tongue, or you will have no friends, no happiness, and no future."

She had never called me a disappointment, but I could taste it in the silence between us. I was not the daughter she had always longed for. At least magic would never abandon me.

"You are my daughter, and I love you. I am pushing you to do this because I know Demeine will laugh you out of university. I do this because I love you." She ran her fingers through the strands of her silver necklaces, where she stored small lockets of power. Her illusion settled over me like snow, soft and cold and suffocating, and I knew no one would be able to tell how hot and miserable I looked. "Time to go."

We had stopped at a stable on the south side of town. The noises of Bosquet were louder now, and the shadows shorter, squat stains beneath our feet. The town had an open-air market and church at the center, and we had passed between storefronts and housing and orderly gravel paths shaded by linden trees with interlaced canopies. Our driver had already vanished inside the stable, and the guards lingered on the other side of the carriage. A crowd had gathered in the shade of the trees across from us. Behind them, a white poster with green ink had been stuck to the trunk of a tree.

At the edge of that crowd was a girl, who despite her flax dress dusted with dirt, despite her white skin spotted with sunburn and old bruises, and despite her brown hair in desperate need of styling, looked like me. I might have mistaken her for some unknown half-sister if either of my parents had ever been inclined to such affairs.

Perhaps Lord Sun had finally answered my prayers.

"Wait," I said quickly, grabbing my mother's wrist before she could leave the carriage. "Give me a moment to prepare myself, please."

I did not let go of her immediately as I usually did, and her gaze dropped to my fingers. She took my hand in hers and nodded.

"What do you think that crowd is?" I asked.

Her eyes didn't leave our hands. "Mademoiselle Charron is in town to inspect the artists in your class. I am sure she's providing free scrying and divinations to those who need them. All of her writings are in green for some ill-graced reason, but so goes the odd trends of youth, I suppose."

"That's nice of her." I moved my other hand, palm up and burning in a sliver of sunlight, out of her sight. "Can we wait until there are fewer people? You knotted me up in new clothes and shoes, and I have no desire for an audience."

She laughed, a sound I hadn't heard in ages, and nodded. "Very well."

"Thank you." I channeled the power I had gathered in my free hand to the one holding hers.

It slipped under her skin with the soft sizzle of heat against flesh. Her head jerked up, but I held tight, the magic slithering through the nerves of her arms to the dark little spaces of her mind, until the inner workings of her body shone with my power like a layer of gold silk. We were all nothing but lightning in a bloody bottle. I deleted the alchemical components in her mind that controlled wakefulness. These last moments would be like a dream.

My mother slumped in her seat, asleep, and I stepped out of the carriage. My own body would pay the price for this; I would not be able to sleep for a day or two at least. I had five minutes at most, and no idea if this would work. It was arrogant to think I would get away with it.

But arrogance and magic were all I had.

Even a chance was worth it.

I was far too overdressed for the crowd, but the people were more focused on the poster than me. My mother was right—it was advertising Estrel Charron's services—and the girl who looked like me was mouthing the words to herself as she read. I slipped into place next to her and tilted my head till my mouth was even with her ear. I was slightly taller and certainly heavier, but we had the same hazel eyes. The silver moon necklace at her throat glowed with power.

"Wouldn't you love to meet her?" I asked the girl.

She couldn't pull her eyes from the poster. "Love to, but it's tomorrow, and I've got to be home tonight."

"What if I could offer you the chance to not only meet her but learn from her?"

Her face whipped to me, and her eyes widened. She whispered with all the gentleness one said a prayer. "What?"

"I am Emilie des Marais, comtesse de Côte Verte, and I'm supposed to start my training at Mademoiselle Gardinier's today but would much rather study the noonday arts at university," I said, smile growing. She didn't stop me, so some part of her was listening. "How would you like to pretend to be me and study the midnight arts at Mademoiselle Gardinier's with your beloved Estrel while I take your last name and study the noonday arts?"

She stared. She did not say no.

"It will be dangerous, and I will do what I can to protect you if we are caught," I told her softly, "but some dangerous things are worth the risk."

"Yes," she whispered. "Yes."

I would prove myself, prove I wasn't a disappointment or insult, and I would change Demeine. If the world wouldn't give me the chance, I would take it myself.

two

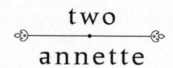

annette

I ATE DIRT AS A CHILD. NOTHING GREW THE SUMMER I turned six; Vaser's dry fields filled only with cicada husks. Lord Sun had not been merciful, giving us endless days of heat without rain, and Monsieur Waleran du Ferrant, comte de Champ, whose family watched over our lands, hadn't sent near enough help. Maman was pregnant with Jean, Papa was busy working, and Macé was seven and going through a growth spurt, crying till I gave him my supper. I'd cried too, but quiet, and pulled at my sides like I'd be able to pry open my ribs and scratch the hunger out of me. I'd been a good sister, then, and dirt was better than Macé crying. Tasted like the air after Alaine's funeral pyre.

"Your family must be proud." The shopkeeper smiled up at me and handed over the little satchel of everything Macé would need in Serre. "A varlet. There's a good career for a country boy."

I was not a good sister now.

"They're very proud of him," I said, tucking the packet into my bag. It wasn't a lie. They were. Of him. "He's leaving next week, and I'll be sad to see him go."

I'd be sad to see him go alone.

It was supposed to be us going—to university, not to Serre—to be hacks. We were supposed to study together, him the noonday and me the midnight arts, so we could both get jobs channeling magic for some rich artists who wanted all the results without getting worn down. I was supposed to go with him.

I'd always known I wasn't as good as him, but I didn't think Maman would make me stay in Vaser. Figured she'd be happy to see me go.

Probably why I'd been sent to pick up his supplies in Bosquet.

"Thank you," I said. "There a baker in town? I'm supposed to buy him something sweet to celebrate."

Our parents wanted to have a nice dinner before he left, and make sure he had some nice things to take with him so he wouldn't be too out of sorts from the others training to assist the chevaliers. So long as no one asked him to do something that required paying attention for longer than five minutes, Macé would make a good varlet. Macé would be a step above a hack, helping Chevalier Waleran du Ferrant stay alive and channeling the noonday arts for him during fights so his noble body didn't wear down too fast. They were honorable, varlets.

They were worth the money and time and sacrifice. I wasn't.

The shopkeeper told me how to find a baker—said Bosquet was too small for a proper pâtisserie, which I didn't believe for one second because there were more people and buildings here than I'd ever seen. As I'd left his store, he said, "Good luck to your brother, girl."

I froze.

"You're not as good as you think you are, girl," Maman had said yesterday morning. We'd been standing in the root cellar, she and I. The magic I'd been gathering to scry the day's weather had scattered when I heard her steps, and I itched to draw it all back to me and lose myself in the one thing I knew for sure. "Your brother's real good. The comte de Champ offered him this, and chances like these are once in a lifetime."

I'd run my finger along the rim of my bowl and refused to look at her. "He's not that good."

"Annette Boucher, keep that jealousy out of your mouth, or I'll wash it out." She'd bent over me, wobbling, and patted my cheek too hard. Like she'd forgotten how. "We're family, and family makes sacrifices. Now, you're going to Bosquet and picking up what he needs. You can get something small for yourself too."

She never asked. Just watched. She narrowed her eyes, the little crinkles of age bundled up in the corners like a handful of nettle cloth.

Bosquet was so much bigger than home. I slipped through one of the narrow alleys between two towering buildings, and wrapped and unwrapped my necklace around my fingers. The market was taking advantage of school starting up too, and nearly every available space was someone selling something. Country people brushed past rich merchant kids, and a rich girl glittering like gold in mud stopped at a stall serving food from our eastern neighbor Kalthorne. She bought dumplings topped with poppy seeds and dripping plum jam for her and her guards. She was nice at least.

She was still one of those destined for school, though. They'd use hacks, country kids like me who had magic but no money for training, to channel Mistress Moon's power for them. They'd get to do the magic with none of the consequences.

How noble.

I stopped, a rock in a river of people who couldn't care less about me. I couldn't see the end of the market, and the rows of trees leading past it were spotted with couples and families resting in the shade. A stall next to me sold sage water faster than the identical twins distributing it could pour, and the twin on the other side of the stall, clothed in a dusky purple and so focused on her work that her look of concentration made me feel like I should be working, lifted a jar of honey to the sunlight. A ribbon of power burned in it, the midnight arts trapped in a lemon slice. I leaned closer to get a better look.

"Drink it right before you need the illusion," the girl said. "It'll make it last a few minutes more than normal."

There were three types of midnight arts—illusions, scrying, and divining—and illusions were the easiest to master. Scrying was harder, but it let you observe what was happening anywhere in the present, so long as you had a looking glass to see through and knew what you were looking for. The hardest art, divining the future, showed artists all the different possible futures and let them puzzle out which one was true. Most artists never mastered it.

I'd never been trained in the midnight arts, but I could do them without wearing myself down too fast like most people. Even on dark, new-moon nights, magic called to me, thrummed in my heart and urged me to use it. Magic was the only thing that wanted me.

"Something small," I muttered to myself, walking away from the stall and onto the gravel-lined path beneath a line of trees. The interlaced branches were a blessing for my sunburned skin. There'd been no shade on the walk here. "Something small."

At the end of the wall was a crowd, and a kid holding a twig like a knife ran past me.

"Ask her where Laurel is!" someone shouted after the kid. "I want that five-hundred-lune reward on his head."

"Like His Majesty would ever pay up," someone else shouted. "Ask her how to join Laurel."

I took off for the crowd. Vaser got news two days late and two truths off, but everyone was waiting for news of Laurel. They'd started a petition for the king to release how much money the crown was spending, called the king a coward when he hadn't answered, and pamphlets had started peppering Demeine with copies of nobles' ledgers too specific to be fake. Papa had clucked and said they had a death wish. Macé had talked about nothing except the reward money His Majesty had offered up for Laurel's capture. Not even the royal diviner Mademoiselle Charron had been able to find them.

I nudged my way to the front of the crowd till I could read the evergreen words on the parchment.

MADEMOISELLE GARDINIER,
WITH GREAT THANKS TO THE GENEROUS DU FERRANTS,
IS PLEASED TO ANNOUNCE
MADEMOISELLE ESTREL CHARRON, ROYAL DIVINER
TO HIS MOST BRIGHT MAJESTY HENRY XII,
WILL BE PROVIDING HER SERVICES AS A MIDNIGHT
ARTIST FOR THREE DAYS TO THOSE IN NEED
OF SCRYINGS AND DIVINATIONS.
THE SESSIONS WILL BE HELD AT TOWN HALL
AND BEGIN AT DUSK.

Estrel Charron was here. The best midnight artist in the country, the only royal diviner of this century not born from a noble family, was in Bosquet. And I could see her.

I twisted my necklace till the silver crescent moon was pressed against my palm and drew out the magic I had hidden in it. Solane, who'd been a physician's hack before moving to Vaser for safety when the court and university started going after those "outside of Lord Sun's dawn and Mistress Moon's dusk and upsetting the traditional order," had taught me how to do it. Solane had said I had promise. They were nice to lie.

I read through the poster again, certain I'd missed something, and rubbed my eyes. The words itched at me, a little twitch on the back of my neck. Someone had written over the poster in red ink and hidden it with an illusion, ensuring that any artists, no matter how untrained, would be able to see the red message for at least three days. After that, the magic stored in the paper to fuel the illusion would wear down the poster. It'd rot before anyone without magic even noticed the secret note.

A KING CANNOT REST ON HIS LAURELS
NOT ALL ARTISTS DIE YOUNG
ONLY COMMON HACKS DO
WHY

A dripping red crown of laurel leaves had been painted above the words.

It was the symbol and call of Laurel, but they couldn't be in Bosquet. And why were they writing over Mademoiselle Charron's papers? She didn't use hacks.

Nearly all artists rich enough to afford them did. Magic corrupted, wearing down the bodies of artists who channeled it, so people paid country kids to channel for them. The artists directed the magic, but the hack bore the brunt of the power. After a few years of channeling, the hacks' bodies broke down till they couldn't channel or died. The artists were fine.

Most of Laurel's posters said using hacks was amoral. They were right, but being right wasn't much good when the folks we were up against had armies and weapons and decades of training in the arts. Without training, an artist channeling too much could wear their body to nothing but bone dust in a few days. I mouthed the words to myself.

A king cannot rest on his laurels. A king could rest on an army with weapons and magic, though.

"Wouldn't you love to meet her?" some girl next to me asked.

Didn't matter what I wanted. Maman and Papa would send people after me if I didn't get Macé's things home. "Love to, but it's tomorrow, and I've got to be home tonight."

"What if I could offer you the chance to not only meet her but learn from her?"

I turned to tell her to jog off, but the words stuck to my teeth. "What?"

She was all full moon, the sort of pretty only money could

buy. Her silver dress was cinched tight, showing off the thick curves of her waist and hips, and a spill of pearls like snowfall was sewn into the silk. She'd long, brown hair twisted into an intricate crown of braids that were so slick, they looked fake. A signet ring, one of five, glittered on her left hand.

"I am Emilie des Marais, comtesse de Côte Verte, and I'm supposed to start my training at Mademoiselle Gardinier's today. I would much rather study the noonday arts at university," she said, as if comtesses said those sorts of things to me every day. She smiled, red paint smeared on her white, rich teeth, and all I could think about was how Maman would've chided me for such poor dress and manners. "How would you like to pretend to be me and study the midnight arts at Mademoiselle Gardinier's with your beloved Estrel while I take your last name and study the noonday arts?"

I'd no words for this.

Was I even allowed to say no? Did I want to?

"It will be dangerous, and I will do what I can to protect you if we are caught," she said, voice low, "but some dangerous things are worth the risk."

Nobles never risked anything. Only we did. We studied and learned, and none of it mattered because they used us as hacks and wore down our bodies before we hit thirty. Even midnight artists channeling Mistress Moon's mercifully gentle powers died sooner than later.

Midnight artists observe the world. You've already proven that's too much responsibility for you.

Maybe the world was as it was because we'd let folks do things without looking too closely at them for so long. Maybe Maman wasn't looking hard enough at me.

But I could make her see me.

"Yes." I nodded, glancing round. No soldiers. No chevaliers. "Yes."

"Brilliant." She looked back, gaze on a carriage bright as

the sun, and touched my hand. "I only have a moment before my mother wakes up, but she will walk me to Mademoiselle Gardinier's estate and leave me there, assuming I will not be foolish enough to run off without money or a plan. However, if you meet me in the gardens, I can tell you everything you need to know."

Pulling away, she yanked a silver cuff prettier than anything I'd ever seen from her wrist. One of her hands was raw and red, the skin looked like it had been burned. Least she hadn't worn herself out too much. Her body could fix that.

"Understood?"

I nodded. "You'll have to send my family what I bought today. So long as they get everything back, they won't look too hard for me."

"Of course." Her nose twitched, and not even the red paint on her lips could pretty her scowl. "I can complete whatever tasks are necessary." Her expression shifted back to a wide smile. Mistress, this girl was fickle as fire. "Meet me near the cherry trees. If they don't let you in, tell them you saw a girl drop this and wish to give it to Mademoiselle Gardinier yourself because there's magic in it, and you don't want it to hurt anyone."

She pressed the silver cuff into my hand and darted away before I could speak. I tucked it into my purse.

Only a noble would throw away being a noble, but this was everything I'd ever wanted. Even if I were only there for a day, I'd come out knowing more than I did today.

And Estrel Charron was there.

She was as common as me and a genius. I could learn to be like her.

I could see the world and make it see me.

about the author

Linsey Miller holds an MFA in fiction and has previously worked as a crime lab intern, lab assistant, and pharmacy technician. She can be found writing about science and magic anywhere there's coffee. She is also the author of the Mask of Shadows duology and *Belle Révolte*. Visit her at linseymiller.com.

FIREreads

#getbooklit

Your hub for the hottest young adult books!

Visit us online and sign up for our
newsletter at FIREreads.com

 @sourcebooksfire

 sourcebooksfire

 firereads.tumblr.com